W9-BAF-255
T 38627

DISCARD

FAIR GAME

Also by Rochelle Majer Krich:

Till Death Do Us Part
Where's Mommy Now?

FAIR GAME

ROCHELLE MAJER KRICH

THE MYSTERIOUS PRESS

Published by Warner Books

A Time Warner Company

Publisher's Note: This novel is a work of fiction. Names, characters, places, and incidents either are the product of the author's imagination or are used fictitiously, and any resemblance to actual persons, living or dead, events, or locales is entirely coincidental.

Grateful acknowledgment is given to quote from the song "Lady in Red" courtesy of Rondor Music International, Inc. Used by permission.

Mysterious Press books are published by Warner Books, Inc.,
1271 Avenue of the Americas, New York, NY 10020.

A Time Warner Company

Printed in the United States of America

First printing: September 1993

10 9 8 7 6 5 4 3 2 1

Library of Congress Cataloging-in-Publication Data
Krich, Rochelle Majer.
Fair game / Rochelle Majer Krich.
p. cm.
ISBN 0-89296-507-X
I. Title.
PS3561.R477F3 1993
813' .54—dc20

92-50661
CIP

For Anita, who encouraged me to make the right moves
and
For Phyllis—a friend for all seasons

Acknowledgments

To Det. Paul Bishop, West L.A. Division of the Los Angeles Police Department; Dr. David Fox; Howard Gluck, Deputy City Attorney, Criminal Branch; Leonard Korobkin; Philip Orbanes; Det. Dennis Payne, Robbery Homicide Division, Homicide Special Section; Dr. Sara Teichman; and Dr. Ronald Wilbur.

To my agent, Mike Hamilburg, and his assistant, Joan Socola.

To my husband Hershie and our children—Eli, David, Sabina, Chani, Meira, and Daniel—for being the unwitting inspiration for *Fair Game* one Saturday afternoon.

And to my editor, Sara Ann Freed, for her clear guidance, flawless judgment, and friendship.

Many thanks.

RMK

FAIR GAME

1

Los Angeles, California
Thursday, June 18

The skin was puckered and discolored but not badly bruised.

Mae Sung Lee hesitated, then put the cantaloupe in her basket. She would eat that one first. She sniffed the green, buttonlike depression at the end of several other melons and selected one whose sweet, almost cloying fragrance assured her it was ripe.

At the cash register, she watched the new girl weigh the tomatoes, squash, and celery. When the girl rang up sixty-seven cents for the melons, Mae Lee stopped her.

"Sixty-six," she told her in Mandarin Chinese, pointing to the sign. "Three for dollar. Two melons, sixty-six."

The girl deducted a penny and rang up the total. "Two dollar forty-three."

"Two bags, please. The melons are heavy, yes?"

Smiling politely, the girl opened two white, opaque plastic shopping bags, placed a melon in each, and carefully distributed the vegetables, conscious of the old woman's scrutiny.

Mae Lee nodded approval, handed the girl two dollars and two quarters, and waited patiently for her change.

He had waited while Mae Lee had browsed through the shops in Kowloon Market on Hill. She'd seemed interested in a tablecloth, had apparently been negotiating the price with the saleswoman, but had left empty-handed. Even from a distance he could see disappointment pulling down the corners of her mouth. (Or was it old age?) He'd followed her to the produce market on Ord Street, had observed her petite, yellow-cotton-shift–clad figure through the poster-filled plate-glass window as she made her purchases. She'd spent forever choosing melons as if they were works of art (as if her careful selection mattered, as if anything she would do in the next thirty minutes mattered), and his eye had started to twitch until he reminded himself that there was no rush.

Yesterday she'd bought pea pods and ginger root; the day before, tenderloin. He'd gone inside the market both times, had bought three pippin apples the first day, a pound of cherries the second. The apples were too tart. The one he tasted had irritated his teeth, tongue, palate. He'd tried to finish it ("*Waste not, want not!*"), but after four bites he'd pushed it into the sink hole and waited until the garbage disposal eliminated all traces of the apple. He should have bought the golden delicious. Now he had two more pippins, and what would he do with them?

She was at the cash register now. He wondered why she went to the market every day. Maybe she couldn't handle heavy packages. Of course, she could buy a shopping cart. His mother had owned a collapsible gridded-metal cart years ago, when they lived in New Jersey. She always let him push it to the market—and back, if it wasn't too heavy. Of course, she had to ease it up and down the curbs herself. One time she let him pull the cart onto the curb and it fell on him, pinning him to the cement. The celery, cold and heavy and damp, landed on his face, and he sealed his eyes against the invasion of its serrated pale-green leaves and waited for his mother to rescue him. *There now, I told you, didn't I?* she said wearily, but she didn't spank him, even though she had to pick up all the canned vegetables that had rolled into the gutter, and two of the cans had been dented. *You can thank the good lord there were no eggs,* his mother said. And he had.

After that, he'd been content to roll the cart along the pavement. Then one of the wheels had started to squeak, and soon it had started turning the wrong way, like a recalcitrant child. Finally, when two of the wheels were broken, his mother had discarded the cart. She had never bought another one.

He had liked going shopping with his mother.

The woman was leaving. He inhaled sharply, felt inside his jacket pocket, then studied his reflection in the glass. He looked calm. He *was* calm. Keeping his eyes on one of the posters (SHORT RIB—SPECIAL TODAY! SEE INSIDE!), he watched her exit the store, a shopping bag in each hand, and start toward Hill Street. She turned left. He waited a minute and began walking.

He knew where she lived. He'd followed her home on both previous days, had watched her turn left from Hill onto Alpine and make her slow, deliberate way up the hilly street past several faded stucco apartment buildings to Bunker Hill Avenue. The real Bunker Hill was the site of an important Colonial victory during the War of Independence. He'd learned that in fifth grade. When he'd read the street name after watching Mae Lee disappear into a ground-floor rear apartment, he'd known it was a sign. (He hadn't chosen her because she lived on Bunker Hill. He hadn't known where she lived, so it *was* a sign. He knew it was.)

He had established that she lived alone. She was probably a widow, like his mother. He had no idea how old Mae Lee was—probably in her sixties, judging from the gray in her braided hair, although his mother was fifty-nine and looked much older, much wearier. He felt a familiar tightening in his chest and paused to catch his breath. The woman was more than a block ahead of him, her short, sturdy legs undaunted by the steep incline. In his mind's ear he could hear the rhythmic slapping of her sandals against the pavement. He didn't know how she made it up the hill every day. She hadn't stopped, not even once.

He waited on Alpine while she turned the corner at Bunker Hill, gave her several minutes to reach her apartment and enter it. When he rang the bell, she came to the door immediately.

"Mrs. Lee? Mrs. Mae Sung Lee?"

"Yes, yes. What you want?" She eyed him through the peephole.

"I have a package for you, a gift." He held up a large square parcel wrapped in red glossy paper.

"What kind gift?" She sounded skeptical more than suspicious.

"It's an advertising promotion." He saw that she didn't understand. "A free sample? You're the third person on this block to get one, by the way, and all the others were happy with theirs." He smiled. "But first I have to see some identification."

"What?"

"A driver's license, or something like that. I can only give you this after you show me proof that you're Mae Sung Lee."

She frowned. "No car. No drive."

"Oh. Well, what about a credit card? Social Security card?"

"Ah!" She nodded rapidly. "You wait." She was gone and

back within a minute. She held up a Social Security card to the privacy window for his scrutiny. "This here?"

"Great! That's it, then. The gift is yours, Mrs. Lee."

"You leave by door, yes?"

He held the package in his right hand, a clipboard in the other. "You have to sign for it. And I have to ask some questions. Like what's your favorite store, and why. How you like the gift." He knew he looked respectable. Clean shaved, neatly dressed.

She eyed the red package. She opened the door but left it secured by a chain.

"I don't blame you for being careful. I'd hate for you to lose out on the gift, but if I don't get the information from you, I could lose my job." He smiled again. "Look, I'll give you the number of the store. You call, give my name—it's Jim Miller, by the way—and check me out. Believe me, I won't be insulted."

She hesitated, then unchained the door. "OK. You come in."

She moved out of the doorway and let him into a small, musty living room. She closed the door. He handed her the package.

"Thank you." Her eyes crinkled with pleasure. She sat on a worn apricot brocade sofa with heavy wooden arms. "Sit, please."

"I'll write some notes first while you open your gift. Then a few questions, and I'll be on my way." He took a pen from a pocket of his camel sports jacket and busied himself with his clipboard.

She placed the package on an ornately carved, dark wood coffee table. It was a large box, but not heavy, and she wondered what it contained. She worked carefully with her short, blunt-edged fingers to peel away the transparent tape without tearing the paper. Her granddaughter's birthday was three weeks away; she would use the paper to wrap the ribbon doll she'd made for her. Mae Lee was concentrating on the last strip of tape when he slipped behind her and clamped the handkerchief across her nose and mouth.

Her hands flew up, and she locked them around his forearm, struggling to force his hands away from her face. Within a minute she was unconscious, and he eased her body onto the sofa. He noticed a violent tear in the glossy red paper, but he felt no pity as he bent over her, syringe in hand.

2

The damn light was never going to turn green, Jessie thought, her foot resting impatiently on the brake pedal.

She checked her watch. Seven-twenty. Her sister's flight was due to arrive in twenty-six minutes. The airport was still fifteen minutes away, and Jessie would need at least another five minutes to park the car in the lot, several more minutes to get to the gate. Helen and Neil and Matthew would probably be waiting. And her sister hated waiting.

"Well, who asked you to come?" Jessie said aloud, irritated with herself for being late and with Helen for inviting herself and arriving this evening, just as Jessie had started making headway on one of her cases. Jessie had been engrossed in reviewing the case file when her partner had come by her desk. "Don't you have to pick up your sister?" he'd asked. "You'll be late."

She'd grabbed her purse, bolted down the stairs, and run out of the police station to her Honda. She'd pulled out of the lot and headed toward Overland and the airport, then remembered her gun. She couldn't be carrying, not at the airport with security and metal detectors, not unless she gave prior notification, or unless she was picking up a prisoner. And she never left her gun in her car—too risky, considering how often cars were stolen in L.A. Cursing softly, she'd made a sharp right turn and driven home and put away her gun and holster.

The light turned green. Jessie moved her foot to the accelerator.

There she was.

Helen was wearing sunglasses, and her blond hair was unfamiliar in its short, blunt cut; Jessie almost hadn't recognized her sister as she exited the walkway with the crush of other passengers. But the heart-shaped face was the same, and so was the petite, elfin figure in white slacks and a green cotton knit sweater that matched her eyes.

Jessie waved to attract Helen's attention, but just then Helen bent down—to Matthew, Jessie knew, although she couldn't see her nephew. She didn't see Neil, Helen's husband, either. He was probably on the plane, collecting the carry-on luggage.

"Helen!" Jessie called, but she was drowned out by a voice over the loudspeaker that announced a boarding call for a flight to New York. "Helen!" she called again.

Helen looked up and smiled. "Jessie!" She took off her glasses. "Look, Matthew, Aunt Jessie's come to meet us."

Jessie's heart lurched. She looks so much like Mom, she thought. A moment later the sisters were embracing. At five feet six inches, Jessie was four inches taller, and although she was slim, she always felt oversized next to Helen's diminutive form.

She's aged, Jessie realized. My twenty-nine-year-old baby sister has aged in the past three years. Especially around her eyes. And how much have recent events added to my thirty-four years? Automatically, she ran a hand through medium-length, wavy dark-brown hair that needed a trim.

"You look great, Jess," Helen said, as if reading her sister's thoughts. "Really great. Matthew, say hi to Aunt Jessie. Remember she visited us in Winnetka? Matthew?" Helen repeated.

He was playing with a small electronic toy he was holding with both hands. Game Boy, Jessie read. "Hi, Matthew."

"Matthew," Helen prompted softly, but now her voice held shades of embarrassment and irritation.

"Hi," Matthew said without looking up.

A handshake or a hug? Jessie hesitated, then hugged the boy lightly, but he was stiff in her arms. Small wonder, she thought, releasing him quickly. He hardly knows me, and isn't eight the beginning of that awkward age for boys?

"Are you still a cop?" Matthew eyed her jeans and T-shirt.

"Yes. A detective." She didn't add, *with Homicide.*

"So where's your holster and gun?"

"Matthew!" Smiling, Helen shook her head in mock despair.

"I don't wear them when I'm off duty."

Right now they were in a hall closet, behind a pile of winter sweaters, the clip removed. So was her personal gun, an Airweight revolver she usually kept in her purse. At night she kept it between her mattress and box spring, and the department-issue 9mm Smith & Wesson in her nightstand. With Matthew around, she'd have to remember to keep both guns out of reach, out of sight.

Gary hadn't liked seeing her guns. He hadn't liked her job, either, had told her so often, even though she'd made it clear long before they married that she had no intention of quitting. But her ex-husband was no longer there to tell her what to do.

She looked at Matthew, wondering if she should continue the conversation, but he'd resumed playing, his small thumbs working the keys furiously, his lips compressed into a serious line.

"I can't believe how much he's grown, Helen," Jessie said in an undertone. "He looks exactly like Neil." Same thin, lanky body; same coal-gray eyes and almost-black hair, parted neatly on the left. She frowned. "Where *is* Neil?" She looked toward the walkway. "Didn't he take the same flight?"

Helen put on her sunglasses. "I thought I told you. Neil's in Saudi Arabia; he'll be there another nine or ten weeks."

Like hell you told me, Jessie thought, wondering what her sister was covering up, aside from her eyes. Helen, she knew, was less than happy with the occasional long absences Neil's work entailed. A civil engineer, he traveled all over the world supervising projects for development companies.

"That's why I thought this would be a great time for Matthew and me to come, Jess. He's going to camp when we get back." She paused. "Do Mom and Dad know we're coming?"

Jessie shook her head. "I haven't talked to them lately." Their parents lived an hour and a half south of Los Angeles in La Jolla, a beautiful beach resort near San Diego.

"Maybe I'll call them tomorrow."

"Whatever." Jessie picked up one of the two tapestry-design satchels Helen had deposited on the floor. "Let's go. I'm parked in the lot just across the terminal."

Helen picked up the other bag. "Come on, Matthew."

She touched his elbow. With his eyes still on the game, the boy followed his mother and aunt down a hall and onto an escalator that led them to a moving walkway. Helen didn't seem nervous, but Jessie glanced back several times to make sure Matthew was all right. He must have radar, she decided.

"It's been too long, Jessie." Helen gripped Jessie's hand.

Jessie turned to her. She'd been surprised when Helen had called two days ago and said she was thinking of coming for a vacation. Did Jessie mind? No, of course not, Jessie had said, but she'd thought, *company,* and immediately felt guilty about the annoyance that had fluttered through her.

And it wasn't as if the solitude was all that great.

"Too long," Jessie agreed, meaning it, and hugged her sister again. "I feel bad I can't spend time with you during the week. Weekends should be OK, unless we have a load of new cases. I—"

"Matthew and I will keep busy. I'll rent a car, and we'll go to Disneyland, Universal. It'll be fun, won't it, hon?"

No answer from Matthew.

"Kids." Helen's mouth curved into a smile. "You know how they are. I'm sorry, Jess," she said quickly. She touched her arm.

"It's OK."

"I wasn't thinking. And I'm sorry I didn't come last year, when you and Gary—" She stopped. "You needed me. I should've—"

"It's OK. Really. *I'm* OK."

The moving walkway ended suddenly, and Jessie half stumbled onto the floor. A few seconds later she stepped into a compartment of the revolving doors and pushed her shoulder against the glass walls that warned NO EMPUJE—DON'T PUSH.

What a gesture, she thought wryly.

"Here we are," Jessie announced twenty-five minutes later as she pulled the white Honda Accord into the driveway of her house on Tennessee Avenue.

"Matthew's asleep," Helen whispered from the backseat. She opened the door carefully, got out, and looked around. "This is pretty. Much nicer than in the photos you sent."

"Thanks."

Helen was being kind, Jessie knew. She and Neil lived in Winnetka, an upscale suburb of Chicago along Lake Michigan, in a two-story brick home that made Jessie's house look like a bungalow. A pale-blue stucco bungalow. Not a color Jessie liked, but Gary had chosen it, and she didn't have money for a paint job.

"I'm glad you got to keep it," Helen said. "This is a lovely area. What's it called?"

"West L.A. The station is minutes from here." She looked at her nephew. His eyes were closed. "I'll open the door. You get Matthew. Unless you need help?"

"I can manage. He doesn't weigh that much."

Jessie hurried up the petunia-bordered concrete path, unlocked the front door, and held it open for Helen, who arrived a minute later leading Matthew by the hand.

"He woke up when I tried to lift him," Helen whispered. "But I want to get him to sleep. It's eleven our time."

Jessie led the way through a small octagonal tiled entry hall down a carpeted hallway. She stopped at the first open door and switched on the light. With the exception of a made-up folding bed and a stack of toys on the white linoleum (a bright-yellow Tonka dump truck, a Lego helicopter kit, Junior Scrabble, and other games that the Toys Я Us salesgirl had recommended for eight-year-old boys), the pale-yellow room was empty.

"Oh, Jess, that's so sweet of you, getting all this for Matthew. This is the second bedroom?"

"Yes." It was the room Jessie rarely entered, because of the memories. "I borrowed the bed from a neighbor. I hope it's comfortable. The closet has shelves, but there's no dresser. Sorry."

"That's OK." Helen sounded uncertain.

"I can try to get some more shelves. Boxes, maybe."

"It's not that. It's—" Helen leaned close and whispered. "Matthew has bad dreams sometimes. And this house is unfamiliar to him. Is there a way we could be together?"

There was a leather couch in the den, but the room was too small to accommodate another bed. "Use my bedroom."

Helen shook her head. "No. This will be fine." She turned to Matthew. "You'll sleep here, hon. Mommy won't be far, OK?"

"Helen, I was going to put you and Neil there anyway, because the den has just a couch. Tomorrow I'll get another folding bed."

Helen hesitated, then said, "Just for tonight, then."

Jessie led Helen and Matthew to her bedroom. The country French headboard, bed, dresser, and nightstands were new; Gary had taken their black lacquered set and the living-room furniture as part of their settlement. Jessie had painted the bedroom herself, a pale peach. She'd removed the carpeting and splurged on having the wood floors bleached and sealed.

The peach-and-green floral quilted bedspread lay folded in a corner of the room. In the morning Jessie had put fresh linens on the king-size bed but had left the spread off, then put it on, then decided the room looked more welcoming with it off. She'd put coral roses from the backyard in a crystal vase on the dresser. For Helen *and* Neil, she thought, then told herself, *let it ride.*

Helen sat Matthew on the bed and unlaced a Reebok.

"I'll get the luggage." Jessie pointed to a door on the right wall. "This is the bathroom. I put out fresh towels."

"Thanks. The smallest case has Matthew's things. If you could get that first?"

Helen was gazing out a window when Jessie returned. Matthew was still on the bed. He'd removed his denim jacket but was clothed except for his socks and shoes.

Jessie placed the suitcase near the bed. "Need any help?"

"Jess, Matthew's shy about undressing in front of other people." Helen's voice was awkward with soft apology.

"Oh. Sure." Jessie took a step backward. "Are you hungry, Helen? I could make sandwiches, some soup."

"No, thanks. We had dinner on the flight. Maybe some fruit."

"Fine. Well, good night, Matthew." Jessie smiled at him.

"Say good night to Aunt Jessie, Matthew. And say thank you for inviting us to stay with her."

"Thank you, Aunt Jessie, for inviting us." Matthew yawned.

"And?" Helen prompted with a smile.

"G'night, Aunt Jessie."

Jessie took the rest of the baggage from the Honda and put it in the spare bedroom. Then she prepared a platter of fruit. She was sitting at the oak-trimmed white Formica table in the breakfast nook, eating a cube of cantaloupe, when Helen entered.

"You started without me!" Helen grinned and sat down. "I'll bet melons are much cheaper here. How much were the cantaloupes? In Winnetka, I pay sixty-nine cents a pound."

"Three for a dollar. I bought them on special at a small market on Pico. But you have to pick the right ones." And not just melons, she thought, lifting another pale-orange cube.

"I know. Matthew once left some slices in his knapsack. It took me forever to get the smell out. Gross." Helen wrinkled her nose. "What's wrong?" she said when Jessie put down the cube.

"Nothing." Nothing Helen would want to know about, anyway. Her comment had reminded Jessie of a conversation she'd had two days ago with Brenda Royes, a detective in Central Division. Close friends from their police academy days, the women were in constant touch, and Brenda had told her about a sixty-three-year-old Chinese woman whose death she was investigating.

"The body was on the living room sofa, but there was this godawful stink coming from the kitchen and I thought, hell, what now? But it was just two cantaloupes rotting on the counter for God knows how long. The flies were having themselves a feast. Good thing you weren't there, Jess. Your nose was always sensitive!" She'd laughed. "Tell you the truth, between the death smell and the cantaloupes, I almost tossed my cookies."

"Jess?" Helen said. "Are you there?"

Jessie looked up. "Sorry. What were you saying?"

Helen took a cluster of flame grapes. "I asked if you've been dating since you and Gary. . ."

"No one special." Her partner had fixed her up; so had Brenda. There had been a few pleasant dates. But Jessie wasn't ready for a relationship, or intimacy. "No one as cute as Matthew." She smiled.

"Thanks." Helen looked pleased. "We think he's terrific. He's impressed that you're a detective, by the way. Before he fell asleep he said, 'Can Aunt Jessie show me her gun?' "

Jessie frowned. "Guns aren't toys, Helen."

"I know that! He's just curious and—" Indecision played across her face. "I told you he has dreams? Sometimes he talks about the bad man coming. But I told him his Aunt Jessie won't let the bad man hurt him. He liked that."

"Who's the bad man?"

"No one special. The school psychologist said it's normal for kids his age to have dreams like that. I guess we had them, too, when we were Matthew's age, huh?"

"I guess," Jessie said, although she couldn't remember dreaming about a bad man. About other things, yes. "He seems kind of quiet, Helen. Is he OK?"

"Of course he's OK!" Helen laughed. "He's exhausted, poor thing. Tomorrow he'll be himself, and you'll wish he were quiet again. By the way, is it safe around here? Winnetka's great, but Chicago . . ." She shook her head.

"It's pretty safe, but you have to be sensible. Don't open the door to strangers, that kind of stuff. Common sense, really, when you live in a big city."

Not that people always used common sense, Jessie thought. Even if they did, sometimes it wasn't enough. Thirteen years on the police force had taught her that.

3

Thursday, June 25

Norma Jeffreys hitched her brown vinyl purse higher on her shoulder and sandwiched it between her arm and side. She strode down the street, her crepe-soled white shoes leaving the predawn quiet undisturbed. The bus stop was only six blocks from her apartment, but the gray-black landscape of the neighborhood emerging from the amorphous, inky night always filled her with a fluttery feeling that was close to, but not quite, apprehension.

"Boogly-wooglies," five-year-old Jolene would call it.

Not that Norma worried. She was a tall, imposing, large-framed woman, strong enough to single-handedly lift even the heaviest patients in the orthopedic wing at Cedars-Sinai Medical Center. She'd been working the early shift there for three years (she'd given up private nursing after Lloyd had died; the pay was good, but the hours too erratic in her new status as a single parent), and the one time some junkie had pulled a knife on her, demanding her money, she'd swung her handbag into his face with such vehement strength born of indignation and fury that it had knocked him, senseless, to the ground. (Later, she'd marveled at her boldness; still later, she'd sat shaking, immobilized by the thought that she could have orphaned her three children.)

That had been a year ago. Claudine had been twelve, too old and grave even then for her years and dubious about the wisdom of her mother's action. But ten-year-old Jerome had basked in the vicarious glory, embellishing the story for classmates and friends. And after a few weeks, Norma had stopped tensing whenever she passed the spot where the junkie had suddenly loomed, the knife barely visible in the half-light of the early morning.

Still, she'd taken a self-defense course at a Watts community center and listened carefully to the young policewoman's lecture on safety in the streets: "Walk briskly. Don't look around as if you're nervous. It's your street. Look confident. Be prepared."

She was prepared, all right, and so was the neighborhood. The shops, including a shoe store, a beauty salon, a liquor store, and drugstore, were all armored with gates and padlocks. Lonely veterans, they stood amid the ruins of other shops that had been looted and torched during the 1992 riots that had blazed through the city and left fifty-eight people dead. Gates and padlocks had been no protection then. If Norma closed her eyes, she could still see the fires, exploding balls of hot orange spiraling madly upward. She could still smell the smoke. The fear. There had been talk of rebuilding, but so far it had stayed mostly that—talk.

The bus stop at 103rd and Central Avenue was deserted. The bench was filled with colorful graffiti carved into the wood and a lewd invitation from Tony R. to Wanda S. Norma settled herself on the bench. She hoped Claudine would remember to give Jolene the amoxycillin. There were six tablets left, and you had to take all of them or the strep could come back. Maybe she'd call Claudine from the hospital. Better not. The girl would resent the reminder. Norma sighed. She was a good girl, Claudine, and not just because she gave the kids snacks after school and started supper. Starting to look real pretty, too, but she was more interested in her studies than in boys, thank goodness. There was time for that.

Norma heard the man approaching the bench before she actually saw him standing in front of her.

"Excuse me, ma'am. How can I get to Third and La Cienega?"

"Take the fifty-three bus. Transfer to the one-oh-five on Vernon." It was the route she took every morning. She shifted to the right and moved her handbag onto her lap, the flap with the clasp pressed against her abdomen. She wasn't worried; her mind had registered the necessary details—Caucasian, shorter than average, slight build, beige jacket and tie, pleasant-looking face—but you never knew.

The man sat on the left edge of the bench. "Bus coming soon?"

He sounded nervous, she thought. Probably *was* nervous, a white man in an all-black neighborhood. She wondered what he was doing here. She checked her watch. "About eight minutes."

He nodded. *Seven and a half,* he wanted to tell her. He'd verified the schedule. On Monday morning he'd reached his observation site at 6:00 but had been disconcerted. Too much human traffic. On Tuesday and Wednesday he'd arrived by 5:10, and on both days he'd seen the large black woman approaching the bus stop, looking like an ambulatory lighthouse in her white uniform.

Angels of mercy, they called nurses. Well, some were angels, he guessed, although as a rule he'd found them to be ordinary humans at best, with a "roll-up-your-sleeve" efficiency that fell just short of brusqueness. His mother's nurse—what was her name? Maria? Marina?—now *she* had seemed caring, but she probably just put on an act when he came to the nursing home on Saturdays.

Marianne; that was it. She looked like an angel, too, with a halo of wispy blond curls around her face. He'd invited her for coffee last time, and she'd said, oh, I'm sorry, I'm married, but he hadn't seen a wedding band. Which didn't mean she was lying; she could've taken it off to wash the dishes and forgotten it at home. His mother used to leave her wedding band on a heart-shaped porcelain ring holder he'd bought her for Mother's Day when he was ten. (*"Junk,"* his father had said, but his mother had said, *"Ooooh, it's so pretty, I'll treasure it always."*) And the next Saturday when he visited his mother, Marianne was gone, so now he'd never know if she was really married. Probably not. She probably didn't want to have coffee with him. The ring holder was long gone, too, lost in one of their many moves across the country.

The black nurse had moved over and was cradling her purse like a newborn. She was staring straight ahead, avoiding eye contact. This morning she'd showed up a minute earlier than she had on the previous days. That was good, because he was cutting things close, and he wondered again if the bus stop had been a good idea after all, so public and exposed. His eye twitched and his breathing quickened, and he felt inside his jacket pocket for the reassuring presence of the readied syringe.

She was married. He could see two yellow gold bands, one with a miniscule diamond, embedded into her finger. There were probably children, too, but he couldn't let that stop him, although the elderly Chinese woman had been easier in that sense. But Norma Jeffreys (he'd read her name tag when he'd stood in front of her) wasn't his choice. Chance had dictated the area; chance, not he, had brought her to this bus stop in Watts, and he had to go through with it (*"Sissy!"*), couldn't stop now (*"You're a mama's boy, is what you are!"*). He had to play fair.

He sneezed loudly.

"Bless you." Out of the corner of her eye Norma saw him take out a white handkerchief from his jacket pocket. "Allergies," she heard him say, almost apologetically, and she wasn't surprised, because his eyes had seemed watery to her, and she wanted to tell him tissues were more sanitary, but suddenly he was lunging toward her, and the handkerchief with its sickly sweet odor was over her nostrils and mouth, and she couldn't yell, couldn't breathe.

4

Jessie had forgotten how uncomfortable it was to sleep in the den. All night the sheet had slipped over the leather sofa cushions, and Jessie with it; several times she'd had to disentangle herself from her mummylike wrappings. She'd also stubbed her toe on the desk under the window that faced the backyard. She'd been disoriented when she'd awakened in the night to go to the guest bathroom—she could have switched on the halogen floor lamp near the sofa, but she hadn't wanted to be blinded by its light.

Who was the guest here, anyway?

On the strip of space between the sofa and desk, Jessie did her twenty-minute academy fitness-maintenance routine. In the bathroom she turned on the stall shower faucets, took off her nightshirt, and reached for the shower cap. Which she'd forgotten to take from her bathroom when she'd moved some clothes into the den closet, and toiletries and makeup into the guest bathroom.

Damn.

She shut the faucets and put on her nightshirt. One of

the two doors from the master bathroom opened onto the hall, but it was locked. She walked to her bedroom and eased the door open. Mother and son were asleep, curled up in semifetal positions at opposite sides of the bed. Like Gary and I used to sleep at the end, she thought, and quickly banished the memory.

She tiptoed to the bathroom and took the shower cap from the cabinet under the sink. She looked around to see if there was anything else she'd forgotten, then remembered she'd be back in her bedroom tonight. If she could borrow another folding bed.

After she showered and put on makeup, Jessie dressed with special care—she was testifying in court this afternoon. A gray skirt (part of a suit), a white, short-sleeved silk blouse, black pumps instead of her usual flats, gold earrings. A spritz of Anne Klein cologne. Businesslike, with a touch of femininity.

She was back in the bathroom, brushing her hair (she'd pinned it up, but it had made her look too severe), when she suddenly sensed someone behind her. She whirled, brush in midair, then immediately relaxed and smiled.

"Oh, hi, Matthew. I thought you were sleeping—that's why I was startled." And my training sometimes goes into overdrive.

Matthew had taken a step back. He was wearing a pair of jeans and a cotton knit Guess? shirt. His hair was damp and flattened, the neat furrows of a comb clearly visible.

"I'm sorry," he said in a small voice.

Jessie realized he was staring at the brush. She put it on the counter. "No, *I'm* sorry. I didn't mean to scare you." She smiled. "I guess we scared each other, huh? Is your mom sleeping?"

Matthew nodded.

"How about breakfast? Eggs? Toast? Cereal?" On Sunday

she'd make pancakes. She hadn't made pancakes in a hundred years.

"Cereal, please."

She was reminded of the orphan in *Oliver. "More, please."* "Come on, Matthew," she said cheerfully. "We'll eat together."

He followed her to the kitchen. It was a small rectangle with white-and-green speckled ceramic tile counters and a white linoleum floor. After Gary had moved out, she'd added hanging plants and placed pots of basil, oregano, and dill next to the radio on the wide window ledge above the sink. The oak cabinets had been painted white by the previous owner. Someday Jessie wanted to strip the paint and refinish them into a bleached oak.

Jessie opened the cabinet she used as a pantry. "I didn't know what you like, so I bought a few brands. So what'll it be—Frosted Flakes, Fruit Loops, Kix, or Cocoa Puffs?" Her partner, Phil Okum, had passed on his two sons' recommendations.

"I'm not allowed to have junk cereals."

He sounds wistful, she thought. And strangely proud. "Maybe your mom'll let you, 'cause you're on vacation." If not, what am I going to do with all this stuff? Have a slumber party?

Matthew hesitated, then shook his head.

They settled on Raisin Bran for Matthew, Product 19 for Jessie, orange juice for both. He filled his bowl with cereal and poured the milk. When a drop of milk spilled onto the table, he looked at her and quickly wiped it with his napkin.

What do I talk about with an eight-year-old nephew I hardly know? "I'll bet you miss your dad, huh?"

"Uh-huh." Crunch.

"He must have interesting things to tell you about his trips." Neil had been to Europe, Africa, China, and several Arab countries. "And pictures. He must take lots of pictures."

"Some." Another crunch.

Dead end. Jessie ate a few spoonfuls of cereal. "I thought we'd go to Universal Studios on Saturday. Would you like that?" According to Phil, Universal, Disneyland, and Magic Mountain were the Big Three for kids.

Matthew looked up. "Is it all rides? I throw up sometimes."

Forget Magic Mountain then, and most of Disneyland. Helen, Jessie recalled vividly, had suffered from a sensitive stomach, too. "There's a tour of famous places used in movies and TV. And stunt shows. An E.T. show—that's pretty new. Plus a fake earthquake."

"Is it scary?" His eyes were darker somehow, larger.

"No. But we can skip the tour and just see the shows. I think you'll like Universal, Matthew."

"OK." Matthew resumed eating.

About a four on the enthusiasm scale. "Are you looking forward to going to camp when you're back home?"

"I liked camp," Matthew said. "My mother says—"

"There you are, Matthew." Helen was standing in the doorway in a short white eyelet robe. "You were so quiet, hon, I didn't hear you get up." She yawned.

"I folded my pajamas."

"I saw. I'm proud of you." She walked slowly to him and hugged him, then looked at the table. "Raisin Bran is Matthew's favorite. You must be psychic, Jess." She smiled and sat down.

"Not quite. I bought some other cereals, but he says he's not allowed to eat junk."

Which was funny, because Jessie remembered how, as kids, she and Helen had sneaked sugary cereals into the house on the rare occasions they'd gone marketing with their father. *"When we have kids,"* they'd vowed, *"we'll let them eat whatever they want."*

"Neil's strict about Matthew's eating right. But if you

want something else, hon . . . ?" Helen's mouth looked suddenly pinched.

Matthew shook his head.

What else was Neil strict about? Jessie wondered. Occasional visits over the past ten years had reinforced her original impression of her forty-three-year-old brother-in-law: pleasant, caring, responsible, ambitious, with a need for order and structure.

Jessie checked her watch: 7:55. "If you want me to drop you off at the car-rental place, we'll have to leave soon."

"Not today, Jess. I have a migraine. Fierce." Along with her blond hair and petite figure, Helen had inherited her migraines from their mother. They came on with no warning and lasted hours. "I'll lie down with a compress. We can get the car tomorrow."

Jessie went to the hall closet for her gun and holster. She inserted a clip in the gun, belted the holster around her waist, and slipped in the gun. Her suit jacket obscured its bulge. When she returned to the kitchen, Helen was talking quietly to Matthew.

". . . will be OK. You believe Mommy, don't you?"

Jessie cleared her throat. "Helen?"

Helen turned and smiled at Jessie. "You look so professional. My sister, the detective. Are you leaving?"

"Yes." She handed Helen a key. "This is for the front door. Don't forget it if you leave the house."

"Unlikely." Helen shook her head, then winced. "Matthew can watch TV or read one of the books he brought. He's a trooper when Mommy has a headache, aren't you, hon?" She kissed him.

Jessie hesitated, then said, "Matthew can come with me. I'll be in court this afternoon, but my morning's pretty clear." She had to drop off papers at the D.A.'s, and she'd planned to shoot to qualify at the academy range, an LAPD bimonthly requirement for all its officers. "How about it, Matthew?"

The boy looked at his mother. "Can I?"

An eleven on the scale; Jessie would have to tell Phil.

"Aunt Jessie's just being kind. She's a busy woman."

"It's no problem, Helen, or I wouldn't have offered. I'll have him back by noon." Actually, it would be a pain—driving back to West L.A., then downtown again, but she felt sorry for Matthew.

"Please, Mommy? Please?"

"Matthew, you know I don't like to be nagged. Another time, Jess. He's still tired from the trip."

He doesn't look tired to me, Jessie thought as she backed the Honda onto the street. But it was her sister's child, her sister's call. She wondered what Helen had been discussing with Matthew—what would "be OK"? Her headache? The vacation? Or was it—?

Shit, she told herself, shaking her head. She grinned and turned on the car radio. Always the detective.

That's what Gary had said, too.

Her partner was in the station. Jessie spotted his green Cutlass in the police lot on Butler Avenue. The lot was crowded with black-and-whites, which meant roll-call hadn't ended. She circled once, then parked in the first space at the lot's entrance, right next to a row of aluminum trash cans that shimmered in the reflected light of the already intense sun.

It was going to be a scorcher. No breeze in sight. The American flag suspended from a pole above the two-story station was drooping. As she walked through the curved entry, she wondered for the thousandth time who had chosen its orange-red glazed oblong tiles. They made a sharp contrast to the taupe-colored stone building—more commercial, somehow, and better suited to a Pizza Hut than a police station.

She passed through Records, said her good-mornings, picked up some folders, then took the stairs to the second-floor reception room. The row of attached mustard-colored molded plastic seats along the left wall was empty.

"Morning, Elsa," Jessie said to the receptionist behind the large, L-shaped wood-tone desk. Like a number of the clerical staff in the city's underbudgeted police stations, she was a volunteer. "Messages?"

"Hi, Jessie. Just one." Elsa handed her a slip.

"Thanks." It was from Brenda Royes, Jessie read. "Can't make lunch. Call me." At the half-door along the left side of the L, Jessie waited for Elsa to buzz her in, then passed through reception into the large partitionless room that had become her home.

No Pizza Hut decor here. Industrial brown-gold carpet that almost camouflaged the coffee spills. A freestanding bookcase filled with "blue books"—loose-leaf binders with grim data and grimmer photos for each case. A bank of orange lockers at the back of the room. Another bank of pale-green lockers next to it. A rummage-sale collection of beige metal desks and scarred oak tables arranged to form the various detective "tables." Assorted chairs.

There was a shortage of chairs. Jessie smiled, remembering how she'd had to scrounge around the station to "appropriate" hers when she'd made detective seven years ago.

She'd studied damn hard for the test. She'd scored ninety-seven percent on the written civil-service exam, but she'd *had* to score high to have any chance of passing. She knew they'd deduct from her oral. She hadn't put in the years.

But she'd made it—on the first try, too. She'd gotten looks for that, more than a few grudging ones. She'd rotated among all the tables—Juvenile, Robbery, Auto Theft, Sex Crimes, Burglary, CAPS (Crimes against Persons). She'd done extremely well, had made a stir when she broke up a major auto-theft ring that targeted homes in Brentwood. Another when she'd disarmed a kidnapper who had snatched the twelve-year-old son of a Pacific Palisades doctor. That had made all the papers: JESSIE DRAKE SAVES THE DAY. DRAKE TO THE RESCUE. BEAUTY TAMES THE BEAST.

She hadn't loved the last headline—she wanted to be recognized for her prowess, not her looks. And she'd taken a lot of kidding about it at the station. But her name had risen on "the list," and then a spot on the Homicide table had become available.

"Why Homicide?" the department psychologist had asked. It was a routine question, and he'd asked it in a routine voice.

"Why Homicide?" Gary had asked in a not-so-routine voice.

"Homicide?" Helen had shuddered two thousand miles away.

Her parents hadn't even asked. They'd stopped questioning her career choices long ago.

Jessie's answer had satisfied the psychologist—and most of the time, herself.

"Hey, Drake," Phil called. "About time you got here."

She looked diagonally across the room at her partner and grinned. "Hey, yourself. Not my fault you have to work twice as many hours to keep up with me."

"Now you've hurt my feelings." He went back to typing on the keyboard of the only PC in the room. Most of the detectives wrote their reports, but Phil's handwriting was illegible. "You should've been a doctor," Jessie always told him. "Like my dad."

Phil Okum was a big, burly man with a walrus mustache and a ruddy complexion. And a big heart. He'd never treated her with a hint of condescension, never given her reason to believe he resented being partnered with a woman. Which wasn't the case with all the cops she'd encountered.

Some of her friends had war stories to tell, too. Like Brenda. Which reminded her. Jessie called Central. Brenda was away from her desk. Jessie left a message.

She looked at the opposite wall. Lieutenant Kalish was in, and alone; the miniblinds on his office windows were open. She walked around several tables, exchanging hellos with her colleagues—some were sitting, writing notes; two were drinking coffee and talking. She knocked on Kalish's door and entered.

Kalish was sitting at his desk, which was littered with papers and folders. He was a tall, angular man with a long, thin face, an aquiline nose, and keen brown eyes. He reminded Jessie of Sherlock Holmes, and she'd often wondered whether he smoked a pipe in the privacy of his home.

"You ready for this afternoon, Drake?"

When it was court appearance time, Kalish called her Drake. Otherwise, it was "Jessie." Rarely "Jess."

"I'm ready."

"Don't let Slater rattle you."

Slater was a high-priced Beverly Hills attorney defending a higher-priced film celebrity charged with the first-degree murder of her real-estate tycoon husband and his male lover.

A not-atypical West L.A. case. And understandably high profile. Jessie had been hounded by the media from the start, but she'd been polite, unruffled, not giving anything away. (Something she'd learned to do over the years. At a price.) She felt good about the way she'd handled the reporters and the anchors.

All except one. Gary Drake, her ex, was a crime reporter for the *L.A. Times*. (That's how they'd met six years ago.) With him, she'd been on the defensive, had bristled at his "you-owe-me-after-everything-that-happened" tone. He'd be in the courtroom today, she knew. Was that why she'd fussed with her hair?

"I won't let him get to me," Jessie promised Kalish, meaning Slater. Or did she?

Kalish went over some questions Slater might raise. Then he said, "Sounds good. This is for the D.A." He handed her a manila envelope. "Nice going, Jess." He smiled and gestured thumbs up.

"Thanks." She turned quickly before he could see her blush.

Jessie walked back to her desk and tried Brenda again. This time the receptionist told her Brenda was out in the field and would be back sometime in the afternoon. So much for that.

And so much for going to the academy. It had seemed like a good idea, but that was when she and Brenda were going to have lunch. And gossip. And Jessie *was* wearing a silk blouse and pumps.

What the hell, she decided. I'll go tomorrow. Instead, she and Phil went over lab reports that had come back from the medical examiner's office on a case they were working. Then she made calls to follow up leads on the fatal stabbing of a homeless man who'd been found on Santa Monica near Bundy. In West L.A., she'd learned right away, you got the most affluent and the most destitute.

When she finished writing up her notes (Phil was hogging the computer), she called home to see how Helen was doing. After four rings, the answering machine picked up. She must be sleeping, Jessie thought, and hung up before the recorded message came on.

Jessie checked her watch: eleven-thirty. Time to go downtown, deliver the papers to the D.A., grab a quick lunch. And testify.

Jessie was scheduled to appear at two o'clock, but she arrived at the courthouse at one o'clock—just after the lunch recess, judging by the crowds in the lobby and on the elevators.

Gary was there. His back was toward her, but she recognized the broad shoulders, the curly dark-blond hair. She hoped she could avoid him, but just as she was about to pass through the wide double doors, he turned and saw her.

Their eyes made contact. He looks great, she thought with a familiar pang as he loped over to her side. She smiled tightly, wondering when she would no longer be a hostage to memory.

"Hi, Jess. I heard you were going on this afternoon. Nervous?" His dark-blue eyes studied her.

He made it sound like an audition, she thought with a flash of irritation. "I'm prepared."

"Any surprises in store for us?"

"No." Just the facts, ma'am.

"You'd tell me first, right? For old times' sake?" He smiled.

It was a lopsided smile, a wonderful smile that had once worked magic. "I can't play favorites, Gary. You know that."

"Oh, yeah. Don't I." He leaned close. "You look great, Jess. I like your hair like that, a little too long, a little wild. Isn't being too feminine against department regulations?"

"Good-bye, Gary." She took a step toward the doorway.

"Sorry." He touched her arm. "Just kidding. How *is* everything, Jess? Really?" He sounded sincere.

"Fine. Helen and Matthew are visiting. Neil's in Saudi Arabia." She saw Gary's expression. "He hasn't been going as often lately." Gary had always criticized Neil's extensive absences. Family's more important, he'd said.

"Mind if I stop by to say hello? If it's all right with Helen, that is."

It would be childish to say no. And selfish. Helen would be uncomfortable at first, feeling in the middle, but she'd love seeing Gary. She'd liked him from the start, had encouraged Jessie to marry him, had been devastated when Jessie had phoned about the divorce. "But why?" Helen had cried. A no-fault divorce, Jessie had explained. An amicable parting, an equitable settlement. The "why" was too difficult, too complicated to explain. Too painful.

"Sure, Gary. Call first, OK?" Jessie would try to be away.

"No problem. Good luck on the stand. I mean it, Jess. I'm still your friend, you know." He leaned over, as if to kiss her on the cheek, but at the last second pulled back.

His action left her flustered, although she wasn't sure why, and she walked into the courtroom without looking back.

A little over an hour later, her name was called. She was on the stand for twenty minutes. Slater was everything she'd heard, but she kept her cool. Answered his questions, didn't volunteer anything. She could see from the jurors' expressions that she'd made points, points that Slater's dismissive hand gestures and skeptical tone couldn't erase. Still, she was relieved when Slater finished and the judge excused her. She stepped off the witness stand and walked out of the courtroom to a water fountain. God, her mouth was dry! She bent down to take a sip.

"Great ass."

Jessie stood up, then laughed when she saw the tall, slim, olive-skinned woman standing near her. "What are you doing here, Brenda? I didn't see you in the courtroom."

"I got your messages to my message. I was in the area, so I figured I'd come see you perform. Great job." Brenda clapped. "Great legs, too. Slater couldn't keep his eyes off them. Every time you crossed them . . ." Brenda rolled her eyes and laughed.

Suspects had been mesmerized by those cavernous, liquid brown eyes, Jessie knew. The same eyes that could turn as cold and relentless as granite. "It's the Hanes Ultra Sheer." Jessie grinned. "I thought you were in the field."

"I was. Mae Sung Lee, this Chinese woman I told you about?" Brenda shook her head. Her long dark-brown waves danced. "The guys at Central are ribbing me, calling it the Cantaloupe Caper, but let me tell you, it's weird."

"What do you mean?"

"Well, first we thought heart attack or stroke. She was on the sofa, eyes closed. Looked like she died in her sleep. 'No, no,' the daughter insists. 'My mom was healthy as a horse, saw a doctor two weeks ago.' The doctor confirms. So OK. The M.E. does an autopsy. He calls me this morning, says he found a puncture wound on the inside of her arm. But we didn't find a syringe."

"So someone killed the mother. What's the M.E.'s guess?"

"He's running tox screens. He doesn't know what he's looking for. It could take a while."

"So why is that weird?"

"That's not the weird part. The first time I was in the old lady's apartment, I found a hundred-dollar bill attached to a bank deposit slip in plain sight on the coffee table."

"So you're wondering why the killer didn't take the money?"

"I'm wondering whether he *left* it. And if he did, why. See, the daughter says Mae Lee *never* left money lying around. She didn't keep it in banks, either. Didn't trust 'em. I checked with the bank, Jess. The First Public Savings Bank on Hill and Alpine. Mae Sung Lee never had an account there."

"That *is* weird," Jessie said.

5

Thursday, July 2

He slipped the twenty-dollar bills into his wallet. The first time he'd counted only nine and felt a rush of anger and frustration, convinced he'd been shortchanged. But he'd counted again, and they were all there, all ten bills. Two had been stuck together. He shouldn't have allowed himself to become so upset; that was something he had to work on, he knew. He had to stay in control.

But it wasn't the twenty dollars. It was the enforced hiatus, the lull in the play. He'd have to wait an entire week before he could make his next move. He felt flat. Dead, somehow.

He'd checked the *Times* every day, but there had been no mention of the Oriental woman or of the black nurse. Well, *he* knew; that's what counted, wasn't it? Soon they would all know.

Later that night, after supper, he wondered who would be next. But it was a waste of time to engage in idle speculation.

Tomorrow night he would know.

6

Thursday, July 9

"So," Alek Radovsky said aloud to the empty room. He closed the anesthesia textbook, dropped his pen onto his notebook, and massaged his eyes.

Alek was familiar with the material—overly familiar; he'd studied it and all his other medical courses in Moscow and received top scores, a special commendation, even, when he'd graduated. But none of that mattered. Here in the United States of America, his medical degree was worthless.

Before Alek had applied for an exit visa, he and Galina had discussed the disadvantages—the wasted years of education and experience; the separation until he could afford to bring her and the two boys to join him in Los Angeles (he had a cousin here who had sponsored him); the harassment Galina and the boys might suffer because of his request to leave. In the end they'd decided that leaving was best for all of them.

Now, eighteen months since he'd left Galina at the Moscow airport, he felt discouraged. Not regretful, never that. There was no future for them in Moscow. But it was frustrating to sit in classrooms with men in their twenties—boys, really—when you were a thirty-six-year-old doctor with eight years of experience who should be healing the ill, not listening to a professor explain a procedure you'd performed hundreds of times.

And he was so lonely. He'd been unprepared for the empty nights, the empty bed. He couldn't blame his cousin; there had been nothing grudging about his helpfulness. Victor Malinov had met Alek at the airport and taken him to this one-bedroom apartment on North Orange Grove that he'd found for him.

A good neighborhood, Victor had assured him; he lived nearby, in one of the two-story pastel stucco apartment buildings filled with Russian Jewish immigrants. A few blocks to the west was Fairfax Avenue with clothing stores, fruit stands, groceries, kosher pizza shops, a falafel stand, several small restaurants. Even a movie theater. To the south was Melrose, a once-sleepy street occupied by hardware stores and funeral monument shops that had metamorphosed into a trendy, funky boulevard crowded day and night with cars and people. On Melrose and Fairfax there was a high school where Alek could take an adult education English course if he wanted. There were also several synagogues nearby; Alek was considering going to one of them to learn about the religion that he and his parents had been forbidden to practice in Russia.

It was Victor who introduced Alek to the consumer wonderlands of Pic N' Save and K mart, who took him to a used-furniture store on Vermont, who helped Alek find a job as an auto mechanic in a body shop on Pico. "Just temporary," they'd assured each other. Victor and his pretty, smiling wife Elena invited him often, but Alek didn't want to increase the debt he owed them. And the truth was that being with them—savoring home-cooked brisket and browned potatoes (almost as good as Galina's) instead of consuming almost cold pizza while he read, speaking in his native tongue instead of breaking his teeth on the English language, reminiscing about faces and places back home— the truth was that all this intensified his aloneness, his longing to caress his wife's face and body, to crush the boys to his chest in a giant hug.

He would write home tonight, a short letter to let Galina know he was all right. Galina's letters were never short, and she wrote at least twice a week. He could hear her low, musical voice through her beautifully scripted words, and he read the letters with the stories about the boys' escapades, about her job as a kindergarten teacher, about the situation at the market ("Still no toothpaste, can you imagine, Alek?"), he read them over and over until he knew them by heart. He always carried the latest letter with him, folded in his wallet. At the auto shop he had little time to glance at it, but during class, with one ear listening so that he wouldn't miss anything or be caught daydreaming, he would unfold the thin parchment and be instantly transported home.

The ringing of the bell startled him. Who could be visiting him so late at night? Victor? But he would have called first.

Alek walked to the door. "Who is, please?"

"Mr. Radovsky? Sorry to bother you, but your neighbor downstairs said you're the person I should talk to."

Alek opened the door. "I no can understand what you are saying."

The man stared at him. "Your—your car, Mr. Radovsky. You do own that blue Chevy Caprice parked in front of the building?"

"Yes, yes. Is mine. But—"

"I bumped into it trying to park. I don't think there's

any damage, but your neighbor came out and looked like she was going to call the police, and I don't want any trouble."

"You hit my car? *My* car?" Disbelief had been quickly strangled by indignation. Alek stepped into the hall, yanked the door shut behind him, and headed for the stairs. He'd bought the used Chevy from one of his boss's customers just six months ago, had spent a great deal of the precious free time he had between his work and school hours to repair the mechanical flaws and perform some cosmetic surgery on the body. The thought that some reckless, half-brained driver had injured the car infuriated him.

The man followed him down the narrow staircase. "Look, if there *is* some minor damage, which I doubt, I want to pay you in cash. I don't want to go through the insurance."

"We see." He would say nothing, accept nothing until he could see the damage. Should he call Victor? He sprinted down the last few steps and headed for the car.

The man was right behind him. "That's mine, the Buick in front of your car. There's a dent on your front bumper, but that must have been there before because if you look closely, you can see that it looks rusty. Anyway, if I did something, I'm sorry."

Sorry. In America, you say "Sorry" and everything is all right. Alek maneuvered himself between the two cars. "Where?"

"Near your left headlight."

Alek bent down and peered at the bumper. He fingered the area. It felt smooth. "I no see—" he said, turning toward the man impatiently, and then a handkerchief was smothering him, a handkerchief with a sickeningly sweet odor that was so familiar.

If Alek Radovsky had regained consciousness, he would have experienced several of the initial effects of the substance injected into his vein: dizziness, blurred vision, a strange sensation in his toes, ears, and eyes, facial paralysis. And since he was an experienced doctor, though not a practicing one, he would probably have identified the substance.

But Alek Radovsky never regained consciousness.

Even if he had, it wouldn't have mattered.

He'd almost lost his nerve. He always rehearsed in front of his bathroom mirror so that he'd look and sound just right, but at the first instant that he and the Russian were standing face to face, he'd been terribly flustered, almost immobilized.

Radovsky was so small! On the previous day he'd watched the Russian to see which car was his, but he hadn't realized he was this slight, this short. Almost as short as *he* was. In the end, of course, he'd gone through with it. Later, he felt the satisfaction of another transaction successfully completed, but the heady excitement he'd experienced after the first two killings wasn't there. The Russian had disturbed him; he'd felt an instant, unwelcome affinity for the small man. . . .

"Eat your steak, boy. You need steak to put a little muscle on you, to make a man out of you, not all that sissy-prissy crap your mother's been feeding you."

"I ate most of it. I can't eat any more."

"You'll finish it, or you won't leave the table. You will not leave this table, I tell you."

"Ed, it's too much for him. He ate more than half."

"Shut up! Was I talking to you, huh? Did you hear me ask your advice? He knows this is for his own good, don't you, boy?"

"Yes."

"Yes, what?"

"Yes, sir."

"Damn right. What did the doctor say today, Ella? Aren't there shots? Steroids or something. Did you tell him I'm five feet eleven inches and his brother's over six feet?"

"Ed, he doesn't need shots. He won't reach your height, but the doctor says he's absolutely normal in development."

"Normal? Look at him, will you! Sixteen years old, and he looks ten. It's your fault, Ella, for not carrying him to term."

"Ed, please. Can we talk about this later?"

They always talked about him as if he weren't there. His father, his teachers, the kids at school. In later years, his coworkers, his bosses. He was invisible to all of them.

"Well, let me tell you something, missus, that is not a normal height for someone in my family. What's he going to be? A chimney sweep? A bowlegged jockey who spends his life getting thrown on his ass by some dumb horse? Not my son. Ella, bring him a glass of milk to go with that steak. Milk is what makes your bones grow, boy, or don't they teach you that in school?"

"Ed, you know he can't have milk products. He—"

"Don't you start about the allergies, do you hear me? Allergies is just the doctors' excuse for taking our money. How the hell can the boy get stronger if they keep poking him with needles every week? The boy knows I'm right. Don't you?"

"Yes, sir." Choking on the steak, forcing it down his gullet, praying he wouldn't gag. If he cut it into small, very small pieces, maybe it wouldn't be so bad.

"Good boy. Your mother, she means well, but she doesn't know how to raise a son—she doesn't know that a man's gotta be strong, that power's everything. I seen that in the service. I seen it every day on the job. Power's what counts, boy. Don't forget it."

Well, he had power now, didn't he? He'd proved it three times. With the Chinese woman. With the big nurse, sitting like a hulking monolith. With the Russian.

Very soon, he would no longer be invisible. Everybody would know who he was. Everybody would pay.

7

"Think we have enough?" Jessie asked Matthew.

He'd helped her load the natural-tone wicker basket with napkins, cups, sandwiches (tuna for Helen and Jessie; peanut butter, no jelly, for Matthew), fruit, apple juice, and seltzer.

Matthew nodded.

"Too crowded for cookies, huh?"

"There's lots of room," he said seriously.

She filled a plastic bag with the Duncan Hines chocolate chip cookies she'd baked last night (OK, not totally from scratch, but wouldn't Gary be impressed, she'd thought), twisted it shut, and handed it to Matthew. He placed them in the basket.

Jessie handed him a cookie and took one for herself. "We have to make sure they taste all right, don't we?"

He took the cookie. "Right," he said in the same serious tone, but a smile turned up the corners of his mouth.

He looks cute, she thought. He was wearing the cap and yellow police academy T-shirt she'd picked up at the academy shop. Still no tan, though. On Monday Helen had rented a Taurus, but a trip to the beach had never materialized.

"To tell you the truth," Helen had said, "I don't love the beach. All that sand! And Matthew's skin is sensitive to sun."

Helen and Matthew had gone to the park one day, to the La Brea Tar Pits on another. On Wednesday Helen had planned to take him to Knott's Berry Farm, but she'd suffered another migraine.

Matthew seemed to take everything in stride. Jessie wondered if all eight-year-olds were like that. But then, he *had* been to Universal—she'd taken him and Helen there that first Saturday. He'd enjoyed the tour, tolerated the earthquake and King Kong, although he'd squeezed Jessie's hand throughout.

Today they were going to the zoo and for a picnic in Griffith Park (Phil had recommended against Disneyland—"Don't do two theme parks in a row"). That is, if Helen ever got out of bed. Matthew had been up since seven—he was an early riser, and Jessie generally found him coloring or watching Sesame Street in the den when she got up—but when she'd checked at nine-thirty, Helen had just been stretching in bed (the second folding bed; Jessie had borrowed it from Phil). That had been half an hour ago. Jessie hoped her sister wasn't having another headache. If she does, Jessie decided, Matthew and I will go ourselves.

She didn't have to go to the zoo, of course. She could go in to the station. She often did, on Sundays, more often now that Gary had left. Her desk was piled high with paperwork—two new murders to investigate, several older cases to follow up. So far, the leads on them had led nowhere. Typical, and frustrating, and she was eager to work on the cases, to make some headway before the trails got cold. But she had promised Matthew.

The doorbell rang. Jessie wiped her hands on a towel and wondered who it could be. "Be right back, Matthew."

At the front door, she looked through the privacy window and tensed. Forcing a smile, she opened the door. "Hello, Mom. Hi, Dad. This is a surprise." She stepped aside to let them enter.

Arthur Claypool was fifty-nine with thick gray hair, a square face, and a cleft chin. He was wearing a lightweight gray suit, a white custom-tailored cotton shirt with monogrammed cuffs, and a silk tie. Frances Claypool was six years younger and as many inches shorter than her husband. Petite and slim, she looked fragile next to him. She was wearing a white linen Chanel suit with navy braiding and navy-and-white Bally pumps. Her expensively tinted honey-blond hair was brushed back in a sleek chignon. Her face was sleek, too, the product of a face-lift two years ago.

"Hi, Jessie." Arthur hugged his daughter lightly.

Frances brushed her lips against her daughter's cheek. "Jessica."

"Helen called last night, said she was here. Your mother and I drove in for the pop art show at the museum. We thought we'd stop by, take you girls and Matthew along."

"Jessica obviously has more casual plans." Frances glanced at her daughter's white shorts, red tank top, and white espadrilles.

"We're going to the zoo."

Frances smiled. "How nice." Her nostrils quivered, as if she were sniffing the air for elephant dung. "Where *is* Helen?"

"Probably getting dressed. I'll tell her you're here."

"And Matthew?" Arthur said. "Where's my only grandchild?"

Thanks, Jessie thought. "He's in the kitchen, helping get a picnic basket ready. Do you want to wait in the breakfast room?"

Frances eyed the empty living and dining rooms on either side of the entry. "As there's no furniture here, that would be a good idea. I don't know why you let that person take everything."

Gary had been "that person" until Frances had seen that Jessie was serious about marrying a crime reporter instead of one of the doctors or lawyers or business executives of good breeding and high income to whom Frances had given Jessie's phone number.

"You're doing this to spite me, aren't you?" Frances had fumed. "Well, don't cry to me when your marriage fails." But Gary had charmed Frances into submission, and at the engagement party she'd insisted on having at the country club, she'd introduced her future son-in-law to her friends as a soon-to-be Pulitzer Prize–winning journalist. She had also promoted Harry Drake, Gary's father, from a Phoenix, Arizona, insurance salesman to a corporate executive; Martha Drake, Gary's mother, had remained a housewife, but Frances had involved her in numerous charitable organizations.

"See what I mean?" Jessie had said to Gary, annoyed and embarrassed. But Gary, ace crime reporter, pursuer of truth and accuracy, had laughed. "What's the harm?" he'd asked. He found Frances delightful, not to mention beautiful, and what was Jessie so upset about? "Why don't you two put your past behind you and start over?" She'd wanted to tell him that she couldn't stuff the past into a box like outgrown clothes and seal it shut; that she'd tried, and it always forced its way out. But he wouldn't understand, and the fault was hers. She'd been sharing her bed with him for months and planned to share her life with him, but there were thoughts and experiences too shameful and painful for her to share with anyone.

She tried to "start over." With Gary as buffer, she visited her parents more often. And pressured by her father and sister and then her fiancé (*"Et tu, Brute,"* she said, only half-joking), she yielded to Frances's "request" to have a formal wedding and a champagne reception at her parents' home.

Frances, in fact, had found an ally in Gary and his parents. They all wanted Jessie to give up police work: Frances was burdened daily by her daughter's breach of good taste. Gary and his parents were concerned about Jessie's safety and thought she should begin a family. The phone lines between Los Angeles and La Jolla and Phoenix hummed with benevolent conspiracy.

Three years later, when Jessie told her parents she and Gary were getting divorced, Jessie wasn't surprised that Frances blamed her for the failure of the marriage (*"You can't do anything right, can you, Jessica?"*). Gradually, though, Frances's anger expanded to include Gary—he, too, had failed her and was a source of embarrassment; and to her friends, Frances couldn't very well blame her own daughter. And so Gary had become "that person" again.

(Later, as she had mentally sifted through the ruins of her marriage, Jessie had decided that there might have been a shade of truth to her mother's charge, that Jessie was marrying Gary to spite Frances. Only a shade, though. She *had* loved him.)

"That was the settlement, Mom," Jessie said now. "He took the furniture. I bought his half of the house." And I told you all this the last time you were here. How many months ago was that? Seven? Eight?

"She'll get new furniture, Frances," Arthur said. "If you need help, Jessie . . . ?"

"I'm fine. But thanks."

She led them to the breakfast room. Matthew had disappeared. "I'll get Helen and Matthew." As she was leaving, she saw her mother brush the vinyl chair seat before she sat down.

Jessie opened Helen's door. "Mom and Dad are here. I wish you'd told me you called them. Did you know they were coming?"

"Of course not." Helen yawned. "But I told you I might call. Is Matthew with them?"

"No. I thought he was with you. I'll look in the den."

Jessie found Matthew sitting at her desk, drawing with the markers she'd bought him. "Matthew, Grandpa and Grandma Claypool are here," she said to his back. "They want to see you."

He didn't turn around. He put down a yellow marker and picked up a purple one. "Does that mean we can't go to the zoo?" He resumed his drawing. Neat, careful strokes.

"We can still go, but a little later. Let's say hello to your grandparents now, OK?" She waited while he capped the marker and pushed the chair under the desk.

In the breakfast room, Helen, Arthur, and Frances were sitting and talking quietly. Helen was wearing a robe. Frances had put her Gucci purse on the table.

"Here he is!" Helen exclaimed when she saw Matthew.

Arthur stood. "Well, hello there, young man." He walked over to Matthew and pumped his hand.

"Come here, dear." Frances turned and extended a ringed hand.

"Say hello to Grandma Frances, Matthew," Helen said. "Take off your cap." She sounded nervous.

Matthew removed his cap. "Hello, Grandma Frances." With his mother's eyes on him, he went to Frances and shook her hand.

She drew him forward and pecked at his cheek. "What a darling child. Isn't he, Arthur?"

"Sure is. Eight years old, are you? The last time we visited you in Winnetka, you were six." Arthur shook his head.

"We would have brought you a gift, dear, but we only found out last night that your mommy and you were here."

Strike one, Jessie thought.

"Where did you get that shirt, dear?" Frances pointed to Matthew's police academy T-shirt.

A shy smile. "Aunt Jessie bought it for me. The cap, too."

"They're training police young these days." Arthur smiled.

"You're not going to be a policeman, are you, dear?" Frances asked.

You forgot to add "God forbid," Mom, Jessie thought.

"Of course he's not," Helen said, then blushed and avoided Jessie's eyes.

"When your father was Matthew's age, Helen, he knew he would be a doctor. What do you want to be, Matthew?"

"An engineer like his dad," Arthur said. "Right, son?"

"He's so young, who knows what he'll be?" Helen said.

Matthew played with the visor on the cap. "Please can I be excused, Mommy?"

"Go ahead, hon."

She's relieved, Jessie thought. She's afraid he'll fail a major test if he stays. Which means Helen will fail.

"You are the cutest thing!" Frances pinched his cheeks.

Jessie winced for Matthew, then watched enviously as he left the room. Arthur sat down again.

"So polite," Frances said. "You've done a wonderful job with him, Helen. But he looks pale and thin. Why is that, dear?"

A wonderful report card, Jessica, but . . .

A fine job cleaning up your room, but . . .

A handsome young man you're dating, but . . .

A lovely dress, dear, but . . .

It never changed, Jessie thought. Why did I think it would?

"He isn't pale," Helen said.

"Of course he's pale. Isn't he pale, Arthur?"

Helen looked at Jessie. Her eyes implored, Save me.

"Can I get you something to drink?" Jessie asked.

"Perrier would be nice," Frances said.

"I have club soda or iced tea."

"Club soda's fine, Jessie," her father said. "No ice."

"Nothing for me, thank you," from Frances.

Jessie went to the refrigerator and took out the club soda.

"Helen, when did you say Neil will be back?" Frances said.

"In about eight weeks."

"And how long will you be staying with your sister?"

Translate that into "Why aren't you staying with us in our beautiful home and swimming in our pool and drinking our Perrier and meeting our wonderfully affluent friends?" Figure it out, Mom. Jessie poured soda into a tumbler and brought it to her father.

"Oh, I don't know exactly."

"A week? Two weeks?"

Funny, Jessie found her mother's tone annoying, but she was curious herself about Helen's plans. She hadn't wanted to ask— Helen would think she wasn't welcome. On the other hand . . .

"Until I wear out my welcome, I guess." Helen's lips formed a smile, but her eyes were anxious.

"What's going on, Helen?" Frances asked. "I told your father after you hung up that something was wrong. Tell me what it is."

"It's nothing, Mom."

"Tell me!" A shrill note had entered Frances's voice.

Here we go, Jessie thought.

"Frannie, calm down." Arthur put his hand on hers.

She jerked her hand away. "I demand an answer, Helen. Now!"

Like a supplicant in church, Helen folded her hands and bent her head. "I've left Neil," she whispered.

Jessie stared at the top of her sister's golden head.

"Why?" Frances's tone was a sliver of ice. Her eyes narrowed.

Helen didn't answer.

"You're lying. He threw you out, didn't he? Did he grow tired of you? I warned you about that. I tried to teach you."

"No! *I* left *him!*" Helen darted a glance at the doorway. "Matthew doesn't know. *Neil* doesn't know, or his family. It's . . . it's complicated, Mom."

"Don't beat around the bush, Helen. You always did that when you were a child. You know you're going to tell me."

"Please, I don't want to discuss this now."

"Frannie, she's upset. She'll tell us later."

"She *wants* to tell me, Arthur. She'll feel better once she has. Isn't that right, Helen?" Her mouth formed a smile, but her gray eyes were like small granite pellets in a pinball machine. Her voice was deceptively low, deceptively soft. Cunning.

Tell me why you broke the vase. If you do, I won't punish you.

Did you use my lipstick, Jessica? Tell me the truth. Mommy won't be angry. Mommy just wants to know.

Each time, Jessie had wanted to believe her beautiful blond mother's silkily seductive voice, so compelling, so irresistible, a voice that promised love, understanding, a feathery caress. It had taken her years to learn that it was a Siren's song, that the only promise it offered was the promise of pain and betrayal. Helen had learned, too. Or had she?

"Neil is . . . it's just—I can't! I just can't!" Helen pushed her chair away and rushed out of the room.

Frances fixed her gaze on Jessie. "Now I have two daughters with failed marriages." She paused. "You know why she's leaving Neil. You're protecting her, like always. Teaming up against me."

"Leave it alone, Frances," Arthur said wearily.

"Stay out of this, Arthur!" Her sleek face threatened to crack. She turned to Jessie. "What did she tell you?"

"I didn't know she left Neil." Jessie started to get up.

"I'm talking to you. Don't you dare leave while I'm

talking to you." Frances grabbed Jessie's forearm and dug her manicured nails into her skin.

"Take your hands off me," Jessie said quietly but firmly.

"Jessie!" her father said.

Frances removed her hand. "Well." She stood up. "Let's go, Arthur." She smoothed her skirt and brushed off imaginary lint.

"Apologize to your mother." It was part command, part plea.

"It's too late," Frances said.

You're right, Jessie thought, looking at the half-moons embedded along her arm. Much too late.

Jessie and Matthew went to the zoo alone. Helen had stayed sequestered in her room; she'd refused to talk to Jessie. Jessie had told Matthew that his mother had a headache.

Matthew was quiet in the car. Jessie didn't force the conversation—that didn't work with Matthew, she'd learned—but she wondered whether he'd overheard the yelling. Helen said he didn't know she'd left Neil, but Matthew must have picked up the signs. That probably accounted for his general reticence. It also accounted for Helen's behavior from the time she'd arrived.

At the zoo Matthew was subdued, but he enjoyed seeing the animals. He even stroked a lamb in the petting zoo. Afterward, Jessie and Matthew picnicked in Griffith Park. She'd brought along a deck of cards, and they played Go Fish. Matthew won both games; his grin seemed to make his freckles dance.

Then she took him to the pony rides. She'd been there years ago with her father and Helen, when they'd lived in L.A. The place hadn't changed much in twenty years; even the ponies seemed the same, although of course they weren't. But as a cop she knew that Griffith Park *had* changed, had lost its innocence. Two years ago an armed robber had held up the owner of the pony ride concession and made off with five thousand dollars. A nearby picnicker videotaping his family had taped the entire incident, including the gunshots fired by the robber and his escape into the hills. Last year the engineer of the minitrain, a man beloved by everyone, had been fatally shot while struggling with a robber.

Jessie was wary all the time they were in the park and at the ponies—part aunt, part detective, her hand continually feeling the bulge in her purse that was her gun. Sometimes, she wondered whether there was any place in the city that was safe.

"I had fun," Matthew said when they were back in the Honda.

"Me, too." Jessie smiled at him, and although he didn't talk on the way home, the silence was companionable. And then she saw Gary's black Audi in front of the house. Shit, she thought, then told herself, Calm down. At least he didn't park in the driveway.

Helen and Gary were in the breakfast room, drinking coffee and eating the chocolate chip cookies Jessie had baked. Helen was wearing a floral print sundress and had put on makeup.

"I thought you were going to call first, Gary!" Jessie blurted, immediately annoyed with herself. She blushed.

"Hi, Jess." Gary grinned. "Great cookies. I *did* call. Helen said you were at the zoo and to come over. Hey, Matthew. How's it going? How was the zoo?"

"Great."

Helen said, "Your remember Uncle Gary, don't you, hon?"

Matthew nodded. "You gave me a Batman piggy bank, and you said if I came to visit, you'd show me how they make newspapers."

"That's right!" Gary smiled, pleased. "Great memory, Matt."

"But my mother said you don't live here anymore, so I guess you can't take me. But that's OK," he added quickly.

There was a beat of silence. Then Helen said, "Uncle Gary's very busy, Matthew, so—"

"I can take you, kid. I'll try to set something up soon."

Helen said, "Your shorts are dirty, Matthew. Let's get you changed." She led him out of the room.

The phone rang. Jessie picked up the receiver in the kitchen. "Hello?"

"Hi, Jess," Brenda Royes said. "Tony and I are leaving in ten minutes. I wanted to say so long." Brenda and her husband, a detective in Rampart Division, were going river-rafting in Colorado and then hiking in Yosemite.

"Have a great time, Brenda. I'll miss you."

"I know." Brenda laughed. "But I'm dying to get away. No phones for three weeks. No newspapers. Just Tony and me and the glories of nature. What's that, Tony?" She laughed again. "Tony says 'and the glories of sex.' We agreed on one thing: no shop talk. Speaking of which, Jess, I've got everything under wraps except this Cantaloupe Caper. It's getting weirder and weirder."

"Hold on a sec, Brenda. I'm switching to the den phone." Jessie turned to Gary. "Hang up when I tell you to, please."

"No problem." He smiled and took another cookie.

Jessie put the receiver on the counter and went to the den. She picked up the phone. "OK, Gary," she called. She heard a click, then said, "So what was the cause of death?"

"Curare."

"You're kidding! The last time I heard of someone using curare to kill somebody was in a Sherlock Holmes movie."

"*The Spider Woman.* I saw it. Well, that's the M.E.'s official report on Mae Sung Lee. Look, I have to run. Tony's honking. I'd promise to drop you a postcard, but why lie? By the way, how's everything there with Helen and the kid?"

"Fine," Jessie said, wishing it were. She hung up and went back to the kitchen. Gary was leaning against the table, his legs crossed. Eating another cookie.

"You'll get fat," she told him.

"You hardly ever baked cookies when we were married."

"You're not as cute as Matthew." Although he was, dammit.

"You used to think I was *more* than cute. I guess I'll be going." He walked over to her and kissed her lightly on the cheek. "Curare, huh? That's a new one."

She shoved him. "You bastard! You had no right to listen in!"

"I can see it now: 'Blow-Dart Killer Strikes Again.' In thirty-six point. What do you think?"

"You're not going to print this, are you? Brenda could get into real trouble."

"We could do a sidebar on the Amazon Indians. People love sidebars." He smiled. "So how about some cookies for the road?"

Jessie frowned. "I'm serious, Gary. This isn't funny."

"Hey, this is my job, remember? Learning information about crimes, reporting it. Anyway, what if there's some nut case out there planning to off a few more people with curare?"

"There isn't. It's just this one case. Will you leave it alone, Gary?" Her hands were clenched.

"You do your job. I'll do mine." He headed for the side door.

"A job isn't everything," she called after him.

With his hand on the knob, he turned and looked at her with amusement. "Coming from you, that's kind of funny."

"Are you going to print it, Gary?" she demanded.

"I guess you'll just have to read the papers and find out."

8

Thursday, July 16

"Excuse me," he whispered to the blond woman as he entered the library alcove. He was holding the books he'd checked out from this branch two days ago. "I hope you don't mind?"

Monica Podrell did mind. She'd come here for some privacy, dammit, to study for her real estate exam. She and Andy had fought about it. You're leaving me to make supper again, he'd said, and I suppose I'll have to do the kids' homework with them? And she'd said, Yes, yes, I am, and I'm thinking of going to a motel for two days to study in peace. And she'd slammed out the door.

"No problem," Monica said to the man, who took the seat across from her. She moved to the right, sliding her materials with her, and returned to the question in her exam kit:

> Judy Loy bought a piece of property for $160,000. The land was appraised at $30,000. The economic life . . .

OK. Monica cleared her calculator and started computing, but after a few seconds gave up. The man was being considerate, turning the pages almost silently, but she could hear his labored breathing and couldn't concentrate. And she felt bad about Andy, who'd just come home when she'd told him she was leaving. She'd go back and help him with the kids. Then she'd find a quiet place to study. Lock herself in the bathroom if necessary.

In a flash, she pushed herself away from the table, grabbed her materials, and headed for the entrance to the alcove.

"You don't have to leave!"

The urgency in his whisper made her turn. Now he was taking a handkerchief out of his pocket, and he was half out of his chair, leaning toward her. God, he was going to sneeze all over her!

She smiled in apology. "Sorry. I can't concentrate with anyone around. Not even my husband. It's just me. Really."

Halfway to the car she realized she'd left her purse under the table. Shit, shit, shit! The idea of going back didn't thrill her. I'll stay ten minutes, she told herself, make up some excuse and leave. It won't kill me. She turned around, retraced her steps on the brick walkway, and found her way back to the alcove.

"Look, I know I was kind of abrupt before, but—"

He wasn't there. His books were, two books about railroads.

". . . but he was gone," Monica Podrell told her husband. "I'm sure I hurt his feelings, and he looked so pathetic, you know?"

"Forget about it, Monica. He'll survive."

He sat in the bathroom cubicle, his head between his knees, until his breathing returned to normal, until he was sure the expression and color of his face wouldn't betray his agitation. In that first minute that the woman had left the alcove, he'd thought he was going to faint because the blood had rushed to his head, to his eyes and ears and scalp, and he'd felt the arteries and capillaries of his face filling with blood and pulsating, pulsating, and his head had been throbbing with the unbearable pressure, throbbing until he was sure he was going to pass out.

He couldn't believe it, he still couldn't believe she'd walked out. Something had alarmed her. Had he been a little too intense? *Had he?* Maybe it wasn't that. Maybe she'd left because she thought he wanted to get friendly (*"a skinny runt like you"*). That's why she said she had a husband, just like Marianne, I'm married, she said. But he hadn't seen a wedding band. Lying bitch.

He couldn't sit here forever. He had to get out of this bathroom, this library, and . . . And what? He couldn't go home; he had to act tonight or he'd lose a whole week. He looked at his watch. Seven-fifteen. If he hurried, he could get to another library. He couldn't stay here. What if she remembered him, what if she came back?

He studied his face in the water-spotted mirror above the sink. He'd loosened his tie, trying to get air; he tightened it now and smoothed his hair with his palms. His forehead and upper lip were beaded with sweat. The paper towel dispenser was empty; he reached for his handkerchief and remembered the other handkerchief in his other pocket—had the fumes evaporated? But that was OK; he could douse it again in the car. He was glad now, so glad he'd decided to keep the bottle in the glove compartment. At the time he hadn't been sure, because what if a policeman stopped him for something and asked to see his registration and asked him about the bottle? That could happen. And how would he explain it?

Five minutes later he was in his car, belted, the books lying on the seat next to him.

He glanced at the wall clock as he entered the library. Seven-thirty-five. That was fine. This room was smaller, more open, but he'd formulated a new plan. Some people were sitting at tables, some standing at the circulation desk. There was a young man working the circulation desk. Was another staff member somewhere in the room? He'd have to take the chance. The librarian was at her desk, reading, which is what a librarian should be doing, setting a positive example. He passed right by her but she didn't look up.

He forced himself to browse through the stacks as he worked his way toward the back of the room. There were lots of books on gardening, he saw. Now that he'd moved back into his parents' house, he might plant vegetables. He would love to plant flowers, but his allergies would probably act up. He was pretty sure vegetables would be all right, but he'd check first, just in case.

There was the door he wanted, the one next to the rest room: DO NOT ENTER. LIBRARY STAFF ONLY. He glanced around. No one was looking his way. He turned the knob, pushed open the door, and slipped inside, prepared with an explanation (*"Thought this was the bathroom"*) in case someone was there. But the room was empty. All he had to do was wait for someone, anyone, to enter.

It was the librarian. He smelled her perfume (roses?) as she entered; she didn't know he was there, hidden in the narrowing triangle between the opening door and the wall, didn't sense him until it was too late, until his hand was pressed against her mouth, the newly doused handkerchief firmly in place, silencing her strangled scream. She fell, limp, into his waiting arms, and it was only after he positioned her on the floor that he saw her face and the red, angry bruises where his fingernails had dug into her skin. It wasn't the way he liked to do it. It wasn't his fault he'd been more nervous than usual, it was the woman's fault, the one who had left him sitting there like a fool in the alcove.

After he was done, he left the room as carefully as he'd entered it, armed with an excuse; but again, no one was looking. Then he meandered among the stacks until he had made his way back to the circulation desk and out the door.

The fresh air was wonderful. For a minute he'd worried that her perfume would make him sneeze, but he'd willed his body into control. Back in his apartment he took a long, hot shower, inhaling the steamy vapor in greedy gulps until the wheezing stopped. Then, dressed in freshly laundered pajamas and a robe, he went to the table in the living room, found the card he wanted, and added it to his collection.

Now he had four.

9

Helen was at the market and Matthew was reading in bed when Jessie got the call. She waited impatiently—how long did it take to buy shampoo?—and jerked the door open when she heard Helen's footsteps along the driveway over half an hour later.

"My partner called," Jessie said as Helen stepped inside. "I have to go, Helen. Don't wait up for me." She spoke calmly, but she was never calm when she was about to start on a new case.

In a way she was relieved to get out of the house. Since Sunday things had been strained between the two sisters, especially when Matthew wasn't around to force counterfeit cheer to their faces. Jessie had tried several times to talk about Neil, to offer a shoulder. (Had Helen finally tired of his long absences? Or was there another person involved—for Helen, because of the absences? For Neil?) Each time Helen had rebuffed her.

"Look," she'd finally told Helen, "if you don't want to talk to me, fine. But you have to level with Matthew."

"I'll handle Matthew, Jessie. Just leave it alone, please."

Have it your way, Jessie thought again as she drove to the West L.A. library. But in seven weeks, Neil would be back from Saudi Arabia, and Helen would have to deal with her problems.

Phil was waiting for Jessie. "We're just about done, so I called the M.E.," he said as he led her to the staff room. "I knew you wouldn't mind. It's the librarian, by the way. Enid Schmidt. Driver's license says she's twenty-eight."

And dead, Jessie thought as she looked at the woman. Someone's daughter, sister, lover. God, she was only a year younger than Helen! She had blond chin-length hair. Fair skin marred by scratches around a pink-lipsticked mouth. There was nothing else to suggest violence. She was lying on her back with her eyes closed, her arms at her side, her skirt covering her knees. Like Sleeping Beauty, Jessie thought, except that there would be no Prince Charming to wake Enid Schmidt with a magical kiss.

The medical investigator, Carl Groch, was still in the small room with the body. Jessie had met him at several crime scenes. He was calm, emotionless. Jessie pretended to be the same. Seeing a corpse still did strange things to her stomach.

Why Homicide?

Groch peeled off plastic gloves. "Hard to say what killed her. Suffocation, maybe. Not strangulation—no ligature marks on her neck. No apparent head contusions. No evidence of rape."

Phil said, "I checked her wallet. Credit cards are there, plus thirty-six dollars cash. So it doesn't look like robbery was the motive."

Jessie said, "Maybe she surprised the killer when he was going through her purse. He panicked, killed her, ran."

While the coroner's van removed the body and Phil talked to the crime lab technicians, Jessie sat at a library table facing Benny Lefton, the young man who had phoned the police.

Lefton was in partial shock, his freckles standing out almost in bas relief against his chalky skin. The bleached spiky hairs on his head were standing on end, too, a product not of fear but of the mousse that had lacquered the hair into stiff attention.

He'd been busy at the circulation desk until a little after eight, he told Jessie. "There's always a few people who check out books at the last minute." Irritation flickered across his face. "Anyway, I hadn't seen Enid in a while, but I figured she was in the staff room getting her stuff, and I had to get my things, too." He stopped, took a breath. "That's when I found her. Jeez, it was awful. Just awful." He closed his eyes, as if that would prevent him from reliving the experience.

"You didn't move the body?"

"No way! I knew right off something was wrong, 'cause there was blood around her mouth. I just knew something was wrong."

"Do you have any idea when she went to the staff room?"

"Nope. Like I said, I was busy, and I'm not facing her desk when I'm checking out books. I'm supposed to keep my eye on people who are leaving, make sure they're not taking books without having them checked out. You'd be surprised how many people try to get away with that—old people, too."

After thirteen years on the force, Jessie was surprised by little. "Did Miss Schmidt seem upset lately? Did she mention having problems with anyone? A boyfriend, maybe?"

"No" to everything. Benny hadn't seen anything suspicious. He hadn't noticed anyone entering or leaving the staff room.

"Did you notice these books on the floor near the body?" Jessie pointed to a pile of texts on the table. She'd taken them from the staff room after they'd been checked for fingerprints.

"I didn't touch them, if that's what you're thinking. I know you're not supposed to touch anything if there's—in case . . ." He didn't seem to know how to finish the sentence.

"Was Miss Schmidt interested in railroads?" Jessie held the front cover of the book toward Benny.

"Not that I know. Could be she was looking something up for someone. See, people call to find out about presidents or capitals or inventions. Anything."

"But then wouldn't she have the books on her desk?"

"Yeah." He nodded. "Yeah, 'cause that's where her phone is, if she wanted to pass on the information she found. So do you think that maybe the . . . uh . . . killer left the books there?"

"Possibly." Jessie pulled over one of the books, opened the cover. "This book is due July twenty-eighth, which means it was checked out two days ago, right?" She turned it toward Lefton and pointed to the manila card tucked into the pocket on the inside of the cover. "You don't remember checking this out to anyone?"

Benny hesitantly drew the book toward him. "No, I don't, but—" He frowned, then relaxed. "This isn't from our library. See this stamp at the top? That tells you which library the book comes from." He returned the book to Jessie, obviously relieved to be rid of it and its morbid association.

Jessie looked at the stamp. The branch had an address on the 1400 block of North Gardner; that was near Sunset Boulevard. "Can we find out who took out this book?"

"I wouldn't know how. I've only been working here a couple of weeks, see. The best thing would be for you to talk to one of the regular librarians tomorrow afternoon. We open at one."

Jessie thanked Benny and told him he could leave. She

planned to call the library. It was unlikely that the killer—if in fact he was the one who'd left the books in the staff room—had taken them out on his own card. He'd probably found a lost card. Or stolen one. But maybe the person working the circulation desk at the other library would remember someone who'd checked out books on railroads.

She looked at the book she'd opened. *The Trans-Continental Railroad.* She liked trains. As a young girl, she'd traveled once with her parents and Helen by train up the coast to San Francisco. It was faster than traveling by car, and you could enjoy the scenery, not like in a plane forty thousand feet above the ground, where everything blended into anonymity. She and Gary had talked of going to Europe someday and spending a month traveling from country to country with a Eurail pass.

So much for plans.

Why had the killer left books on railroads? Was that arbitrary? And why books from another library? If the killer wanted camouflage, he could've pulled books off the shelves here. But *had* the other books come from the same library?

The second one had, Jessie saw; it was due the same day, July 28. She opened the third book and her eye was immediately drawn to the twenty-dollar bill in the inside pocket. There were more bills under the twenty, she noticed. Presumably, they'd been checked for prints, but just in case, she slipped on a pair of latex gloves to separate them as she counted. There were 10 twenty-dollar bills. Two hundred dollars. That would take care of a hell of a lot of overdue fines, she thought.

And then she froze. Underneath the last bill was a First Interstate Bank of California deposit slip. She flashed to Brenda's case, to the hundred dollars someone had attached to a bank deposit slip and left in the Chinese woman's apartment, and was transfixed with a curious mixture of excitement and dread.

* * *

"I realize it could be a coincidence," Jessie said.

It was the next morning, and she was sitting in Kalish's office. The night before she'd called her supervisor. He'd called his supervisor, who had called Kalish.

Kalish drummed his fingers on his desk. "But you think it's the same guy. Just because of the deposit slips?"

"Mostly that," she admitted. "I can't imagine anyone leaving two hundred dollars in a library book. But Detective Royes said that Mae Lee looked like she died in her sleep. Schmidt looked peaceful, too, except for bruises around her mouth. Her eyes were closed, too."

"Groch didn't find a puncture wound."

"He didn't do a complete exam. By the time I found the deposit slip, they'd already bagged her and taken her to the morgue. She was wearing a long-sleeved blouse," Jessie added.

Kalish's eyebrows rose. "In this heat?"

"The library was air-conditioned. Cold, actually."

"So if they find a puncture wound, they'll look for toxins. That could take days. In the meantime send a teletype to all eighteen divisions about homicides with similar m.o.'s."

"I prepared a memo." Jessie handed Kalish a copy. "I also ran what I had through Hitman. Nothing." Once in a while the Parker Center computer data bank worked magic, matching up crimes or criminals with similar patterns. But not this time.

He smiled. "A step ahead of me, huh, Jessie?" He scanned the memo, then nodded in approval. "I don't have to tell you not to mention this to anyone. If word got out . . ." He ran a hand through his thick, graying hair.

Jessie hesitated, then said. "My ex-husband knows about Mae Lee and the curare. He eavesdropped on my conversation with Detective Royes." She was uncomfortably warm.

"But he obviously hasn't told anyone about it." Every morning since Sunday, she'd anxiously checked the *Times* and been relieved to find nothing.

Kalish studied her. "Not a nice thing to do, eavesdropping," he said softly. The smile had vanished. "See that he doesn't get the opportunity to do it again, Drake." He paused. "Let's hope the killer doesn't get another chance, either."

10

Thursday, July 23

"Close your eyes," he told her. "Just for a minute."

Angelina Balderas wondered if she was doing the right thing. Jaime would be home soon; he'd probably worry, because she'd told him she'd be back before seven. But the man had stopped her, a free offer, he'd said, and it had sounded like a good idea. She hoped it wouldn't take too long, but even if she was a little late, Jaime wouldn't be angry. He always said you only lived once.

He leaned over her. Her eyes were closed but not sealed, and she could see his hand approaching her mouth with a white tissue that emitted a strong but not unpleasant odor. He pressed the tissue firmly against her lips.

"It tingles," she said.

"That's the mint." He swabbed around her lips, then on her eyes, cheeks, and forehead. "I'm going to use the number two astringent. Then an oil-free moisturizer—you're dry around the cheeks and forehead, but you have that oily T-zone we want to keep clean. Then makeup. Close your eyes again, Angelina."

Before she closed her eyes, she read the name on the pin on his white lab coat. Nicholas. He'd introduced himself when he'd offered her the makeover, but she hadn't paid attention. She had no idea what any of the products cost; they were probably expensive, but she'd have to buy something even though he'd said there was no obligation. She didn't want him to think she was cheap.

"I'm using a light, water-based foundation with a hint of rose to pick up your natural coloring," Nicholas said. "I'll write down everything so that you can think about it later."

In a way it was luck that he'd stopped her; she wanted to look special tonight. She'd planned it all out. Dinner was ready; she just had to reheat it. She'd set the dining room table. Why the dining room? Jaime would ask. Just because, she'd say. After dinner she'd take out the box. It's for Father's Day, she'd say, an early gift, and he'd say, but I'm not a father, and she'd smile, and he'd stare at her. Then he'd grin. When? he'd ask. And she'd tell him she'd found out today, the doctor said sometime in March, and wasn't it the most wonderful news in the world?

"This combination of peach and taupe is marvelous on you," Nicholas said. "Look how it brings out your eyes." He held up a mirror. "You look luminous, dear, you really do."

If luminous meant glowing, that's exactly how she did feel, how she'd felt the minute the doctor told her she was pregnant. They'd have to get a two-bedroom apartment, although the baby could be in the room with them for a while in a port-a-crib. And she'd have to take maternity leave. And if Jaime got a promotion, she could quit until the baby was in nursery school.

"And there you are." Nicholas smiled. "I used a tawny powder blush. The lipstick is Carmine Fire. It has a moisturizer that protects against sun and wind. How do you like it?" He swiveled the stool so that she was facing a lighted mirror on the counter.

She liked it very much, she told him. Did she want to purchase something now? Well, the astringent; that had felt wonderful. And the cleanser and moisturizer? Because you don't want dry, flaky skin. The makeup works best on properly prepared skin; the essentials are the cleanser, moisturizer, and astringent. The moisturizer and cleanser, too, she agreed.

Her car was parked quite a distance from the escalator. Her high heels clacked on the concrete floor, and she thought that soon she'd have to buy some sensible, low-heeled pumps; she had read that pregnant women lost their balance easily.

She heard footsteps behind her, footsteps that sounded as if they were coming closer, and she was surprised because she hadn't heard anyone get off the escalator after her. She stopped and pretended to look at her watch, and out of the corner of her eye she saw a man approaching. She wasn't actually worried. He was obviously just going to his car. But there were no other people around, and she walked faster, one hand groping in her purse for her ignition key. Now the staccato, metallic music of her stiletto heels on the concrete, amplified in the vast echo chamber of the parking structure, seemed urgent and shrill to her ears, but it didn't block out the heavy sound of the footsteps that were coming closer and closer, louder and louder, and just as she was about to break into a run, the footsteps stopped and she saw with a quick turn of her head that the man was getting into a car. Silly, she told herself, but her neck and underarms and thighs were drenched with perspiration and her heart was still pounding rapidly as she opened her car door and got in.

She put Jaime's gift and the skin-care products on the seat, then locked the doors and belted herself. She studied herself in the rearview mirror. She really did look nice; the makeup was subtle. Jaime probably wouldn't even notice. She smiled. She was turning away when she saw him staring at her; their eyes locked for one brief, endless moment, and then she opened her mouth to scream, but a hand was on her mouth and nose, jerking her head backward, an iron hand with a white monogrammed handkerchief whose embroidered edge she could see through eyes widened in terror; and she tried desperately to move out of reach, tried twisting her face to the right, but succeeded only in smearing the handkerchief with the Carmine Fire; and she strained to reach the steering wheel, to sound the horn, *someone help me, pleeeeeeeease,* but another arm was girdling her chest and arms, pinning her against the back of the seat until her hands fluttered to her lap like wounded butterflies and she stopped resisting and was still.

He had withdrawn sixty dollars and redeposited fifteen. Then he'd gone to the parking lot and done reconnaissance (he liked the word and its association) until he'd chosen the right car.

The hardest part had been waiting, crouching in the back of the stuffy Mazda every time he saw someone approaching. It had seemed like an eternity before the woman had finally returned to her car, and he'd worried that his knees and back, stiff from their bent position, would creak as he moved and alert her that someone was there. But everything had gone flawlessly.

The handkerchief was probably ruined. Maybe if he soaked it in bleach. He didn't think hot water; his mother had said hot water sets a stain, but that had been after his nose bled all over a shirt, and this wasn't blood, there hadn't been any blood, not like last time; it was lipstick.

It was a shame about the handkerchief, but he wouldn't let it upset him. Everything had gone so well, not like at the library. The memory rankled, but the important thing was that he *hadn't* failed. Saturday he'd seen proof of his success in the *Times:*

> LIBRARIAN SLAIN
>
> Enid Schmidt, twenty-eight, was found dead in the staff room of a West L.A. library. . . . Anyone with information should call 312-8441 and ask for Det. Jessie Drake.

Well, *he* had information. But he wouldn't call the detective. Not yet.

11

The minute Jessie saw Angelina Balderas, she knew.

There was an uncanny similarity between her posture and the librarian's. This woman's eyes were closed, too; she was lying with her arms pressed to her sides, her head facing the passenger door. There were no bruises on her face, but there was a garish streak of red across one cheek.

Jessie didn't need bruises to tell her this was homicide. If Angelina Balderas had suffered a heart attack or stroke, she would have slumped against the seat or onto the steering wheel. And people don't nap in the parking lot of the Century City shopping center, wedged in the coffinlike space between the doors of a car. Someone had arranged her body; Jessie was certain it was the same person who had arranged Enid Schmidt in the library staff room.

If Phil were here, she could run this by him. But he was at a cousin's wedding. Jessie approached Paul Andrews, one of the men from Scientific Investigation Division (SID).

"Did you find any money attached to a deposit slip?" she asked.

He looked at her curiously. "Nope. Were you expecting to?"

"Kind of." Say little, Kalish had instructed her and Phil.

Paul said, "We *did* find a parking lot ticket. Entitles you to three hours' free parking. It was in both hands, like a bouquet of flowers. Kind of weird, I thought."

Weird. There was that word again. Jessie had a prickly sensation. A minute later she was examining the ticket. The time stamped was 5:26 P.M. That might help the M.E. determine time of death. There was nothing else on the ticket, only a printed message stating that the facility "does not guard or assume care, custody, or control of your vehicle or its contents and is not responsible for fire, theft, damage or loss" in connection with the vehicle or with any property left in said vehicle.

Or for murder committed in said vehicle, Jessie added. Why had the killer left the ticket, not money, as he'd done with the Chinese woman and librarian? Because Jessie *knew* that all three women had been killed by the same person. Instinct. Her academy instructors had told her not to rely on it alone, but never to ignore it, either. And it had served her well in the past.

Jessie had received responses to her teletype, but none fit the killer's m.o. Wilshire was investigating an apparent stroke victim. The lab results weren't expected for another week. Foothill was investigating a forty-year-old woman who had died in her sleep. No suicide note, no pills. No history of heart disease. Lab results not back. There were two possible overdoses: Hollenbeck reported a twenty-two-year-old male with a history of drug abuse; Rampart, a sixteen-year-old girl whose brother had been arrested for dealing. Both cases were awaiting final lab results.

The lab results on Enid Schmidt hadn't come back yet, either. Kalish had said to investigate the death as a regular homicide, and she'd done so, but with meager results.

She'd learned little of value from the staff at the library where the railroad books had been borrowed. According to the main librarian, Donna Fletcher, only when a book is overdue does the main branch computer print out the title and name of the person whose card was used to check out the book. A printout with all overdue books for a certain time period is then sent to all city libraries. That process can take four weeks to six weeks, Donna Fletcher said. Had anyone requested help in finding books on railroads? Jessie asked. No, not that she recalled.

Jessie had also talked to Virginia Ekker, the middle-aged brunette at the circulation desk. No, she didn't remember checking out books on railroads, but she rarely looked at books she was processing unless an unusual book jacket caught her eye.

"Maybe Larry can help you," she said.

Larry didn't recall checking out books on railroads, but he'd seen two on the table in an alcove. He remembered because he'd been annoyed about having to reshelve them; they were heavy, and why couldn't people return books when they were done?

"Do you have any idea who that person could have been?"

Larry looked at Jessie, his eyebrows raised in an exaggerated you've-got-to-be-kidding arch. "Uh-uh."

Then Virginia said, "There was a woman here last night who's used the alcoves a few times a week during the past month. I remember her because she left, then came back in a hurry and said something about leaving her purse. I don't know her name."

But Virginia Ekker had promised to keep an eye out for the woman and get her name and phone number if she came again.

So far Jessie hadn't heard from Virginia. She wasn't holding her breath. She'd talked to Enid Schmidt's parents and boyfriend and acquaintances, all of whom had been visibly—and genuinely, Jessie believed—horrified by the librarian's death.

Now she'd have to repeat the process for Angelina Balderas.

On the floor of Angelina's car there had been a package and a Broadway bag with skin-care products. Opening the package, Jessie wondered whether it belonged to the dead woman or, like the railroad books, was camouflage for the killer.

The box contained a velour robe, burgundy with navy trim. There was a small envelope, the kind stores provide. A message from the killer? Even though SID had dusted for prints, Jessie handled the envelope and the note inside carefully but saw immediately that her caution had been unnecessary.

> Jaime—Happy Father's Day to the father-to-be. I'm the luckiest woman in the whole world. *Tu eres mi vida.*
>
> *Te amo,* Angelina

You are my life. I love you.

She was taken by surprise, and the pain, honed on the strop of memory, sliced through her.

She had waited until they were in bed to tell him.

"I'm pregnant, Gary." The word trembled on her lips, then floated like a soap bubble in the air.

"You're sure?"

She nodded.

"God, Jess!" he whispered. "That's so goddamn wonderful!"

He kissed her lips, her neck. His hand, then his mouth, moved across her breasts, traced a line down her body until it rested on her still-flat abdomen, beneath which was her womb.

Womb. The word had an echolike, cavernous sound, full of import, of mystery. Of the unknown.

She hugged him fiercely to her. They made quiet, tender love. He handled her gingerly, as if he were afraid to shake loose what had just begun to form.

"You're happy, aren't you, Jess?" Gary asked afterward.

Happy, happy, happy, happy, happy, happy, happy, happy . . .

A stone sending ripples across the waters of her mind.

It was after one in the morning when Jessie got home. Helen had left on the front porch and side entrance lights, just as Jessie had asked. One thing Jessie had to say for her sister—she was a thoughtful house guest. Neat, too. Almost compulsively neat, tidying up Jessie's things as well as her own and Matthew's. Clearing away dishes. Dusting. Maybe it took her mind off Neil.

Except for the faithful droning of the refrigerator and the whirring of the central air-conditioning unit, the house was quiet. In the bedroom, Jessie undressed, put on a nightshirt, and crawled under her comforter. She was too tired to think anymore about Angelina Balderas, about her husband Jaime's grief, about the killer who she knew had claimed three victims. She was half asleep when she heard a crash from the front of the house.

She reached immediately between the mattress and box spring for her revolver, then remembered that it was in the closet with her Smith & Wesson. Shit! Her heart hammering, she tiptoed with practiced speed and stealth across the wood floor to the hall, eased open the closet door, and grabbed the revolver.

With the clip inserted, she moved toward the front of the house, her back hugging the wall. There was a sliver of light from the kitchen area. Was the intruder using a flashlight?

Five seconds later she was in the kitchen.

"Freeze!" She stood with her feet apart, the gun in both hands aimed at the figure crouching on the floor. And immediately lowered the gun. "Jesus Christ, Matthew! You scared the hell out of me!" Her heart was still beating rapidly.

"I'm sorry," he whispered. "It was an accident."

The light she'd seen was from the refrigerator. Caught in its glare were a broken glass, spilled milk. A boy quaking with fright, his eyes black holes in the white sphere of his face.

"It's OK," she said softly. "I'm sorry I yelled. I thought you were a burglar."

"I tried to clean it up. I'm sorry."

She noticed now that the paper towel he was holding had a red stain and that his hand was bleeding. With the gun in her left hand, she reached to pick him up with her right arm and remove him to a safer, glass-free place.

He recoiled. "Please," he whimpered. "I'm sorry. I'm sorry. I'm sorry." Like the bleats of a lamb.

She realized with a shock that he thought she was going to hit him. Do I look that fierce? she wondered, then remembered the gun. She reached over and put it behind the toaster. She would get it when he was back in bed. "It's OK, Matthew. I'm not angry. I know it was an accident. I want to take you to the bathroom, to rinse your hand and check for glass. All right?"

He nodded.

Slowly, as though she were attempting to stroke a butterfly, she picked him up and carried him to the bathroom. His legs were locked around her waist, his arms around her neck. He was trembling. She smoothed his cheek. It was moist with tears.

She felt an ineffable something stirring within her and wanted to cry. For Angelina and her husband and their unborn child, for Helen and Neil and Matthew. For Gary. For herself.

She caught a glimpse of herself in the large mirror over the bathroom counter. A thirty-four-year-old woman. A little boy cradled against her breast.

You're happy, aren't you, Jess?

12

On Friday he found the article in the Metro section:

> Early Friday a guard discovered the body of Angelina Balderas in the Century City shopping center parking structure. According to Det. Jessie Drake of West L.A. . . .

Drake. Wasn't that the detective they'd mentioned in the other article? He opened his folder and looked at the clipping he'd pasted to a piece of paper. Yes, there it was. Jesse Drake. He wondered what the detective looked like. He continued reading.

> . . . revealed that Mrs. Balderas was eight weeks pregnant and was poisoned, but Detective Drake refused to comment.

He couldn't have known she was pregnant. He didn't like thinking about the eight-week-old-fetus, a viable human life according to people against abortion, but this wasn't the same as abortion; he hadn't made a conscious choice. He couldn't understand how anyone *could* make a conscious choice to kill a baby. He clipped the article and pasted it onto a piece of paper.

He was glad he hadn't known about the baby, but even if he had, he would have gone through with it (*"Toughen up, boy!"*). It wouldn't have been fair if he'd changed his mind, not to the Russian or to the black nurse or to the young librarian, all with their own lives and expectations. Even the Oriental woman. And what if the librarian had been pregnant, too? He couldn't allow emotion to cloud his thinking, to weaken his resolve.

"Give him another chance, Ed. He's just a boy."

"Butt out, Ella. Get me another beer, will ya? Come on, boy. Fair's fair. It's your turn. Let's see how far you get."

"I give up. You win."

"You'll play till it's over, and that's an order. I'm not raising a kid to be a quitter. Go on, make your move."

"I don't want to play. I hate this game! Mommy, do I have to play?"

"Ed, don't you see that he's crying? He doesn't understand it's just a game. Can't you give him another chance this once?"

"You're not crying, are you, boy? 'Cause you know I'm teaching you a valuable lesson in life. You play fair, but you show no mercy. There's winners and losers, nothing in between. It's you or the other guy, and if you give one inch, well, hell, it's your ass. Remember that. Your grandfather didn't, and look where it got him. A bankrupt and a suicide. And look where it left us."

This time he was determined to be a winner.

13

On Friday morning, Jessie was halfway to the Honda when Helen caught up with her.

"I didn't want to talk in front of Matthew, Jess. I need a lawyer. And I want to establish California residency."

"What?" Jessie asked, startled, and wondered immediately, *In my house?* She squinted at Helen in the early morning sun. "What's going on? And why can't you handle this in Winnetka?"

Helen squeezed her hand. "I'll talk to you about it later, Jess. I promise. But I need the name of a good lawyer, OK?"

Driving to the station, Jessie wondered what Helen was up to, but once there, thoughts of Helen flew from her mind. A written response to the intradivision memo had come in from Det. Henry Piggott of 77th. He'd seen her memo when he'd returned from sick leave; he thought she might be interested in the death of Norma Jeffreys. Jessie immediately contacted him.

"She was killed Thursday, June twenty-fifth," Piggott told Jessie. "Injected with curare. Guy did her right on a bus stop bench, can you believe it? Now that takes balls. There was liver damage, too. The M.E. says the killer probably chloroformed her first."

Jessie felt her stomach muscles contract. "Was there money attached to a deposit slip?" She held her breath.

"Yeah. That's why I called you. There was a hundred fifty dollars clipped to a Bank of America slip. So what do we have, a serial killer?"

Play it cool, she told herself. "We don't know yet. Keep it under wraps, OK?" Jessie thanked Piggott and hung up.

One hundred dollars. A hundred fifty. Two hundred. Was there a meaning to the pattern? And if Angelina was his victim, why hadn't he left money with her?

Aside from the money, Jessie had noticed other similarities: All the victims were females. All had been killed on a Thursday (Jessie had verified the date of Mae Lee's murder). She was pondering the significance of Thursdays when a classmate from the academy, Howard Thompson from Hollywood Division, called.

"Got your memo, Jessie. I have a case that may fit your m.o.—then again, it may not. Victim's name is Alek Radovsky."

Jessie frowned. "A male?"

"I didn't do a physical, but yeah, a male. Why?"

There went that pattern. "Nothing. Go ahead."

"Body was found four A.M. on July tenth, but the M.E. says he could've died as early as eight P.M. on the ninth. I thought heart attack or stroke even though he was in his thirties."

"Cause of death?" Jessie asked, ready to write "curare."

"Don't know yet. Maybe it's *not* a homicide. It wasn't a mugging. Radovsky's wallet had some bills. But there was a deposit slip in his shirt pocket. That's why I'm calling."

"How much money did you find, Howie?" If Radovsky

had been killed two weeks ago, he was number three and Enid Schmidt was four. Which meant that Howard would have found a hundred seventy-five dollars.

"Three twenty-dollar bills. Sixty bucks. So what's going on?"

Sixty dollars? That didn't make any sense, Jessie thought glumly after thanking Thompson and hanging up. She reported her findings to Kalish.

He brooded in silence, then said, "All we have is two definites—the Chinese woman and the nurse. We don't have the tox screens on the librarian or the Russian. But there *are* those damn deposit slips. I'm passing this on to Parker Center."

"Don't forget to mention Angelina Balderas."

"No deposit slip."

"She was killed on a Thursday. The killer substituted the parking ticket for the money. I'm sure of it."

"Supposition." Kalish looked at Jessie with interest. "Good job, Jessie. I'm noting it in your file."

"Thanks." She was pleased. "So what do you think?"

"Same as you. That we're sitting on a goddamn time bomb."

Before she left for lunch, Jessie called Helen. The phone rang four times, then the answering machine picked up. She waited for the beep, then said, "Helen, it's Jessie. I just—"

"Jess? I couldn't get to the phone fast enough. What about the lawyer who handled your divorce? Was he good?"

"Margaret Lasky. She's *very* good. But why are you moving back to California? Don't you want to give it some thought?"

"I've given it a *lot* of thought, Jess. What's her number?"

Jessie told Helen the number—she still knew it by heart. "Helen, wait till I get home. What's the rush?"

"Neil will be back in seven weeks, Jess. That's the rush."

"What about Matthew's going to camp? Isn't he—"

"Thanks for the number. See you later." Helen hung up.

"You're welcome," Jessie muttered to the dial tone.

She used her lunch break to shop at Nordstrom—the store had advertised a sale and she needed a new dress and a pick-me-up. Because of Helen. And because she felt deflated, now that Kalish had removed the cases from her hands and was turning them over to Robbery Homicide at Parker Center. That was routine for serial killers or crimes that involved more than one division. Still . . .

After Nordstrom (no luck with the dress), she interviewed a witness reluctant to testify about a shooting that had erupted from a quarrel in a computer store near Beverly Glenn. (No luck with the witness, either.) When Jessie returned to the station, Phil intercepted her as she entered the detective room.

"Kalish is looking for you, Jess." Phil handed her the *Times*. It was a special edition, she noted, and her eyes were drawn to the bold headlines:

BLOW DART POISON KILLS THREE!

> Informed sources revealed today that at least three Los Angeles residents have been fatally injected with curare. . . .

Oh, shit! Jessie moaned silently. She handed the paper back to Phil and walked to Kalish's office. She knocked, opened the door, entered, and shut the door behind her. "Phil showed me the paper. How did they find out?"

He was glowering. "My question exactly. Did you look at the by-line, Drake?" He tossed the paper at her.

She read the name, knowing what she'd find: Gary Drake.

"Your ex-husband the reporter do a little more eavesdropping, Drake? Are you the 'informed source'?"

The unfairness of the accusation angered her. Kalish was treating her as if she were a child. Would he have spoken to Phil or another male detective in the same way, made the same assumptions? *"Can't you do anything right, Jessica?"*

"I haven't talked to Gary in two weeks," she said, trying not to let her anger show. "The article mentioned Radovsky. *I* didn't even know he'd been killed with curare. And when Gary listened in, all we knew about was Mae Lee." But it had been enough, Jessie admitted to herself, to give the son of a bitch a lead on a front-page story. She should've been more careful with Gary around.

Kalish thought for a moment, then said, "OK."

No apology, of course. Maybe she didn't deserve one. "How *did* they know about Radovsky?"

"Thompson from Hollywood called. He just got the lab reports. Curare. Your ex was obviously a step ahead of him. He did his research, by the way. Take a look at the sidebar."

Curare comes from the Indian word *woorari, woorali,* or *urari,* meaning poison. Indigenous to South America, crude curare comes from the bark of strychnos and was used by South American Indians to tip their arrowheads.

Curare has medicinal applications. It is a muscle relaxant, a highly effective therapy for multiple sclerosis, Parkinson's, and St. Vitus' Dance. It is also used as an auxiliary anesthetic, especially in abdominal surgery.

The substance used to kill Mae Sung Lee, Norma Jeffreys, and Alek Radovsky is the purified form of curare, tubocurarine chloride. By blocking a substance called acetylcholine, curare prevents nerve impulses from activating skeletal, or voluntary, muscles. It first affects the muscles of the toes, ears, and eyes, then those of the neck and limbs, and finally those involved in respiration. Death in the three victims was caused by respiratory paralysis.

> The action of tubocurarine can be stopped by an injection of neostigmine, which allows acetylcholine to accumulate so that normal muscle activity can occur. But the drug would have to be injected immediately after the curare, and . . .

Pretty damn thorough, Jessie had to admit as she walked back to her desk. All you ever wanted to know about curare . . .

"Phone for you." Phil handed her the receiver. "You OK?"

"Alive, but barely. Thanks." She sandwiched the receiver between her ear and shoulder. "Detective Drake."

"So what'd you think, Jess? We scooped all the media. Is that a great story, or what?"

She told Gary what she thought in noneditorial words that made Phil's eyebrows rise. Then she slammed down the phone.

Damn Gary. Damn his sidebars. Damn his "informed sources"—probably someone at the coroner's office.

Of course, Gary would say he was just doing his job, just as she was doing hers. He had his sources; she had hers. And in a way he was right. The moment she'd spotted the connection between Enid Schmidt and Mae Lee, notwithstanding the sympathy she'd felt for the librarian, Jessie had been excited by the discovery, eager to see where it led. To solve the puzzle.

Which was why she was a detective.

And the thought *had* crossed her mind that this could further her career. Not a thought she was proud of, but she'd had it.

But that's where the similarity ended, she told herself. Gary wasn't reporting the deaths to solve a crime; he was doing it to get a scoop, to make his journalistic mark. And if his thirty-six point headline incited a citywide panic or inspired copycat murders, well, hell, lady, that's the way it goes.

Gary was committed to the story.

Jessie was committed to finding the bad guys, to bringing some sense of justice and order to this world. And by extension, to her own life.

That's "why Homicide."

14

Helen had prepared lasagna—Jessie's favorite. She smelled the pungent blend of cheese and spinach when she opened the door.

"Matthew set the table," Helen informed Jessie as they sat down to eat. "Didn't he do a great job?"

"Great," Jessie agreed, noting the perfect alignment of forks, knives, plates, napkins. His smile of pleasure. The smile warmed, then pained her; she couldn't help wondering how much he realized, how long the smiles would last.

During supper Jessie couldn't ask Helen if she'd called Margaret Lasky and, oh, yeah, what the hell's going on? After supper Helen was busy with Matthew—a bath, story hour. Then Helen announced that she and Matthew had had a long day (Farmer's Market) and she was going to curl up with the latest Danielle Steele.

Her sister, Jessie decided as she sat cross-legged on her bed doing a crossword puzzle, was as slippery as the cheese-smothered lasagna noodles.

Saturday was the same. Helen made herself unavailable,

pleading yet another headache. Jessie took Matthew to a matinee in Westwood and to a Baskin-Robbins afterward for ice cream. Back at home, they had just gotten out of the car when Paige Trainer, the neighbor who'd loaned Jessie the first folding bed and a small dresser, came by. Jessie introduced her to Matthew.

"Eric's having a birthday party," Paige said. Eric was her seven-year-old. "I thought Matthew would like to join us. Your sister, too, of course." Paige turned to Matthew. "How about it?"

"Can I, Aunt Jessie?" His eyes were wide with excitement.

Jessie grinned. "Sure. It'll be fun."

"Great!" Paige said. "Bring your swimsuits."

Maybe Helen *would* come along. But when Jessie peeked inside the darkened room, she saw that her sister was sleeping. She'd leave her a note.

"Where's your swimsuit, Matthew?" she whispered.

"Inside my suitcase. But I can't bother Mommy when she has a headache. Anyway, I don't really know how to swim."

Poor kid. "Eric's about your size, Matthew. I'm sure you can borrow one of his trunks."

She changed into a bathing suit and thongs and took towels for both of them and a white terry cover-up for herself. When they entered Paige's backyard, the pool was already filled—mostly with children, a few brave adults. Paige found a suit for Matthew. He changed in one of the bathrooms, but left his T-shirt on.

"My mommy doesn't like for me to get sunburned," he told Jessie. "I left my clothes in the bathroom. Is that OK?"

"That's fine, Matthew. Let's test the water. Ready?"

"I can't swim," he reminded her. "I was supposed to have lessons in camp, but Mommy says I'm not going back this year."

His tone was matter-of-fact. Had Helen told him that

they'd be staying in California permanently? And what explanation had she given?

"How about if I give you your first lesson today?" Jessie asked.

He hesitated, then nodded. "But not in the deep."

Holding hands, they stepped into the pool. It was a hot day, but the water raised goose bumps on his arms and legs.

"Fast is better," she told him. She picked him up. With his legs straddling her waist, she walked down the remaining two steps and submerged herself and him up to her shoulders.

"It's freezing!" he squealed. His hands were locked around her neck. His wet T-shirt was plastered against his skin.

She dipped three more times. "Better now?"

"Yup." He grinned. "More, Aunt Jessie."

She dipped again, twirling this time. In the velvety water he was weightless, and she spun him around, again and again, loving his giggles, the bright joy in his eyes, the feel of his thin chest against her. Cheek to cheek.

"Come out of there!" a voice screeched. "He can't swim!"

Jessie stopped midspin. Helen was at the edge of the pool. She was in her robe. Her hair was messy. Panic was in her eyes.

"I'm holding him, Helen. Calm down. He's perfectly safe."

"I want him out of there right now!"

Everyone was staring at them. Jessie made her way to the steps and deposited Matthew on the top one. Helen wrapped a towel around her son. In a quieter, no less intense voice, she said, "You had no right to do this without asking me!"

Through clenched teeth, Jessie said, "You were sleeping, Helen." *As usual,* she felt like adding. "I left you a note."

"That's not the point! He's afraid of the water." Helen turned to Matthew. "Are you OK, baby?" She stroked his cheek.

"It was fun, Mommy. Can I go back in with Aunt Jessie?" His teeth were chattering, but he was grinning.

"No! Find your clothes and let's go."

"But Aunt Jessie's friend said they're having a cake soon."

"You'll have cake another time."

"But there won't *be* another party! Please, Mommy!"

"Matthew!" Helen took his hand and moved away from the pool.

Jessie grabbed Helen's arm. "Let him have a piece of cake, goddammit!" she whispered. "What the hell is wrong with you?"

Helen started to say something, then stopped and turned to Matthew. "You'll have to come home first and change. You'll catch cold, standing around in wet clothes."

"Thank you, Mommy. I'll get my jeans." He threw Jessie a quick, adoring look, then scurried off.

Thank you for what? Jessie thought, simmering with anger and humiliation as she walked to the canvas deck chair where she'd put her towel. For ruining the poor kid's day? For scaring him half to death? She toweled herself dry, slipped on the cover-up, and without a backward glance at Helen, left the pool area.

Paige was nowhere in sight; Jessie would call her later and make up an excuse for leaving early. She walked down the driveway and headed home, half expecting Helen to follow, and felt a mixture of relief and disappointment when she didn't.

Inside the house Jessie had a childish impulse, first to chain-lock the door and bar Helen's entry, then to pack Helen's things and send her sister and all her problems and neuroses back to Winnetka. (Not Matthew. Matthew could stay.) She was tired of having to adjust her schedule and habits to someone who took everything for granted and didn't give a damn about anyone but herself.

She slammed her bedroom door but felt no better. She took a shower. The hot water eased some of her tension but not all of it—part of it had nothing to do with Helen; it had to do with the killer and the curare and Gary, that son of a bitch, and the fact that because of him, Kalish had rebuked her. When she exited the bedroom, dressed in a pair of shorts and a tank top, she found Helen in the hall, and all her resentment came flooding back.

"Where's Matthew?" Jessie said, squeezing emotion from her voice.

"Paige loaned him one of Eric's shirts. I'm sorry I overreacted, Jess. I was frightened. You can understand that, can't you?" She smiled and put her hand on Jessie's shoulder.

Jessie shrugged it off. "What the hell's going on here?"

"What do you mean?"

"You call to say you're coming for a vacation. Fine. Then I find out, and only 'cause Mom forced it out of you, that you left Neil. You ask me for an attorney, but you won't talk about it. You hide behind your damn headaches—"

"The headaches are real! And my life is my business!"

"I'm your sister, for Christ's sake. I want to help!"

"I don't *need* your help! Why can't you leave me alone? I didn't pester you about your divorce. Or about the baby."

Jessie winced. *Not fair!* "You're in my house, Helen. If you wanted to be alone, why come here? This isn't a goddamn hotel!"

"You want me to leave? Fine. Matthew and I don't have to stay where we're not wanted. I didn't realize we were in the way."

"I didn't say that." She'd thought it a while ago, and not for the first time. Had Helen sensed her irritation before now?

Helen had turned and run into her bedroom. Jessie followed and found Helen flinging dresses onto the folding bed.

"Stop this!" Jessie snapped. "You're being ridiculous."

"We'll go to Mom and Dad's. They'll be happy to have us." Helen went to the closet and brought out another armful of clothes. "I try to help. I straighten up. I do our laundry. I cook almost every night, but I guess you'd rather eat alone!"

"That's not true." Despite an occasional urge to eat in solitude, Jessie had found it pleasant coming home to find supper prepared. She liked to cook, but after Gary had moved out, she'd relied on quick meals and take-out food. Sometimes she wondered why she'd bothered to buy the herbs that were sitting on her kitchen window ledge. "I appreciate what you've been doing, Helen. I don't want you to leave. I just feel shut out." Jessie paused. "I thought we were close." Confidantes. Allies.

"We are." Helen clasped the dresses to her. "But there's nothing you can do to help, Jess." Her eyes welled with tears.

"Why did you leave Neil, Helen? Why do you want to set up residency in California? *Talk* to me!"

Helen shook her head. "It's so complicated." She sat down on Matthew's bed, the dresses folded in her arms.

Jessie sat next to her. "Is it because Neil's away so much?" She hesitated. "Is there someone else, Helen?"

"Of course not!" Then she sighed. "Not that I haven't been tempted. I get so damn lonely with Neil away. The nights are especially bad. But it's not just that. Our marriage isn't working. We're so different, Jess. You said so from the start."

Neil was fourteen years older than Helen, his hair already graying when he dated Helen. Solid, dependable. A father figure to protect her? Jessie had wondered.

"I wanted you to be sure that you weren't marrying him just to get out of the house," Jessie said. To escape.

When Jessie was a freshman in a San Diego community college, she had escaped into a six-month relationship with a teaching assistant she could barely visualize now. (Jessie wasn't sure what had infuriated her mother more—that Jessie had quashed another one of her dreams—purposely?—by not earning the grades for an Ivy League school, or that she was "rutting like a pig in a vermin-infested apartment. Don't," Frances had warned, "think about moving back in here. Your father and I are through with you.")

Helen had cried when Jessie had told her she was moving out; Jessie had cried, too. Arthur had surreptitiously sent his daughter weekly checks. Jessie, fueled by pride and anger and a grim determination to be free, had returned them uncashed to his office.

Luck or some nameless protector kept Jessie from making her mistake permanent. After saying good-bye to the teaching assistant, she shared a small apartment in San Diego with a female friend. She took courses during the day and worked nights as a cashier in a supermarket, then as a waitress in the elegant Del Coronado Hotel. Where a friend of her parents saw her. "You're determined to ruin my life, aren't you!" Frances screeched.

Jessie quit her job and moved to Los Angeles. She transferred to Cal State Northridge and received a degree in political science. Then she applied to the police academy. Her one regret—the source of her unassuaged guilt—was leaving Helen behind. But Jessie had known instinctively that her own survival was at stake.

When Helen was sixteen, she turned up one day on Jessie's doorstep. Arthur drove to L.A. and persuaded her to return. Helen came again. And again. Each time Arthur took her back. Then Helen married Neil Bollinger and moved to Winnetka.

Now she had run away again. To Jessie, again. Was she waiting for Neil to come and take her back? Jessie asked Helen.

Helen shook her head. "I want to start over. Here, not in Winnetka." She took Jessie's hand. "You're the best friend I have, Jess. With Neil away so much, it's been hard to make friends. Most of the people I know, I met through Neil. They're his friends, not mine."

His and hers friends. Like the possessions they'd divided, Jessie and Gary had reclaimed the friends they'd brought to the marriage. There were some "joint property" couples, acquired after the marriage. Those were more difficult to inventory; eventually the friendships waned, the couples distancing themselves from the awkwardness and bitterness of divorce and the difficulty of having to choose sides. Divorce, like any war, always takes innocent casualties.

"What about Matthew, Helen? When will you tell him?"

Helen removed her hand. "When the time is right."

"You're uprooting him from his friends, the people and places he knows. You're smothering him, Helen. Look what happened today."

"He doesn't know how to swim!" She twisted the sleeve of one of the dresses she was holding. "He's afraid of the water!"

"No, he's not. *You're* afraid of water, Helen," Jessie said gently, "but you shouldn't pass that fear onto Matthew."

It was more than fear, Jessie thought with a rush of pity. It was terror, a phobia compounded by Frances's insistence, after the move from L.A. to La Jolla, that both her daughters be accomplished swimmers, even though she herself rarely stepped into the large oval pool. ("Chlorine and sun are so damaging to my skin.")

Jessie had loved the water—it always welcomed her unconditionally—and she'd mastered it effortlessly. Helen, fussy as a baby even about taking baths, had balked.

"Maybe she's too young, Mrs. Claypool," the instructor had said after trying to coax Helen into the water for ten minutes.

"Nonsense, Jeffrey. Go into the water, sweetheart," Frances had cooed. "Do it for Mommy." She took off her sunglasses to beam at her five-year-old daughter.

Helen didn't budge from the top step of the pool. Thirty minutes later Jeffrey left, accompanied by Frances's smile and her sunny assurance that "next time Helen will do better." Then Frances, her smile eclipsed by a scowl, turned to Helen, who stood quivering at the edge of the pool in her red bikini.

"Get into the water, sweetie. One step at a time. I know you can do it." The voice was like honey.

Helen shook her head and thin body. The flounces on the red panties fluttered.

"Get in, I said!" There was no honey now, only steel.

"I don't want to, Mommy!" she whispered.

Brave words, Jessie had thought even then. Foolish words.

"You don't want *to? You don't* want *to listen to your mother? Have you ever heard anything like that?" Frances addressed an invisible, sympathetic audience. She shook her head. "I have been patient with you, Helen, so, so patient, even though you embarrassed me in front of that nice young man."*

"I'm sorry, Mommy." A whimper. "I don't like the water."

"Well, I'm sorry, too, Helen Felicia Claypool, but I think it's a little too late for 'sorry,' don't you?"

In her bathing suit and high-heeled sandals that clacked on the hand-painted Italian ceramic tiles, Frances made her way to the pool in a graceful Miss America stride. Helen's eyes were riveted on her mother; she knew better than to run away.

Jessie had been sitting near the edge of the pool, her legs dangling in the water. Now she jumped up and hurried over. "Mommy, maybe she'll go with me. I—"

The slap caught her on her cheekbone and mouth. She cried out in pain, then compressed her lips. They were bleeding.

"Don't you ever, ever, ever interfere again, Jessica!"

Each word was punctuated with venom and a blow to her body. Jessie's hands performed wild calisthenics, trying to shield first her face, then her arms, chest, legs.

Frances kicked off her sandals and turned to Helen. The blond little girl, shivering in the sunlight, started crying even before the slim arm came down and circled her waist like a snake.

"Please!" Helen begged. "Please!"

"Stop that!" Frances smacked her on the back of her stick-thin legs. The handprint was instantly red against her skin.

Jessie put her fist into her mouth to stifle her moan.

Dragging a shrieking Helen with her, Frances walked down the steps until the water was up to her waist. Grasping Helen around her middle with both hands, she plunged the girl under the turquoise water, then yanked her up again. Helen was sobbing and sputtering. Water was pouring out of her mouth, her nose.

"Well, that wasn't so bad, was it, baby?" Frances said. "Next time, I know you'll cooperate with Jeffrey, won't you?"

At dinner, Arthur asked Jessie about the bruises on her face.

Jessie stared at her creamy porcelain Lenox plate. She could feel her mother's stiletto eyes. If you tell . . . if you tell . . . if you tell. . . . *"I bumped it against the side of the pool." Underneath the table, she gripped Helen's small hand.*

Arthur was quiet for a moment, then said, "Be more careful, Jessie," and she knew that he knew, and in that moment, as in the ones that had come before it and the ones that would follow, she hated her father and the betrayal of his silence and cruel abandonment as much as she hated her mother. Maybe more.

Frances smiled brightly. "We had a lovely time, didn't we, girls? Helen had her first lesson. I think she'll do beautifully."

At night, after she knew that Frances was asleep, Jessie tiptoed down the hall to Helen's room. "I'm sorry," she whispered to the sleeping child and smoothed the silvery-blond hair.

It was a different time now, a different house. But the guilt and pain were the same.

"I'm sorry," Jessie said. She moved closer to her sister on the folding bed and put her arms around her, crushing the clothes between them. "It'll be OK. You'll see."

15

Monday morning, Jessie sensed that something was going on the minute she entered the squad room. Two detectives at the Robbery table stopped talking when they saw her, then resumed their conversation. Phil was on the phone, but there was an odd expression in his eyes as he waved to her. Catella, a detective in Juvenile, was definitely staring at her. There were others staring, too.

Another headline? What had Gary written this time? Jessie put her purse on her desk and was waiting for Phil to get off the phone when she heard Kalish call her name.

"In here," he ordered and disappeared into his office.

Great. Feeling as though she were marching to her execution (although she didn't know what crime she'd committed), and conscious of all the eyes that followed her, she walked across the room and into his office and sat down.

"You're going downtown."

She frowned, puzzled. That was it? Why the big production?

"Chief Hanson has set up a task force to find the curare killer. I told him you linked the deaths. He's impressed. He wants you on the team." Kalish's eyes held paternal pride and something else Jessie couldn't define.

Jessie's mouth was suddenly dry. "Thank you."

"Don't thank me. You'll be up nights until this is solved. You'll have the whole city breathing down your neck. The mayor. The press. But you have an in with the press, don't you, Jess?"

This time his reference to Gary was a light one, she noted gratefully. So that was behind her. "I don't know what to say."

"Don't say. Do. Make us proud, Jessie." Kalish cleared his throat. "OK. Enough sentimental bullshit. You're expected at Parker Center by twelve. I told them you'd need till then to get your cases in order. Give everything to Phil. At Parker, report to Lt. Peter Corcoran. He's in charge of the task force. He wants you to bring all your notes on the curare cases, including Balderas."

She stood up.

"It's a terrific opportunity, Jessie. But you knew that the minute you found the money in the library books, didn't you?" Kalish smiled at her instant discomfiture. "Don't apologize for being ambitious. But don't blow it, either."

Phil was waiting for her outside Kalish's office. He gave her a bear hug. "Way to go, Jess!"

So Phil had known. That explained his earlier look, the aborted conversation, the stares. Jessie knew they were all happy for her—she was one of them, wasn't she?—but she wondered whether there wasn't a bit of envy in their good wishes, wondered how she would have felt in their places.

"This is Det. Jessica Drake from West L.A.," Peter Corcoran said to the three other members of the task force. "She'll be working on this investigation. Detective, this is. . . ."

Jessie made preliminary assessments as she shook hands

with each of the men. Corcoran was about five feet nine inches tall and had a stocky build. His graying blond hair was clipped. His face was jowly. He reminded Jessie of a bulldog.

John Takamura was short and trim with delicate, almost feminine features. He was wearing an expensively cut light-gray silk suit—interesting on a detective's salary, she thought—and looked like a bank executive. Ray Barrows was a tall, solidly built black with a neatly trimmed Afro, a warm smile, and a firm handshake.

Frank Pruitt was tall, muscular, and ruggedly handsome. He had dark-brown wavy hair touched with streaks of gray, dark-brown eyes that looked impenetrable, well-defined lips, and a nose that had obviously been broken. He held her hand for a fraction too long, and his eyes brushed over her body. She flushed and was instantly annoyed with herself and with him.

Corcoran and Pruitt were in their forties; Takamura and Barrows, in their midthirties.

The task force had a great racial mix—but not a great gender mix. Typical. She wondered how they were assessing her: tall, good figure, pretty; gray-green eyes; wavy brown hair (still too long; she hadn't gotten around to that haircut). She was wearing taupe slacks and a short-sleeved pale peach rayon blouse. She'd wanted to change into something more sophisticated, but there'd been no time. As it was, she'd barely made it to Parker Center by noon.

Every time Jessie came to Parker Center, the multistory building seemed to have slipped farther into decrepitude. The exterior was passable—turquoise stucco and endless glass (which explained why suspects called Parker Center the Glass House). Inside, everything was terminally beige. The walls were cracked and missing chunks of plaster; the floors pitted. The elevators posted No Smoking signs, but the smell of cigarettes pervaded.

On the third floor a maze of corridors led to Robbery-Homicide, off of which was the Operations Room, a narrow rectangle with black-and-gray speckled linoleum and a window facing San Pedro. There were four desks (one, empty except for a stapler, a tape dispenser, and two stacked in-and-out trays, was clearly waiting for Jessie); a blackboard; file cabinets; a water cooler and a beat-up coffeepot. On one wall was a map of L.A. County dotted with five red pins, one for each victim. Jessie wondered how many pins would be added before they found the killer.

Corcoran stood near the doorway and waited until Jessie and the others were seated. "You'll be working as a team, but we need someone to coordinate the investigation. That'll be you, John." He nodded in Takamura's direction. "We also need a media spokesman. Jessie, your name's been linked in the media to two of the investigations. Somebody has information, your name will be familiar. Makes it easier all around. Since you've checked out all five cases, you can brief the others."

Jessie had to admit that appointing her media spokesman made sense, but she hoped it wouldn't arouse any resentment. She was aware that the other members of the task force, all from Robbery–Homicide—all male—were well acquainted with each other. Family.

"As far as manpower," Corcoran continued, "we have four guys on loan from Metro if we need them. Next point: I've talked to the chief and the mayor, and it's our joint decision to hold a press conference sometime today. Jessie, that involves you."

"Won't that create more problems for us?" Barrows asked.

"It's a double-edged sword." Corcoran folded his arms. "We don't want to start a panic. But if we say nothing and our guy strikes again, the media will say we recklessly withheld information. So we'll let people know there's a killer, tell them to exercise caution—but make them feel we're on top of the situation."

"Which we're not." Pruitt was half sitting, half leaning in his brown vinyl armchair. "Who're we kidding?"

"Keep your feelings to yourself, Frank. That goes for all of you. Not a word to your wife or girlfriend or mother or sister or barber." Corcoran looked at Jessie. "Or boyfriend."

Whom would I tell? Jessie thought. Not Helen; she was fearful by nature. Brenda was still on vacation—no phones, no newspapers, she'd said. Jessie imagined her friend's reaction when she learned what had developed from her Cantaloupe Caper. She wondered suddenly whether Brenda would be jealous of Jessie's being catapulted onto the task force; after all, it was Brenda who'd brought Mae Lee's deposit slip to Jessie's attention. . . .

After Corcoran left, Jessie handed out copies of the report she'd typed. (Phil had surrendered the PC.) "I thought this would make it easier as we go through the cases."

"Good idea, Jessica." Ray Barrows nodded. He had a deep, rumbling James Earl Jones voice that resonated in the room.

"Jessie," she told him.

"A for efficiency, Jessie." Frank Pruitt smiled at her.

She returned the smile, unsure whether his voice had held condescension or whether she was being sensitive. Probably the latter. From the minute she'd arrived, despite Corcoran's pleasant introductions, she'd felt awkward, like an uninvited guest. Well, she'd just have to get over that. She'd done it before.

"OK," Jessie said after she'd given the men a chance to look at the report. "From what we know, the killer uses chloroform to knock out the victim, then injects the curare into a vein. Curare acts quickly—death can occur within six minutes. My guess is that's why the killer chose it. Curare works by—"

"We all read the sidebar," Pruitt interrupted. "Your husband wrote it, right?"

"My ex." As if it's any of your damn business, she thought, taking a dislike to Pruitt. And she was irritated that they'd obviously been discussing her. But wasn't that natural? "What the sidebar *didn't* tell you is that I spoke to the M.E. He says pharmacies don't carry it. I thought we should check with local hospitals and labs to see if there've been any thefts of the substance. I've prepared a list of hospitals and clinics, and nursing homes that treat patients with Parkinson's, multiple sclerosis, any disease treated with curare." She handed out additional papers.

Pruitt glanced at his copies and tossed them behind him onto his desk. "Shit! You're talking weeks. And it's a goddamn waste of time. The killer's managed to kill five people without being seen. He's not going to be stupid and leave a trail."

Jessie flushed. This isn't personal, she reminded herself.

Barrows said, "It's worth a shot, Frank. Right now, we have diddly-squat. We don't know whether the killer's male or female. We sure as hell don't know where he's going to strike next."

Pruitt threw an imaginary dart at the map on the wall.

Jessie said, "As far as we know, the first killing took place in Chinatown, the second in Watts, the third in Hollywood, the fourth and fifth in West L.A." This morning the lab results on Schmidt and Balderas had come in: curare.

Takamura's well-groomed fingers had formed a tent; he'd been tapping them against his thin lips. "The victims are all members of minority groups. The Lee woman is Chinese, Jeffreys is black, Radovsky is Russian, possibly Jewish, Balderas is a Latina. Schmidt is German. I wonder if that's a coincidence, or whether the victim was chosen *because* of his nationality."

It was an interesting idea; Jessie had been about to

mention it but had hesitated. She was new on the team—and female. It was more politic to let one of the regulars score some points.

Barrows frowned. "You think the killer's a white-supremacy nut, John? A skinhead or something? Jesus, that's all we need!"

"You want to explain how he knew their nationalities, John?" Pruitt's voice was snide.

"The Asian woman and the black nurse are obvious." Takamura's reply was as unruffled as his maroon silk tie. "Maybe the killer looked up Russian-sounding names in a phone book and picked Radovsky. He was found near his apartment, correct?"

Jessie nodded. "But how did he know that Angelina Balderas was a Latina? Or that Schmidt was German? They weren't killed at home, and there's nothing strikingly ethnic about them."

Barrows said, "Maybe he picked their names from the phone book and followed them from their homes. The Schmidt woman to the library, the Latina to the Century City shopping center."

Takamura frowned. "Why didn't he kill them at their homes, then, as he did the Russian and the Chinese?" The fingers formed a tent again.

Jessie said, "Because the Russian and Mae Lee lived alone. Schmidt had a roommate. Angelina Balderas was married."

The room was silent. Through the window, Jessie could hear the traffic. Pruitt's chair creaked as he tilted it back.

"There *are* some constants," Jessie said. "So far, he's killed on Thursdays. The only possible exception is Radovsky. He was found around four A.M. Friday, but the M.E. who did the autopsy says Radovsky was probably killed late Thursday night."

"So we shut down the city on Thursdays till we find this

guy?" Pruitt tilted his chair back until it was almost a couch.

Jessie pictured him crashing to the floor. It was a satisfying image. "The killer did skip one Thursday. July second."

"Holiday weekend." Pruitt returned his chair to its normal position. "Maybe he had front-row seats to a Janet Jackson concert. I wouldn't give those up, would you?"

"Get serious, Frank." Barrows shook his head and smiled.

"I *am* serious. Do you have any idea how much tickets to a Janet Jackson concert cost?" He stood and walked to the cooler.

"Maybe the killer tried and missed," Barrows said.

Takamura nodded. "Good point. We'll check the precincts. If anyone reported an attempted murder that fits our killer's m.o., we may have a witness. You mentioned *several* constants, Jessie?"

"All the victims were posed to make it look like they were sleeping. Except for the nurse, they were found on their backs. And all of them had their eyes closed—again, obviously by the killer." She hesitated. "It's as if he doesn't like violence."

"A kinder and gentler killer." Pruitt grinned. "I love it."

"Go ahead, Jessie," Barrows said, frowning at Pruitt.

"Finally, there's the money and the deposit slips he leaves. But there's no discernible pattern: a hundred dollars, then one fifty, then sixty, then two hundred. And with the Balderas woman, he left a parking ticket. The deposit slips are all from different banks. Each bank is near the area where the victim was killed, but none of the victims had an account at the bank named on the slip. I think the deposit slip is the killer's way of making sure we know he left the money."

Barrows said, "So why didn't he leave money with Balderas?"

Pruitt said, "Maybe he goes to Vegas before the kill. He wins big, he pays big. He loses, he leaves nothing."

"He left a parking ticket instead," Jessie said. "He put it in her hand. That must mean something." What? she wondered.

Barrows said, "Something else bothers me. How'd he get into the Chinese woman's apartment? The report said no forced entry."

Pruitt snorted. "He made up some story and she bought it. Happens all the time. People are dumb, believe anything. Same thing with the Russian. The killer lured him out to the street."

Takamura said, "That's if the Russian was a specific target. He may just have been walking when the killer was on the prowl."

"In his slippers?" The same snide tone. "That's what the report says. Why would the guy be walking around in the middle of the night in his slippers?" He crumpled his paper cup.

"I think Frank's right, John," Barrows said.

"None of this will help us figure out where the killer will strike next," Takamura said. "We should concentrate on that."

A hint of irritation had flashed across his face. If Jessie hadn't been watching, she wouldn't have seen it. Barrows, she decided, was the peacemaker. Pruitt was the jerk. And Takamura?

"You got a crystal ball, John?" Pruitt turned to Jessie. "If you're right, and Thursday's his special day, we have two days before he strikes again. I'm going to take a leak. By the time I get back, you hotshots better have it figured out." He lobbed the cup into a wastebasket and sauntered out of the room.

Definitely a jerk, Jessie thought.

"Frank's uptight," Barrows told Jessie. "Personal stuff." He turned to Takamura. "I'll talk to him, John."

"This was Corcoran's decision, not mine," he said without looking up from the gray notebook in which he was writing.

"Yeah," Barrows said. He sounded unhappy.

Great, Jessie thought. The task force was an hour old, and they were already knee-deep in personality problems. She knew that this was a great career opportunity and that working at Parker Center had its perks—overtime, a car, accessibility to all the manpower and facilities she needed. She wouldn't have any other cases to distract her; she wouldn't have to check in every few hours, as she did at West L.A. She would make the most of the opportunity, would enjoy the perks, but she thought longingly about Phil and the others—what were they doing now? And how long would she be away? Weeks? Months? She wondered suddenly whether her "chair" would be waiting for her when she returned.

From her canvas satchel she took out her Rolodex, a calendar, and a framed five-by-seven color photo she kept on her desk in West L.A. of Helen, Neil, and Matthew, taken a year ago in their backyard in Winnetka. A year ago she'd kept a picture of Gary on her desk, too. Right now the photo was in a box in the den closet, along with her wedding album and other photos that had brought first remembered joy, then pain. She hadn't looked at any of them since Gary had moved out. She wasn't sure why she'd kept them, knew she wasn't quite ready to discard them.

Takamura said, "We'll start with the hospitals and labs to look for the source of the killer's curare."

Jessie said, "Maybe we should check with Narcotics first about recent drug thefts in medical facilities."

"Good point." He smiled. "We'll check with all the divisions. And we'll follow up on your idea, Ray, that our man botched an attempt on July second. Who knows? Maybe we'll get some answers."

They had no real answers, Jessie thought four long hours

later on her way to the ground-floor Police Commissioner's Room, where the press conference would be held, and each hypothetical answer generated ten new questions.

She'd asked Corcoran if she should go home first and change, but he'd said no, she looked fine. The room officially accommodated sixty people, but she knew it would be crowded well past its capacity. Gary would probably be in the front row, positioned to be the first to shove his microphone into her face. Grinning. Well, she was ready for him.

She wondered if the killer would be watching.

16

It was on the six o'clock news.

He was sitting on the living room sofa, watching TV while he folded the clothes he'd just laundered. The lead story was about an airliner that had crashed on takeoff, killing all 144 passengers. Terrible, he murmured, all those people. And then, while he was smoothing the puckered knit of his T-shirt, he heard the words "special report," and there was a picture of the librarian! Now the anchorman was talking, ". . . was killed with a lethal injection of curare," and then there was a picture of the woman in the parking lot, Angelina Balderas, eight weeks pregnant, but there was no way he could have known.

"Police have confirmed that the two deaths are related, and we understand there may be other related deaths. We take you now to Brad Clement, reporting live from Parker Center in downtown Los Angeles, where we'll be hearing from Det. Jessie Drake."

Which one was Jesse Drake? he wondered, studying several somber-looking men huddled together, and then a tall, beautiful woman approached the maze of microphones.

Another anchor, he thought, but then she said, "I'm Detective Drake," and he gasped.

A woman! *Jessie*, not Jesse. They'd put a *woman* on the case! And then he understood: they were trying to insult him, to get him angry, to belittle him. He listened intently, unaware that he was twisting the T-shirt into a coil.

". . . no cause for alarm," Jessie Drake was saying, "but caution is advisable, five people have been killed. Be alert and wary of unfamiliar faces, lock your doors. We have several leads—"

What leads? They didn't have any leads, couldn't possibly know what he looked like, who he was, where he lived. They were lying, trying to frighten him, but it wouldn't work.

". . . that's all for now. Thank you." Jessie Drake turned away from the podium, ignoring the cacophony of reporters' questions that continued to bombard her.

He flipped rapidly to another channel, but now she had started walking away; he turned to another, and another, but on each one she was a little farther. It was like watching in slow motion, frame by frame, watching the detective walking away from him, out of his reach, until she was gone.

The news would be on again at ten on the local stations, and at eleven on the major networks. He was glad he'd bought the VCR; he could use it to tape the newscasts. He could watch the segment over and over, in slow motion, if he wanted to.

And he could stop Jessie Drake from walking away.

17

"Thanks for seeing me so quickly, Manny."

It was early Tuesday morning, and Jessie was sitting in the LAPD psychologist's office in Parker Center. Dr. Emanuel Freiberg was in his late forties. He had curly light-brown hair, warm brown eyes magnified behind tortoiseshell-framed glasses, a thin nose, and a long neck with a pronounced Adam's apple. He was tall and lanky with a springy stride. Even sitting behind his desk, he exuded energy.

Jessie had been in this office several times—for periodic psychological evaluations (mandatory after the department's overhaul following a critical report of the LAPD by a City Council–appointed commission), for job-related stress, for personal stress, including the end of her marriage. The help was available, and she'd taken advantage of it.

"You said it's about the serial killer, Jessie." Freiberg buffed his glasses with a linen cloth and put them on. "That's important enough for me to shuffle around a few appointments."

Serial killer. God, she hated that label as much as the

press loved it. There was something about it and its previous associations—the Hillside Strangler, Ted Bundy, Son of Sam, the Night Stalker—that revived the public's latent fears and intensified new ones. (There was something tantalizing about it, too, Jessie had to admit—macabre and grisly and chilling, but definitely tantalizing.) Now it was the Curare Killer.

"I need your input, Manny," Jessie said. "We have some patterns, but nothing concrete to go on."

He smiled. "No one would know from yesterday's press conference. You sounded great, Jessie—like you were hot on the killer's trail."

"I wish." Helen had said the same thing: "You looked terrific, Jess—so confident, so pretty. Will you be making an arrest soon?" Matthew had been in awe: "I saw you on TV, Aunt Jessie!"

Even her parents had called—primarily because they were worried and wanted Helen and Matthew to come to La Jolla. But Arthur had said, "Proud of you, Jessie." And Frances had said, "You were wonderful, Jessica. All of our friends thought so. Next time, though, wear a suit. And you should have your hair cut and styled." You could laugh or cry, Jessie had thought.

And of course, there was Gary. After the press conference, he'd come up and said, "Way to go, Jess. Today the task force. Tomorrow—a woman chief of police. Looks like the Blow Dart Murderer's been good for both of us."

"You're beneath contempt," she'd told him, wondering how she could have ever thought him sensitive. Gary had grinned.

Freiberg leaned back in his chair. "You want me to give you the guy's name and address, right?" He shook his head. "I'm not a goddamn magician, Jessie. If I were, I'd be raking it in. I can't tell you what this guy looks like, what his ethnic makeup is. I sure as hell can't tell you who his next target will be."

"You said 'his,' Manny. Do you think the killer's a male?"

"Typically, males commit multiple murders. It's the male-female culture thing. You're dealing with someone who's emotionally disturbed, who's suffered real or imagined abuse. Someone extremely angry. Women who are abused or traumatized feel shame and internalize their anger. Males act on it." He leaned forward. "Look, I could be wrong—women's roles are changing. But if I had to bet, I'd say you're dealing with a male."

"What else can you tell me?" It was odd, in this office, to be asking the questions. Usually, she revealed; Manny listened.

"You first," he said. "Tell me everything you know."

She slipped almost gratefully into her role. She spoke slowly, referring to her notes from time to time. Freiberg listened intently, scribbling on a yellow legal-size pad. Occasionally, he interrupted to ask her to clarify a point or repeat a fact. When she was finished, she looked at Freiberg expectantly.

"My turn, right? Give me a minute." He flipped through the pages he'd filled, then looked up. "My guess is schizoid personality. The killer's obviously in control of his behavior and can make a good impression—the Chinese woman let him into her home; the Russian followed him into the street. Also, he didn't look out of place at the library, so he's probably nondescript." Freiberg tapped his pen against his pad. "The nurse at the bus stop and the woman in the parking lot—they add a different dimension. Maybe your killer likes voyeuristic involvement."

Your killer. As though they had a relationship, as though he were her responsibility, no one else's. *"She's your daughter, Arthur."* But Jessie *had* "discovered" him.

"So what about all these ethnic groups, Manny? Are we dealing with a psycho racist?

Freiberg shook his head. "From studies I've seen, racists concentrate on one ethnic group and limit their victims to one gender. Plus this guy's method doesn't fit. Hate groups are volatile, vicious. They want to draw attention to themselves and their causes. Your killings are relatively nonviolent—if you can call murder nonviolent. No beatings, no torture, no sexual violation, no swastikas or crosses or hexagrams or any of that symbolic shit they leave for the cops and the public to find."

So much for that theory. If the killer *was* a racist, at least the task force would have some direction. They could check membership lists of racist organizations, check police files for names of those with prior involvement in similar episodes.

"So why is he killing, Manny?"

Freiberg shrugged. "Why is the sky blue? Why did Donald Trump dump Ivana? Why did the stock I just bought three months ago take a nose dive?"

"Seriously."

"Seriously? I've never met the guy, so how can I unravel the workings of what's obviously a sick mind? Sometimes it takes years of therapy to figure out a patient's motivation."

"We don't have years, Manny. We have two days."

Freiberg sighed. "Point well taken." He scanned his notes again. "One thing that stands out is the *way* he kills. He closes the victims' eyes. He arranges victims so they're comfortable—those are caring actions that suggest an almost maternal touch. And it's a painless death, Jessie—a mercy murder. That's a hell of an oxymoron, isn't it?"

It was. Jessie nodded.

"He uses chloroform to render the victims unconscious," Freiberg continued. "They don't feel the injection or the effects of the curare. And the curare's a telling choice. Sure, it's a poison, but unlike arsenic or strychnine or cyanide, it *is* used as an anesthetic. Gary mentioned that in his sidebar, I saw."

Jessie groaned. "If I hear about that sidebar again . . ."

"Sorry about that." Freiberg smiled. "I should've realized it would be a sore point. You OK? In general, I mean."

"I'm OK." More or less. But she was here to talk about the killer, not her personal problems.

"Anyway, it's possible the killer's convincing himself that he's not killing his victims. He's just putting them to sleep. In a sense, he's sorry to see them go."

"So why *does* he kill them?"

"Back to square one, huh?" He frowned, twirling his pen between his fingers. "Maybe killing is a way for him to relieve his tension. Also, the need to kill may have been triggered by a couple of things. One, he may be frustrated by the world situation—economic, political, societal, moral. Like who isn't, right?" Freiberg sighed. "So he wants to draw attention to it. Or he thinks he's doing his victims a favor by removing them from such an uncaring world."

"Some favor."

"Yeah," Freiberg agreed. "Two, and this is a little trickier, he may have gone through a recent period of significant personal achievement and feels uneasy being a success."

Jessie frowned. "That doesn't make sense. He's successful so he kills? We'll have to lock up all the lottery winners."

"I told you it's tricky. See, performing acts of violence is his attempt to restore his equilibrium. Hey, it's just a theory, Jessie," he added when he saw her expression. "Three, his actions may have been triggered by the death of or contact with the person who caused his trauma."

"Too bad we don't know who that is, huh? What about a personality profile, Manny?" And a name. And an address.

"I'd feel on safer ground if I could give him a Rorschach and an MMPI. What if you guys catch him and he proves me totally wrong?" Freiberg grinned. "OK. Emanuel Freiberg's armchair analysis." The grin had disappeared; the eyes were serious. "In my opinion, Jessie—and it's just opinion, remember—the guy is passive-aggressive. He's furious, but too passive to act viciously—hence the chloroform and curare. The chloroform isn't deadly, but using it gives him a feeling of power. Same thing with the Thursday pattern. He enjoys causing the acceleration of fear—you know, making the public worry 'Who will it be tonight?' That kind of thing. It gives him another measure of control."

"What about the week he skipped?"

"Who knows? Maybe he got sick. Maybe he muffed an attempt."

"We're checking into that possibility. What about the money? A form of atonement?"

He smiled. "Pretty good, Jessie. That was my thought. Thing is, it doesn't fit with passive-aggressives. They have miserly tendencies. Maybe that's why he didn't leave anything with the Balderas woman. He got cheap." The smile had deepened into a grin.

"You sound like Frank Pruitt. He's on the task force. God, what an asshole."

"I know Frank," Freiberg said quietly. "He's a good cop."

"Could be." And good-looking, and sexy, but so what? "He's got a major chip on his shoulder."

Freiberg shrugged. "Maybe once you get to know him—"

"No, thanks. What else can you tell me about him, Manny?"

"About Pruitt?" Freiberg said with a straight face.

"No, dammit. About the killer." But she smiled. Manny was entitled to his jokes.

"Your killer is a fairly intelligent, moderately affable guy who has a vendetta against something or someone. People who know him casually would never suspect his anger. He's very brittle emotionally. A rebuff or slight makes him angry. He's probably suffered emotional deprivation. Possibly a parent has withheld affection or abused him. That's about all I can tell you."

"Christ, it's the same old thing! Aren't there any killers who weren't abused by their parents? People who were just born crazy or evil or with some aberration that makes them kill?"

"Hey," he said softly. "You asked."

"I know." She sighed. "Shit. I'm sorry, Manny."

"It doesn't mean that every kid who was abused is going to turn into a killer, Jessie."

"Of course not. I know that."

"Or that cycles of abuse always perpetuate themselves."

"So you've said." She stood. "Thanks for everything, Manny. You've been a real help. I'll pass on what you've told me."

"We joked earlier about Gary. But I had the feeling the last time we talked that you had unresolved feelings about your divorce. I have some time now before my next appointment."

She hesitated, then shook her head. "It's over. There's no point in rehashing my mistakes."

"Your miscarriage wasn't a mistake, Jessie. It wasn't something you did. It just happened."

She was straddling a suspect, about to cuff him, when an accomplice appeared from nowhere and pushed her from behind. She broke the fall with her palms, but her body made contact with the concrete and the impact rumbled through her.

"You OK?" Phil asked later, after the suspects were in custody.

"Fine," she told him. "I'm fine."

But the next morning, there was bright-red blood on her panties and she had menstruallike cramps. Gary had already left for the paper; she called her obstetrician and drove herself to Cedars-Sinai. When Gary arrived, it was all over.

He kissed her and held her close. "Thank God you're OK," he whispered. There were tears in his eyes. They rocked together on the hospital bed.

Her doctor walked in. "I'm not sure it was the fall, Jessie," he said. "Don't blame yourself."

"What fall?" Gary asked. "What fall?" he repeated after the doctor made a hurried, awkward exit from the room.

She told him.

"You had to go chasing someone, didn't you?" Gary said. "I begged you to take a leave. I begged you. But you never wanted this baby, did you, Jessie? You wanted to lose it, so you wouldn't have a setback in your damn career.

"Are you happy now, Jessie?"

Freiberg said, "It might help to talk about it. I noticed how tense you were when you talked about the Balderas woman. And she's the only one you refer to by her first name."

Jessie smiled tightly. "That's why you're a shrink, Manny."

"Guilt's a heavy package to lug around, Jess."

She shrugged. "Everybody feels guilty about something."

"You're telling me? I have a Jewish mother." He smiled. "It's in our genes."

"Well, blame the Jewish gene I got from someone on my mother's side of the family," she said lightly. "I have to go, Manny. Duty calls." She headed for the door, knowing he was watching her, then turned around. "Look, you're right. I *haven't* resolved my feelings about my miscarriage or Gary or my fears. I *will* talk to you about all this, but some other time."

"Whenever you're ready." Freiberg smiled.

She hesitated. "One more thing. This is about my nephew."

"Your sister's son, right?"

Jessie nodded. "Helen and Matthew are visiting me. She told me she and her husband Neil are separating."

"I'm sorry to hear that."

"Me, too. Neil doesn't know about it. Neither does Matthew. To tell you the truth, I'm worried about Matthew. He's awfully quiet. He's shy. He's warming up to me, but sometimes he's still jittery, jumpy." She paused. "He reminds me of Helen when she was his age. Fragile, somehow. Timid. Helen hovers over him constantly. She's so overprotective." Just like I was toward her, Jessie thought. The big sister, shielding the little one.

"He's probably aware that his parents are having problems. You can't hide something like that from kids. Sounds like he could benefit from talking to a therapist. I can give you the names of some competent people." He reached for the Rolodex on his desk.

Jessie frowned. "Helen will probably think I'm interfering, trying to be his mother because I don't have kids of my own."

"Are you?" Freiberg asked gently.

"I'm worried about him, Manny!" And then, "I don't know. Maybe I am. What do *you* think?"

18

The press conference had depressed him, but seeing the published proof of his power (UNKNOWN KILLER SLAYS FIVE IN LOS ANGELES; POLICE BAFFLED) had been a tonic, restoring his self-confidence and filling him with renewed purpose. He clipped the entire article and added it to his folder.

His tooth ached. The pain was radiating toward his left eye, and he was glad he hadn't canceled today's appointment even though he was so busy. A cavity in your upper left molar, Dr. Stoltz had said, showing him the X ray. He hated the cardboard forms the X-ray technician had pressed into his gums, hated the cold tip of the machine against his cheek, wondered why, if the dosage was safe, she scurried out of the room to activate the machine that would send invisible rays into his body.

Maybe he'd see the new hygienist again. She was pretty and he liked her soapy scent, with no perfume to assail his nose and make his eyes water. I'm Teresa Barnett, she'd said as she adjusted his bib. I'm taking over while Lucille's out. Then she put on a mask. The mask ballooned out, and he didn't think it would smear her pale pink lipstick. Even if it did, it was disposable, not like his handkerchief; the bleach had turned the blood into pale rust. He'd decided not to use the handkerchief again.

Teresa had a gentle touch, and as she leaned over him, he studied her face. She had wavy, shoulder-length brown hair and large brown eyes with flecks of amber near the centers. Her lashes were naturally long, not spiky or matted; the ends were blond. Even close up her skin was smooth, with tiny, almost invisible pores, and he had an urge to stroke her cheek. Then she moved back and said something, but he'd been concentrating on her skin so she had to repeat it. You can rinse now, she said, and he saw in the deep pools of her eyes that she cared, he sensed the smile behind the mask that billowed with her warm breath.

She turned discreetly away as he rinsed and spit into the basin. He shut his eyes, because he'd never been able to stand the sight of blood (*"Look at that punch! The guy's nose is gushing blood like a goddamned geyser!"*), but he knew his blood was swirling around in the basin, swirling and swirling, and soon it would be sucked into the whirlpool and disappear.

When she finished flossing, she held up a mirror for his inspection, but his eyes turned from his polished teeth to her now-ungloved hands. He didn't see a wedding band or engagement ring. Unmasked, she smiled warmly. I hope I didn't hurt you, she said, I know there are some tender areas, and she smiled again, so he knew she cared, and he almost said, Teresa, may I call you Teresa? I'd like to see you sometime. But as his chair finished its descent and thudded to a stop, he lost his nerve. And when he finished making his next appointment, she was with another patient.

If she was there today, he'd ask her out. He didn't think she'd say no, not like Marianne, not after the way she'd smiled at him. They could go to a movie over the weekend—

not on Friday night; Friday night he had to stay home. Maybe on Saturday or Sunday night, whichever she preferred. A Sunday matinee would be fine too; afterward they could go for coffee or take a walk. He couldn't go to a Saturday matinee. He always visited his mother on Saturday afternoons, and he didn't want to disappoint her.

He knew his visits made a difference, even though she wasn't fully conscious most of the time, and when he stared into her eyes, trying to see if comprehension lay behind their glazed surface, more often than not they only mirrored his anxiety. I'll see you next week, Mama, he'd whispered last Saturday, and he thought she'd gripped his hand a little. He mentioned that to the nurse—not Marianne, she'd lied about being married, he knew that now, they all lied—and the new nurse smiled and said she'd make sure to tell the doctor. What a devoted son, she said, they say you come every week, call every day. He *was* a devoted son, and he wished his mother were more alert, so that he could tell her everything he was doing. She would be so proud of him.

Most of the time she was disoriented. Where's Ed? she'd asked lately. He'd told her Ed was dead, his father was dead; cirrhosis of the liver and a final heart attack, the doctor had said. And she'd nodded, and her eyes had blinked back tears, but then the following Saturday she'd asked again, where is Ed?

It pained him that she was lying in a strange bed, cared for by strangers. His father had placed her in the nursing facility two years ago (*"Best thing for her, boy"*). After his father's death, he'd moved back into his parents' house and wanted her released to his care, but the doctors had convinced him he wasn't equipped to handle the round-the-clock nursing. The disease is advanced, they said, she's debilitated, almost no motor function, there's partial paralysis and impaired speech from the stroke. He knew the multiple sclerosis was genetic, but he'd read that mental stress accelerated its course, and he knew who was responsible for that, and for the stroke, too, even if he couldn't prove it.

She was as helpless as a baby. He fed her when he visited, custards or jello or puddings, sometimes lukewarm broth or farina. But it was a slow process, and after every spoonful he had to wipe the food that dribbled out of the corner of her mouth and down her chin. The muscles of her arms and legs were flaccid, despite the therapy the nurses assured him she was receiving. And she was swaddled in diapers. He'd seen that once when the nurse had changed his mother's sheets; his mother's gown had crept up past her thighs, exposing the latest indignity she had to suffer. She can't always wait for the bedpan, the nurse had said in answer to his protest, and we can't have her lying in urine, now can we?

"You wet again last night, didn't you, boy? Your mother tried to sneak out of bed to change your sheets, but I heard her. What do you have to say about that?"

"I'm sorry, sir. I drank too much before I went to sleep."

"You're a liar, is what you are. Ten-year-old boys don't wet their beds unless they want to. Ed, Jr., never wet a day in his life, and as far as I know, you boys were born with the same equipment. Admit it, boy—you did it to get me angry."

"It was an accident. Can I be excused, please? I have to go to the bathroom."

"Tell me the truth, and I won't smack you. I just want to hear you say it. Just tell me you did it 'cause you know how crazy it makes me when you wet. Come on, tell me the truth."

"It's not like that! I dream I'm in the bathroom. And then I wake up and I'm all wet. I don't do it on purpose. I don't! Can I go now, please, because I can't hold it in. Please, sir."

"I'm not your mother, boy. You can't fool me like you do her, making her change your smelly sheets like some slave. And that is going to stop, do you hear me? You wet your sheets, you'll sleep in

them. Maybe we should put you back in diapers like a baby. What do you think of that, huh?"

"I have to go right now!" Without looking, he knew the telltale circle of his shame was already there. It was small now, barely visible, but if he stayed here one second longer, it would spread wider and wider, darkening the crotch of his jeans.

"You'll stay here until you tell me the truth, boy. Now just say it, say that you wet on purpose and you can go."

"I didn't—"

"Say it, goddammit! Say it, you little shit!"

"I did—I did it—on purpose. Please can I go now, please?"

"Get out of here. Just get the hell out before I puke."

All these years later the humiliation still gnawed at him, and when he thought of his mother, he felt like crying at the unfairness of it all. It was worse than pain, worse than deprivation. Worse, even, than death. He looked at the grainy photos of the five people on the front page and closed the folder.

Helen told Jessie to mind her own business, thank you very much; she didn't need her sister's advice on how to raise her child. Then she stormed out of the kitchen. So much for the closeness they'd shared Sunday night, Jessie thought. And the tears. Maybe Helen was right to be hurt—maybe Jessie *was* interfering—but Matthew seemed forlorn so much of the time.

Tonight he'd been particularly subdued. After supper, while Helen had been busy circling ads for job opportunities and apartments, Jessie had looked in on him. He'd been lying on his bed on his side, facing the wall, his knees drawn almost to his chest. She'd stepped into the room (she ought to thank Helen for transforming into a guest room what had been "the baby's room" long after the baby and her marriage no longer existed). Hey, Matthew, she'd said, how about a game of checkers? No, thanks, Aunt Jessie, he'd whispered, a tremor in his voice. Want to talk? she'd offered, but he'd answered with a shake of his head.

So she'd gone back to Helen and mentioned the idea of Matthew's seeing a psychologist. And now Helen was angry.

Sighing, Jessie finished wiping the supper dishes, then went to the den and turned on the television. She couldn't concentrate. Instead, she opened the folder she'd brought home.

Five victims. Five nationalities, five parts of the city, five occupations. And aside from the curare, and the fact that all the murders had taken place on a Thursday, the only common denominator she could see was money attached to deposit slips from different banks. And that applied to only four of the victims. And the amount of money varied in each case.

Some common denominator.

But the deposit slips and the parking ticket *had* to be significant. Jessie checked her notes again. The Chinese woman had been found with a slip from First Public Savings Bank; there was a branch on Hill and Alpine, a few blocks from Mae Lee's apartment. Norma Jeffreys' slip was from Bank of America; there was a branch across the street from the bus stop where she'd been found. Next, Radovsky. The slip was from Security Pacific; there was a branch three blocks from the Russian's residence. Finally, Enid Schmidt: a slip from First Interstate Bank of California.

There was no risk for the killer in helping himself to a blank slip from the stack in the bank lobby. No one would notice him. And he'd gone to different banks each time, chosen banks within close proximity of the murder site.

That was interesting. Why hadn't he chosen a bank closer to the library? There were several within walking distance, she knew, whereas the First Interstate closest to the library was on Wilshire and Oakhurst, almost a mile away. She'd talked to the manager there and learned about Enid Schmidt's nonexisting account.

Maybe there *was* a closer branch. Jessie called the twenty-four-hour phone number of the Wilshire branch. A recording told her she could have assistance with her checking account, with reporting a lost bank book. . . . Even the phones were conspiring against her. She slammed down the receiver.

In the morning she learned that there was no closer branch.

"We have branches on Wilshire and Detroit, on Highland and Santa Monica, and on Sunset and Spaulding," the receptionist told her. "But they're all farther away."

The Sunset location sounded familiar. Jessie reread her report on Enid Schmidt. Halfway through her interview with Benny Lefton, she found it: the books had originated from the branch half a block from Sunset. Spaulding was four blocks from Gardner.

Jessie nodded, pleased with her discovery, then frowned. That fit into the pattern of the other deposit slips only if the murderer had killed someone at the Gardner library. But he hadn't; he'd killed Enid Schmidt at a branch miles away.

But what if Schmidt wasn't his first choice? What if he muffed the attempt at the Gardner library, then tried again at another branch? It was evening, too late to get a slip from another bank, so he'd had to use the one from First Interstate.

If that was so, and Enid Schmidt wasn't a specific choice, then her ethnic background wasn't a factor. But why had the killer gone to another library? Why hadn't he picked someone on the street? And why had he brought the railroad books with him and left them on the floor near the dead librarian?

Clearly, it was the library that was important, Jessie decided; the library, not the librarian. Maybe the killer had chosen his victims not on the basis of who they were, but of *where* they were. Jessie looked at the report again.

Mae Lee was killed in her apartment, not in a public facility; so it was the neighborhood that was significant. Chinatown. With Norma Jeffreys, it could be the bus stop or, more probably, the neighborhood. Watts. Radovsky was puzzling. The man had been found in the gutter of a street that technically belonged to Hollywood, but the connection seemed vague. If the killer had wanted a "Hollywood" association, he would've chosen a flamboyant area—Sunset or Hollywood Boulevard or Melrose Avenue. Jessie would have to get back to Radovsky. That left the library and the parking lot of the Century City shopping center. And . . .

And it left Jessie nowhere. She threw down the report, too tired to think. She'd run this by the other members of the task force. Maybe one of them would see something she hadn't.

But it probably wouldn't be in time.

19

Thursday, July 30

Adrian Boyd tied the laces of his Reebok running shoes and stepped outside. The night air was cool, with a salty breeze that fanned his face as he began a slow trot, and he thought again how much he enjoyed living in Venice. It was quaint and charming, and provided him with the best of both worlds: the grand vista of the Pacific Ocean, with an endless expanse of beach that served as his backyard, and the convenience of small shops and department stores. And Venice was less expensive than other beach communities like Pacific Palisades or Malibu.

It was more colorful, too, and had a carnival air he found appealing. On weekends throughout the year and most summer days, Venice was a mélange of local residents and Angelinos and tourists from all over the country and the world. Some came to enjoy the sun or pedal along the bicycle paths (there were rental shops for those who didn't own bikes); others to be entertained by muscle-flexing males, each a hopeful Mr. Universe, whose oiled, undulating bronzed torsos glistened in the sun; still others who admired the choreographic feats of roller-skate dancers who rumbled along the boardwalk as they performed—pirouetting, leaping, executing perfect ball-bearing pas de deux. And for the tourist, there were kiosks and boutiques that offered sunglasses and T-shirts (THREE FOR $10) stenciled in bright colors with "I Love Venice" themes.

Adrian turned up Windward and increased his pace. He jogged daily, usually before he went to the loft he'd converted into a studio; but tonight he'd had to get out of the apartment. He didn't know what to do about Paula. Lately, she'd been dropping hints about this friend or that one who'd gotten married—"I think it's wonderful, don't you, Adrian?" Or, "Don't you want to practice law again? You have to think about the future." She sighed loudly (she was a great sigher, Paula) whenever they passed a cute toddler on the beach—and the beach was full of cute toddlers.

The last few weeks, after they made love, she'd murmur, "I'm so happy" or "I hope this lasts forever"; and he'd tell her that he was managing fine by selling his art, that he'd left law because it had bored him to tears, that he wasn't ready for a wife and children and a mortgage. Then she'd cry, "Who said anything about getting married? Don't do me any favors, Adrian!"

That had happened tonight, and it was getting to the point that he'd have to ask her to move out. He'd miss her for a while, but he was looking forward to having the apartment to himself again. She was crowding his closets and his life.

It was time to head back. He completed the U he'd started with Windward and turned onto the boardwalk, his breathing more audible than it had been before. He'd talk to Paula in the morning. There was no point in putting it off. Life was too short.

He was getting winded; the air felt raw as he inhaled. He

slowed gradually until the pistonlike motion of his legs all but stopped. He looked out toward the gray-black fusion of sky and sea and saw that the moon, his sole companion, had adjusted its pace to his. He could hear the surf pounding against the sand, advancing and retreating.

Life went on. Paula would cry but she'd be OK. He'd give her a week or two to find a place. That was fair.

The hand came from nowhere, snaking its way around his neck, *what the—!* jerking his head backward, and a handkerchief covered his nose and mouth, a handkerchief with a sweet, heavy odor, and he tried not to inhale, *ohmyGod,* tried to hold his breath, but the fumes overpowered him and he sank to his knees on the boardwalk.

The moon bore silent testimony, and the surf pounded relentlessly against the sand, advancing and retreating.

The body was lying faceup on the boardwalk.

Takamura and Jessie approached it, escorted by Det. Kevin Stevens of Pacific Division. Stevens had been awakened at 2:20 A.M. by a patrolman who'd discovered the body while verifying an anonymous phone call about a homicide on Venice Beach.

There was no gunshot or knife wound, Stevens told them. Possibly a heart attack or a stroke, the M.E. had said; jogging can be dangerous if you're not in good shape, although the dead guy seemed fit. Then Stevens had remembered the memo from Parker Center. He'd contacted Takamura; Takamura had called Jessie.

Venice Beach after midnight was strange, Jessie thought, inhaling the salty, sea-perfumed mist. She and Gary had come here often during the day. Now there was an absence of color and an eerie silence broken only by the sound of the surf slapping the shore; it was like watching a muted TV show in black and white. Instead of a multitude of bodies, all in bright-colored bikinis and trunks lying on bright-colored towels, paying homage to the orange sun, there was a solitary figure in a gray sweat suit resting under the indifferent gaze of the blank-faced moon.

It was the same killer. Someone had arranged the body so that it wasn't on the sand. From a distance, it had looked like a large package on a stalled conveyer belt. The dead man's eyes were closed; his arms were at his sides. Jessie knelt, picked up his arm, and exposed his right elbow. There was a small puncture. She wouldn't have found it if she hadn't been looking for it.

"Do we have an ID?" Takamura asked Stevens.

"No. We found keys in his shirt pocket, but no ID. No wedding band. If no one reports him missing, we'll have to go door to door with his picture, see if anyone can ID him."

"Who placed the call?" Jessie asked. "Male or female?"

"The desk sergeant's guess was a male, but the caller's voice was muffled. I figure the killer called. But why?"

Takamura said, "He wanted us to find the body. He placed it in the middle of the boardwalk. I see what you mean, Jessie, about the body being arranged. Practically ready for the undertaker."

Except for the sweat suit, Jessie thought. "Did you find anything else on him?" she asked Stevens.

"Not a thing. I checked the back pocket of his pants, too."

Jessie bent down to check the waistband of the sweat pants. No deposit slip, no money. She checked beneath the elastic edging at the bottom of both pant legs. Nothing. Then she noticed the dead man's shoes. "Did the M.E. untie the guy's shoe?" The laces of the left Reebok were undone. The right one was tied securely.

"Not that I know of. Why would he do that, anyway?"

Jessie slipped off the left shoe and felt inside it. Her heart skipped a beat. Something was there. Using tweezers from her purse, she pulled down and removed it. She looked at the Great Western deposit slip and the attached money and wondered how much the killer had left. She counted the bills. Four hundred dollars.

The price of atonement was going up; either that, or the killer was feeling generous. And why not? The son of a bitch was winning the game.

He was tired. He was always tired afterward, drained physically and emotionally after the release of the excitement and tension that had been building up all week (and the fear of failure; there was that, too); he usually fell asleep filled with the buoyancy of success. This time he was still keyed up, and he couldn't think about anything else, not his mother, not even Teresa.

She'd said yes. He'd been pretty sure she would, but he'd been nervous (*"a runt like you"*) when he asked her out for Saturday night. I'd love to, she said. They decided to go to a movie. Is there a particular film you want to see? he asked. Well, a comedy or a drama, but nothing like *Silence of the Lambs*, I don't like violence or gore, do you? No, he didn't like violence or gore, either. Movie tickets were expensive (he could rent a video for two dollars) and there would be popcorn and soda, and coffee afterward, if she wanted. But Teresa was worth it.

Four hundred dollars was a great deal of money, he thought, but he'd been determined from the start to play by the rules. The good thing was that this was the most expensive payment he'd have to make.

"The dead man is Adrian Boyd," John Takamura announced the next morning. "Boyd's girlfriend reported him missing and ID'd him. He was a free-lance artist."

"Good thing you found the deposit slip and money, Jessie," Barrows said. "Otherwise, we'd have to wait for the tox screens to show curare before we could tie this murder in with the others."

"Real nice detecting." Pruitt saluted her with the Diet Coke can in his hand. "A-plus, in fact."

Jessie glanced at him; his smile looked sincere. Since Monday, he'd been civil if not overly friendly. What had Manny said? Pruitt's a nice guy; get to know him.

"He leaves the Balderas woman with zip, then leaves four hundred bucks with this guy." Barrows shook his head. "And Boyd is white, so there goes the racist-killer theory. Jessie, I think you're on to something with the locations. Chinatown, Watts, Hollywood, the library. Why Venice? You think he chose that beach specifically?" He walked to the map and fingered the new stickpin.

"The deposit slip fits," Jessie said.

"Come on," Pruitt said. "Venice Beach, Santa Monica, Malibu, Laguna. Makes no difference. A beach is a beach."

She shook her head. "I don't think so. Something's niggling at me, but for the life of me I can't figure out what it is."

"Maybe it's PMS." Pruitt grinned and took a swig of soda.

She felt the heat rising up her neck. The others, she noticed, were watching her. "How sensitive, Pruitt. Is this how you charm all your women?"

The barb, she saw from the sudden red on his face, had struck home. Manny was wrong. On the pad in front of her, she scribbled "Frank Pruitt—Asshole." Or was she overreacting? she wondered suddenly. Being defensive? She'd call Phil and get his opinion.

Takamura said, "Corcoran doesn't want anyone to know about Boyd. He thinks if word leaks out, it'll alarm the public."

"No shit," Pruitt said. "Hey, Jessica"—he drawled her

name—"you'd better make sure your ex didn't put a tap on your phone or he'll be writing another Pulitzer Prize story."

"At least he's literate, Pruitt. Can you spell *literate?* Or can you only handle initials?"

"Touché." Pruitt smiled.

"There's some good news," Barrows said. "The killer won't strike until next week. And maybe he'll skip a week—he did it before."

"And I'm going to win the lottery," Pruitt said.

Ernest Moody looked at his watch. "I gotta go, Lester. Visitin' hours is just about over. They real strict here."

"You just got here, Ernie. Cain't you stay five mo' minutes?"

"I'll be back. I got me a real busy schedule tonight." Dinner and a movie with Denise. The main thing was to get out of here.

"What about Odette? She's mad at me, I know that. But not to come see her ol' man? That ain't right, Ernie."

Ernest leaned closer to the mesh barrier that separated him from his brother-in-law. "The cops trashed the place searchin' for stolen e-lectronic goods, Lester. Odette's pissed. She didn't even want me comin' here, but I make up my own mind what to do."

"Odette, she's always moanin' that I don't give her enough money. And then when I give her more, she never asks me where's this money from? She never asks, 'cause she don't wanna know."

"I'll work on her, Lester. You just stay cool, you hear? Don't say nothin' to no one. There's informants all over the damn place." Ernie should know. He'd been arrested twice for possession, served six months the second time, but that part of his life was over. He'd turned over a new leaf, gotten a job as a pizza delivery man. Not a great salary, but it was a start. And it beat worrying about the men in blue.

"What about the five hundred dollars bail? Can you ask around, Ernie?"

"I'll try, but don't count on anythin', 'cause times is rough, and money is tight." He stood up. "Well, I gotta go. I'll tell Odette you're sorry. You take care now, brother."

No matter what side of the screen he sat at, Ernest Moody decided when he left the visiting room, the place still unnerved him. That's why he'd come so late, why he'd felt like leaving the minute he sat down. Too many uniformed policemen. It was probably his imagination, but he felt they were studying him, seeing him not as Ernest Moody, rehabilitated citizen, but as a two-time loser who was bound to lose again.

He squared his shoulders. Don't be lookin' for me, he wanted to tell them, 'cause there's no way I'm goin' back in there. He looked straight ahead as he walked out the door.

Lester was miserable. Ernest would talk to Odette, try to convince her to see the poor son of a bitch. He done it for you, woman, he'd tell her. Can't you see that? Poor, dumb Lester, selling stolen goods to an undercover cop.

His car was at the end of the lot. Not much of a car, with the torn upholstery and cracked windshield and doors that wouldn't lock. But it was his. On the plus side, it was unlikely anyone would steal it. Not that he had to worry about that here, Ernest thought as he got in. You didn't have to worry about having your car stolen in front of the LAPD.

Friday morning, the faces around the table were grim.

"Lemme get this straight," Barrows said to Takamura. "You think this Ernest Moody was murdered by our killer? But that makes twice in one day! He's never done that before."

"Jessie's sure of it, and I agree. I asked her to come with me last night after I got the call from Central."

"You two going steady or what, John?" Pruitt laced his hands behind his head and leaned back in his chair.

Takamura's eyes were onyx stones. "I asked Jessie because she's had the most firsthand experience with the killer's m.o."

"So how is the m.o. the same, Jessie?" Barrows asked.

Ray to the rescue; Jessie repressed a smile. "The body was lying on the front seat of the car. Eyes closed, arms at his sides. A small puncture wound on the inside of his elbow."

"He could've OD'd," Pruitt said.

"The M.E. is conducting the autopsy right now. He said he'll rush the tox screens. But there was no syringe. If Moody shot up, what happened to the syringe? And why would someone shoot up in front of the LAPD? That's crazy."

"But it's not crazy for the killer to choose that location?" Pruitt said.

"Maybe. But he's done it before, remember? And he's not afraid of taking risks. He killed at the bus stop, in a library. Manny says the risk factor increases his excitement."

"Did you find a deposit slip and money?" Barrows asked her.

She shook her head. "No parking ticket, either. I'm stumped."

"Did you check his shoes, Jessie?" Pruitt asked.

"Why don't you just shut up, Frank," Barrows said quietly.

"I checked his shoes, Pruitt. I checked every place. If I missed something, the morgue attendants will find it."

They stared at each other. Pruitt looked away first.

"What do we know about Moody, John?" Barrows asked, breaking the uncomfortable silence.

"He did time for possession. He was at the jail visiting his brother-in-law. According to the sister, Ernest had a job and was going to get his high school diploma. He had plans."

Plans that didn't include being murdered, Jessie thought. On a pad listing the other killings, she'd drawn three columns: "Name of Victim"; "Site of Homicide"; "Amount of Money Left by Killer." She added Moody's name in the first column, under Boyd.

"Too late for Moody's plans now," Barrows was saying. "It's just his dumb luck he was visiting his brother-in-law."

Under the column headed Site of Homicide, Jessie wrote "JAIL—VISITING." In the third column she wrote a circle with a line through it to indicate that the killer had left nothing.

Pruitt said, "It's the end of the line for Moody. No second chances, no second roll of the dice. Life sucks, then you die."

Driving home, Jessie was so preoccupied she almost missed the turnoff from the Harbor onto the Santa Monica Freeway. The rush-hour traffic was heavy, but she barely noticed it, and when she pulled up in front of her house, she couldn't remember having navigated the streets to get there.

She'd brought her pad home, and long after Matthew and Helen were asleep, Jessie was still at the breakfast room table, drinking iced tea as she studied the lists she'd made.

The answer was there—not the identity of the killer, but his method of selecting his victims. There was a chain that linked Mae Sung Lee of Chinatown to Ernest Moody visiting his brother-in-law in jail. That morning, sitting around the table with the others, she'd almost had it, but the hazy half-thought had receded from her grasp, like a dream that deserts the dreamer as soon as she awakens. There was also something someone had said, but the more Jessie tried to remember what it was, the more it eluded her.

At one o'clock she gave up. A half-hour later she was

almost asleep, but the names and numbers and locations were still dancing in her head, grouping and regrouping like fragments of colored glass in a kaleidoscope, until they formed one final image.

And then she had it.

Tingling with excitement, she hurried into the den and found what she wanted. It was after 4:00 A.M. when she finally returned to bed. She fell asleep immediately.

The next morning, when she arrived at Parker Center, the others were already there. "Sorry I'm late," she said. "I overslept."

"What's that in your hand?" Barrows pointed to the oblong box she was carrying. "Looks like a game."

"It is. I think I—"

"Let me guess." Pruitt closed his eyes. "I see a game. I see a game that's going to help you solve this case and be a hero." He opened his eyes. "It's Clue!" He grinned. "Am I right, Detective?"

"B-minus, Pruitt." Jessie set the box on the table. "Monopoly."

20

Jessie unfolded the game board and placed it on her desk.

"Can I be green?" Pruitt asked. "I never get to be green."

She ignored him. "A couple of things were staring at me. Boardwalk, for one. I kept thinking about the word, wondering why it rang a bell. And then we were talking about Moody, and the fact that he was visiting jail. Actually, Frank, you helped me put it together." She smiled, knowing it would irritate him.

Pruitt frowned. "What are you talking about?"

"We were discussing Moody, and you said something about 'no second roll of the dice.' Later, it made everything click. The killer is playing a *real* game. He rolls the dice, makes his move, and chooses a victim according to an association he makes with the place where he lands."

Everyone was quiet, even Pruitt—a moment in history, Jessie thought. "Let me show you what I've figured out. Every property on the board has a purchase price printed on it. To buy a property, a player pays the stated amount to the bank."

"We know how to play Monopoly, Jessica," Pruitt said.

"Let her talk, Frank," Barrows warned.

Jessie didn't care about Pruitt. Nothing he said could annoy her today. "My point is the killer's been 'buying' properties and paying the 'bank'—with cash attached to a deposit slip. Take Boardwalk." She pointed to the space. "The purchase price is four hundred dollars. That's what we found on Boyd. Boardwalk was obvious once I figured it out. In some cases I had a harder time seeing the connections."

She placed a game piece on Go. "The first victim, Mae Lee, was a Chinese woman killed in Chinatown." Jessie moved the piece to Oriental Avenue. "The purchase price is a hundred dollars. That's what Detective Royes found in Mae Lee's apartment. Next was Norma Jeffreys, killed in Watts. I tried to ignore the ethnic aspect of the neighborhood and find logical associations with the word."

"Light bulbs?" Barrows said. "That's what 'watts' reminds me of, but I don't see—" He frowned, then whistled. "I get it! Electric Company." He located the property on the board. "A hundred fifty. Is that how much he left with the nurse?"

"Exactly," Takamura said quietly. He stared at the board.

"Holy shit!" Barrows exclaimed.

"Radovsky was a puzzle. I couldn't figure out a Russian or Hollywood angle, so I reversed the procedure. The killer left sixty dollars. The only property on the board that costs sixty dollars is Baltic Avenue."

Pruitt said, "How does that fit? Radovsky's Russian."

"It fits perfectly," Takamura said. "The Baltic area includes Germany, Poland, Russia, and Estonia and Latvia."

"Go to the head of the class, John," Pruitt said.

"I had to check my atlas," Jessie admitted, taking pity on Pruitt. "Next, Enid Schmidt. The library is the setting, and the killer left two hundred dollars in a railroad book he placed near the body."

"So he landed on one of the railroads, right?" Barrows checked the board and nodded. "A railroad is two hundred. But there are four railroads. How do we know which one he landed on?"

"*Library* is the clue," Takamura said. "*Library* plus *railroad*." He pointed to Reading Railroad. "It's pronounced 'redding,' but not everyone knows that."

"Lucky we have you, right, John?" Pruitt said, and Jessie had to agree that Takamura did sound smug. "Why didn't he leave any money with Balderas or Moody?" Pruitt asked Jessie.

"Angelina had the parking ticket." Jessie pointed to a corner of the board. "Free Parking. Moody is Just Visiting Jail."

Barrows shook his head. "Monopoly. Jesus! Everybody plays that. Jessie, you're amazing." He hugged her.

"This could all be a coincidence," Jessie said, knowing that it wasn't. *Takamura may know his geography and how to pronounce Reading Railroad,* she thought, *but I solved the puzzle!* She'd love to tell Phil and Kalish and everybody at West L.A. *Her* family.

Takamura said, "Yesterday he killed twice. One week he didn't kill anyone. How do you explain that?"

"Yesterday he rolled doubles and had a second turn. The week he skipped, he landed on Chance or Community Chest and picked a card. Community Chest involves collecting money from the bank or other players or paying fees. Chance cards instruct the player to advance to a property, but if the killer took a Chance card, he would've picked another victim."

Jessie picked up the Chance cards and read: " 'Advance to Illinois,' 'Boardwalk,' 'nearest railroad,' 'St. Charles Place,' 'Jail,' 'nearest utility.' See what I mean?" She replaced the cards. "There *is* one Chance card that could fit: 'Advance to Go.' Community Chest has the same card."

"Wait a second," Pruitt said sharply. "How'd he get from Electric Company to Baltic Avenue in one week? They're way across the board from each other." He traced the route with his finger.

"Thirty-three spaces apart. Twenty-six from Community Chest if that's where he landed after Electric Company. At first I thought he got two doubles and rolled again. But then he would've landed on properties along the way and picked additional victims."

"So how did he do it?" Pruitt asked.

You're interested, aren't you? "I think he picked up an 'Advance to Go' card, either from Community Chest or Chance. That placed him three spaces from Baltic Avenue."

"That means he was only two away from Reading Railroad, which was his next kill," Takamura said. "But that doesn't fit, because if he rolled two, he'd go again—that's a double."

"Right. So he didn't roll a two. But if he rolled a four—meaning a three plus a one—he'd land on Chance."

"So?" Pruitt asked.

"There's a Chance card that says 'Take a ride on the Reading Railroad.' Then, to get to Free Parking, he rolled two sixes—there were no intermittent killings, so we know he didn't land on any properties between Reading Railroad and Free Parking. That put him on Community Chest, three spaces from Free Parking. I was up till four working out the moves." Her eyes were bleary, but she was floating, tingling with the emotional high she'd felt a number of times in her career, the high that compensated for endless hours—weeks, sometimes—of paperwork and tedious routine.

"What about the double kills?" Barrows asked.

"First he rolled a pair of ones. That put him on Chance, where he picked up 'Advance to Boardwalk.' That's the only way it works. Then he rolled eleven. Just Visiting."

Barrows said, "So he passed Go again. Does he pay himself?"

"Maybe. He's leaving real cash with his victims, Ray, so he's obviously taking this game seriously."

"What if he lands on the same property twice?" Barrows asked. "Will he kill again?"

"I don't know that, either." She was sobered by the thought. "He may. Then again, since he 'owns' that property, he may not."

"Very fancy detecting, Jessie," Pruitt said. "I mean that," he added, and there was no irony in his voice. "But even though we know what game he's playing, there's no way we can figure out where he'll land next or who his next victim will be. Right?"

"Whoa!" Manny Freiberg exclaimed. "Talk about weird!"

"So does this tell you anything?" Jessie asked.

"It tells me I'm gonna get rid of my Monopoly set. Let me think a minute, OK?" He swiveled back and forth in his chair. Finally, he said, "Monopoly's a game of power. Power and control. And unlike other games where you win by getting somewhere before the other guy, here you have to force all your opponents into bankruptcy. There's no room for compassion or second chances."

"Tell me about it. Gary had a radical personality change whenever we played the game. It was embarrassing when we played with other couples. It's probably for the best that we got divorced," she said solemnly, then grinned.

Freiberg's eyebrows rose. "A sense of humor? There's hope for you yet." He smiled. "You feel good about figuring this out, huh?"

"Pretty damn good." Although Pruitt, not unkindly, had brought her down to earth. Her grin faded. "What else can you tell me, Manny?" She waited. The room's familiar quiet, usually so comforting, seemed to throb with urgency.

"Not much. Not enough," he added. "The killer's actions speak of his need for control—the chloroform, the stalking, the curare. The game is just his vehicle for choosing his victims."

She leaned forward. "But why Monopoly? Why not chess? That involves defeating an opponent, crushing him. So does checkers."

"Maybe he loved it as a kid. Maybe it has a deep significance rooted in his psychological problems." Freiberg shrugged. "Something else strikes me. By making his moves and associations, he absolves himself of guilt. *He's* not choosing the victims. It's the roll of the dice. That goes along with the passive-aggressive personality we discussed. See what I mean?"

Jessie thought for a moment. "I think so. How does this information fit in with your previous assessment of the killer?"

"I said he's intelligent. It takes a certain cleverness to make these associations. He's proud of being so goddamn smart, frustrated 'cause he can't share it with anyone."

Especially if that "anyone" is dead. "Anything else?"

"The fact that he didn't kill during the week you think he landed on Go is significant. It tells us he's playing according to the rules. So does the fact that he left real money—the exact purchase price of the properties with the victims."

"But why did he kill on Free Parking and Just Visiting Jail? Those aren't properties. That's been bothering me."

"Good question." Freiberg thought for a moment, rubbing his chin. "Maybe he's proving that he's in control of his actions, of the entire board. I think that's very important to him. Even though he's playing by the rules, it's his game, see."

Jessie nodded. "Makes sense, as much as any of this does. So who's he playing with, Manny?"

"He could be playing solitaire, or he could be playing an imaginary opponent, someone he's always wanted to defeat—a parent, a sibling, an employer, a rival, a spouse. Of course, right now he has a very real opponent." He looked at Jessie.

"Me?" The thought made her mildly uncomfortable.

"And what you represent. His goal is to win, to control the board by establishing monopolies. Your goal is to stop him."

21

Fridays were the longest. The minutes inched by, especially after dinner, and it was physically painful to wait until he could play, so painful that his breathing became labored and he had to use the inhalator.

He could start earlier. There was no one to tell him what to do, but he wanted it to be the same. So after supper he'd put the pretzels into his mother's glass bowl with the pineapple motif, and he would get a beer and put everything on a TV tray next to the card table and two chairs in the living room. He didn't like beer (*"Drink it—it'll put a little hair on your chest"*), but he'd discovered that if he added Seven-Up, it wasn't bad.

He used to hate Friday nights, hearing his laughter (*"Not even a contest, boy, like taking candy from a baby. Ed Jr., now, he knows how to put up a fight"*), laughter that had no pretense of good sportsmanship (*"It isn't how you play the game, boy, it's winning that counts. Anyone tells you different, that's 'cause he's a loser"*), laughter that haunted him throughout the week, that made his hands clammy with fear and frustration and his heart beat so wildly that sometimes he really believed that it was going to pound its way right through his chest as he took his seat on Friday night again and again and again and again.

At precisely nine o'clock he sat down.

Some people kissed the dice or rubbed them together or blew on them for good luck, but he didn't believe in doing that. It was silly and childish, and it didn't work—not for him, anyway.

"You get a two, you're on Park Place. A four, you're on Boardwalk. And before you roll those pretty little dice, I'm going to improve my properties and build a fancy hotel on each one."

"Can he do that, Mommy? Can he?"

"'Course I can do that. It's in the rules. Fair is fair. I'll bet you're sorry now you traded me Park Place for those two railroads, huh? That was a dumb move, boy."

"But you said it was a good trade. You said so."

"Not my fault that you're so gullible, now is it?"

"What's 'gullible'?"

"'Gullible' means—"

"He's asking me, Ella. 'Gullible' means stupid, boy, and that's the one thing a man can't afford to be. I'm teaching you a valuable lesson here: you can't believe the other guy, 'cause he will lie every time. If I had your grandfather's money and chances, believe me, I wouldn't have gone bankrupt. No, sir. Go ahead, no more stalling. Roll those dice. Two or four, you are dead, and I'll be sitting pretty, counting all your money."

"Ed, you don't have to gloat, for God's sake. Can't you see you're upsetting him?"

"Shut up. Will you shut the hell up and let me enjoy the game, for Christ's sake? Go ahead, boy. Stop rubbing and kissing those dice before you wear them out. Come on. Choose your death."

A three or a five. Please, God, please, please, please.

"All right! Four! Come to Mama."

It had never, ever worked for him.

He picked up the dice and shook them in his cupped

hands. He hoped he wouldn't get doubles again. At first the idea of two killings in one day had seemed exciting and practical, a test of his mettle and a way to compensate for the week he'd been stalled. But after he'd completed the Boardwalk transaction, he'd been so disoriented and tense and his wheezing had become so pronounced that he'd considered postponing his second move.

Somehow, though, he'd regained control of his emotions and his breathing, and in the end everything had gone smoothly, especially since he'd only had to repeat the method he'd used in the other parking lot. (There was nothing wrong with repeating a method; the important thing was not originality but success.) Doubles made him nervous too because if he rolled three doubles in a row, he'd go to jail. That was the rule. He didn't have to worry about that right now; he had a Community Chest "Get Out of Jail, Free" card that he'd picked on his first turn. But what if he landed in jail twice? He could try to get doubles on his next three turns, or pay fifty dollars to get out immediately. That was a lot of money, but it was better than missing his turn.

He shook the dice one final time, closed his eyes, and let the off-white cubes drop onto the board.

He could see immediately that he wouldn't land on St. James Place. He was disappointed. He'd contemplated St. James, toyed with choosing someone connected with the British Embassy. He could picture the headlines in the local papers; maybe there would be national coverage, too. International, even.

He sighed. Maybe on his next circuit around the board.

He took his purple piece and advanced slowly, resting on each space, past St. Charles, past St. James Place. . . .

22

Pruitt, damn him, was right, Jessie thought dejectedly Saturday. There was no way of predicting where the killer would strike next, almost no chance of identifying him. He was a damn good planner or loaded with luck—maybe both. The son of a bitch had left no forensic clues; no fingerprints on or near the victims or on the money or deposit slips; no blood or saliva or other body fluids; no clothing fibers or strands of hair or skin cells.

He'd left no witnesses, either. The task force had talked to people who lived or worked near the various crime scenes, to the victims' neighbors, relatives, employers, colleagues, friends. They'd investigated dozens of "suspicious-looking" individuals whom concerned (nosy?) citizens had reported spotting at the crime scenes. The individuals had turned out to include a gas meter reader (Jessie had loved that one), an Amway salesman, a deaf handyman, a Baptist minister, and an undercover cop. The reactions of the "suspects" had ranged from wry amusement (the minister) to fear (the handyman) to petulant indignation (the salesman).

But they couldn't ignore any call. Someone *could* have

information that would lead them to the killer. So far, Jessie thought, he's the invisible man, a phantom messenger of death who disappears without a trace. Except for the curare—the poison found in the seven victims proved that the phantom was real.

The curare was, in fact, their only clue. Corcoran had asked them to work through the weekend to try to locate its source. They'd all groaned—Pruitt, of course, had groaned loudest—but they knew Corcoran was right. So Jessie had stayed late on Friday and apologized to Matthew for canceling their trip to Disneyland. Her disappointment had matched his.

"'Cause you're trying to catch the killer, right, Aunt Jessie?" His eyes had glowed with pride and a little fear.

"Uh-huh. When this is over, I'll make it up to you, OK?"

By Wednesday Jessie wondered when that would be. They'd called hundreds of hospitals and labs, investigated dozens of leads that had led nowhere. They were exhausted, tense. Now Takamura had announced that they would have to search outside of L.A. County. Corcoran, he added, was pressuring him for results.

"He's calling every five goddamn minutes!" Pruitt snapped.

Barrows said, "Don't blame him. Blame the press."

SERIAL KILLER SLAYS TWO! BODY FOUND IN LAPD'S BACKYARD! the Saturday headlines had screamed. The police had received hundreds of calls from citizens panicked by the daily front-page coverage and "Special Report" status the media accorded the killings. Nice going, Gary, Jessie thought. But of course, it wasn't just Gary.

"Can you imagine if they find out about the Monopoly angle?" Barrows shook his head. "Corcoran will croak."

After he kills us, Jessie thought, remembering the lieutenant's reaction when she told him about the Monopoly.

First incredulity. Then, "Great job. But one word to the press, Drake, and I'll have your ass." He'd smiled, but his eyes had been bullets.

"Not a bad idea, Corcoran croaking." Pruitt smiled.

"Would you like to be in his shoes?" Takamura demanded.

"Too tight. Anyway, he's saving them for you, isn't he?"

Takamura's face reddened. "Listen, Frank—"

The phone rang. Saved by the bell, Jessie thought and picked up the receiver. Although if it was Corcoran . . . "Detective Drake."

"I come back from vacation and the first thing I hear is that you're a celebrity!"

Jessie grinned. "Welcome back, Brenda. How was it?"

"Exhausting. I pulled every muscle in my body. And Tony was right. The sex *was* glorious, even on the raft. But forget about me. My God, Jess, how the hell did you get onto the task force? Do you realize how spectacular that is?"

She sounds genuinely happy for me, Jessie thought, relieved. "It's a long story." The men were looking at her, she saw. Any minute Pruitt would make some comment about women and gossip. "Can I call you later, Brenda? I'm sorry, but we're real busy."

A pause. "No problem, Jess. I'm sure you are." She hung up.

Great. Something else to worry about in addition to finding the killer (that was number one). And Helen. Helen had started looking for an apartment near Jessie, and a car. "Dad said he'll help until I get my finances straightened out," she'd told Jessie. And she was checking into schools for Matthew— September wasn't far away. Everything sounded reasonable (Jessie didn't approve of borrowing money from her parents—the price was always stiff—but that was Helen's business). But what about Matthew's needs and fears? The boy needed to see a therapist. Helen did, too.

Takamura's face had regained its normal pallor. "Jessie,

you'll be giving another press conference tomorrow or Friday. Corcoran wants to wait until we have some reassuring news, but Chief Hanson says we have to give the media something soon."

Pruitt said, "Tomorrow night you'll give them the name of the next victim. Or two, if the son of a bitch rolls his dice right."

At night, Jessie reached Brenda and filled her in on what had happened. "Sorry again about today, Brenda. I'm the only woman there. I feel like I'm on probation. And Frank Pruitt is getting on my nerves." She told Brenda about him and his snide comments.

"Don't let him get to you, Jess. You're as good as he is. As good as *all* of them. Better."

"Yeah." She wished she could tell Brenda about the Monopoly angle, and that she'd figured it out. But Corcoran had been specific: no one outside the task force was to know. "Are you upset that I picked up on the curare lead? Be honest with me, Brenda."

"Honestly? I wish it were me on the task force. But if it's not me, I'm glad it's you. Hey, I was on vacation. You were there on the spot. Those are the breaks. Listen, you got the exposure. I got a great tan." She laughed. "But you *did* put the cases together. Don't let those macho detectives forget that. So what else is new? The house must seem empty now that your guests left, huh?"

Jessie paused. "Actually, Helen and Matthew are staying until Neil returns from Saudi Arabia. So tell me about the trip, Brenda. Skip the sex stuff, though. I'm too jealous to hear it."

She half listened to Brenda, interjecting "Oh" and "You're kidding," telling herself that she hadn't told Brenda the truth about Helen because it wasn't her truth to tell. It was Helen's.

But that was only part of the reason, she admitted to herself after she said good night to Brenda. The truth—Jessie's truth, not Helen's—was that she'd always found it difficult to confide in people, that she had surrounded herself for the most part with colleagues and acquaintances who wouldn't trespass on her privacy. She had only a few close friends—Phil for one, and Brenda. They confided in Jessie. To them Jessie was more open, but still selective in what she revealed. They knew she'd lost first her baby, then her husband; she'd accepted their comfort but had locked the door to her grief, realizing she was wounding them with her silence. She had done the same with Gary—her friend, her lover—and had frayed the fabrics of both friendship and love.

There had been so much promise in their marriage. They had similar interests—he reported crime; she tried to solve it—and she'd been drawn to his boyish good looks and charm, to his candor and lighthearted humor. And to the fact that he was an emotionally healthy son of emotionally healthy parents whom he loved. She had wanted to tell him her innermost feelings, to tell him about her tortured relationship with her mother. But she had learned long ago to doubt her perceptions, her reality.

To the world that included Jessie's childhood friends—and until the divorce, Gary—Frances Claypool was a beautiful, charming, sophisticated woman. The perfect mother. As a child, and later as a teenager, Jessie had often thought that maybe everyone else was right—maybe her mother *was* everything she appeared to be; maybe it was Jessie's fault that her mother beat her. Jessie was inconsiderate. Jessie was selfish. Jessie was irresponsible. Jessie was clumsy. Jessie was a bad, bad, bad, bad girl.

When she'd moved to L.A., a therapist helped her see that she'd been abused (she'd paid for the sessions by taking an additional job as a photographer's assistant). But by then, silence had been ingrained in her. And the shame was still there. How could she reveal to anyone, even the man she loved, the catalog of horrors that was her childhood and adolescence without evoking his revulsion? How could she describe a mother who pinched her and raked her skin with elegant, manicured fingernails; who yanked her half-asleep from her bed in the middle of the night to confront her with a chipped dinner plate; who slashed the hems on all her clothes because Jessie had said that a newly hemmed skirt was still too long; who locked her out of the house for two hours (her father was out of town at the time) because she'd come home twenty minutes late on a date, then dragged her to a gynecologist to verify that she was still a virgin; a mother who inflicted welts and blackened eyes and sprained arms and fractured ribs. A mother who battered not only her child's body, but her soul.

The therapist helped Jessie deal with her past, but it was always there, her albatross. When she'd joined the force, there had been difficult moments when her sense of right and wrong, of law and order, of justice, had been clouded by sympathy for a suspect with a history of abuse. (Juvenile had been the hardest; she'd been relieved when that stint ended.) Ultimately, she'd come to terms with the fact that her job was to find the guilty party; defense lawyers would present mitigating circumstances. Juries would decide. Judges would mete out sentences.

She thought about the Monopoly killer. Manny had said he was probably a victim of abuse. But for this faceless, nameless person, Jessie felt no sympathy, only dread, and anger, and frustration. She was up most of the night, waiting for the phone call that would announce another death. Was the killer sleeping soundly in his bed, she wondered, or was he stalking his next victim, his invisibility aided by the cover of night?

During her thirteen years on the force, she'd seen her

share of grisly murders, of gaping wounds and exposed organs and viscera and mutilated tissue, of mangled, tortured, dismembered limbs and shattered bones and skulls and vertebrae, of blood-smeared shirts and skirts and sheets and walls. She'd seen enough blood to last a lifetime. But these bloodless, painless killings—"mercy murders," Manny had called them—were far more chilling. It was easier dealing with brutal crimes motivated by greed or revenge or hate or lust or envy, crimes that ultimately revealed a link between victim and killer, crimes whose insular nature left the average citizen horrified, but safe.

No one was safe. Somewhere today a person would engage for the last time in morning rituals, would leave home unaware that there would be no returning, would kiss a spouse or a lover or a parent or a child good-bye with a quick casualness born of the mistaken certainty that other, more-lingering embraces would follow.

No one was safe, but there was nothing the police could do beyond warning people to be careful, to lock their car doors, to be wary of strangers—commonsense precautions when you lived in a large city filled with desperate people driven to violence by desperate needs. But Angelina Balderas apparently hadn't followed precautions; neither had Ernest Moody, or Mae Sung Lee, who had allowed a stranger into her apartment.

No one was safe, but you couldn't shut down the city; you couldn't tell people to lock themselves in their homes. You couldn't keep people from going to work or to school or the park (she thought of Helen and Matthew and felt her stomach tighten), or jogging along the beach, or shopping for groceries or a velour robe for a husband who was about to become a father for the first time. You couldn't do a damn thing but wait and hope that the killer would make a mistake. Sooner or later, Jessie knew, he would slip. But how many victims would he add to his list before that happened?

By five Jessie admitted defeat. She exercised, showered, and dressed, then brought in the *Times*. The front page featured the gang-related murder of yet another child—this time, an eighteen-month-old girl. Jessie's eyes smarted with exhaustion and despair. Death goes on. The serial killings, she noted with relief, had been relegated to page three. "Police still have no clues as to the identity of the murderer who has taken seven lives."

Tell me about it, Jessie thought. She resisted an urge to wake Helen and make her promise to stay indoors all day with Matthew. You couldn't live your life as if you were under siege.

Conversation among the task force that morning was minimal, burdened with the heaviness of ominous expectation. Even Pruitt was subdued, Jessie noticed. Every time the phone rang, they all tensed, waiting to hear if the inevitable had happened.

At 12:23 P.M., the call came.

"That was Detective Lowell from Manhattan Beach PD," Takamura said after he hung up. "There's a body. Female Caucasian. No signs of violence. Could be an OD, but they thought of us."

"Manhattan Beach," Barrows said. "What would that be?"

Jessie went to the table where the open Monopoly board was lying. "It could be New York Avenue. That's nine spaces from Just Visiting. If that's the case, at least he didn't roll doubles. New York is two hundred dollars. Did they find a deposit slip with money, John?"

"Lowell didn't say. We'd better check this out."

Pruitt stood up and flexed his fingers. "I'll go with you. I need a break from calling all those damn hospitals and labs."

"OK, but Jessie should come too. She's had the most—"

"Don't give me that 'most experience' shit! By now we're all experts on the killer's m.o." Something twitched in his cheek.

"Calm down, Frank." Barrows put his hand on Pruitt's arm.

Pruitt flung it off. "You trying to keep me out, John? Is that what Corcoran told you to do? I should've been in charge here! Everybody knows that! I have the years, the seniority." He grabbed his jacket from the coat tree and stormed out the door.

"Where are you going, Frank?" Barrows asked.

"The beach," he called without turning. "Anybody for a swim?"

"What's with Pruitt and Corcoran?" Jessie asked on the drive to Manhattan Beach. She had gone with Barrows. Takamura had taken his own car. To brood or to gloat? She couldn't decide.

"They've been competing since the academy. Corcoran made lieutenant years back. Now he's OIC, and Frank's boss. Frank isn't thrilled—he was hoping to be Officer in Charge himself."

"What happened to Pruitt's career?" And why do I care?

"Frank's rough around the edges, too independent. He says what's on his mind. He won't play the game—you know what I mean. Corcoran is diplomatic, knows how to talk to the mayor, to the press." Barrows hesitated. "Plus he backed the right horse."

"What do you mean?"

"A couple of years ago, when the commission was questioning members of the department, Corcoran came out against the former chief. And he really kissed up to Chief

Hanson when he took over. So now he's top gun of Robbery-Homicide. And John Takamura is his fair-haired boy. Or dark-haired, in this case."

Jessie had seen Hanson several times even before she'd joined the task force. He was trim and distinguished looking but had always struck her as aloof. "Do you think Frank should've been heading this investigation?" Pruitt was a good cop, Manny had said.

"A year ago I would've said yes. John's methodical, thorough. A good organizer. But Frank—well, he's got instinct and that extra edge. A cop's cop. But he's run into a number of problems. About a year ago his wife ran off with a boyfriend. She took the kids."

"That's tough," Jessie said, trying to imagine Pruitt with a family. Barrows kept assorted snapshots of his wife and six-year-old daughter underneath the protective plexiglass sheet on his desk. Takamura had posed against a blue background with twin pigtailed, immaculately dressed little girls and a demure wife for the silver-framed photo on his desk. Pruitt's desk held no photos—just the usual paraphernalia and an ever-present can of Diet Coke.

"Yeah. Then a while ago a good friend of his, a cop, died. So everything's eating at him. He's pissed with Corcoran, with John, with the whole department. With himself, if he'd admit it."

"And me?" Because I'm a woman, like the wife who left him?

Barrows smiled. "Actually, he's impressed with you. I can tell. You're just an easy target for his frustration."

"Lucky me," Jessie said quietly.

23

Jessie was familiar with Manhattan Beach, a bedroom community south of El Segundo; she would have loved to live in one of the homes that hugged the beach or perched along the bluffs overlooking the Pacific. They were reserved for the well-to-do—doctors, lawyers, engineers, other professionals. The less-affluent resided in more modest, pedestrian dwellings farther east. Several aerospace firms abutted the community, which had a string of car dealerships and a large mall with major department stores.

The alley in the rear of one of these stores was cordoned off by yellow police tape when Jessie and Barrows arrived. Pruitt was there. So was Takamura. A race to the finish? Takamura introduced Jessie and Barrows to Det. Christopher Lowell.

The body was stretched out on the litter-strewn concrete, wedged between a chipped mocha-colored stucco wall and a dusty black dumpster. The woman's eyes were closed, Jessie noticed. Another mercy murder? She'd been young and pretty, but there was an obscene incongruity between her pallid lifelessness and the riot of color in her clothing and makeup. She was wearing a canary-yellow cotton halter top that barely met the waistband of her chartreuse miniskirt. Her long, sculpted fingernails and the toes of her bare, sandaled feet were painted a high-gloss tangerine, and the bright coral on her lips, together with patches of rose on her cheek and charcoal on her eyelids, gave her a macabre, Halloween-like appearance. Her complexion and hair were ashen, as if the blood had been drained out of both.

"Her name is Joyce Dehoff," Lowell said. "Twenty-two, according to her license. A couple of singles in her wallet. No credit cards, but the slots on the leather say she had some. No sign of assault or rape. The M.E. noticed a puncture on her arm that could've been made by a syringe. I thought you'd be interested." The curiosity in his blue eyes belied his flat recital.

"Could be," Takamura said, leaving Lowell's unasked question unanswered. "Who found her?"

"A sanitation worker. He was plenty shook up."

"Could he have taken money from her wallet?" Barrows asked.

"Nope. The wallet wasn't visible. It was in the back pocket of her skirt—hard to get out, as a matter of fact. And the guy was here with a crew. Somebody would've seen if he'd done anything. They were all standing around gawking when I got here."

"Did you check anywhere else?" Pruitt asked.

Pruitt seemed calmer after his outburst, Jessie thought, although he hadn't made eye contact with Takamura. Or her.

"Not too many places she could've kept anything. That halter top's pretty thin, and she wasn't exactly hiding anything. Something was there, I would've seen it, but you might want to check out the merchandise for yourself." He grinned knowingly.

"What kind of merchandise is that, Detective?" Jessie said.

Lowell glanced at her, then quickly looked away. He seemed startled, as if he'd suddenly remembered she existed. "I just—sorry." He assumed a somber expression and turned his head to hide his reddening face.

Barrows looked uncomfortable; Takamura studied his watch. Pruitt was scowling at Stevens. My heroes, she thought.

Lowell's remark hadn't surprised her. Over the years she'd overheard lewd innuendos in squad rooms and courtrooms, at crime scenes. It was a product, she and Brenda had decided long ago, of stupidity and chauvinism and a puerile attempt at male bonding. And in some cases, it was sexual harassment or a way of making a female cop know "her place." When Jessie had joined West L.A., a Vice detective had stared unabashedly at her breasts. Jessie had stared at his crotch. The guy had turned away; he'd never bothered her again. And she'd saved the article the *Times* had done a while back about the LAPD—"Female Officers Unwelcome—But Doing Well." It was an important reminder.

Jessie bent down and touched the woman's neck. It was cold. "She's been dead for quite some time."

Lowell said, "The mark is on her right arm. She may have OD'd or maybe someone injected her with a drug or some other lethal substance. I had the patrolmen who responded to the call search up and down the alley. They didn't find a syringe. The dumpster had already been emptied, but we didn't check the garbage truck." His tone was crisply professional now. "Excuse me a minute." He walked toward the medical examiner's van, clearly eager to make his getaway.

Jessie checked the arm. The puncture site on the inside of the elbow, an angry purple oval, was clearly visible. She carefully probed the cotton surface and then the interior of the halter top, apologizing silently to Joyce Dehoff for the undignified intimacy she was forcing upon her defenseless form as she checked under her large, unencumbered breasts that lay heavy in death. There was no money in the halter. There was nothing hidden under her skirt or in her panties, either.

Takamura said, "Someone could have taken the money and credit cards after she was killed, before the sanitation crew arrived. From the body temperature, I'd say she's been here five, six hours. The killer couldn't stand guard over her wallet all that time. Actually, it's amazing that none of his other victims were ripped off before the police arrived."

"A small miracle," Jessie agreed.

The money was gone. It didn't matter whether it was ten dollars or a hundred dollars or a thousand dollars. It was his money! He felt himself becoming agitated again and forced himself to focus on the TV.

L.A. Law was on. He enjoyed the stories, the dialogue, the courtroom scenes, the characters. He especially liked Stuart Markowitz, the cherubic middle-aged tax specialist. He was kind and generous and decent. And he was married to beautiful Anne Kelsey. Taller-by-several-inches-than-Stuart Anne Kelsey, who didn't seem bothered that her chin rested on his balding, graying, curly head. And the best part was that the actors who played this loving couple were really married. He'd read that in *People* and kept the article because it proved his father wrong.

"Showing a little scalp, boy? Guess the girls won't be running their fingers through your hair, huh?" A chuckle. "Not that they're pounding down the door, are they? Not like they do with Ed, Jr. Jesus, he's something, isn't he? You ever see the way the girls look at him? They are sizzling, boy, absolutely sizzling. Am I right or am I right?"

"Ed, Jr., is great. All the girls love him." That is the

catechism, and he knows it by heart, but still the words stick in his throat, like lumps of mashed potatoes.

"Reminds me of myself, Ed, Jr., does. I was a lady-killer in my time. There was no one I couldn't have, and why I settled for your mother, I'll never know, though she was kind of pretty and I didn't want her to die of a broken heart." Another chuckle. *"Well, I can't bring back those days, and you can't bring back your hair, so I guess we're in the same miserable boat."*

He never showed his father the *People* article. It was a spark of comfort too vulnerable to withstand the icy gusts of his father's disdain. And now he had Teresa.

Teresa was just an inch or so taller than he was, and that was in midsize heels. She had looked lovely, so lovely in a dark green dress with a paisley print that he felt like crying with pleasure and pride. Her hair looked even prettier than he remembered, fuller and wavier, and she wore it brushed back to expose her small ears.

She was wearing earrings, and he was disappointed to see they weren't clip-ons. The idea of pierced ears bothered him, it was so fundamentally barbaric. As a boy he'd always gone with his mother to the bakery and stared with fascination and dread at the hawk-nosed, Gypsy-like woman with the heaving bosom and floured hands who served them. Her earrings were huge, gaudy, pendulous affairs that pulled at the slits in her ears, and on each visit it had seemed to him that the slits were getting longer, threatening some day to sever her lobes in two.

His mother had always worn clip-ons. He had loved watching her sort through her wooden armoire-shaped jewelry box and try on pair after pair. *You choose,* she'd say, and he'd choose the topaz or the pearls or the opals or the turquois, and his mother would say, *oh, thank you, that's exactly what this outfit needs, and aren't you the cleverest young man in the whole world?*

Teresa's earrings were tiny pearls, and he was certain that the holes in her ears were tiny, too, probably not noticeable.

Come in, Teresa said, and he stepped into a small living room that smelled pleasantly of lemon furniture polish. She pointed to two glasses on a dark wood table in front of a green sofa. I thought we'd have iced tea, she said; the night's so warm. He watched her fingers as she held her glass. They were graceful and slender, with short nails covered with clear polish, not like the long, curved, predatory orange claws he'd noticed on one of the women. (Or was it two? He couldn't remember. And he didn't want to think about that, not now, not with Teresa.)

He'd chosen a comedy that had received wonderful reviews. He worried at first that she wouldn't like the movie but would feel obligated to laugh. But her laugh was genuine, a tinkly, silvery sound that he wished would go on forever. And when the movie was over, she turned to him and rested her right hand lightly on his. That was wonderful, she said, I don't know when I've enjoyed a film so much. And then she removed her hand and stood up, the folds of her green dress swishing against her thighs, but the warmth of her touch lingered for a long time.

After the movie they strolled through the mall, and she told him about herself. She was thirty-one, an only child. Her parents lived in San Diego, but half a year ago she'd moved to Los Angeles to make a fresh start. After my divorce, she said, and he felt a stab of disappointment. But it was silly to think she wouldn't have been married. She was pretty and intelligent and special. Anyone could see that.

Thank goodness we didn't have children, she said. She asked about him, and he told her his father had died recently, and his mother was in a nursing home, the doctors don't have hope. Oh, Teresa whispered, her face so close he could read the dismay in her eyes, that's so sad. She blinked and ran a finger across her right eyelid. Something in my eye, she said, but he saw the tears and offered his handkerchief. I don't want to smudge it, she said. But he insisted, and after she used it, she admired the monogram: What beautiful work. My mother, he told her, she liked to embroider. It's a satin stitch. And then Teresa said, Well, it's beautiful, and I'll launder it and return it the next time I see you. And then she blushed. Oh, I only meant on your next appointment, if I'm still there, if Lucille isn't back. Her color deepened. And he said, but I want very much to see you again. And then she smiled. I'd like that.

He saw her home. He didn't kiss her. He wanted to, he wanted so much to feel the soft, smooth pillowy lips with only a hint of pink gloss on them, but he knew it was too soon.

L.A. Law was coming to an end. Stuart and Anne were in bed, and you could tell they'd just made love, and she was stroking his cheek, and you could see the swell of her breasts above the sheet that covered both of them. I adore you, Markowitz, she was saying, and he grinned along with Stuart, and thought how wonderful it would be if someday, with Teresa. . . . He didn't want to finish the thought. It was like announcing your wish after you blew out the candles on the cake; it would never come true.

But the world was full of possibilities. He had the article from *People* to prove it.

The news was on next. The lead story was about a multiple gang shooting in East L.A., and he didn't want to hear about it, not now. He was on the way to the kitchen when he heard ". . . new development in the Curare Killer case." He hurried back to the sofa, and there was Detective Drake, her beautiful face filling the screen, repeating what she'd said last time, ". . . urge you to use extreme caution until the killer is apprehended."

Her face receded, and the screen was filled with reporters

saluting wildly into the air with their microphones. And he had to admit she was good, so calm in the face of the questions that came hurling at her, one on top of the other, "What evidence do you . . . ?" and "What are the police . . . ?" and "When will you . . . ?"

Now the camera focused on a tall, handsome reporter whose strident voice was asking, "Is it true that . . . ?" And the camera switched quickly to Detective Drake, whose face expressed surprise and—was it anger? But why would she be angry? And suddenly everything was wrong, terribly wrong, he couldn't believe what he was hearing, the lies, the outrageous!—how could she?—and he couldn't breathe, the knifelike pain in his chest was so sharp, slicing through his lungs. He grabbed the inhalator from his pants pocket and plunged it deep into his mouth and sent the blessed albuterol into his constricted bronchi and waited.

Thirty-five minutes passed before the squeaking sounds of his breathing (*"Jesus Christ, you sound like a goddamn pig!"*) returned to normal, but even then he sat on the sofa, clutching the inhalator, because just thinking about what he'd heard was still potent enough to threaten another attack.

Well, she wouldn't get away with it. *She would not get away with it.* Somehow, he would have to stop her.

24

"Goddamn press!" Barrows slammed his fist on his desk in an uncharacteristic display of anger. "They've got connections that put the CIA to shame. They probably have reporters and photographers stashed in the morgue drawers, ready to pop out just in case there's a story."

That's where I'd like to put Gary now, Jessie thought—in a morgue drawer. Of course, it had been Gary who'd asked about Joyce Dehoff: "And is it true, Detective Drake, that there's been another victim of the Curare Killer?" She'd felt like stepping down from the podium and wrapping the damn microphone around his damn neck.

"I've gotta hand it to your ex, Jessie," Pruitt said. "He's got some great sources."

"Back off, Pruitt!" Maybe she'd wrap the microphone around his neck, too. A double loop would be nice. Too bad she'd never joined the Girl Scouts.

"Hey, I didn't mean anything." Pruitt sounded offended.

She glanced at him. He looked sincere.

The phone rang. Takamura answered it, then thrust the

receiver at Jessie. "For you." His tone was curt, with none of his usual politeness. The stress was getting to all of them.

Jessie took the receiver. "Detective Drake."

"I want you to stop the lies."

The voice was muffled. Jessie wasn't sure she'd heard correctly. "I'm sorry, sir, but I can't hear you clearly."

"I said, I want you to stop the lies. It isn't right!"

Another jerk. "I don't know what you mean, sir. If you—"

"Stop it! You stop it right now! You're playing with me, telling one lie after another about me at the press conference."

Jessie froze, then scribbled a note and motioned furiously to Takamura: "Could be killer. Start tap!" She spoke into the phone. "Try to calm down, sir. What lie are you talking about?"

"You know! Don't pretend to be stupid!"

"I really *don't* know. Why don't you tell me what you mean."

"All right, Detective, I'll play your little game. That Joyce Dehoff. You know I didn't kill her, but you said I did. I killed the others, but not her, and I don't want you saying I did."

"How do I know you're telling the truth?" Jessie asked with a nonchalance she hadn't known she possessed. "We've had calls from many people who've confessed to the killings." That *was* the truth. In cases with extensive media coverage, it was almost inevitable that disturbed people would claim credit for the crimes.

"Did they mention the deposit slips?" the voice hissed. "I'll bet they didn't say that, did they, Detective Drake."

Jesus, it *was* him! The press, thank God, had no idea about the deposit slips. *Nobody* knew about them. Jessie signaled to Takamura, who had his ear to the receiver of his own phone, monitoring the progress of the tap.

"They're working on it," Takamura mouthed, his eyes adding the exclamation point.

"Sir, I believe you," Jessie said quietly. "I really want to help you. I can appreciate why you're so upset. I'd like—"

"You'd like to keep me on this phone long enough to put a tap on it! I see it now!" the voice shrieked. "That's why you lied—to trap me, to make me so angry I'd make a mistake!"

"If you could just try—"

"You can tell more lies, you can tell a million lies if you want to, Jessie Drake, but there's no way you can stop me!"

"Listen—" The line was dead. Jessie looked at Takamura.

Takamura spoke into the receiver, then shook his head.

The room was deathly quiet. Then Barrows said, "If he didn't kill Joyce Dehoff, then who *did* he kill?"

It was bad enough that his turn had been wasted, but to have Jessie Drake mock him was more than he could bear.

Last Friday night, when he'd rolled the dice and moved his piece seven spaces, a wave of disappointment had rippled through him. Community Chest. Community Chest meant a lost opportunity.

He picked up the yellow card. "You have won second prize in a beauty contest. Collect $10."

Second prize . . .

"So how come you lost, boy? Your mother's been telling the whole goddamn neighborhood what a good speller you are. I was kind of expecting to see you win first place. What happened?"

"He got out on egregious. *That's a very hard word, Ed. Very hard. He won second place. Danny Morton was just lucky."*

"What's it mean?"

"It means exceedingly bad. I looked it up, sir."

"Locking the barn door a little late, don't you think? You want to win, you've gotta be prepared. You're in combat and you're

unprepared, you're in second place, and you know what you are? You're dead, boy. D.E.A.D. Understand?"

"Yes, sir."

"He did real well, Ed. We're all proud of him, aren't we? We'll frame that certificate and put it someplace special."

"'Course we're proud of him, but it's my job to put things in perspective for the boy. Second place isn't exceedingly bad, it isn't egreeeegious, *but it isn't exceedingly great either. Second place means loser, even if they give you a fancy piece of paper that says otherwise. That's just a lot of crap, and everyone knows it. Doesn't prepare you for the real world. Deep down, you know it too. No point in fooling yourself, is there."*

"No, sir."

"You're not crying, boy, are you? Men don't cry. Babies cry. I'm telling you this for your own good, so you'll do better next time, come up on top, show Danny Morton what for. Second place is second-rate. Remember that."

His father had tossed the award certificate onto the table. The upper left corner had fallen into the hashed browns. His mother had removed it quickly and wiped off the greasy blob with a napkin. Maybe it'll dry, honey, his mother had said. I hardly see it now, it's so small. But he'd known that the stain would remain forever, and in his bedroom he'd ripped the red paper into tiny pieces that floated to the bottom of the trash can like dying embers, and he'd stood there, ripping and crying, until he'd spent all his shame and frustration and rage.

He had seen his father cry only once. His father hadn't cried when his career plans had been thwarted in a series of transfers from Fort Dix, New Jersey—first to Fort Benning, Georgia; then to Fort Bliss, Texas; finally to Fort Ord in California. He'd announced each transfer with an identical mixture of anger, resignation, and contempt.

"Well, boys, looks like we're moving again. Seems the army don't appreciate the way I train recruits. According to my superior,

I'm too hard on those boys. If I did things his way, those boys would have caddies carrying their gear. But you mark my words, boys, they'll be sorry they let me go."

His father hadn't cried when his army career had ended when he was thirty-eight years old. I'm quitting, he'd said one night, after fifteen years I am not about to take any more of their shit. But Ed, Jr., had said, Dad's quitting before they fire him. And then, He's an old fart, isn't he? And oh, how shocked he'd been! And he wondered what his father would say (*"That boy, he's one in a million!"*) if he heard the pride of his loins (*"Jesus, he's something, isn't he?"*) speaking about him like that.

He's an old fart. For nights he'd fantasized about throwing the words at his father, watching them explode like shrapnel in his still-handsome, beefy face, waiting until his massive form dissolved into a puddle of nothingness, like the Wicked Witch. Because it was only partially true that sticks and stones can break your bones; the other truth he'd grown up with, the truth that had seared itself into his soul, was that names *can* hurt.

He'd never acted out his fantasy. His father would never have believed him. But the knowledge (*"an old fart"*) was a wonderful, if unshared, joke, and for a long while it was his secret weapon that helped deflect some of the barbs his father hurled at him with flawless aim. Some, but not all.

He had seen his father cry only once, the day the uniformed officer brought the news that Ed, Jr., had been killed on maneuvers. Maneuvers, his father had repeated dully, what the hell kind of—? I don't understand. And his mother had moaned, oh, my God, and clutched her throat with both hands and shrieked until his father told her to shut up, to shut the hell up before he smacked her. And then his father turned to the officer, who was clearly uncomfortable. There must be a mistake, his father said, because my boy Ed, Jr., my son—He shook his head.

There must be a mistake, he said again, but he said it softer this time. Then the officer handed him a document, and his father read it for what seemed like an eternity, and finally nodded.

The officer left. At some time his mother had started moaning again, but his father walked past her imploring arms to a makeshift bar, where he took the bottle of Jack Daniel's he saved for special occasions and filled half a tumbler with the whiskey. He held the tumbler and squeezed so hard that the veins in his right hand stood out, squeezed so hard that the glass shattered into angry fragments that embedded themselves in his skin. And then his shoulders began heaving, and he started to cry with a gurgling sound that finally erupted into a thundering, volcanic roar, and the rivulets of tears and whiskey and blood mingled into a burgundy stream that trailed down his white shirt.

His father refused to go to a hospital, but he let his mother remove the glass slivers from his hand and bandage it. Then his father disappeared for three days, and after he returned, he never mentioned Ed, Jr.'s, death again.

"You have won second prize in a beauty contest. . . ."

He'd withdrawn twenty dollars and had been about to redeposit ten when they'd grabbed him, two juvenile delinquents with greasy hair who appeared out of nowhere on either side of him. They pulled him into a recess of a nearby building.

"Scream and you're dead, man," the taller of the two said, and he believed him. "Hey, whatcha got there, huh?" His face loomed close, and he made obscene smacking noises.

"He's got a present for us, ain't that right, mister?" the other one said. He whisked the bill from his hand. "Ten bucks?"

The tall one pinned his arms behind his back while his friend pulled his wallet from his pocket. "There'd better be more'n ten bucks, or we're gonna be real disappointed, man. And if we're disappointed, guess what you're gonna be?" He laughed hysterically, amused by his witticism.

"Put your hands behind your heads!" The voice, booming in their direction out of the still night, was accompanied first by a flashlight and then by a policeman with his weapon drawn.

The two boys froze.

"Do it slowly, or I'll shoot." He waited until they had obeyed, then walked over and handcuffed their hands behind their backs. "You OK?"

He nodded. "They grabbed me at the ATM. If you hadn't come by. . ." His voice shook. "I don't know how to thank you."

"What'd they take?"

"Ten dollars and my wallet. There it is, on the floor." He pointed to the short boy. "He must have dropped it when you yelled." He bent down, retrieved the wallet, and slipped it into his pants pocket, thanking God that the punk hadn't had time to open it or pocket it, that the policeman hadn't had to demand it and ask him to verify his ownership. And give his name.

"Wait here while I put these nice young gentlemen into the squad car. I'll need you to come down to headquarters and file a report." He turned to the two boys. "Move it!"

He'd taken advantage of the policeman's absence to disappear down the block and into a Thrifty drugstore, where he'd spent what seemed like endless minutes pretending to study the paperbacks until he was confident that the policeman had driven away. The clerk, a tall bleached blonde wearing a skimpy, scoop-necked knit top, had come up to him. Can I help you? she asked, leaning close, her freckled cleavage almost in his face. She was doused in cheap perfume, and his eyes began to itch. Looking for something to read, he told her. Whaddaya like? Adventure? Mystery?

Romance? We got all the Robert Ludlums. Maybe I'll come back, he said, starting to move away, but she stopped him. Say! Here's something you'll like. *Misery*. It's by Stephen King. Kinda scary, but that's Stephen King, and ya know what they say. What's that? he asked, knowing he had to play the game. Misery loves company. Get it? she squealed, and her breasts jiggled like twin water beds.

His eyes started watering, but he forced himself to laugh and paid for the book. Lemme know how ya like it, she said, and he promised to do just that. Then he returned to the automatic teller and deposited ten dollars.

It wasn't until he was in his apartment that he started shaking, frightened by his encounter with violence, frightened even more by his close brush with exposure. Then he remembered the ten dollars the punk had yanked out of his hand, and the $5.36 he'd spent on a book he didn't want, and he was suddenly angry, because it didn't matter whether it was ten dollars or a hundred dollars or a thousand dollars. And just when he succeeded in calming himself by thinking about Teresa, he saw the press conference.

That had been yesterday. And today, Jessie Drake had tried to dupe him into exposing himself, but she'd failed, because he was smarter than she was, and now she knew it, too.

Tonight he would roll the dice and move his piece the appropriate number of spaces even if he didn't like where he landed. He'd played fair till now and would continue to play a fair game, not like the police, who had tried to trick him ("*You can't believe the other guy, 'cause he will lie every time*").

In a way, he understood their actions. They were in a desperate race against time, whereas he didn't care how long it took to play the game because he knew he would eventually win.

There was no one to stop him from purchasing property after property, no one to stop him from amassing monopolies, from getting even with a world that had rendered him invisible and insignificant for as long as he could remember. No one to stop him from ultimately beating his father, for the first and last time, at the game he hated almost as much as he hated the man who had forced him to play it for over twenty years.

And then—oh, God!—then he would be free.

25

"The *Times* called." Corcoran's voice was dangerously quiet. His short, wiry gray hair seemed to bristle with anger. "They heard about the Monopoly."

Oh, shit! Jessie thought. And then, Please don't let it be Gary's by-line. She shifted in her seat.

"I told the *Times* that was bullshit, but they're printing a special Sunday edition. The mayor called. The *Times* had called *him* to see if he knew. Which of course he didn't." He looked around the room. "The mayor isn't happy with the story about the Monopoly angle, or with the fact that he didn't know about it. He sure as hell isn't happy with me."

Corcoran's eyes made another slow survey of the room. "I hope you're proud. We'll have everyone in the goddamn city calling to tell us his neighbor or hair dresser or mechanic plays Monopoly. The guy at the *Times* knows how every victim is connected with the game. So every jerk in town will know too. Ten to one we'll have copycat murders. After that, who knows? Bingo killings, lotto, chess, Chinese checkers. Shit, the possibilities are endless."

Corcoran was right, Jessie knew. The idea was chilling.

"Do they know about the money?" Pruitt was leaning back in his chair, as usual. "Or that all the victims' eyes were closed?"

"The guy didn't say. I sure as hell didn't ask him." Corcoran stared at Pruitt. "Maybe the *reliable source*"—he said the two words with contempt—"didn't do a thorough job. Or maybe he's saving that for another installment. Spreading the glory."

Takamura said, "Lieutenant, with all due respect, why would any of us leak this? It makes our job harder. We all know that."

Corcoran's smile was a slit. "Then how do you explain the article, John? This information's accurate, and the only people with access to that information are in this room."

Jessie tensed for a remark from Pruitt, but he was silent.

Barrows said, "Will the *Times* identify the source?"

Corcoran snorted. "Sure, and donkeys can fly. Get real, Ray." He turned to Jessie. "Gary Drake's a reporter for the *Times*. He's your ex-husband, right?" His eyes studied her.

Did the world know? "Right."

"Still have the same name, huh? You talk to him lately?"

She tried not to bristle at Corcoran's tone and implication. "No. I haven't discussed this with anyone." And I keep all my papers locked in my desk. And my Monopoly set's been right in this room ever since I spent all night figuring this out.

Corcoran said, "Are you sure you—"

"Come on, Corcoran." Pruitt straightened his chair. "What's the point? What's done is done. We have to go on from here."

Pruitt to the rescue? That was a switch, Jessie thought.

Corcoran shifted his attention to Pruitt. "No big deal, huh? Doesn't bother you?"

"It bothers me, but there's not a hell of a lot we can do

about it. So OK, we'll get phone calls. So we'll handle them."

"I wonder if the rest of your task force feels the same."

Pruitt stood up. His hands were clenched. "Meaning what?"

"You figure it out. You're the ace detective."

"You think *I* leaked this? Is that it?"

"Calm down, Frank," Barrows said. "Nobody accused anyone."

"But that's what you think, don't you?" Pruitt said to Corcoran.

"Now why would I think that, Frank?" Corcoran smiled.

"I didn't do it." Pruitt spoke more to the others than to Corcoran. "Why in hell would I do that?"

"Methinks you doth protest too much. Isn't that how it goes?"

"Screw you," Pruitt said.

Jessie parked the Honda on the street and walked briskly to the apartment building entrance. She pressed the buzzer, again and again, until Gary answered.

"It's Jessie." She tapped her foot on the tile floor.

"You heard, huh? Look, I know you're upset, but I'm half asleep. Can we talk about this later?"

"Buzz me in, Gary, or I'm going to tear off my clothes right here and say you raped me."

He sighed. "What are my choices again?"

When he opened the door, she saw that he was wearing the black terry robe she'd bought him last year. He was barefoot. He ran his hand through his tousled hair and yawned.

"I don't know why this couldn't wait." Gary moved aside to let her into the small entry. "So what's up?"

She slammed the door shut behind her. "You're scum,

Gary. Do you have any idea the damage you're doing with this story?"

"Oh, shit. Let's not go through this again, OK, Jess?"

"You don't care, do you? We'll have copycat murders, but you'll have your goddamn story. Corcoran gave me the third degree an hour ago, because we were married. He thinks—"

"I'm having coffee. Want some?" He started walking.

She followed him and grabbed his arm. "You're doing this on purpose, Gary! To get even! You know what a tough spot I'm in!"

He removed her arm. "Get a grip on yourself, Jess." He wasn't smiling. "First of all, I'm not trying to get even. Hell, we both agreed the marriage wasn't working, right?"

"Right." But there had been anger and hurt on both parts, confusion and guilt on hers. *You had to go chasing someone when you were four months pregnant, didn't you, Jessie?*

"Second, Corcoran's *your* problem, not mine. Don't lay this guilt shit on me. You want to play with the boys, toughen up."

He was right again, damn him. "That doesn't excuse your recklessness, Gary. You're putting—"

"It's not my story. Surprised, huh?" He grinned. "I wish it were, but it's Vic Ballowsky's. Someone called late last night."

"Who?"

"How the hell do I know? What's the difference? It'll be on the news this afternoon, all three networks."

"I want to get Corcoran off my back, Gary."

Gary hesitated, then said, "I'll see what I can do." He yawned again. "As long as you're here, how about that coffee now?"

She shook her head. "Thanks, but I have to get back downtown. Another press conference." She grimaced.

Then, for the first time since she'd entered the apartment (she'd been so angry), she looked around. It was a strange, disjointed feeling. She'd been here once before. Gary had insisted on showing her the apartment—"We're still friends, aren't we? "—but it had been bare then. Now she noticed "their" furniture. A black lacquered bookcase. Stereo components. A cream leather sofa. They'd made love on that sofa several times.

"Call Vic, Gary."

"I will. By the way, Helen told me about her and Neil. That's tough. She said she's staying in L.A. How's Matthew?"

"Helen hasn't told him yet."

Gary frowned. "I promised I'd take him to the *Times*, but things came up. Now that they're staying, I can still do it. Tell him, OK? And if he needs me for anything, call. I'm available."

More than I've been in the last week. She smiled at Gary. "That's nice of you."

"I *am* nice. And I like kids."

"I know," she said softly. She turned to go.

He put his arm on her shoulder. "You're a good detective, Jess. Don't let Corcoran throw you."

"You're getting soft in your old age, Gary." She kissed his cheek. The stubble was pleasantly scratchy.

And then his lips were on hers. She didn't resist. It was so familiar, so natural. Latent feelings stirred in her.

"I still think about you, Jess," he whispered. "I miss you." He kissed her eyes, the hollow of her neck, her lips again. "Maybe if we started over..."

The words hovered in the air. So tempting.

Sighing, she slipped out of his arms.

Corcoran had been right.

By midmorning, after another press conference, the Parker Center switchboard was swamped with frantic callers. In between answering calls, Jessie wondered about the leak. Had one of the detectives been indiscreet? She realized again how little she knew about Barrows and Takamura. And Pruitt?

He was an enigma. He'd been riding her from the minute she'd stepped into Parker Center—about Gary, about everything. And, then, two hours ago, he stopped Corcoran from grilling her and made himself his new target.

"Another call for you, Jessie," Takamura said.

Many of the callers requested Jessie because they'd seen her on the televised press conference. She took the receiver. "Drake."

"Detective? I'm Monica Podrell. I saw you on TV and I read the article in the paper. I think I met him. The killer, I mean."

This was the fourteenth identical call today. "What makes you think you saw him?" Anchoring the receiver between her ear and shoulder, she used both hands to rifle through some notes.

"At the time I didn't think anything of it. I didn't even know that a librarian had been killed. But today's article said the dead librarian was connected with Reading Railroad. And then I remembered seeing him. And the railroad books."

Jessie grabbed the receiver. Don't get your hopes up, she warned herself, but she had a tingly sensation. "Where?"

"I was studying in the library alcove when he came in, but I left because I couldn't concentrate. Then I went back because I'd forgotten my purse. He wasn't there, but the books were. Not all of them. Maybe he took the others with him."

A half-hour later, Jessie and a police sketch artist were sitting in Monica Podrell's den. Monica was a pretty woman in her thirties with streaked blond hair and serious brown eyes. She seemed a little nervous. Who could blame her? Jessie thought. She asked Monica to describe the man she met in the alcove.

Monica bit her bottom lip; her brow was creased in concentration. "He has a long, thin face, no mustache or beard. An average nose, light-brown hair, kind of mousy, and thin on top. My kids would say he's geeky looking."

"How old do you think he is?"

"Thirty-ish. And very short, Detective. I noticed that when he came in. Average weight, but not muscular. He was pale, too."

"Was he wearing glasses?"

"No. Brown eyes, I think, but I can't be sure. I remember they were watery. And oh, something else! He had an allergy or cold, because he was holding a handkerchief, and he was breathing heavily. That's why I couldn't concentrate. So do you think it could be the killer?"

"It's possible. You have a great memory, Mrs. Podrell." Jessie smiled at her encouragingly. "When did this take place?"

"Mid-July. I took my real estate license exam the second week in August. I think I passed. I haven't heard yet." She smiled.

"You don't know the day of the week?" Jessie held her breath and willed Monica to say "Thursday."

"Not Friday. The library closes early on Fridays." She concentrated. "And not Monday, because I had a review class on Monday. But I'm not sure . . ." Her voice trailed off.

Shit, Jessie thought, the woman can't remember.

"Thursday." Monica nodded. "After I got my purse, I stopped at Mayfair Market on the way home. They were advertising Pepsi at ninety-nine cents a two-liter bottle. And they always start the new ads on Thursday." She smiled triumphantly.

With forced calm, Jessie said, "The middle Thursday in July?"

"Yes. I'm sure now. Does that make a difference?"

All the difference in the world. "That would be July sixteenth, the date the librarian, Enid Schmidt, was killed."

"Oh." Monica's tone was hushed. "I didn't realize—" She frowned. "The article said there were railroad books next to the librarian. So if it was the killer, why did he take some of the library books from one library to another library? Unless . . ." She looked at Jessie. "Oh, my God! He was going to kill *me?*"

When Jessie returned from Monica Podrell's, Takamura told her Gary had called. Ignoring the curiosity in the detective's eyes, she called her ex-husband at his home.

Gary said, "Vic wouldn't say at first, but I twisted his arm. He couldn't tell if it was a male or female—the caller had a whispery voice. Very polite, Vic said. He or she told Vic everything over the phone, refused to meet with him, said Vic could contact the police for confirmation."

"That's it?"

"The caller left a name."

"Why didn't you say so, Gary! Who was it?"

"*You,* Jess."

"Quit kidding, Gary." Sometimes, he was so infantile.

"I'm not kidding. That's what Vic said. He recognized your name, of course. He figured someone was playing a trick on you. Or on me. So what's the game?"

26

The game was simple, Jessie realized as she hung up. The *killer* had called the *Times,* to get even with the task force for saying he'd killed Joyce Dehoff. (Lab results had shown an overdose of heroin as the cause of death.) She repeated what Gary had told her—to the task force, then to Corcoran. Takamura had notified the lieutenant, who had been with Hanson in the chief's sixth-floor office, and he'd come down to the Operations Room.

"But why use your name?" Corcoran gazed at her.

As if that's my fault, too, she thought. She met his eyes.

"She's the one he talked to the other day," Barrows said. "She's in the public eye. The killer knows her name, her face. When he thinks 'police,' he thinks 'Jessie Drake.' "

"Hey, Jessie, you're a celebrity." Pruitt was half sitting on his desk. His tone was affectionate. His smile reached his eyes.

"Wonderful," Jessie said. "Can you get me on *Donahue?*"

Takamura said, "But why would the killer want to tell

the press about the Monopoly angle? Why would he give that away?"

Jessie said, "He didn't say anything that would help us catch him or stop him. And killers are show-offs. Manny Freiberg says the guy's probably dying to show the world how clever he is."

Most criminals, Jessie had learned, liked to show off—especially to a woman cop. That's why Phil usually left the interrogations to her. She'd gleaned a great deal of incriminating information from smirking males who relaxed their guard because they were sitting across the table from a "harmless" female detective.

"Makes sense." Corcoran nodded. "All right. I'll tell the chief. I never really thought it was one of you." He smiled.

Jessie stared at him. Was this the Twilight Zone?

In one swift, seamless, pantherlike movement, Pruitt was off the desk and facing Corcoran. "So what was all that shit yesterday? Grilling Jessie? Grilling me? Your idea of fun?"

Takamura said, "Peter, we know you're under pressure. It's—"

"One day you're gonna slip on all that grease, John, and break your neck." Pruitt's voice was dangerously soft. He turned to Corcoran. "You know, I'm not convinced the killer called the paper." There was a glint in his eyes. "Maybe *you* did it so you could make all this up about the killer calling in the info."

"Frank." Barrows' eyes darted from Pruitt to Corcoran.

"You're an asshole, Pruitt." Corcoran's complexion was mottled. "Why in hell would I do that?"

"Maybe you thought you'd flush the killer out, but you knew the chief and the mayor wouldn't go along with it."

"You're crazy, Pruitt. I didn't do it."

"Methinks you doth protest too much. That's from *Hamlet*—I checked it in my *Bartlett's*. Surprised I have one, Corcoran?"

"You have an attitude problem, is what you have." Corcoran poked his finger at Pruitt's chest. "Stay the hell out of my way!"

He stormed out of the room. Takamura followed him.

"Wouf, wouf." Pruitt's smiled was tired and a little sad.

"What the hell got into you, taking him on?" Barrows shook his head. "I need some air," he said. He took his jacket and left the room.

"Your turn, Jessie." Pruitt's hands were in his pockets.

"It's not my business." She picked up her purse and rummaged through it, wishing Barrows hadn't left.

"But you have an opinion, I'm sure." He smiled.

Jessie hesitated, then said, "Antagonizing Corcoran is pointless." She paused. "And he *did* try to apologize."

"Is that what you think that was?" Pruitt came closer. "You don't know the man. Corcoran doesn't apologize. He evaluates. He plans. He figures out everything. How many bowel movements he's gonna have per week, how much toilet paper he's gonna use."

"What does that have to—"

"He's a calculating son of a bitch." His eyes flashed with anger. "This morning he was ready to throw you to the wolves. Now you saved his ass, so you're safe for a while. He didn't want you on this task force. He doesn't want me, but he's stuck with me."

"Why?"

"Because I've got friends in the department, and Hanson insisted. He knows I'm damn good. And the others? Barrows is black. Don't get me wrong—he's a terrific cop and a terrific guy, but his color helps, especially since the commission came down on the department for bias against minorities. Then there's John Takamura, number one sycophant, looking to move up right behind Peter Corcoran. Takamura is *always* careful. *Always.* So let's see. We've got a black, an Asian, a white male. And you." Pruitt smiled.

She felt like smacking the smile off his face. "I pulled the cases together. I earned the chance."

"You still don't get it, do you? This has nothing to do with merit, sweetheart. This is politics. You're here because you look good on camera and you have nice tits and a great ass."

"You're disgusting." But she didn't leave. She had to hear.

"But honest. If you were a lesbian Latina, you'd be perfect."

"Why don't you admit it, Pruitt. You hate women cops."

"You don't have to worry about me, sweetheart. I've been partnered with women. No problem. Ask around. And Ray's cool with you. But John believes a woman's place is in the home. That's where he keeps *his* wife. He was pissed when you figured out the Monopoly bit, but he's a good actor. And Corcoran?" Pruitt smiled. "His famous line is, 'When a female cop reaches into her purse, you don't know if she's going for her gun or lipstick or tampon.'"

"Hanson appointed me. He knows I figured out the Monopoly—"

"Of course he appointed you. Smartest move he could've made. Everybody's been screaming about women on the LAPD, how they don't get chances for advancement. Hanson sees a great opportunity. And the beauty is, he wins either way."

Jessie frowned. "What do you mean?"

"You think they needed a 'media contact'? Bullshit. Corcoran could've handled it. Or Hanson. Would've made more sense, a case this important. Now you're the high-profile cop. Your face is all over the TV and the papers. We find the bastard who killed all these people, you look good, the department looks good. Hanson looks good. We don't find him—sorry, folks, that's what you get when you put a woman in a man's job."

Bastard, Jessie thought, but she wasn't sure whom she meant.

* * *

"Is it true?" Helen whispered, her eyes wide with fear and excitement when Jessie came home late that night. "There was a special report on the news. Mom's been calling nonstop. . . ."

"Monopoly, huh?" Brenda said, and it was a relief for Jessie to be able to talk about it with her friend; a relief, too, to confide that she felt diminished by what Pruitt had said, that she'd been chosen for the task force just because she was a woman.

"What the hell do you care *why*, Jess? You figured it out, not those testosterone-heavy jerks. Come on, girl, you've been there before. We all have. You can beat them at their own game."

Phil called. "Great going!" he said when Jessie told him she'd figured out the Monopoly angle. He'd broken a suspect he and Jessie had been working on for weeks. "Small potatoes compared to the Monopoly. Guess you'll never want to come back to West L.A., Jess," and they both laughed, but she thought she'd heard a tinge of not-quite envy in his voice. Not Phil, she thought—he's my partner, my friend. But she didn't mention what Pruitt had said.

When Jessie arrived at Parker Center the next morning, Pruitt was alone. He was on the phone and didn't acknowledge her. She put her purse on a table and took out her notes on her interview with Monica Podrell. At least they had their first lead, she thought. And finally, a drawing of the killer.

A copy of the police sketch had been tacked to the wall, next to the large map of L.A. which now had two more pegs—one in Venice, the other on San Pedro Avenue, the parking lot across the street. What balls, she thought again. She felt suddenly vulnerable and touched her gun for reassurance.

She looked again at the face of the killer. So ordinary—just what Manny had predicted. The sketch would be aired on TV and printed in the paper. Copies would be circulated all over the city. But Monica Podrell had looked dubiously at the finished sketch. "I don't know," she'd said. "It's not really him." And she hadn't been able to say why.

Jessie sensed that Pruitt was standing behind her. What now? she thought as she turned to face him.

"I was rough on you yesterday," he said. "I'm sorry."

"You were right. I should probably thank you." She'd been giving this some thought since yesterday. *You want to play with the boys, toughen up,* Gary had said.

"Another thing," Pruitt said. "I've been a real bastard, needling you since you got here. I was pissed because they picked you and John to run this dog and pony show. And I'm going through a tough time. Personal stuff. But I shouldn't be taking it out on you." He was looking somewhere over Jessie's head.

"Forget it." She felt uncomfortable and fought an urge to reciprocate with an apology for something she hadn't done.

"Thanks." Pruitt came closer. He extended his hand.

He had a firm grip; her hand felt small in his, and she was suddenly, acutely aware of his maleness. He stared at her.

"How about a drink sometime, Jessie? A peace offering."

Takamura entered the room. Jessie pulled her hand away. She knew she was blushing and she felt awkward, as though Takamura had interrupted her and Pruitt in an embrace.

Takamura's face was inscrutable. "The desk sergeant gave me something for you, Jessie." He handed her a manila envelope.

There was no return address, but JESSIE DRAKE was typed on the front. "Who's it from?" she wondered aloud. She'd been getting tons of mail from L.A. residents. Fan mail, she'd joked to Brenda. Jessie tore open the flap and emptied the contents of the envelope onto her desk. "Oh, my God!" she whispered.

Takamura and Pruitt joined her. They all stared at the desk.

There were five Monopoly property cards: Oriental, Electric Company, Baltic, Reading Railroad, and Boardwalk. There were three Chance cards: "Advance to Go," "Take a ride on the Reading Railroad," and "Advance to Boardwalk." And there were two Community Chest cards: "From sale of stock you get $45" and "You have won second prize in a beauty contest. Collect $10." The second one was paper-clipped to a folded piece of paper.

Using her tweezers again, Jessie removed the card and opened the paper. She read the typed note aloud.

> Dear Detective Drake,
>
> I decided to let you in on my game, to make the contest more even. I've enclosed the cards for the properties I've purchased. Don't bother to dust them or this letter or the envelope for fingerprints.
>
> For your edification, last Thursday I was collecting a prize for a beauty contest. It's only $10, but it's money in my account. But you knew I didn't kill that young woman. You were playing a game to provoke me into exposing myself. You enjoy games, don't you?
>
> Well, Jessie Drake, I can play games, too. By now you probably know that I used your name when I called the *Times*. This time, Jessie, the joke's on you. Fair game, wouldn't you say?
>
> This week I won't be using a Community Chest or Chance card. And I won't be landing on Go. I'll be purchasing another property. I'd love to tell you which one, but I won't—not yet. Maybe I'll tell you later today, or tomorrow. Maybe I won't tell you at all.
>
> You shouldn't have lied, Jessie. It wasn't fair, and I always play a fair game.

27

"You can't trace the note?" Manny Freiberg asked Jessie an hour later in his office.

"No. The dot matrix means it's from a printer. The killer doesn't have to own one. He could've typed and printed his note in a computer store. No one would've noticed him."

Freiberg frowned. "There's a lot of anger here, Jessie. Repressed anger, hiding behind a facade of politeness. Scary."

"He thinks we tricked him with the Dehoff woman."

"That's only part of it. There's a more general, underlying rage. What bothers me is that he's personalized this. He gave *your* name to the *Times*. He called *you*." Freiberg pointed to the paper. "He mentions your name four times. 'Detective Drake,' then 'Jessie Drake,' then 'Jessie,' twice. And he refers to *your* liking games."

She felt a flutter of unease. "Isn't that natural? I'm the one he sees on TV." As Frank Pruitt had so eloquently told her. "And my name was in the papers with the first cases."

"He's trying to engage you, Jessie."

"I'll tell him I'm taken." She tried a smile.

"Not funny!" Freiberg's tone was sharp.

"Hey! Now who doesn't have a sense of humor?"

"This guy's dangerous, or hadn't you noticed? I don't like the fact that he's focusing on you. You shouldn't, either."

"We could take turns doing the press conferences." And foil Hanson and Corcoran's plan, she thought with remembered anger.

"The killer's already identified with you. The fact that you're a woman may play into it, too. We don't know how he feels about women—whether he's married, has a sister. He may connect you with his mother. She may have abused him or stood by while he was being abused. In either case—"

"Why did he assume we tried to trick him, Manny?"

He paused. "It's indicative of the pathology of his personality. He thinks everyone's watching him and his actions."

"Paranoia?"

Freiberg shook his head. "Not quite. But he's desperate to be the center of attention. My guess is that at some point he's suffered severe narcissistic injury, so he's got a poor sense of self. Of course, not everyone with low self-esteem kills."

"Thank God."

"Yeah." He looked at her, then again at the note. "He's also showing you how smart he is, using words like 'edification,' 'provoke,' 'purchase.' And he enjoys teasing you, telling you he *may* let you know something about his next move."

"Any guesses, Dr. Freiberg?"

"I told you—I'm a shrink, not a psychic." But this time, he wasn't smiling. "Think about what I said, Jessie. Be careful. By the way, how's your nephew? Is he seeing someone?"

Jessie stood up. "I suggested it to Helen. She told me to mind my own business. I can't push it."

"Too bad. Any chance she and her husband will reconcile?"

"I don't even know why she left Neil. He used to be away frequently on business for long absences. She hated that. But he's cut down." Jessie frowned. "Neil *is* domineering. Particular. A stickler about neatness and punctuality. But Helen knew all that before she married him." Jessie shrugged. "Thanks again, Manny."

"Where to now? Any ideas?"

"I have an appointment with an expert."

His eyebrows rose. "I'm crushed. You're replacing me?"

"A different kind of expert, Manny."

The address was for an apartment on Havenhurst, but Jessie had forgotten that south of Santa Monica, Havenhurst turned into Kilkea. Just one of the fun things about L.A., she thought.

Finally she found it. Minutes later she was identifying herself to Henry Malloy. When he opened the door, she couldn't help staring. He was gorgeous! A Kevin Costner face and a torso, partially covered by a tank top, with muscles rippling à la Schwarzenegger above low-slung, acid-washed jeans.

"*You're* a mathematician?" she heard herself asking, and blushed. Thank God Pruitt wasn't here. She'd never live it down.

"*You're* a detective?" He grinned. "I saw you on TV, so I had an advantage. You're even prettier in person. I guess you were expecting someone from *Revenge of the Nerds,* huh? Sorry if I disappointed you."

"No problem." *Dear Brenda, wish you were here. . . .*

"You didn't say on the phone, Detective Drake, but it's about the Monopoly killer, isn't it? It's freaking me out, that he's using the game to choose his victims. It pisses me off, too."

Join the crowd. "You're a champion, I understand." That's what the toy store owner had told Jessie. Talk to

Henry Malloy if you want to know about Monopoly. Henry's only twenty-three, but he's tops. What he didn't say is, Henry is a hunk.

Henry shrugged. "I haven't won any international competitions yet, but I plan to enter the next one. They're hoping it'll be in Moscow. Can you believe it? Until recently, you couldn't even *buy* a set there."

"How many sets do you own, Henry?" Jessie looked around a living room furnished with a brown-and-gold tweed sofa, a pole lamp, and a bookcase. No Monopoly sets in view.

"Hank. Three working sets, plus my dad's. That has the silver tokens. I use that only for special games. Parker Brothers doesn't make a big variety. Well, Dunhill made a set with solid gold pieces. It cost about twenty-five thousand dollars. And in 1978 Neiman Marcus sold an all-chocolate set for six hundred. There are about twenty-three foreign editions, too. The British one has London streets; the Japanese, Tokyo streets; the Greek, Athens, and so on. They have editions in French, German, Spanish, Hebrew, Russian, Italian, Portuguese, Afrikaans. I don't remember all of them. Come on, I'll show you my sets."

Hank led Jessie to a dining alcove. The walls were filled with laminated plaques and trophies. On a large oak parson's table were three Monopoly sets, all in various stages of play.

"I've been playing since I was seven. I've researched the game. How it started, what was the longest game, stuff like that."

"How long?" Jessie found it hard to concentrate. God! she thought, I must be horny as hell. I let Gary kiss me, I held Frank Pruitt's hand and imagined a meaningful look, and now I'm salivating over a guy who's ten years younger than I am.

"Fifty-nine days, with substitutions. The longest game in

a bathtub took ninety-nine hours. The longest underwater was forty-five days. The longest played upside-down was thirty-six hours. In an elevator in a Holiday Inn in Torrance, California, for a hundred forty-eight hours. More?" He smiled.

Jessie nodded, fascinated.

"Guys in the *Nautilus* played Monopoly under the polar ice cap. Parker Brothers made a set for astronauts. British robbers played with real money while they were waiting to pull off a train robbery. In World War II, escape maps, compasses, and files were smuggled into POW camps in Germany. Real money was slipped into the packs of Monopoly money." Hank grinned. "Cool, huh?"

"Cool," Jessie echoed. A person could drown in eyes that blue. She turned her attention to one of the sets, and Hank the Hunk was suddenly unimportant. The board was identical to the one she'd used to plot the killer's moves. Identical, too, to the one the killer had used to choose seven victims and would use to choose the next one. And how many after that? *You're fair game,* he'd basically said. Everybody was fair game.

"You know who invented Monopoly?" Hank asked.

"Charles Darrow." She'd done some homework in the library.

He shook his head. "Darrow *discovered* it and changed it around a little. The person who *invented* it was Elizabeth Magie-Phillips. That was in 1904. She called it the Landlord's Game."

The original game, Hank explained, had a continuous path of forty spaces, including four railroads, a water and electric utility, and twenty-two rental properties which increased in value as one traveled clockwise around the board. There were other similarities: a park space, a jail, a "Go to Jail" space.

"Instead of Go, the starting space was called Mother

Earth. Anyway, in 1924 she took it to Parker Brothers. They turned it down, and said it was too educational and political." He threw Jessie a "can-you-believe-it?" look.

Jessie reciprocated. "Then what?"

"College students started playing her game. And they started calling it Monopoly, because if you owned all the utilities or all three railroads, you could charge higher rents."

"Just like today's game."

"Not exactly. That rule didn't apply to other properties."

"But Darrow's the one who named the properties after streets in Atlantic City, right?" Darrow, Jessie had read, had loved Atlantic City and the life of ease it represented. Unfortunately, in 1933, in the heart of the Depression, he'd been an unemployed heating engineer living in western Philadelphia. Atlantic City could have been the moon.

"Sorry." Hank's smile was apologetic. "Ruth Hoskins did that. She moved to Atlantic City with an updated version of Liz's game called Finance. Then Darrow came across *her* game."

Darrow made a new gameboard but kept the Atlantic City names, Hank explained. He inadvertently kept the misspelling of Marven Gardens—spelling it Marv*i*n Gardens. "Anyway, Darrow made changes and took the new version to Parker Brothers."

"And they turned it down again," Jessie said, hoping she'd gotten something right.

"Yup. They said there were fifty-two things wrong with the game. Like it took too long, and it was too complicated." Another grin. "But after Charlie sold twenty thousand sets on his own, they came to him. From rags to riches. It's the American dream, don't you think?"

For Charles Darrow, who'd imagined himself a real estate tycoon and become a real millionaire, it was. For Jessie and the task force and all of Los Angeles, it had become a nightmare. "Tell me something, Hank. Why do you play Monopoly?"

"I like the power," he said simply. "I'm very competitive. It's not just luck, you know. It takes strategy. Which properties pay off the most. When to build houses, hotels. When to cut your losses. I have a *Science Digest* article that talks about how to win. It's based on matrix math. A little tricky, but if you're interested, I could show it to you."

Would it help Jessie figure out where the killer would strike next? Unlikely. "I don't think so."

"You know why else I like it? It's the great equalizer. I play in tournaments all the time, and it doesn't matter how old you are, what color, how much money you have. Anyone can win."

Or lose. "But it's a ruthless game, Hank. Basically, you have to force all your opponents into bankruptcy."

"Like Ed Parker said—he was a former president of Parker Brothers—'People just like to clobber the next guy.' But it's just a game." Hank frowned. "Of course, this psycho's playing for real."

"Hank, can you figure out where he'd go next?" Of course not, she realized. It had been a vain hope, a wasted trip.

Hank sighed. "I wish I could. But there's no way. You know what I was thinking, though? What if this guy was unhinged to begin with and was forced into *real* bankruptcy and figured this was a way of getting even? Or maybe someone in his family went belly up, and that ruined his life, or his parents' life, or both? Wouldn't *that* be a twist."

Wouldn't it, though. But they couldn't check into everyone who'd ever gone bankrupt. And gone bankrupt where? In California? Who knew where the killer originated?

"And even if he's getting away with the killings," Hank said, his blue eyes somber, "he's got to be empty inside, don't you think? It's kind of like a bankruptcy of the soul."

Bankruptcy of the soul.
The phrase haunted her as she drove home.

She needed a hug. Matthew no longer shied from her embraces, and she could picture his freckled face, hear his "Hi, Aunt Jessie." Helen's Taurus was parked in front of the house, but inside, taped to the refrigerator, was a note from Helen.

> Matthew and I are spending a few days with Mom and Dad. Mom's nervous about this crazy Monopoly killer. I figured I'd humor her, and Matthew will enjoy seeing San Diego. Dad picked us up; he has a great deal on a car in La Jolla. If so, I'll drive it back. Matthew says to throw you a kiss.
>
> P.S. I tried to call you, but you were unavailable.

Unavailable. Hadn't Jessie just told herself the same thing, standing in Gary's living room? It was unreasonable to feel abandoned; yet that was exactly how she felt.

She called Brenda; Tony said she was out shopping. She picked up the phone to call Phil, but changed her mind.

She broiled a lambchop for dinner. Later, she showered and washed her hair (she'd probably never get that haircut; she'd end up looking like Rapunzel). She turned the radio on to a classical station (she really should get a compact disc player to replace the stereo Gary had taken) and listened to a Mozart sonata while she put pink nail polish on her fingernails and toenails.

She thought about calling Gary. Not a good idea.

She wondered idly what Frank Pruitt was doing.

All day Tuesday, in between calling hospitals and following up leads, Jessie and the others waited for the phone to ring.

They waited all day Wednesday, too. At ten o'clock, when they finally went home, the room was filled with the pungent remains of the deli suppers they'd ordered and the stale, acrid odor of cigarettes and defeat.

At seven Thursday morning, when Jessie entered the lobby of Parker Center, the desk sergeant handed her an envelope.

There was no postmark. "Who delivered it?" she asked.

"Don't know. Somebody slipped it under the door."

The envelope contained a single card: Water Works.

28

The Water Works card has a black-and-white drawing of a faucet. On the back was a message printed in green ink:

> This should give you a glimmer of an idea, Jessie—sorry I can't be more help, but it would clearly be against my best interests.

The envelope had also contained disks of green mylar confetti.

"Why the confetti?" Barrows picked up one of the disks.

"The son of a bitch is celebrating, that's why!" Pruitt swept the disks onto the floor. "What the hell good is it to know where he landed? It doesn't tell us a goddamn thing, and he knows it!"

Takamura's fingers had formed their usual tent. "Jessie, did your expert have any idea as to how the killer makes his associations?"

Your expert. Was he being snide? "Not a clue. I just spoke to Manny again. He doesn't know, either. Sometimes the killer's literal—like Free Parking. Other times . . ." She shook her head.

"The Department of Water and Power?" Barrows said. "He didn't use it for Electric Company. Maybe he's using it now."

Aside from the DWP, Jessie learned, the yellow pages listed fifteen water-utility companies. "What about water heaters? Or independent plumbers, or distributors of plumbing parts."

"Or water beds," Pruitt added.

Or water softening and conditioning systems. Or ice plants. Or hot tubs or spas. Or fountains. The possibilities were endless.

Jessie frowned. "If it's a fountain, odds are he won't do it in broad daylight. He'll either do it at night, or—"

"Or he's already killed his victim early this morning, and we just haven't heard yet." Pruitt frowned. "What about a private pool? He got Mae Sung Lee to let him into her apartment."

Barrows shook his head. "People are more cautious now, Frank. There's been so much media talk about the killer. Plus the papers printed the sketch based on the Podrell woman's description."

"Which shows what? An average guy, brown hair, brown eyes, no distinguishing features." Pruitt turned to Jessie. "You said she wasn't sure about the sketch."

"She wasn't."

"See? You never think it's going to be you. She said he was polite. He got one person to let him in, he can do it again."

He rang the doorbell, waited, then rang again. He was about to ring a third time (someone was home; he could hear the sound of vacuuming) when the vacuuming stopped and footsteps approached.

Dark-brown eyes studied him through the privacy window.

"I have a delivery for Mrs. Jean Tiller. Pickup, too."

"You got the right place, but I don't know you." Her tone was flat with accusation.

"My name is Leonard Stuckey. I just started today."

"Uh-huh. Well, Leonard Stuckey, I don't know nothin' 'bout no delivery an' pickup today. The other man, he comes Fridays."

He smiled disarmingly. "My dispatcher gave me the orders this morning. Maybe there's been a change in the schedule."

"My missus didn't tell me nothin' 'bout no change in any schedule. Whyn't you come back aroun' two. She'll be here then."

He smiled again, determined to be patient. "It'll throw off my schedule, ma'am, and I'll get in trouble with my boss."

"Well, I guess that's your problem, isn't it? Why don't you set those in the driveway."

"That's fine." He nodded. "But I have to get the empties."

"How do I know you're not that killer the po-lice has been talkin' about? Leave those in the driveway, and come back some other time for the empties." She started to shut the small window.

"Please, ma'am!" This time the smile was nervous. "Look, I don't blame you for being careful. I hope my wife would be, too. Why don't you call the company. They'll tell you I'm who I say I am. Leonard Stuckey." He spelled the name for her.

"Well." She looked at him. He was short, she noticed, with a slight build. "I guess it's all right." She opened the door.

* * *

Jessie looked again at the message on the card. "Water's blue, so why green ink and confetti? Why the message altogether?"

"He's taunting us, Jessie," Takamura said. "That's obvious."

Was he patronizing her, as Pruitt had suggested? "Sending the card did that. Maybe there's a clue."

"You wish," Pruitt said kindly. He smiled at her.

Since yesterday, their relationship had taken a significant turn. It was like driving a car, she thought, straining noisily in the wrong gear, then suddenly shifting into the right one.

She read the message again. "Why *'glimmer'?* He could've said, 'This should give you an idea.' Why 'a glimmer of an idea'?"

"I think you're reading too much into this." Takamura was writing notes with his fountain pen in a gray spiral pad.

Jessie ignored him. Aloud, she said, "Glimmer. Shimmer. Shine. Glisten."

Pruitt bent down and retrieved a handful of disks and let them rain onto a desk. "Glitter."

"Glitter," Jessie echoed. "Sparkle. Sparkle," she repeated softly. "Sparkling water! And the confetti sparkles, too!"

"So what are you thinking, a fountain?" Barrows frowned.

She nodded. "Or drinking water. Bottled drinking water." She pointed to the cooler.

"Which one?" Pruitt asked. "There's lots of companies."

"You're right. I don't—" She sat up straight. "Sparkletts water has trucks that are green with spangles. Sparkling green."

Takamura capped his pen. "It could be bottled water. It could be fountains. It could be anything." He sounded irritated.

Pruitt said, "We should send an APB to all units to keep a watch on utility companies and fountains. Deploy some plainclothes detectives, too. And we have to call the bottling companies."

"We don't have the manpower," Takamura said curtly.

"All the companies, Frank?" Barrows asked.

Who's the leader now? Jessie wondered.

"The major ones. I don't see him choosing a small firm. He may have chosen Sparkletts, but we can't take the chance."

"So what's he doing, Frank?" Barrows said. "Pretending to be a Sparkletts man?"

"Why not? He could take one or two bottles, maybe his own, ring the bell. The person answering the door isn't going to ask him where his truck is. Once he's inside . . ."

"You forgot something." Takamura sounded smug. "He'd need a uniform."

"What if he *is* working for the company?" Barrows said. "What if he took the job just so he could pull this off?"

He emerged from the house and looked at his watch. It had taken longer than anticipated, but he was only fifteen minutes behind schedule.

He shifted the empties onto his shoulders. They were much lighter than the filled ones. He hadn't expected five gallons to weigh that much, had been surprised when he'd started loading the containers onto the truck that morning.

"Sure you can handle the job?" the plant foreman had asked, squinting at him. "You need muscle for this kind of work."

"I can handle it. I'm short, but I'm built solid."

The foreman watched him load ten more bottles. Then he gave him a delivery route. "Be real polite. If the pickups are empty, ask if they'd like to add to the order. But don't be pushy, OK? And always offer to set the container on the stand."

"Right."

"One more thing. Don't leave any empties. And remember: any broken bottles, I've gotta deduct from your pay."

"Yes, sir. Don't worry, sir. I won't break any."

"'Course you won't, Stuckey. They're all polycarbonate nowadays." He laughed. "Lighten up, man. You'll be fine."

"He wouldn't take a job with a bottling company," Jessie said. "People could identify him." She drummed her fingers on the desk, then said, "He's following a truck."

"He drives around till he sees one?" Takamura said with unconcealed irony.

He was beginning to annoy her. "He gets to the plant early and follows one on its route. This is it!" Her voice betrayed her excitement. "We have to alert the water companies and have them contact their drivers. Where the hell is that yellow pages?"

It wasn't how he'd figured to be spending his life—hoisting bottles of water—but it was a job, and he needed a job. Connie had read him the riot act last week.

"I'm giving cuts and tints and perms and manicures six days a week, Lennie. You've gotta do your share. This school business is fine for rich folks, but it isn't getting us anywhere. Work during the day, finish at night. Nothing wrong with that."

"I already signed up for the summer session. Let me at least finish that. In the fall, I'll take night classes."

"Lennie, either you get a job now, or I quit mine."

On Saturday, Connie had brought him the classifieds and they'd run down the possibilities. He'd gone for interviews on Monday and Tuesday at Sears, Pacific Bell, and two major department stores. He thought he'd made a good impression, but the people who'd interviewed him had said they'd have to get back to him. His last stop on Tuesday had been at the bottling plant.

"Can you start Thursday?" the personnel manager had asked.

He'd told Connie the good news as soon as she'd come home.

"Why don't you get something with more potential?" she'd said. "Management, maybe. That's what Mel, Bernice's husband, is doing, and he's earning enough so's they can buy a house."

He'd wanted to strangle her at that point, he was so mad. "Get a job," she'd said, "any job," and now he'd gotten one and it wasn't good enough for her. She could be incredibly sweet one minute and then impossible the next. That was Connie.

She must've seen how upset he was, because she snuggled up to him and kissed him. "I'm sorry, Lennie. I just don't want you being lured into sin by one of those lonely, half-naked housewives." She grinned. "Why don't we just wait and see if you hear from any of those other places tomorrow, OK, honey?"

But no one had called on Wednesday. And on Thursday he'd reported to the plant at 6:00 A.M., ready, if not eager, to work.

"Keep your hands off those housewives, you hear?" Connie had said when he'd left, her words half swallowed in a yawn.

Leonard deposited the empties in the slots along the side of the truck facing the street. Then he walked around to the cab and got inside. As he turned on the ignition, the radio came to life. He adjusted the volume, made it louder. If he had to drive all day, at least he could relax with the music. He didn't hear the muffled sound of his beeper, sitting in the back pocket of his pants, cushioned by the upholstered seat.

"Timothy Chrisman, Gordon Polk, Leonard Stuckey, and Louis Danczak." Takamura read the names of four drivers who hadn't called in yet. Chrisman worked for Arrowhead; Polk, for Indian Head; Stuckey and Danczak, for Sparkletts.

"OK. We have approximate locations for all these drivers." He turned to Barrows. "Ray, you take Chrisman. Frank, you take Polk. Jessie, Stuckey. I'll take Danczak."

His next four stops had been uneventful, and he'd made up five of the fifteen minutes he'd been behind. He was getting into the truck after the second stop when the beeper signaled. Maybe he should go back to the last house, ask to use the phone.

He shook his head. It was probably the foreman, checking up on the new man. Leonard had heard the beeper two or three times but had turned it off for a while, it was so annoying. He'd turned it back on, but decided not to call in. The foreman would be upset to hear that Lenny was behind schedule. If Leonard waited until he completed deliveries at two or three more stops, he'd be right on target. If the foreman asked him later why he hadn't called in, he could say he'd accidentally turned the beeper off. No big deal.

He was looking in the rearview mirror before moving away from the curb when he spotted the man running toward the truck, waving his arms. Leonard turned off the ignition and waited.

"Out of gas." The man was out of breath from running. "Out of shape, too." He smiled sheepishly.

"Where's your car?"

"Couple of blocks back, on Durango." He pointed. "There's a gas station not far from here, on Pico near Beverly Drive. I figured I'd walk there, get some gas, maybe get a ride back. Then I saw your truck. OK if I get a lift with you?"

"Pico and Beverly Drive, did you say?" Leonard checked his route. "Sure. Why not? It's on my way to my next stop."

"Can't keep the customers waiting, right?" He smiled, opened the cab door, and climbed in.

"What do you figure to put the gas in?"

"I knocked on some houses near where my car stalled, finally got someone to give me an empty juice carton." He showed Stuckey the container. "I appreciate this. I really do."

"No problem." Not for Leonard anyway. It was probably against company regulations, but no one would know. If you couldn't help a fellow human being, what was the point of living?

The man had taken out a handkerchief. "Hot day," he murmured. And then, "Seat belt's stuck."

"What? Oh, well, it's just a few blocks. I'm a safe driver." Lucky for him he'd had experience driving a truck. That was the first thing the personnel manager had asked him about.

"I know, but it's a habit with me. I hope you don't mind?" He smiled apologetically.

"No problem." He felt a momentary twinge of irritation but suppressed it. The guy was entitled. "My wife Connie, she's always bugging me about seat belts."

Leonard leaned over and tugged at the shoulder harness. "Here you go."

Their faces were inches apart, and suddenly the man's hand was around the back of Leonard's neck, an incredibly strong hand for such a small man, and Leonard thought, Oh sweet Jesus, he's a fag! "Hey, man, I'm not—" But then the handkerchief was pressed against his nose and mouth, and he couldn't breathe, and his eyes, eyes that had registered first shock, then disgust, were frozen with horror. The two men stayed locked in a grotesque embrace until Leonard's face slumped heavily against the man's shoulder.

Jessie had gone to an address on Camden first, but the woman who answered the door had told her no, the Sparkletts man hadn't come yet, and as a matter of fact, he was usually prompt and was something wrong? So Jessie had backtracked two stops to Reeves.

"You just missed him," the black housekeeper told her. "This is his first day, you know. Somethin' wrong?"

Maybe nothing was wrong. Maybe everything.

Jessie turned the corner and there, up the block, was the truck! It was glittering, the green plastic catching the sun's reflections, dancing in the mild breeze.

She pulled up alongside the truck and ran out of her car. She looked inside the cab of the truck.

Too late, goddammit! Too late!

She smashed her fist against the side of the truck, sending waves of pain up her arm. The water in the bottles nestled in the slots on the side of the truck sloshed in agitated protest, then quivered mildly before resuming its translucent placidity.

From somewhere under the still form of Leonard Stuckey, the beeper was emitting pathetic bleats.

Jessie found it and turned it off.

29

He had come too close this time.

He hadn't realized *how* close until he'd watched the Thursday evening news and learned that the police had discovered the body of Leonard Stuckey at a little after nine that morning. Which meant that Jessie Drake (he *knew* it was Jessie) had found the body not more than ten minutes after he'd completed his move.

He'd expected her to decipher the clues, had wanted her to, but he hadn't expected her to do it so quickly. Of course, there were other detectives on the case, but he knew it was Jessie who had made the connection between "glimmer" and the confetti, knew it was Jessie who was the smartest of them all. And that was fine, because it made the game more interesting, more challenging. He'd been telling the truth in the note.

The sketch in Wednesday's paper had startled him. Not that it looked like him—far from it. His forehead wasn't that high, his hair not that sparse. The eyes were too close together, too small. And his chin wasn't that sharp. But there had been something in the sketch that had been vaguely familiar, and he'd felt as if he were looking at a distant relative, recognizing shared features that didn't quite add up to the whole.

He'd wondered who had helped the police with the sketch. The paper hadn't said, of course. No one had seen him, no one. . . . And then he'd remembered the woman in the library who had almost thwarted his move. And he'd remembered, too, the panic and anger and frustration that had coursed through him as he'd sat in the bathroom cubicle, trying to calm down.

But in the end, she hadn't been able to defeat him, not in the library, and not with the sketch. No one would connect him with the man the police artist had drawn.

"Glimmer" had been a fine clue. He'd liked *glimmer* because it meant hint and sparkle and because it started with *g,* like *green*. His tenth-grade English teacher, Mrs. Ballinger, had read them a wonderful poem by Edgar Allan Poe filled with alliteration. "The Bells." He still knew bits of it by heart. Jessie Drake, he was sure, knew all about alliteration.

Glimmer and *green.* He'd often noticed the Sparkletts trucks making their way across town, like mobile oases in the desert of the city. At first he'd wondered why green—after all, water is blue. But then he remembered that the Pacific is sometimes green. He was sure that was the reason.

Glimmer was better than *glitter,* too; it was softer and reminded him of *shimmer,* and that's what he thought of every time he saw the curtain of green strips of connected plastic disks at the back of the truck, strips that caught the light and bounced it back and forth (*"with a crystalline delight"*), strips that swayed with a silent motion that made him think of gentle waves and the undulating rhythm of hula dancers. If the strips had a sound, he was sure it would be light and tinkly, like Teresa's laugh.

He loved Teresa's laugh. They'd gone out again last Saturday night, had seen another comedy, and he'd listened to her laughter (*"the tintinnabulation"*), had watched the faint rise of her softly rounded breasts beneath the thin, rose-colored cotton knit of her dress. Her breasts weren't small, but they weren't large, either, not as large as his mother's, and that was fine, because sometimes when his mother had pulled him to her (*"Oh, baby, Daddy didn't mean it"*), and his nose and mouth were pressed against the downy cushion of her chest, sometimes he'd felt as though he were suffocating. His mother's breasts were flat now, shriveled along with the rest of her body.

He'd visited his mother Saturday afternoon, but she was barely alert. She had a bad morning, vomited all over herself and soiled herself, too, the nurse said. I had to change everything. There was recrimination in the nurse's eyes, which wasn't fair, because it had never been his idea to put her here (*"Best thing for her, boy"*), and the doctors insisted he couldn't care for her at home. He apologized to the nurse, and thanked her for the care she was being paid to give, and she said, well, and left the room. Maybe she'd been expecting a tip.

Alone with his mother, he'd tried to talk to her, to make at least minimal contact with the person who he was sure existed behind the glassy, red-veined eyes. After more than half an hour he'd given up and released the hand that had lain, limp and rubbery, in his. He'd been doubly disappointed, because he'd wanted so much to tell her about Teresa, about her soft hair and her beautiful eyes and her tinkly laugh, and the fact that she really liked him (*"a runt like you"*), and that they were going out for the second time. Instead, he'd bent over to kiss her and almost gagged on the rank perfume of fetid breath and residual vomit that had met his lips. I love you, Mama, he'd whispered.

Teresa's lips had tasted of popcorn and lip gloss. He'd kissed her that night. He had known he would in the theater, when their hands, brushing against each other on the arm rest between their seats, had locked. He kissed her that night in her living room, and even though she was a little taller (only in her pumps) and his approach a little tentative, their lips met perfectly, so soft! and he found a world of promise in her eyes. They kissed a second time, lips not quite so firmly sealed, and he probed the even surface of her teeth with the tip of his tongue and was instantly aroused. And then she pulled slowly away, and sighed. Good night, she said, I had such a lovely time. And he knew then that there would be other times, other kisses, kisses that would lead to . . . He knew that she was right, that it wasn't time. She wasn't that kind of girl.

And then he left. Halfway down the stairs, he heard her calling, Wait, and he almost sprinted up the stairs, his heart thumping, to meet the urgency in her voice. But then, This is for you, she said, smiling, I almost forgot, and she handed him a slim, oblong white box. I hope they're all right. What? he said, pleased puzzlement slowly replacing the chagrin that had suffused his face with color. I don't . . .

And he opened the box and there, cradled in stiff white tissue, lay three white linen handkerchiefs. I had them embroider your initials on the bottom right-hand corner. Are they all right? she asked. Beautiful, he said, they're so beautiful, but I can't. . . . Oh, but you have to, she said, the one you gave me is ruined, the mascara wouldn't come out. Please, I'll feel terrible if you don't. . . . So of course, he had to take them.

Back in his house, he opened the box and fingered the handkerchiefs. They were beautiful, the edges thinly rolled and finely stitched, the embroidery skillfully executed. He would show them to his mother. And suddenly, he was overwhelmed with the thought that Teresa had given him the handkerchiefs, because it proved, didn't it, that she really liked him?

It was a bittersweet thought that made him at once exhilarated and strangely sad. It was the first time in his life that a woman other than his mother had given him a gift.

30

It was amazing, Jessie thought Monday morning, how ready people were to suspect others of vicious crimes. Eager, even.

Ever since the *Times* had printed a sketch of the killer and revealed the Monopoly connection, people had been phoning in, certain that they knew his identity. By Thursday the calls had abated, but the Friday morning media announcement that Leonard Stuckey was the Monopoly Murderer's latest victim had initiated a fresh spate of calls. Jessie had listened with strained patience to tens of finger-pointing callers. If the situation weren't so serious, she thought, it would be laughable.

People had called to report suspicious neighbors: they were too quiet, too noisy, too aloof, too friendly; they refused to lend anything; they always kept their blinds drawn; they disliked children or animals; they had the spirit of evil in them.

"He's always playing Monopoly late at night," one woman told Jessie. "I can see him through my window. He's hiding something—never looks me in the eye. I just *know* it's him!"

Some called to accuse estranged or ex-husbands or -lovers ("He's always had a menacing quality, you know?"), sons-in-law, fathers-in-law. Others named uncles or cousins or nephews, or former friends or business partners or casual acquaintances. Tenants called to report landlords, landlords to report tenants. One man insisted the killer was his ex-wife.

"Sure I saw the sketch, but you can't be sure the killer's a male, can you?" he asked. "'Cause I *know* it's Sheila. She's obsessed with Monopoly. And she's cracked. Over the wall."

Jessie and the others would sift through all the names the callers had given them, dismiss the obviously dismissable, pursue those that sounded even remotely plausible.

The entire city, she decided, was obsessed with Monopoly.

Since last Monday hundreds of people had rushed out to buy the game. By the weekend most of the games had been sold; Saturday's paper had reported that two men had gotten into a fist fight over the last Monopoly set in a major toy store. Toy store managers were frantically trying to refill their stock. And last night's evening news had reported rumors of betting pools across the city: people were wagering fifty cents to a hundred dollars or more on where the killer would land next.

It was grotesque and morbid and pathetic and repulsive.

It's a product, Jessie thought, of the voyeur in all of us that makes us gawk at smashed cars on the freeway and the bodies trapped inside them; makes us stare, from a safe distance, at fires burning out of control and the bewildered, panicked, nightgowned and pajamaed survivors watching their homes and possessions and lives crumble into ashes; makes us watch docudramas that recreate for our edification horrifying examples of man's violence against man, yet force those who would rather forget to remember; makes us listen avidly to reporters as they interview the victims (and their supporting cast of relatives and neighbors) of burglaries and conspiracies and hijackings and rapes and murders; makes us listen to the responses of these victims who stand dazed with grief, their intimate pain broadcast to thousands, millions of strangers.

Strangers like me, Jessie thought. I'm no better. She instinctively slowed when she spotted a traffic accident, if just for a moment. She listened to reporters interviewing victims.

But the betting pools? They were obscene. What kind of person would profit from guessing the killer's next move? It wasn't like betting on a game of wrestling or boxing or football. It was betting on a game of murder. Death across the board.

Hundreds of people—maybe thousands—had rushed to K marts and malls to buy Monopoly and play along with the killer. And it was very possible that one of them could be the next victim. Had any of them considered that possibility?

If they had, they'd probably dismissed it.

We're all convinced of our invincibility, Jessie thought. *It enables us to conduct our lives with a veneer of normalcy in the jungle of civilization. We live with the certainty that God or luck or a benevolent force will keep us safe. So we watch appalled as disaster strikes in another part of the city, or around the corner, or down the block. But we know it won't touch us.*

Until it enters through the back door.

The phone rang again. Jessie picked it up. "Detective Drake."

"Jessie? It's Paige."

Jessie's heart skipped a beat. "Why are you—"

"First, Matthew's OK. I don't think it's anything serious. But he blacked out for about a minute, and his arm is badly bruised. I don't *think* it's broken."

That was "OK"? How could Paige be so calm? "What happened?"

"Matthew and Eric were playing hide and seek in the yard. Matthew fell on the concrete. Helen dropped him off about ten minutes ago to go apartment hunting. That's why I'm calling you. I think a doctor should take a look at him, just in case."

"Of course. Right away." But which doctor? Jessie didn't know any pediatricians or orthopedic specialists. "Can you meet me in the emergency room at Cedars, Paige?"

"No problem. I'll leave a note with my maid for Helen."

Jessie hung up and turned to Barrows. "I have to leave." She told him what had happened. "I'm meeting Matthew at Cedars. I don't know if I'll be back." She frowned. "With John and Frank in the field—"

"Not to worry." Barrows put his hand on her shoulder. "I hope your nephew's all right, Jessie."

Me, too, she thought, and hurried to her car.

Except for Paige and Matthew and an older couple, the emergency room was empty when Jessie arrived. Matthew was sitting on one of the chairs, swinging his legs back and forth. His white T-shirt was dirty, and he was cupping the elbow of his left arm.

He looked OK, Jessie thought. Pale and frightened, with a tear-streaked face, but OK. She forced a smile as she sat next to him. "You had an adventure, huh?" She put an arm around his shoulders and hugged him, careful not to disturb the arm.

"I don't know what happened, Aunt Jessie. I wasn't being wild. I promise!" Fresh tears formed in his eyes.

Paige said, " 'Course you weren't. Eric said you tripped." She stood. "I'll go. It'll be better if I'm home when Helen returns."

"Thanks for bringing him, Paige."

"No problem. See you later, kiddo," she said to Matthew. "You're a real trooper." She smiled at him and left.

"Does your arm hurt, Matthew?" Jessie smoothed his hair.

He nodded. "Some. Will they take an X ray?"

"I don't know." Jessie squeezed his good hand. "But X rays don't hurt. Let's not worry about it, OK?"

A few minutes later, a male volunteer escorted them down a series of halls to a large room partitioned by curtains. The volunteer put Matthew on a bed in one of the "rooms."

"Doctor will be here soon," he said and disappeared.

"Soon" was fifteen minutes. When the tall, gangly resident arrived, Jessie explained what had happened.

"How long was he out?" the doctor asked her.

"My friend said about a minute. He's fully coherent now." She and Matthew had played Geography while waiting.

"Sound's good. Let's see the arm." He prodded it gently with two fingers, then lifted it cautiously.

Matthew winced and bit his lip.

"Could be broken, could be just a strain. We'll take X rays. Ready, kid?" He lifted Matthew off the bed.

"Can Aunt Jessie come with me?"

"Not for X rays. Sorry. But you'll be back in a minute."

Jessie went back to the lobby. The elderly couple had disappeared. In their place was a young mother rocking a sleeping infant in her arms and trying to calm a crying little girl.

Helen would be frantic when she heard about Matthew. Jessie hoped she wouldn't blame Eric. Or Paige, for letting the boys play. Or Matthew, for being a kid. This would probably make Helen more overprotective than ever.

The little girl had stopped crying, but now the baby had taken her place. A middle-aged, stooped man entered the lobby. After checking in at the nurse's window, he sat down next to Jessie. He was coughing—a wet, raspy sound that made Jessie nervous. She wondered whether it would be rude to move her seat.

The gangly young resident reappeared. "No break, just a strain. You're lucky, Mrs. Bollinger."

"Thank God!" Jessie stood up. "I'm not Mrs. Bollinger, by the way. That's my sister. Where's Matthew?"

"He'll be out in a minute. I'd like to talk to you first."

His tone alarmed her. She noticed that he was avoiding her eyes. Her mouth was suddenly dry. "What's wrong?" she managed to say.

They'd given Matthew a sling—just for a few days, the resident had said. When they got home, Jessie called Paige, who told her she hadn't heard from Helen yet.

Matthew had eaten two hot dogs in buns a little stale from the freezer. Now he was sitting in the den, watching TV. Jessie was standing at the breakfast room window, looking for Helen to pull up in the blue Buick Regal she'd driven back from La Jolla on Sunday. Their father had insisted on paying for it—"until things are settled," Helen had explained.

The phone rang. Jessie grabbed the receiver. "Helen?"

"It's Frank. Frank Pruitt."

She frowned. "Is there a break in the case?" Right now the case wasn't the most important thing on her mind.

"What? Oh. No, nothing like that. Ray told me about your nephew. I . . . uh . . . just wanted to know if he was OK."

This was a surprise. For a moment, she was flustered. "Thanks for asking, Frank. Matthew's fine. Just a sprained arm."

"Well, good. Do you think—"

Jessie heard a car pulling up. "My sister's here, Frank. I have to go. Sorry. See you tomorrow." She hoped he didn't think she was brushing him off. She liked the fact that he'd called.

Helen was running up the walk when Jessie opened the door.

"Where is he?" Helen cried. "Paige said—"

Jessie stepped out and pulled the door shut behind her. "Matthew's OK. His arm's just sprained." She paused. "They took X rays, Helen. I saw them."

"See this?" The doctor had pointed. *"And this? Do you have any idea . . ."*

She'd felt sick, dizzy. Not Matthew! Please, not Matthew!

"Oh, God!" Helen covered her mouth with her hand. "Oh, God!"

Jessie clenched her hands to keep from shaking her sister. "You never told me Matthew broke his arm. Why?" She spoke in the calm, inflectionless voice she used with suspects.

"Neil said it was an accident!" Helen whispered fiercely. "An accident! Matthew said so, too, so why wouldn't I believe him?"

"If you tell Daddy, Jessica, I'll be very angry."

"I won't tell, Mommy. I won't."

"I hope that's true, Jessica. Because if you tell, you know what will happen. I'll have to punish you again."

"I won't tell. I won't tell. I won't tell."

In the same matter-of-fact tone, Jessie said, "There were bruises, Helen." Ugly scars that hid uglier secrets. "Those weren't accidents. You must've seen them." They explained Matthew's shyness about undressing, his insistence on wearing a T-shirt when he went swimming. Bruises, not sunburn or modesty. She closed her eyes and saw them again; her careful veneer of calm splintered. "How could you let that happen, Helen?" Jessie cried. "How? He's a child! An eight-year-old, defenseless child!"

"But that's why I left, don't you understand?" Helen

clutched Jessie's hand. "I couldn't let something else happen to him!"

Jessie yanked her hand away. "How long has this been going on? Months? Years? Why didn't you leave right away? What kind of mother lets someone hurt her child? After what we went through, you of all people—"

"You have no right to judge me! I tried to stop him. I threatened to leave, and each time Neil promised that he'd get help, that he'd never hit Matthew again." Helen bent her head. "I knew you'd blame me, just like you blamed Dad. That's why I didn't tell you. It's always my fault. Always." She was sobbing quietly.

I'm supposed to say "I don't blame you," Jessie knew. "When Neil comes back, we'll settle this." Her feelings about her sister were confused. Those about her brother-in-law—the "bad man" who gave Matthew nightmares—were uncomplicated. She hated him.

"I don't want you going after Neil! He can be vicious—you have no idea. That's why I didn't tell him I was leaving him. Neil thinks Matthew's in camp. A friend in Winnetka has been mailing our letters to Saudi Arabia, so the envelope will have an Illinois postmark." She fixed imploring eyes on Jessie. "You'll help me, won't you, Jessie? You won't let Neil hurt us?"

"Move out of the way, Jessica. Helen knows she was a bad girl. Move out of the way or you'll be punished, too."

Poor, timid Helen. Always the victim. Not really a surprise, Jessie thought. She knew all the statistics, and that's what they showed: abused children often marry abusive spouses.

A grim, self-perpetuating irony.

"I'll take care of Neil," Jessie promised.

31

Tuesday morning, it was back to business.

"Detective Drake, I know a man . . ."

"Detective, I think you should know that my neighbor . . ."

Between calls, Jessie cornered Pruitt at the water cooler. "Thanks again for calling last night, Frank."

"No big deal." He seemed uncomfortable, as if he didn't want anyone to hear them. "I'm glad the kid's OK."

"Phone for you, Jessie," Barrows called.

Jessie walked over and took the receiver. "Detective Drake."

"Detective? My name is Carley Caffrey. I'm calling about the serial killer. I think I may know him."

Jessie suppressed a groan. Who was *this* caller—a jilted girlfriend? A frustrated Avon lady? "What makes you think you know him, Ms. Caffrey?" Because he plays Monopoly?

"I'm missing six vials of curare. The hospital where I'm a nurse is, I mean. Bollard Memorial? I think he worked here."

* * *

Even in heels, Carley Caffrey was barely five feet tall; Jessie felt like an Amazon standing next to her. She followed the nurse to a small office and sat down on a chair opposite her.

Jessie smiled. "Carley, Detective Takamura says he called Bollard last week, but the hospital didn't know of a drug theft."

"A week ago I didn't know it *was* missing. We use it infrequently. Yesterday I went to get a vial and found the seal broken. So I checked the other vials of curare; six had broken seals. I have a friend who works in the lab; he analyzed the substance in one of the vials. It was glucose solution."

Clever. So damn clever! "And you know who did this?"

"After I found the tampered vials, I looked at the sketch again." She hesitated. "There's *some* similarity to Jim Miller—I think I mentioned he worked here as a volunteer? He used to help me sometimes in the medication room. But I can't believe Jim's a killer. He was so sweet, so helpful." She sounded wistful.

"How do you think he got the vials of curare?"

"The locks weren't jimmied. I would've noticed. He couldn't have gotten my keys. I keep them on a chain on my person. But once when I was doing a supplies check—we do it daily—Jim ran in to tell me a patient was hysterical and insisted on seeing me right away. When I got there, she'd yanked out her IV. Someone had called her and threatened to poison her IV."

Someone named Jim? "How long were you gone?"

"It took me a while to reconnect the IV and calm her. When I remembered the keys, I ran back to the medication room. I remember how relieved I was to see that nothing was missing. Looking back, I guess Jim could've emptied the vials then."

"How long after this happened did Miller quit?"

Carley frowned. "A little over a week. He found a paying job. In a shoe store, I think he said." She took a slip of paper from her purse and handed it to Jessie. "Here's his phone number and address. I got it from personnel. I tried the number, but an Asian man answered. He said he's had this number for years."

The address would probably turn out to be bogus, too. "Carley, you said Miller doesn't look like the man in the sketch. Why?"

"Jim has a toupee, for one thing. And he wears glasses. Actually, I think he looked better in the newspaper, without the toupee. I had the feeling he lacked self-confidence. It's kind of sad, really."

Sadder for the people he killed. If in fact "Jim Miller" was the killer. "What about his clothes? His car?"

"I don't know if he has a car. As far as his clothes, nothing special. Sorry." She frowned. "Oh, there is one thing. He always had a Proventil inhalator with him."

"Allergies?" That would support Monica Podrell's guess.

"Or asthma. Shortness of breath, wheezing."

Monica had said the man's breathing had been loud. It was the same man! "Where are the vials now?"

Carley pulled a manila envelope from her purse. "I brought five. The prints on the one I gave my friend are probably smeared. I put latex gloves on to handle these." She handed Jessie the envelope. "I hope it isn't Jim, Detective. But if it is . . ."

There were no prints on the vials. The address Jim Miller had given the hospital personnel office didn't exist. Naturally.

There were no Jim Millers in the police computer files. Jessie and the others spent all day Tuesday and half of Wednesday investigating and ruling out the twenty-three Jim Millers they'd found listed in the L.A. County phone directories.

Too old. Too tall. Too fat. Wrong ethnic group.

Too damn bad. Not that Jessie had expected anything else.

Takamura said, "His first name probably *is* Jim. If I were changing my identity, I'd keep John. That way, if someone called me by name, I'd respond."

Barrows said, "So why 'Miller'?"

"It's his favorite beer." Pruitt looked glum. "What's the difference? We're no closer to knowing who he is, where he lives."

Takamura said, "But we don't have to search for the curare anymore. And we *do* know a little more about the killer."

"Yeah, like what? That the guy wore a toupee and glasses for a disguise? He'd be pretty stupid if he hadn't."

"The nurse said he has asthma," Barrows said.

"What do you want to do, Ray, contact every medical facility and doctor in the city for the names of every asthma patient? We spent who knows how many goddamn hours running down hundreds of goddamn hospitals looking for the source of the goddamn curare, and where did it get us?"

Probably nowhere, Jessie admitted.

"Excuse me," a voice said from the doorway. "I have registered mail for Det. Jessie Drake."

Jessie stood and turned toward the doorway and the mailman standing there. She walked over to him. "I'm Detective Drake."

"You'll have to sign for this." He handed her a white envelope with her name printed on top.

She signed. Inside the envelope she found an index card on which someone had used a black marker to write the number "10."

As she hurried to the board, she was aware that she was playing the killer's game, that at this very moment he was grinning as he pictured her moving the game piece the one-two-three-four-five-six-seven-eight-nine-ten frenzied spaces from Water Works to a space that would tell them nothing but would force them to admire his cryptic cleverness and admit defeat.

Ten spaces from Water Works was Luxury Tax.

Luxury could be anything. Jewels. Or furs. A Rolls-Royce. A yacht. Rare art. Along with the others, Jessie went through the motions—making lists, calling jewelry stores and furriers and car showrooms and galleries, knowing all along that their motions were useless, that there was no way on earth they could figure out where the killer would strike.

That the son of a bitch knew it, too.

32

There was a spot on the counter.

Shahram Tabari misted the glass with Windex and wiped it with paper towels, but the spot was still there. He ran his index finger over the area and felt the minute indentation. Another scratch. "So what?" his wife Roya would say. "What is, a few scratches? No one can see them." But he could.

Shahram sighed. He'd asked Roya again and again to take off her rings when she wiped the counters. He sighed, too, because Roya would deny that this scratch (like the others) was her fault, and she would start in about the store, how she'd told him eight years ago not to rent on Santa Monica but on Melrose, only four blocks to the south, but oh, what a difference! Melrose was booming, new shops opening daily, attracting hundreds, thousands of shoppers. Hadn't she begged him to listen? But of course, how could he listen to her, a woman?

The bell rang. Shahram looked up, a smile automatically on his face. "Can I help you?" he asked the short man who entered.

The man approached the counter. "I'd like some earrings."

For the last ten minutes, the man had been eyeing the BMW, walking around it, touching it. And for the last ten minutes Ron Hadley had been sitting alone in the office, watching him through the full-length plate-glass windows. The man was wearing navy slacks and a camel jacket; next to the polished elegance of the steel-gray BMW, they looked shabby. Ron would never have pegged him as a buyer of a luxury car, but experience had taught him not to judge by appearances. Just last week a guy in cut-off jeans had driven out of the showroom with the top of the line, the same one this guy was looking at: 750iL. Eighty-two thousand cash. Go figure.

Ron Hadley buttoned the jacket of his gray double-breasted pin-stripe suit, an Armani knockoff, straightened his burgundy silk Oleg Cassini tie, adjusted his smile, and strolled out of the office. Up close, the man was shorter than Ronald had thought.

"Ron Hadley." He shook the man's hand. "Beautiful, isn't she? Finest-quality leather interior. Genuine burled-wood accents."

He nodded. "I've been admiring the details."

"I could tell that you had an expert eye. You know, Mr. . . . ?"

"Madison. Jim Madison."

"You know, Mr. Madison, I could give you all the technical details, but frankly, you'd get a better understanding of what this beauty is all about if we went for a little spin."

"Could we?"

"Absolutely. Wait here just a moment and I'll get the keys to the manager's demo. Unless you'd rather take this one?"

"The demo would be perfect." He smiled. "Absolutely perfect."

"May I ask what kind of earrings you wish to see?" Shahram smiled again. "We have many-many kinds, many-many prices." The large diamond in his pinky ring flashed as he waved his hand over the display case like a magician about to say "Presto."

"Something dainty, for pierced ears. They're for a friend."

The man's ears had turned pink. A male friend? *None of your business, Shahram.* "Diamonds are always a perfect choice."

"I think that's out of my reach."

"We have all sizes. Allow me to show you." Shahram unlocked the cabinet and selected a pair of earrings attached to a black velvet card. "These are ten points, finest quality. Your price, a hundred seventy dollars. Much less than you would pay elsewhere, I assure you."

The man frowned. "They're so tiny."

"Yes, but of excellent quality. If you combine them with earring jackets, the look is impressive. Shall I show you?"

The man shook his head. "I don't think so."

Shahram lifted another pair. "This is one-fifth of a carat, combined. Quite a bit larger, yes?" He handed him the earrings. "Look at the luster. Four hundred twenty dollars. No tax, if you pay cash."

The man hesitated, then gave back the earrings. "It's out of my budget."

"Cubic zirconium, perhaps? There are times when even I am fooled." Shahram smiled.

He shook his head. "No. I want something real."

"A wise decision. Gemstones, then? What is your . . . friend's birth month?"

"October."

"Ah, October! You have two choices." He brought out

another tray and pointed to an iridescent oval stone encased in a gold setting. "Opals." Then he pointed to two square-cut stones, one rose, the other green. "Tourmalines. They come in different colors, but these are the most attractive."

"The opals are pretty."

"An excellent choice." He checked the tiny tag at the back of the card. "You are in luck. I designed these myself for a customer. The customer has disappeared, and her number has been disconnected. But she left a hundred-dollar deposit, which I will deduct from the cost." He smiled graciously. "For you, one hundred eighty-five dollars."

"I'll take them."

With a practiced eye on the road, Ron Hadley smiled. "I'm doing sixty-five and you don't feel a thing, right? You could take her up to a hundred thirty-eight—if the cops don't stop you." He grinned. "Did you notice how she took those curves on Sunset? Not a sound."

"Amazing. Where are we now?"

"North of Malibu, on Pacific Coast Highway. I'll head back to the showroom, unless you'd like to drive her."

"No, that's fine. I—" Madison leaned forward. "Can you pull over?" He looked pale and started to shake.

"Car sick?" The man was perspiring. Shit! What if he went into cardiac arrest? Ron pulled over and turned off the ignition. "Should I call 911? The cellular phone's connected."

"I'll be OK. Just give me a minute. I know what to do."

Madison reached into his pocket and took out a white handkerchief. *Who the hell uses handkerchiefs?* Ron wondered, and froze as he saw the bottom of what he knew was a syringe. His sister was a nurse, and he'd seen enough of them to recognize one instantly.

"Jesus Christ! You're him! The Monopoly killer!" Hadley

pulled out a gun and aimed it at Madison. "That's why you had me pull over, why you pretended to be sick! So you could kill me!"

"Please, put down the gun! I *was* sick." Madison's color had returned to normal; his shaking had stopped. "I'm a diabetic. I carry a hypodermic in case I need to inject myself with insulin. I thought I was having an attack, but it was nausea. You don't—"

"Keep your arms up!" Hadley gestured with the gun.

Madison obeyed. "You saw a syringe. You think I'm the killer. A normal conclusion. If you let me out of the car, I won't press charges. I could, you know. Do you have a license for that gun?"

"That's none of your business, Mr. Jim Madison, or whoever the hell you are. Ever since that car salesman was killed on a test drive, I've been carrying this, but I sure as hell never thought I'd use it. Keep your hands up, I said!"

"They're up! I'm not moving. Please, be careful with that gun! Just let me out. I'll get a cab, and I swear I won't make any trouble for you." His voice, tightly controlled, betrayed panic.

"I think you're awfully anxious to get away." With the gun aimed at Madison, he picked up the phone with his left hand. "Let's see what the police think."

"You're making a mistake. I can show—"

"Shut up. Just shut the hell up, OK, 'cause I'm very nervous, and my finger's on the trigger."

Jessie was getting into her car after responding to a false alarm in a jewelry store in Pacific Palisades when her radio squawked. "Drake here."

"They got him!" Barrows yelled. "They got the son of a bitch!"

She felt light-headed. "Where?"

"Pacific Coast Highway, south of Malibu." Barrows related what had happened. "The suspect's in custody. A detective from Pacific is on his way there. John says to go there. We'll meet you."

"What's the suspect's name?"

"Jim Madison. Same initials as Jim Miller."

Even though it was an unpopulated stretch of beach, a small group of gawkers had already assembled when Jessie arrived, held in check only by an invisible line of authority.

Stevens, the detective who'd called the task force about Adrian Boyd, was there, talking with two uniformed officers who were leaning against a patrol car next to an unmarked Chevy. Near it was the BMW. The luxury car gleamed in the morning sun, oblivious to the drama surrounding it. Someone was in the front seat. Probably the salesman. There was someone in the back of the patrol car, too. The killer? Jessie tried to contain her excitement.

She walked over to the officers and greeted Stevens; he introduced her to the officers.

The older of the two officers, Joe Stakowski, said, "We found a syringe and a vial in his jacket, plus this stuff in the pocket of his pants." He handed Jessie the items. "The salesman, Ronald Hadley, claims the guy was going to use the syringe on him."

She kept her face blank. "Driver's license?"

Stevens said, "Guy's name is James Madison. He's five feet five inches. Color eyes, brown. Color hair, light brown. All that checks. The thing is, he doesn't look exactly like the picture on the license. Then again, this is a renewal, but with the old picture, which is almost seven years old."

He handed Jessie the license. Her heart pounding, she examined the picture and felt a rush of disappointment. There was only a small resemblance to the face in the police sketch. But Monica Podrell, she reminded herself, had been unhappy with the sketch.

A minute later the suspect was standing in front of her.

He looks so ordinary, she thought. And Stevens was right. Madison didn't look exactly like the picture on the license. Had he stolen it?

"Mr. Madison, I'm Detective Drake. I'd like to ask you a few questions."

"You're making a terrible mistake, Detective. If you don't release me, I'm going to sue you and the city for false arrest."

"You're not under arrest. I'd just like to clear up a few things. Can you explain the syringe the officers found on you?"

He sighed. "For the tenth time, I am a diabetic." He spoke with exaggerated slowness. "I keep insulin on me in case I go into shock. If you check the vial which the officers removed from my pocket, you will find that it contains insulin."

Patronizing bastard, she thought. But did that make him a killer? "We'll do that."

"Look, I know you're doing your job, but this is a waste of my time and yours. If you let me go now, I won't press charges."

"Of course you won't!" a voice exclaimed behind them. "You'll be on your way to South America!"

Turning, Jessie saw the man who had been sitting in the BMW. Ronald Hadley, Stakowski had said. "Stay out of this, sir."

"Don't you think it's strange he's willing to drop charges? He's trying to con you into letting him go!"

"Can I level with you?" Madison said quietly to Jessie. "I'm fighting my wife for custody of our kids. If this gets in the paper, I'm finished. Please! Can't you see I'm telling the truth?"

"Can I see your diabetic identification tag?"

Stevens said, "I asked him. He said he lost it."

Hadley snorted.

"I've been meaning to have it replaced." Madison said. "The vial is labeled insulin. Look at it."

Madison could have placed a label from an insulin vial on this one, Jessie knew. "The officers found this can of mace in your pocket. Do you have a license for it?"

He hesitated. "No. But with all the crime on the streets, lots of people carry it nowadays for protection."

Hadley snorted again. "The only person who needs protection is me. He was going to use the mace on me, then kill me."

Stevens started to say something. Jessie quieted him with a look. "Mr. Hadley, if you make one more comment or sound, I'm going to arrest you for interfering with police business. One more sound, Mr. Hadley." She turned to Madison. "Carrying mace without a license is a misdemeanor."

"That's it. I'm not answering any more questions. I'm carrying a syringe and insulin, and just because this man"—he pointed to Hadley—"decided I'm a killer doesn't prove anything except that he's been watching too much TV and wants to see his name in the headlines. If anyone should be arrested, it's him. He could have killed me with that gun!" He turned to Hadley. "I plan to have my lawyer bring a charge of kidnapping against you."

"Get real!"

Madison said, "If you want to fine me for the mace, go ahead. I'll pay the fine. Right now I am going to leave. I am going to walk along the highway until I find a phone to call a cab to pick me up." He took a step away from the car.

"You aren't going to let him go, are you?" Hadley exclaimed to Jessie. "Can't you see he's conning you?"

Shahram Tabari placed the money and one copy of the receipt in the register and handed the other copy to the man. "Your friend will love the opals. Some say opals bring bad luck, but for you they have brought good luck today." He smiled.

The man took the small box and opened it. Then he frowned. "I think there's a chip in one of the stones."

"Impossible. They are brand-new."

"I see a chip." He removed one earring and placed it on the counter. "It's in the center of the stone. Here." He pointed.

"You are probably seeing the reflection of the light. Opals are so beautifully iridescent, you know." He picked up the earring and leaned over to examine it, his elbows resting on the counter.

"Hold it!" Jessie pointed her gun at him.

Madison turned around slowly.

"Why were you carrying this photocopy of your license?" Jessie showed Madison a white paper Stakowski had given her.

"Say, that's—" Hadley stopped.

"Do you know anything about this paper?" she asked Hadley.

Hadley nodded. "I made a copy of this guy's license just before we left the showroom. Standard procedure, to prevent someone from stealing a car when he's out on a test drive. Especially since that salesman was killed. How the hell did you get this out of the showroom?" he asked Madison.

"I'm not saying anything else until I see a lawyer."

"Told you!" Hadley said to Jessie.

Shahram Tabari was concentrating on the gem and didn't see the handkerchief, didn't sense the man nearing him until it was too late, until the handkerchief was clamped firmly in place.

The flawless iridescent stone fell clattering off the counter.

As he was slipping to the floor in his final seconds of consciousness, Shahram Tabari's hands slid across the counter in a desperate, futile attempt to hold on.

A nick in the otherwise smooth gold of his pinky ring etched another permanent scar in the clear glass of the display case.

Takamura hung up the phone. His face wore disappointment. "That was the lab. The stuff in the vial is insulin." Madison's doctor had already verified that Madison was a diabetic. "They're releasing Madison. Maybe they'll fine him for the mace."

Pruitt shook his head. "What a godawful waste of time."

"He was going to steal a car," Barrows said. "He removed the copy of his license, so no one would be able to trace him. And he goes scot-free." He shook his head. "Amazing."

The phone rang. Takamura answered it, then handed the receiver to Jessie. "A Det. Howard Thompson for you."

Jessie took the receiver. "Howard? What's up?"

"I think your killer just struck again, Jessie."

She closed her eyes briefly. "Where?"

"A jewelry store on Santa Monica near Cahuenga. Small shop. The wife called us to check the place. Seems she's been calling her husband off and on all morning but the phone's been busy. There was a CLOSED sign showing when we got there."

"Find anything?"

"A bank deposit slip plus seventy-five dollars. Does that fit?"

The merchants on either side of Shahram Tabari's shop had noticed nothing unusual. Neither had those up and down the block. If the killer had purchased anything, he'd left no sign of that either. There were no receipts in the register. SID had found prints on the CLOSED sign and on the counter, but they would undoubtedly be found to belong to the victim or other customers.

So what's new? Jessie thought.

They drove back to Parker Center in Takamura's car the same way they had come, in dejected silence. It was almost 7:00 P.M. They were all exhausted. Enough for one day, they all decided.

Jessie was opening her car door when she saw Pruitt walking toward her. "Did you forget something?" she asked.

"I'm too wired. Join me for dinner?"

Not a good idea, she thought. "That would be nice."

33

The lighting in the restaurant was dim, a contrast to the still-bright August sky. The room was frigid from air-conditioning. Jessie heard soft music, but she couldn't tell whether it was from a stereo or from the small nightclub Pruitt had told her was in the back room of the restaurant.

A miniskirted waitress seated them at a table in the rear and took their orders. The tablecloth was white; so were the napkins. There was a red-globed candle in the center of the table.

"Do you come here often?" Jessie asked.

"Here and other places. I eat out a lot. I'm divorced."

She met his eyes. "Ray told me."

"Trying to explain my bad behavior." Pruitt smiled. "Ray watches out for me. How about you? How long are you divorced?"

"A little more than a year."

"Are you over him?"

Was she? There were people and places that would always evoke memories of her life with Gary. Jessie had accepted that. But there were still moments, like the one the other day in Gary's apartment, when she wasn't sure. And sometimes (more often than she liked to admit) she found herself thinking about him, missing him. Was that regret, or loneliness?

"More or less," she said to Pruitt. "Are you over your ex-wife?"

"Sweetheart, I was over her a long time before she walked out. But it still hurt."

The waitress brought their wines. "Ready to order dinner?"

Jessie ordered grilled salmon. Pruitt ordered a steak.

"You on good terms with your ex?" he asked after the waitress left.

"Pretty good. He's a nice guy." Most of the time, he was.

"And a hell of a reporter." Pruitt grinned. "I gave you a rough time."

"Yeah, you did." She smiled. "Why?"

He shrugged. "I told you. I was pissed about John being put in charge. And you walked in like you owned the place with reports and lists. John loves lists. I hate 'em."

"I was nervous as hell."

"It didn't show. And you're beautiful."

"Thanks, I guess." She smiled again.

"I thought you were window dressing. But you're not. You're smart *and* beautiful. I guess my ego couldn't take it."

His dark-brown eyes were on her. She felt herself blushing.

"What about now?" she asked.

"I can take it," he said softly. "Let's drink to that." He lifted his wineglass.

They agreed not to discuss the killer. They talked about their backgrounds, their families. He told her about his two sons.

"They live with Rona in Arizona." He grinned. "I never realized before—that rhymes! Rona's a good mother. I see them a couple of times a year. It's not nearly enough, but they can't live with me, not with my schedule."

"It's hard when you're a detective." Then, not knowing why (maybe it was the globed candle's hypnotic effect), she told him about the miscarriage, about Gary's accusation.

"I'm sorry." He was quiet for a long time. Then he said, "Is that why your marriage broke up?"

She shook her head. "That was part of it."

"And the rest?"

"I haven't figured it out yet." She played with a fork.

"Yeah," he said. "Me, either."

The music was louder now. She took another sip of wine.

Pruitt leaned over. "Want to dance?"

She looked up, startled. "What?"

He smiled. "They're playing your song. 'Lady in Red.'" He pointed to her red silk blouse. "I promise not to step on your toes. I'm a pretty good dancer. How about it?"

Why not? He came around to her side of the table and helped her up. Then he took her hand and led her to the back room.

It was even dimmer here. There was a glittery strobe twirling lazily from the black ceiling, blinking silver flashes of light. On a stage at the end of the room was a four-piece live band. Several couples were dancing. Pruitt led her onto the dance floor.

He put his arm around her waist. He was several inches taller than she was, and the top of her head came just beneath his eyes. They started to dance. Although it wasn't really dancing, she thought, as they moved in place to the music. He drew her closer; his breath was warm on her cheek. She felt a tingling sensation.

"Lady in red is dancing with me," he whispered in her ear.

"Don't tell me you sing, too," she said, trying to dispel

with a light remark what she sensed was starting to happen, because she wasn't ready for this, not ready at all.

He kissed her, his lips grazing hers, and she felt a shock of pleasure. He kissed her again, harder this time, his lips more insistent, his fingers pressing against her back, she could feel each one, and she thought, oh God, what am I doing, and opened her mouth under his. He tasted of wine and the salted peanuts that had been on the table.

"Jessie," he murmured.

Both of his hands were around her now, in the small of her back. Her arms were clasped around his neck. She could hear his heart beating, or maybe it was hers. Her breasts were pressed against his chest, and she could feel his muscular thighs, and he was rubbing against her while he explored her mouth with his tongue, moving with slow, slow circles, and she was overwhelmingly, unbearably excited and flushed with heat.

Suddenly, he pulled away.

A wall of cold air came between them. She looked at his face—it was suddenly stern—then looked away so that he wouldn't see the lingering tint of arousal that was being replaced by embarrassment. And confusion. And hurt.

"Your beeper," he said softly. He pointed to the small black box inside the waistband of her slacks.

Now she heard it, too. "Oh," she said, feeling silly and relieved at the same time.

She called Parker Center from the restaurant pay phone and was put in touch with Officer Knox.

"Some kid just dropped off an envelope for you," Knox told her. "Said a guy paid him five bucks to do it."

Jessie's stomach muscles contracted. "Please open it."

A moment later, he said, "There's a theater ticket and a note that looks like it was printed from a computer. The ticket's for a performance at the Greek on August twentieth. Say, that's tonight!"

Doubles. Five plus five. They'd considered the possibility but discounted it when the killer hadn't delivered another message by the end of the day. Discounted it, obviously, too soon.

"Please read the note." Jessie took paper and pencil from her purse and copied the message as Knox read it.

> Hope you enjoy the second half of the show, Jessie. Sorry I couldn't get this to you sooner—it would have interfered with my plans.

"What?" Pruitt asked after she hung up.

Jessie handed him the message. In her mind, she was opening the Monopoly board. By now, she knew it by heart. She moved a mental finger from Luxury Tax to the first property past Go.

Mediterranean Avenue.

34

He had to be careful.

Soon there would be police all over the amphitheater and the parking lot. He wondered again why he'd sent the note and ticket, why he'd voluntarily increased the danger like last time, with Water Works. It was bewildering, this newborn urge to be daring; he'd never enjoyed taking risks (*"You're a sissy, is what you are!"*), always shied away from confrontation (*"Yes, sir"; "No, sir"; "Yes, ma'am"; "Sorry, sir"; "It's all my fault, sir"*). Now he seemed to revel in it. It was a strangely exhilarating sensation.

He'd read that emotionally disturbed killers wanted to be caught. But he wasn't disturbed, he knew exactly what he was doing. It made perfect sense. And he didn't want to be caught. Nothing could be farther from the truth; he wanted to be free, *had* to be free to continue playing until he was the indisputable winner.

Jessie Drake would be arriving any minute. He pictured her frowning as she and the other police (how many would there be—fifty? a hundred?) began a sweep of the theater.

Would they shine their flashlights into every face in the audience? He didn't think so. More likely, they would remain a quiet presence, bodies taut with tension, ready to jump into protective action, eyes watching warily for some abnormal movement, ears poised to pick up a muted scream.

The Iranian had tried to scream, but the chloroform had silenced him, as it had the others. The sound that had emerged from his throat had been pathetic, like the bleat of a sheep about to be slaughtered. Not *slaughtered,* he corrected himself quickly. He'd been gentle with the Iranian. He'd been gentle with all of them. And he'd been scrupulously fair.

It was the dice that chose. He was merely acting out their stark, black-on-white commands. It was the roll of the dice—five plus five, another double move—that had brought him here tonight and made his path intersect with that of some as-yet-nameless person whom Fate had selected. This morning it had brought him to the Iranian so anxious to make a sale.

Well, he'd been fair there, too, hadn't he? He could have kept the opals without paying for them. He could have taken anything he wanted. But he wasn't a thief. He'd removed the receipt from the register, but he'd left the $185.

It had taken him a while to find the opal—it had bounced off the counter after the Iranian dropped it—but at the last minute, he saw the iridescent stone on the carpeted floor. The opal had been unharmed. He'd returned it to the jewelry box and been about to shut the lid when he noticed the imprint on the silk lining: "Roya's Jewels." Thank God he'd noticed that! He'd have to find another box before he gave the earrings to Teresa.

He'd planned to buy something for Teresa, to thank her for the handkerchiefs. It was too soon for a ring. Earrings had seemed right. He hadn't planned on spending so much. A hundred eighty-five dollars! But the opals were beautiful, and Teresa was worth it. She would know that they were expensive, oh, I couldn't, she'd say. But he would insist.

He'd been fair, too, about the money for the opals. That had come from his own account, not from the money his father had left his mother. He had sole power of attorney and could withdraw a hundred eighty-five dollars, but it was important that the gift come from him. He'd been determined from the day he got *the idea* to use his father's money only for the game and his mother's needs. He'd used it to pay for his living expenses since he'd quit his job, but that was only fair because how could he play *the game* if he had to work?

He'd used his father's money to buy the front-row ticket for Jessie Drake, too. She wouldn't be using it, but he'd liked the panache of the gesture, had derived enjoyment from envisioning her face when she learned about it.

The sky had darkened long ago. Rosy streaks had given way to purple, then to charcoal-gray. He looked around. Night had blurred the distinct shapes of the people in the audience and robbed their clothes of color.

He wondered where Jessie was now.

Jessie and Pruitt and the other members of the task force arrived at the Greek Theater within minutes of each other. The commander of Hollywood Division, Lou D'Angelo, met them.

"You have five units from Hollywood, plus two detectives from Special Problems Unit," D'Angelo said. "Detectives are backstage, coordinating with the theater's promoter and security, which is basically a bunch of college kids and some retired cops. I put uniforms at all the entrances, the rest inside the theater. I took a quick look and didn't see anything unusual. But that doesn't mean shit. It's a full house, by the way. Over six thousand people."

"How far along is the program?" Jessie asked.

"It'll be over in less than an hour."

Takamura looked grim. "More manpower should be arriving momentarily from Northeast, Wilshire, and Rampart Divisions. Until then, we'll have to manage as best as we can."

D'Angelo said, "One of the detectives from Special Problems Unit can wait outside for the others and direct them. These guys are familiar with the theater."

Takamura rapidly made assignments: He and Jessie would be at either end of the middle of section C, which was composed of four segments. Except for section D, where almost no one sat, this was the most elevated area and afforded an overview of the entire arena. Pruitt and D'Angelo were in charge of the four segments in section B; Barrows and a detective from Hollywood, the three segments in section A and the orchestra pit.

"Stay in close radio contact," Takamura said. "If you see anything suspicious, signal me, then check it out. Ready?"

Yes, they were ready, Jessie thought.

The parking lot, filled to capacity, was being searched and patrolled. There was little tension there at the moment—the cars were vacant. The greatest danger was yet to come, when throngs of concertgoers would exit the theater and head for their cars.

Inside the amphitheater, detectives in civilian clothes were seating themselves alongside genuine members of the audience. Like them, they peered through binoculars, but instead of focusing on the stage, they were making periodic sweeps of the area. Uniformed police were positioning themselves in the aisles throughout the amphitheater. Initially, they attracted the stares and whispers of concertgoers; soon, however, they were accepted as part of the background.

The audience probably figures we're here for a drug bust. Jessie looked around. Yes, they were ready. Was that enough?

"Readiness is all," Shakespeare had said.

It hadn't worked for Hamlet, she reminded herself. She had a sinking feeling that it wasn't going to work for them tonight.

Seeing was difficult. Jessie's eyes hurt from the strain. The sun had set long ago, with a brilliant display of color, while Jessie and Pruitt had been racing to the theater. Now the amphitheater was cloaked in shadows.

Her head ached, too. The air reverberated with the high-pitched wailing of guitars and the frenetic, metallic clanging of synthesizers underscored by the deafening rumble of drums. A plane flew overhead, but its drone was barely audible over the electric noise blaring through the loudspeakers.

Jessie followed the blinking red taillights of the airplane as it inched across the sky toward the rear of the theater. And then she saw something white catch the light. Something in the last row in section D, near the outer aisle, a row almost empty except for someone leaning—was it menacingly?—leaning over the person next to him, a flash of white in his hand. Was it—?

Even before she finished formulating the thought, she was moving, her legs propelling her forward with desperate strides, her hand readied on her gun. Now she was almost there, only two rows away, and the man had moved away revealing a woman, a woman falling forward. And just as Jessie was about to draw her gun, the woman sat up.

Jessie came to an abrupt halt several feet from the bench.

The man looked up, frightened. "What are you—?"

She flashed her badge. "Are you all right?" she asked the woman, knowing she was. She felt ridiculous. "You looked like you were falling," she said lamely.

The woman looked bewildered. "Falling?" Then, "Oh,

something got in my eye, and Barry tried to get it out with a tissue."

With muttered apologies, Jessie returned to her station. Her radio burst into static. "Yes?" Her whisper was a bark.

"Takamura here. I spotted you running. What was that?"

"Nothing. False alarm."

Standing there for the next thirty minutes, Jessie decided they were wasting their time. Then, suddenly, she knew with a sickening certainty that they were too late, that the killer, sitting somewhere in the dark—because he hadn't left; she was positive of that—the killer was exercising his control by having them run like rats in a maze, was exulting in their panic and their attempts to prevent what had already been done.

She knew all this even before she saw a uniformed officer run over to Takamura, saw him gesturing, in urgent pantomime, in the direction of the exit, knew it before the radio crackled and hissed the news that a body had been found in a rest room.

"The rest is silence."

The music stopped.

He made his way with a wave of people out of section C and walked toward one of the exits. A long, widening queue had already formed, and more people were hurrying toward it. He allowed several people to move ahead of him, then joined the line.

There were so many police! He'd expected a decent number, of course, but now the place was swarming with them, some in uniform, others in plainclothes, their identities revealed by the radios pressed against their ears. He was strangely excited to see how many police had been brought here tonight, solely because of him. The feeling of power that coursed through him was unlike anything he'd ever experienced.

The line was moving slowly down the incline. He could see that the police had blocked the wide exits, forcing people to exit singly past one of six uniformed men. The crowd was complaining.

"What's the holdup?"

"Why all the cops?"

"What's with the barricades?"

He knew the reason. Someone had found the man. Now all the concertgoers were being checked, one by one, against the composite sketch the police artist had drawn of him. He'd expected no less. He reminded himself that he had nothing to worry about, that he had everything under control, but a tremor of anxiety ran through his body, and he had an urge to push his way through the crowd, to pass through to safety.

There were so many ahead of him! He tried maneuvering around one man. "Hey, bud, wait your—!" Then, "Oh, sorry, go ahead." He maneuvered around countless others, pushing, squeezing, elbowing, until there were only four ahead of him. Then three. Then two.

He was caught by the reflection of the flashlight.

"Just a minute, please," the uniformed officer said.

His heart thumped so loudly that he was sure everyone around him could hear it. How could—?

But the officer wasn't talking to him; he was talking to the man in front of him. ". . . if you could step aside, please."

"What's wrong?" The man sounded annoyed and frightened.

"If you'll step aside, please," the officer repeated. He motioned to another uniformed policeman, who talked to the man, quietly steering him away from the exits and the staring people.

His turn. Now they were face-to-face. He nodded casually to the officer, who looked at him, puzzled.

"How's it going?" he asked the officer.

"Nothing yet. Look's like it's going to be a long night. But why are you in line? Why didn't you just go around?"

A mistake! A stupid mistake! He stopped breathing. He thought he was going to faint. "Trying to . . ." He cleared his throat. "Sorry. A tickle." He coughed. "I was told to maintain an orderly line. People are panicking." He was amazed that any sound had come out of his throat. He'd been certain that his vocal chords, like the rest of him, had been paralyzed with fear.

"Figures. You leaving already?"

"Have to check the parking lot. Just in case he slipped through." He could feel his bronchial passages closing, knew he would start wheezing any second.

"Good idea." The officer let him pass. "Happy hunting."

He was out. He walked with measured steps past the barricades and headed for the parking lot. He felt an almost irresistible temptation to look back, but he knew that would be a mistake, that something terrible would happen. Maybe he'd be turned into a pillar of salt, just like Lot's wife in the Bible.

He walked, eyes resolutely ahead, his uniform blending into the navy-blue night, and disappeared between two rows of cars.

35

"How the hell did he get past us?" Takamura fumed.

It was something basic, Jessie thought, something that would impress and depress them with its simplicity and obviousness. She scanned the parking lot—empty now except for their own cars and police vehicles and the '82 Dodge belonging to the twenty-year-old victim, Joseph Bidwell. Was the killer watching? Gloating?

"He left before we got here," Pruitt said. "The body was found at nine-eighteen. The M.E. thinks Bidwell was dead at least an hour. Which means he was killed close to the start of the program. People go to the bathroom before the show so they won't miss anything. The killer waits in the bathroom. When there's one guy left, he attacks. Then he leaves."

Jessie shook her head. "He stayed. I just know it."

"He sent you a ticket, so he had to figure the place would be full of cops. He'd be crazy to stick around."

From the time she'd made the phone call from the restaurant, his attitude had been strictly professional. Which was only right. "It's part of the game," she said. "Watching us gives him a high. It's like Manny said—the guy has a need for power, control. And he must've been pretty sure he'd get past the police."

"How?" Barrows asked. "He knew we'd be looking for him, that we'd have a sketch. Two sketches." Carley Caffrey had helped a police artist draw a sketch of "Jim Miller."

"Maybe he was disguised," Takamura said.

"With what?" Pruitt said. "The toupee and glasses?"

"Maybe he was dressed like a woman," Barrows said. "A nun, maybe. A habit would be a good disguise."

"I didn't seen any nuns," Takamura said. "Did you guys?"

"No nuns, nobody in drag," Pruitt said. "Just your run-of-the-mill concertgoer. And lots of cops."

Simple and obvious. Jessie said, "He was dressed like a cop."

There was a moment of electrified silence.

Takamura nodded slowly. "Or he *is* a cop."

A half-hour later, they had confirmation of sorts. One of the patrol officers who had monitored the exiting crowd remembered seeing a uniformed officer walking with the crowd and asking him why he'd been waiting in line.

"He said something about having to keep the line in order. It made sense to me." The officer looked tense.

"What did he look like?" Takamura asked.

"He looked like a cop." A hint of defensiveness had crept into the man's voice.

"Was he short?" Takamura said impatiently. "Dark? Blond? Can you tell us anything about him?"

"I didn't notice much. He was pretty short, I guess. I couldn't see his hair, because he was wearing his cap."

"You didn't find that odd?" Takamura asked. Except for formal inspections or special occasions, most LAPD don't wear caps. Takamura didn't wait for an answer. "Motorcycle or patrol?"

The officer thought for a moment. "Patrol. He was wearing a nylon jacket, not leather. I remember that."

"A jacket on a hot night like tonight?" Takamura stared at the jacketless officer, who was in navy-blue slacks and shirt.

"Did the uniform look right?" Jessie was surprised by Takamura's sarcasm; it made her uncomfortable.

"I didn't notice anything wrong. He had his badge over his left pocket. I'm sure I would've noticed if he hadn't."

"Are you?" Takamura asked.

"Yes. Look, I made a mistake, but it was an honest one. He looked like a cop—there was no reason for me to think he wasn't. Are you saying you would've known he was an imposter? Sir?"

The "sir" was clearly an afterthought, an attempt to soften the challenge voiced in the question. Takamura didn't answer.

In the morning, going on the assumption that the killer had masqueraded as a policeman, they called costume-rental companies.

"How about a pirate?" one man suggested to Jessie. "Or Batman. We got a few of those in great condition."

"No, thank you."

"Darth Vader? A gorilla?"

At another place, she talked with a woman who barely spoke English. "You like to be Kaiston?" the woman asked.

"I'm sorry, I don't understand."

"You know, with moustache and big stick? Kaiston."

Keystone Cops. "No, thank you." Not today.

Most of the larger companies said they didn't rent police uniforms to private individuals.

"We rent only to theatrical productions, TV studios, film companies," a woman told Jessie. "We're not allowed to do it."

They didn't do it, Jessie knew, because they didn't want to risk liability for helping someone to impersonate an officer. Which violated sections 146A and 538D of the Penal Code. But some companies weren't that concerned. Jessie came across two, both on Hollywood Boulevard: Costumes to Go and Masquerade.

The woman at Costumes to Go seemed bored. "Yeah, we have a couple of police uniforms. Your best bet is to come down here and take a look. I have another call, OK?" And she hung up.

The man at Masquerade was more talkative.

"What kind of cop?" he asked after Jessie had told him it was for someone's birthday party. "L.A.? New York? Modern? Period?"

"Modern, L.A." Not Kaiston.

"Jeez, not 'Zsa Zsa and the Cop' again? For a while that's all people wanted. Bo-o-o-r-r-r-ing."

"Not 'Zsa Zsa.' So can you help me? I need a thirty-eight short." A rough guess, based on Carley Caffrey's information.

"Short is harder. Maybe we got one or two. Shoes, I dunno. I'll check stock for your size." He was gone for a minute. "You're in luck. I got one in your size. If you come in, ask for Murray."

An hour later, the detectives compared notes. Barrows had located three places in North Hollywood. Takamura was going to Venice and from there to Westwood. Jessie was going to two stores on Hollywood, one on Normandie, the other near Cahuenga.

Pruitt said, "Mine are on Hollywood, too. Western, Vine, and Highland. We may as well go together. I'll drive."

Fate or coincidence? In the car, Pruitt was friendly but still very much the cop, and Jessie wondered whether she'd imagined the other evening.

They stopped first at Costumes to Go on Normandie, then at Show Time on Western. Within five minutes of arriving at each place, Jessie was convinced that the killer hadn't rented the police uniform there. *If in fact he rented a uniform.*

Masquerade was next. The walls were covered with colorful posters of theatrical productions and eight-by-ten glossies of a few famous and more not-so-famous stars, all apparently costumed by Masquerade, all signed with variations of "To Murray, with love."

Murray Pelkowitz, the heavyset owner of the company and of the voice Jessie had talked to on the phone, was immediately on guard. "Cops, right?" He swiveled his seemingly neckless, owllike head from one to the other.

"Right," Jessie said. "We're trying to locate someone who rented a police uniform a day or so ago."

"Say, you're the person who called! So what was that crap about renting a uniform, huh?" Under the twin canopies of thick, bushy brows, his liquid brown eyes stared balefully at her.

"Mr. Pelkowitz, did you rent a police uniform to an individual?" Jessie repeated.

"No, I didn't. Why?"

"We're asking the questions," Pruitt said mildly.

"Well, pardon me!" He looked at Jessie. "You know, I got everything ready—the jacket, the pants, the cap. Everything."

"Can we see your rental account books?" she asked.

"What, you don't believe me? You wanna see books, here's books." He reached underneath the counter and slammed a spiral notebook in front of Jessie. "Check. You'll see that Murray Pelkowitz don't lie."

Jessie flipped through the notebook until she came to the week of August 17. Pelkowitz had neatly entered each costume with a description, rental fee, deposit fee, and estimated date of return. The entries included hula dancers, Puritans (*in August?*), a Cossack, a priest, a clown, and a devil. No cop.

It was possible, Jessie and Pruitt decided on the way to their next stop, that Pelkowitz hadn't entered "policeman" because he knew he was bending the law. Possible, but unlikely. Pelkowitz hadn't given any indication of nervousness.

Three down, two to go.

Custom Costumes inhabited a small, dilapidated, second-floor office with more dust than decor. There were a few mannequins wearing costumes, one of Uncle Sam, another of a Carmen-like Gypsy. The costumes were worn and shabby. Uncle Sam was leering at Carmen, who looked like she'd sung one aria too many.

The not-so-young woman behind the counter, whose shoulder-length hair was red with green accents, was applying a bright purple polish to her nails when the detectives walked in. Her nasal "Yeah?" said she was annoyed by the interruption.

"I'd like to speak to the owner, please," Pruitt said.

"He's filling an order. What kinda costume didya wanna rent?" She raised the hand she'd been working on, admired her handiwork, then waved her fingers to dry them.

"I'm trying to locate someone who rented a police uniform."

She hesitated a fraction of a second. "We don't rent police uniforms to private parties. Just to movie studios, places like that." She studied her hand again, blew on the fingers.

Pruitt leaned forward. "What's your name, miss?"

"Glenda Gibbins. And it's *Mrs.*"

"Well, *Mrs.* Gibbins, I spoke to you an hour ago, and you told me you *did* rent police uniforms. To private parties."

"Unh-unh. You didn't speak to me. Maybe you called another place. Some of these names sound alike."

"Unh-unh," he mimicked. "I called Custom Costumes, and I spoke to you. I never forget a place. Or a voice." He took out his ID. "I'd like to see your rental books, please."

"You got a subpoena?"

"You watch too much television, Mrs. Gibbins. The books?"

Jessie restrained a smile.

"Stan!" Glenda turned around and stepped into a hall toward the back. "Stan, get over here! Now!"

Pruitt picked up a business card from a metal holder on the counter and slipped it into his pocket.

A short, harried-looking man in his forties appeared in the doorway. "What is it now?" He glared at the woman, then noticed Jessie and Pruitt. He smiled. "Can I help you? I'm Stan Gibbins."

"They're cops," Glenda Gibbins told her husband. "They wanna know did we rent a police uniform to someone. I told them we don't do that. They wanna see the rental books."

Stan looked at Pruitt thoughtfully. "There's a problem?"

"We know you rented a police uniform within the last day or so. We'd like some information on the guy who rented it."

"What makes you think I rented it?"

"Stan! Don't say nothing!"

"Shut up!" He turned to Pruitt. "I'm just curious as to why you'd think that, is all."

"We found your business card in the uniform."

Gibbins thought that over. "So am I in trouble, or what?"

"Stan, they don't know nothing!"

Pruitt ignored her. "Possibly. But that's not what we're here for. What can you tell us about the man?"

Gibbins sighed. "I knew I shouldn't have done it."

"Christ!" Glenda Gibbins moaned.

"What did he do, rob a bank?" Gibbins asked.

Neither detective answered.

"All right. He was here Wednesday, a real average guy. Said he needed a police uniform for a costume party. I believed him."

"What was his name?" Pruitt asked.

"I'd have to check." He looked through a ledger until he found what he wanted. "Miller. Jim Miller."

All right! Jessie thought. She and Pruitt exchanged looks.

Pruitt said,"He had to leave a deposit. How did he pay?"

"Cash. Two hundred bucks. I remember I told him he could use a credit card, but he said no, cash was fine. The deposit covers the cost of the uniform."

So there was no need for him to show an ID. "What did he rent?" Jessie asked.

"The works. Pants, jacket, shirt, cap, holster. Shoes, too. It was hard fitting him, on account of he's so short. No badge. He didn't need it." He hesitated. "So do I get the uniform back?"

"Frankly, a lost uniform is the least of your problems," Pruitt said.

Gibbins paled. "Are you going to arrest me?"

"That's up to the D.A. He'll decide your liability."

Gibbins, Jessie knew, could be guilty of a misdemeanor and could face up to six months in county jail and/or a fine of a thousand dollars or more. Not to mention civil liability.

Gibbins licked his lips. "What . . . uh . . . what did he do?"

Pruitt looked at him. "Murder."

"Oh, Jesus!" Gibbins whispered. He closed his eyes.

"You shouldda kept your mouth shut!" Glenda snarled. "They conned you into talking, you stupid shit!" She faced the detectives. "There was no damn card, was there?"

Gibbins looked at the two detectives.

"Sure there was." Pruitt took the card from his pocket and showed it to Gibbins. "See?"

He'd used his father's badge. It was the real badge, the one his father had reported lost a few months before he'd left the force. It was as though his father had sensed that for him there would be no replacement badge fixed in a brass mounting in a shadow box that housed his gun. The gun, of course, would have been incapacitated. Like his father.

His father hadn't left the force, though that's what he'd told everyone. He'd been fired. One night when he'd been drunk, the truth had come belching out, a maudlin story filled with self-pity and recriminations. They said did I want to resign in lieu of, close my record, and I told them hell, no! I'll take it to the Board of Rights, you won't get away with this. And they fired me! After twenty-one years, they fired me! Can you imagine, boy! Those goddamn sons of bitches fired me for no goddamn reason.

"No goddamn reason," he'd found out looking through his father's papers after his death, was "significant and repeated incidents of excessive force in dealing with suspects and apprehended criminals despite repeated warnings." That was after the commission, after the nationally televised videotape of police brutality that had incited a riot and cries for police reform.

The amazing thing was that his father had still been entitled to his pension. By itself, not much to live on. But there had also been monthly payments, since Ed, Jr., had been killed in the line of duty. The mortgage on the house was small, his father's needs simple. He'd lived on a diet of frozen dinners and beer and memories doctored to feed his delusions.

And now the pension was his. And the Social Security. His mother's, really, but that was quibbling. And in addition to the lump sum his father had received when he'd left the force, a reimbursement for the monies he'd contributed toward life insurance, he'd owned a substantial private insurance policy, too. Dying, in fact, had proved to be the one generous thing he'd done in a life filled with obtuse self-centeredness.

He'd enjoyed wearing the badge. He'd wanted to use his father's uniform—that would have been the perfect irony, using his uniform in the commission of a crime. "Excessive force." But as soon as he tried it on, he saw he'd have to rent one.

Of course, he'd known that his father's uniform was too big. He'd tried it on one Sunday afternoon when his father had gone bowling. But when he looked in the full-length mirror on his parents' closet door, he'd disappeared, his arms and legs and neck swallowed by the dark fabric, gone. He could imagine his father's laughter rolling toward him in waves of contempt and pity.

That had been before his father had died. Then he'd started playing *the game,* and with each success he'd felt larger, taller, more powerful. So it had been a shock to see that the uniform still didn't fit, that the sleeves and pant legs, dangling limply beyond his invisible limbs, were still too long. He didn't know why he'd assumed that it would fit, because of course he hadn't grown. Thirty-five-year-old men don't grow.

He'd have to forfeit the two-hundred-dollar deposit for the rented uniform. He couldn't return it. By now Jessie Drake had probably figured out that he'd been dressed like a cop. Maybe at this very moment she was tracing him to the company that had rented him the uniform. If he wasn't careful, she could ruin everything.

He really hated her.

Pruitt dropped Jessie off in front of Parker Center and drove off to park in the lot on San Pedro. As she entered the building, she was so preoccupied with Jim Miller and the police uniform that she almost collided with a mailman who was leaving.

Takamura was back. He was on the phone, his back to Jessie.

"Listen, John, Frank and I—"

"Jessie!" Takamura turned to face her. "You just missed his call!"

"Who?" She saw Takamura's expression. "The killer?"

Takamura nodded excitedly. "We have an open line! He must not have replaced the receiver completely. I've done it myself. The phone company is tracing the call right now." He grinned.

"What did he say? The killer, I mean."

"At first he insisted on talking to you. I told him you were out. He left you a message. He—just a minute, Jessie." Takamura listened to whoever was on the phone. "Right. OK." He turned to Jessie. "So far they've determined that the call originated from a pay phone. Not as good as a residential phone, but it's a start."

"So what was the message."

"What? Oh. He said, 'Tell Jessie I have a monopoly.' "

Mediterranean and Baltic. No doubt the *Times* would have that as its headline in Saturday's edition. Jessie had to admit it made terrific copy. "That's it?"

"He said he'll be in touch. He—yes?" Takamura said into the receiver. "What? Are you sure?" His face showed incredulity, then fury. "Goddammit!" He slammed down the receiver.

"They lost it?" Jessie shook her head.

"They didn't *lose* it. They traced the call to the pay phone right here, in Parker Center. He left the receiver dangling."

He had left them all dangling, Jessie thought. And not for the first time.

36

Teresa loved the earrings.

He'd given them to her as soon as they returned to her apartment. All during dinner he'd been half-listening to her conversation, the other part trying to picture the expression on her face when she opened the box. He'd found an empty jewelry box for the opals among his mother's nightgowns, and he'd placed it in a small white gift box he'd bought. Some glossy red wrapping paper had caught his eye, and he'd been about to buy it when he remembered the old Chinese woman on Bunker Hill Avenue. He decided not to buy the paper.

He showed his mother the opals when he visited her Saturday afternoon. Better today, the nurse told him. She slept right through the night and ate most of her breakfast. We've been having the nicest conversation, and we just had a nice bath, too, didn't we, Ella? He was glad he'd remembered to bring a box of Tobler's chocolates for the nurse, oh, how thoughtful, she said, but he had the feeling she would have preferred a tip.

These are for Teresa, he told his mother, she's a friend, you'd like her. He leaned closer and brought the iridescent stones close to his mother's face, and he thought he saw a flash of understanding behind the glassy membrane of her eyes. His mother blinked and moved her head the fraction of a nod. Pity, she said, and he was confused and angry, why would she say that? why did she have to ruin it? but then she said the word again, and he realized what she was trying to say. "Pretty."

He was sitting with Teresa on her living room sofa when he handed her the box. Open it, he said. It's just a little something. He watched her take out the black velvet box and open it, ohhh, Jimmy, she whispered, looking up, ohhh, they're exquisite. And then, but they're so expensive! I couldn't, just as he'd known she would. I want you to have them, he said, and the look in her eyes was worth far more than a hundred eighty-five dollars.

I'll try them on, she said. She removed the tiny pearl earrings and attached them to their backings before she placed them on the coffee table. And he saw that he'd been right about her ears, they were fine, the holes almost invisible. She removed one opal from the velvet card, and he watched, fascinated, as the tiny gold rod disappeared into her ear.

When she had both earrings on, she smiled at him and pushed her hair back from her face. How do they look? she asked, the tiny dots of rose and aqua on the milky-white background of the opalescent stones changing as she turned her head first this way, then that. Perfect, he murmured, I knew they would. She moved closer to him, so close that the nearness of her made him tremble with longing. Thank you, Jimmy, she said, and then her bare arms were around his neck and she drew his face to hers until their lips met. These are the most beautiful earrings I've ever had, she whispered, and she kissed him again. And then she stood up. Well, she said, and laughed shyly, and he stood up uncertainly. I had a great time, he said, I'll call you soon, all right? And she gave him her hand. Stay, she said.

They undressed silently in her bedroom, and he was acutely grateful for the darkness; it had been such a long time, and in spite of everything that was happening, he felt so . . . He folded his clothes and placed them on the floor. Then he turned around. The slivers of light that stole through the spaces between the slats of the window blinds diffused the shadows, and he could make out the outline of her alabaster body, the long column of her neck, her breasts, her softly rounded hips, slender legs. For a moment he thought he could see the opals twinkling.

Or maybe it was hope.

They moved slowly together, finding each other under the comforter on the double bed, skin on skin, touching, caressing, yes, she said, oh yes, and he had never felt like this before, never, Teresa, he whispered, Teresa, oh God, and he knew that any minute he would be soaring, soaring, that he would get there this time, it would be different, there was nothing to stop him, no one, if he could just . . .

If he could just . . .

I'm sorry, he groaned, turning away, choking back a sob, so sorry, curling into a ball, wishing he could disappear into the black hole of his shame, sorry, this has never happened before ("*not much of a man, are you?*"), never. Shhh, she said, it's all right; she stroked his cheek, traced the outline of his chin. Really it is. It isn't important, is it? Because we have next time, and the time after that. She moved closer, pressed her body against his. We have all the time in the world.

And he wanted to believe her, wanted to more than anything else in the world. But he couldn't turn around now, couldn't face her, because his eyes were wet with tears for his failed manhood and his shriveled expectations, he'd been so sure this time! and he wondered whether he would ever be free of the specter that always hovered over him.

When he was sure that Teresa was asleep, he moved carefully off the bed and dressed in the dark. She was lying on her side, and before he left, he leaned over and brushed his lips lightly against hers. She stirred a little, murmured something, and rolled onto her back. He could see the opals in her ears, but in the filtered light they looked dull and lifeless.

37

At 10:45 A.M. on Monday, Stan Gibbins called for Pruitt.

"Detective Pruitt is out in the field," Jessie told Gibbins. So was Barrows. Takamura was meeting with Corcoran, for a change. "Can I help?"

"It's about this guy who rented the uniform. He—"

"Jim Miller's there?" Jessie grabbed the edge of the table.

"No. Sorry. But I found something that may be his."

Disappointment cut through her. "What's that?" Probably nothing. The man was trying to ingratiate himself with the police, chalking up points against the day the D.A. called him in.

"A handkerchief. I found it this morning in the dressing room, under a bench. I don't know how long it's been there."

A clue? A real clue? "Why do you think it belongs to him?"

"Because of the initials embroidered on it. J.M. I mean, it could be just a coincidence, but then again . . ."

* * *

The handkerchief was stiffly new and had its original creases. It was a fine-quality cotton with a linen weave, Jessie noticed, and the edges were neatly rolled.

The label said "Cotton Club." She checked the yellow pages but found no listing for it. She called the California Clothing Mart, but there was no showroom for a manufacturer of that name.

"What type of garment are you trying to locate?" the receptionist at the Mart asked her.

"A handkerchief."

"You might try showrooms that deal with linens or men's apparel." She dictated fifteen phone numbers. "If you don't find what you want at one of these showrooms, stop by and pick up a directory that lists all the showrooms in the Mart."

Great, Jessie thought. That could take hours. In the end, though, she found what she was looking for on the seventh call. The salesman at World of Linen told her that yes, they were the West Coast distributors for Cotton Club linens and accessories.

"We sell to major department stores in Los Angeles and the surrounding communities. Nordstrom, Robinsons, Bullocks, Saks, I. Magnin. We also deal with specialty shops, like the Custom Shirt Shoppe. I can give you a list, if you like."

It was a long list, but Jessie was able to eliminate many of the places by phone. Most of the department stores, she learned, carried handkerchiefs that were plain cotton or embroidered with only one initial. The one Stan Gibbins had found had two initials. After an hour Jessie was left with four Los Angeles specialty shops and two Beverly Hills establishments that did monogram and embroidery work (a clerk at one of the stores had suggested that).

By the end of the day, she had five possibilities.

At The Cotton Bin on Larchmont, a young woman wearing a Gunny Sax dress and lace cap examined the handkerchief.

"It's not a distinctive item, but we do carry the brand," she told Jessie. "Give me a minute while I check in the back."

When she returned she handed Jessie an invoice dated July 23 for Julian Masony; he'd ordered six handkerchiefs monogrammed with his initials. No, she didn't remember what he looked like.

Jessie's next stop was It's a Man's World (how true!) in the Farmer's Market, a quaint mall in the Beverly-Fairfax area that attracts tourists with food, clothing, gift shops and outdoor cafés. The plump, chignoned, gray-haired owner remembered a young woman who had insisted on ordering monogrammed handkerchiefs.

"I told her that monogramming would cost more than the handkerchiefs. We carry a pre-initialed, fine cotton handkerchief, six for eleven fifty. But she wanted two initials." She looked at Jessie hesitantly. "She's not in trouble, is she? She seemed so nice."

"It's a routine investigation, ma'am. Can you look through your files for her name?"

Several minutes later the older woman returned. "I can't find the invoices for July and August. The bookkeeper may have taken them home with her."

"Can you call her?"

"I did. She's not home. But I'll keep trying. If you leave me your card, I'll call as soon as I know anything."

From the Farmer's Market, Jessie drove to the two monogramming establishments. At Initially Yours, on La Cienega, the Korean owner examined the handkerchief and told the detective the embroidery work hadn't been done at his shop.

"Try place on Beverly Drive. I no can remember name."

Jessie already had the name: A My Name Is Alice. It was her final stop. A half-hour later Jessie left the shop with the names of two customers who had ordered handkerchiefs embroidered with their own initials: Jerome Mattson and John Mercer. With Julian Masony, Jessie now had three people to investigate. And the owner of It's a Man's World was going to give her the name of another.

Back at Parker Center, Jessie told Takamura and Barrows what she'd learned. Pruitt wasn't there—out following a lead, Barrows told her. Oh, she said, hoping her disappointment didn't show.

It was early when she arrived home. Matthew's face lit up when he saw her; Helen looked pleased, too. They ate a quiet supper, then watched TV together in the den.

Matthew's arm was out of the sling; he seemed to be doing fine. Helen had gotten her California driver's license, a step in establishing residency. Margaret Lasky, her attorney, was preparing to start divorce proceedings. Helen, in fact, looked much calmer and more at peace with herself since she'd told Jessie about Neil. She hadn't had a migraine all week.

And all's well with the world, Jessie thought, as she tried to fall asleep in the large king-size bed.

Jessie was beginning to wonder whether the handkerchief would lead them anywhere.

Pruitt had eliminated John Mercer and Julian Masony. Mercer was a short, overweight man in his late fifties. He'd willingly shown the detective the handkerchiefs he'd ordered. Masony had been less willing, but he'd produced the six handkerchiefs. In any case, he didn't fit the profile of the killer. He was in his forties and tall, with thick black hair and a mustache.

Takamura had talked to Jerome Mattson. As soon as Mattson opened the door, the detective had known that his visit was pointless. Mattson was over six feet tall and black. Both Monica Podrell and Carley Caffrey had described a Caucasian.

Then on Tuesday afternoon, the owner of A Man for All Seasons called Jessie and told her she had the invoice.

"She ordered the handkerchiefs on Monday, August third, and picked them up on Friday, the seventh. Three handkerchiefs, a hundred percent cotton, two-fifty each. Two-initial monogramming per handkerchief, six twenty-five. Initials: *J* and *M*."

"What's the name on the invoice?"

"Teresa Barnett. Here are her address and phone number."

The Wooster Street address was in the Pico-Robertson area. Jessie drove there on her way home. Teresa Barnett lived in a two-level white stucco apartment building with a modified Spanish motif. Jessie walked up a long, metal-railed staircase to the second floor and found the apartment, number 8. She didn't see any lights on, but it was still light outside. She rang the bell, waited, then rang the bell and waited again. Nothing.

She dialed Teresa Barnett's number several times from home, letting the phone ring for a long time. By ten o'clock she decided she'd have to leave Teresa Barnett for tomorrow.

On Saturday night he'd realized the handkerchief was missing. He'd opened the drawer where he kept his belts, collar stays, loose change, and handkerchiefs. (Not the other handkerchiefs that he used for *the game*. He kept those in a separate drawer.) He took out one of the handkerchiefs Teresa had given him—he wanted to show her he was using her gift—then noticed that there was only one left, not two.

He tried to remember the last time he'd seen it, knew for a certainty he'd put it in the pocket of his navy jacket before their date on the Saturday night before last. He thought he'd removed it after he'd come home. Maybe he hadn't. It wasn't like him to be careless, but he'd had so much on his mind.

He checked the jacket. There was nothing in any of the pockets. Then he saw the pink receipt from A-1 Cleaners and remembered that on Wednesday he'd given in the jacket to be cleaned. Had they found the handkerchief and removed it before cleaning the jacket? But then, why hadn't they pinned it to the jacket? Or called him? His phone number was on the ticket.

Maybe one of the workers had kept it for himself. It was a beautiful handkerchief, 100 percent cotton, custom monogrammed. That didn't make sense, though, because how likely was it that one of the employees would have the initials *J.M.?* Maybe someone had kept it, even though the initials were different. That's probably what happened, he decided. He was suddenly angry, very angry. The bastard! It was a terrible world where you couldn't give in your jacket to be cleaned without having something stolen from you.

He decided not to say anything to Teresa about the handkerchief. He didn't want her to think that he'd been careless, that he didn't value her gift.

Wednesday afternoon Jessie climbed the staircase and walked to Teresa Barnett's door. Again, there were no lights. She rang the bell anyway. This time she heard footsteps.

"Yes?" the woman said.

"Miss Teresa Barnett?"

"I'm Teresa Barnett. Who are you?"

"Det. Jessie Drake, LAPD. I'd like to ask you a few questions."

She hesitated. "Can I see your identification, please?"

Jessie held out her ID to the privacy window and waited while Teresa scrutinized her face. Then Teresa opened the door.

She was attractive in a quiet way, Jessie thought. Medium-length brown hair, large, expressive brown eyes. Pretty, flawless skin with only a little makeup. She was shapely, too, in a blue cotton skirt and matching cotton knit sweater.

Teresa led her into an L-shaped combination living room–dining room. There were two suitcases on the floor. "I just got back from visiting my parents in San Diego. Please sit down." She sat on one end of a small sofa. "Can I ask what this is about?"

Jessie sat and showed her the handkerchief. "You bought one like this recently in the Farmer's Market. We'd like to know who it was for."

"Is something wrong?"

Teresa looked puzzled and a little nervous, Jessie thought. Not unusual for someone being questioned by a detective. "We're doing a routine investigation, and this handkerchief may or may not be significant in helping us find a witness. Right now we're trying to eliminate as many names as we can from the list of people we have to interview."

"It's just routine, you say?"

"Yes. And don't worry. This will be strictly confidential. So can you tell me who the handkerchiefs were for?"

"I'm afraid it won't help you. I bought them for my uncle Jonathan. Jonathan Merrick. He lives in Canada, and the last time he was in L.A. was ten years ago. He couldn't be your witness."

"I guess not." Jessie smiled and stood up. "Well, thank you for your time, Miss Barnett."

"That's all right." She escorted Jessie to the door.

Teresa had been more than a little nervous when the detective had been questioning her, but she was confident that she believed her. She didn't feel right about having lied, but she knew she'd done the right thing. After all, it wasn't anything serious—"just routine," the detective had said; they were looking for a witness. It was someone else's handkerchief anyway; she was sure of that. In any case, she hadn't wanted to involve Jim. She would mention the detective's visit. If Jim wanted to call her, he would.

She picked up the phone, punched the first three digits, hesitated, then replaced the receiver. She would be seeing him Saturday night. She would tell him about the handkerchief then.

Screw the handkerchief, Jessie decided late Thursday night.

They'd ruled out the three men and Teresa Barnett. They'd checked out names from A My Name Is Alice and shops in the suburbs of Los Angeles and spent hours tracking down all the people who had purchased or received them. And come up with nothing. The son of a bitch probably got the damn thing as a Christmas gift from some aunt in Topeka.

Jessie looked around the room. Takamura was pacing up and down, checking his watch. Pruitt was leaning back in a chair, flying paper airplanes. Barrows was staring at the phone.

She'd waited with taut expectancy all day, dreading the message that would reveal the killer's next move and propel them into meaningless action that would reinforce their helplessness. For the fist time, she understood the torture Sisyphus had endured, perpetually having to roll the damn rock up the damn hill just to have it come rolling down, every damn time.

But this time there had been no message. No phone call. No letter. No card. No ticket. Nothing. To know or not to know. . . . She couldn't decide which was worse.

"He isn't going to contact us." She picked up her purse. "I'm going home. See you tomorrow," she said and left.

She was waiting for the elevator when she heard him

come up behind her. She knew without turning that it was Pruitt.

Dinner first, then a movie—"To take our minds off the goddamn case," he said and smiled wearily. He followed her home so that they wouldn't have two cars. He waited while she parked the Honda in the driveway.

"I'll be right out," Jessie told him.

She went inside to say hello to Helen and Matthew and told her sister she was going. "Don't wait up."

"Oh, God!" Helen put her hand to her mouth. "Who did he kill this time? I didn't hear anything on the news!"

Not a murder, Jessie told her.

"A date?" Helen's eyebrows formed comic arcs.

She sounds so much like our mother—like anybody's mother, Jessie thought, and almost laughed.

They went to a deli in the neighborhood, then to the Avco near Westwood. The theater was half-empty. They sat on the right, toward the back. His arm was around her shoulder, his hands beneath her hair, lightly massaging the back of her neck.

"You're so tense," he said. "Relax."

They watched the trailers; then the feature started. It was a romantic comedy, and she tried to concentrate, but she was too aware of him. At the deli, their conversation had been light, but there had been something in his dark-brown eyes even then.

She thought she was prepared, but when he leaned over, she shivered with anticipation and felt a tightening in her groin. He bit her lower lip gently, then kissed her. And she was back on the dance floor, in his arms, the heat coursing through her, feeling like an adolescent, loving it.

"Let's go," he said.

His voice was husky with desire, and she was suddenly nervous, because it had been so long since she'd been with anyone, there had been no one after Gary, and she thought, God, this is crazy, getting involved with a colleague, *crazy*, but there was no place else she wanted to be, no one she wanted to be with more. They drove in silence, and she wondered if the music emanating from the radio camouflaged the hammering of her heart.

Aside from a new-looking gray leather sofa, a black cabinet with a CD player, and two speakers, the living room was bare. He didn't do much better in his divorce settlement than I did, she thought. Or maybe he got rid of everything that held memories.

Pruitt took off his jacket and put it on the sofa, then walked over to the cabinet, selected a cartridge, and slipped it into the player. The music started. Roberta Flack. "The First Time."

"Dance with me," he said, and drew her to him.

Her arms circled his neck; his hands were on her hips.

"You're so beautiful," he said, looking into her eyes. He bent and kissed the hollow of her neck, then kissed her lips. His mouth was on hers as they danced to the music, moving slowly against each other for what seemed to her like a long time, and she was feeling warm, so incredibly warm, and then he was unbuttoning her blouse and slipping it off, his fingers hot against her skin.

"Jessie," he whispered, "Jessie," and she pressed herself against him.

The music was still playing when he took her to the bedroom.

"Where do you think he is now?" Jessie asked a long time later.

Pruitt put his fingers on her lips. "Sweetheart, I made it a rule after Rona left me. No business in the bedroom."

Who else has been in this bedroom? Jessie wondered. Like the living room, it was mostly unfurnished—a large bed without a headboard, a chest of drawers on top of which was a photo of two young boys, probably his sons. One looked Matthew's age.

"Good rule." She should have followed it with Gary. "Can I ask you something, though? Why did you become a cop?" She ran her hands through the gray-black hairs on his chest.

"To fight for truth, justice, and the American way." He smiled.

"No, really."

"Really. I was an idealistic kid. I thought the good guys should win more often. I thought I could make a difference."

"Do you?"

"Sometimes. Not often enough. What about you?"

"It's complicated."

He propped himself on one elbow and looked at her. "I'm listening." He stroked her arm.

She was silent a moment, then said, "At first, I guess I was rebelling against my parents. My dad's a very successful doctor. My mom—well, she's busy being a rich doctor's wife. It was the last thing they wanted me to do."

"I'll bet." He smiled. "That's it, rebellion?"

She could say yes; he would never know otherwise. But suddenly, it was important that she tell him what she had been unable to tell others. "No, that's just part of it." She looked up at the ceiling; it was easier than facing him. "My mother used to . . . hit me. She'd go into these rages over nothing. If I didn't make my bed exactly right. If I scuffed my shoes, or dirtied a dress. Or looked at her wrong. She was always imagining insults."

Pruitt said softly, "Your dad didn't help you?"

"He didn't want to see what was going on. He just wanted peace." *Try not to get your mother upset, Jessie. Can't you cooperate, Jessie? Please, Jessie, don't make things worse.*

"What about your sister? Did your mom abuse her too?"

Jessie nodded. "But I was my mom's favorite target. She's petite, like Helen, and I think it really bothered her that I was so much taller, as if I'd grown on purpose to show her up. And I wouldn't cry. That made her crazy. I tried to protect Helen, but I left home when I was eighteen. I just had to." She paused. "Helen married young—to escape, I think. Now she's getting divorced." Jessie sighed. "And her husband's been abusing their son." She told Pruitt about Matthew's fall, the X rays.

Pruitt was silent. Then he said, "What about you?"

"I went to a therapist and worked things through—the anger, the guilt. Later, he helped me see that in part, maybe I wanted to be a cop because by bringing order to the world around me, I'm trying to be more in control of my own life." She shrugged.

"Has it worked?"

"Not lately." She tried a smile. "The killer's still on the loose. Helen is terrified that Neil is going to show up any day. But I don't feel intimidated by my mother anymore. Actually, I don't feel anything toward her, which is sad, but there's nothing I can do about it. We keep our distance."

There had been another phone call the other day. *"Why are you keeping Helen and Matthew from staying with us? Do you want them both to be killed by that crazy Monopoly killer?"*

"And your father?" Pruitt asked.

"Still trying to keep the peace. Sometimes I feel sorry for him, but I'm still angry at him for abandoning us. Anyway, that's why I joined the LAPD," she said softly.

There was another reason, lurking in the corner of her mind, one she wasn't ready to verbalize to anyone. Even to herself.

38

Teresa kissed him as soon as he stepped into the living room, and that was before he handed her the wine and flowers. (The salesman had recommended the fragrance-free cymbidium orchids, white roses, and phlox.) She was wearing the opals, so he knew that everything was all right, in spite of last time. . . .

Oh, you shouldn't have, she said. She ran into the kitchen, and when she returned, the flowers were in a tall, cylindrical glass vase, their stems fixed in place by a bed of clear marbles. She placed the vase on the table. Perfect, she said. That's just what this needed.

She had set the round table in the dining alcove with a white linen cloth. Everything looks beautiful, he told her. The china is so pretty, he said, admiring aloud its octagonal design and sparkling, unblemished newness. Mikasa, she said. Silk Flowers.

He still used his mother's blue-and-white stoneware with the windmill design. Toward the end, when Ed, Jr., had been alive, there were only three cups left. His mother had used the mug he'd given her, the one that said "World's Best Mom." The mug was on her nightstand in the nursing home with some other things: her favorite throw pillow, her Bible, some *McCall's* and *Good Housekeeping* magazines, an afghan, and a blue tissue-box cover she'd crocheted. He'd hoped having familiar objects around her would make her feel less lonely, less frightened. But she rarely noticed anything.

Today she'd seemed more alert, and he thought the right side of her mouth had turned up in a lopsided attempt at a smile when she saw him. Hi, Mama, it's good to see you looking so well. He told her Teresa was cooking dinner for him. Next week I'll tell you all about it. When coming? she mouthed. Next week, he repeated. She shook her head. when coming? Again he told her, next week, I'll come next week. And she said, no, when Ed coming? And he wanted to take her by her frail, bony shoulders and shake the truth into her. Ed isn't coming, he's never coming, the old fart is dead! Instead, he said, Ed is coming soon. I have to go, he said; you're still the world's best mom, you know, and he held up the mug to show her. Maybe she smiled again. He wasn't sure.

The salad was first. He was grateful Teresa hadn't put dressing on it. Some made him break out in hives. Scallions did too; he picked those aside and hoped she didn't notice the green mound growing like moss on his plate. The main course was next, glazed Cornish hens with candied baby carrots and asparagus. A little wine would be nice, she said, and waited while he uncorked the bottle. He didn't have much experience with corks, and he worried about it *("Jesus, can't you get anything right, you stupid oaf!"),* about having little pieces of cork drop into the wine like flotsam, but the cork came out easily with a pop.

He filled her glass, then started filling his. I forgot to tell you, she said. A detective was here; she showed me a handkerchief and— oh! Teresa exclaimed softly. And then, Don't worry. The glass isn't broken, and the wine will come out. I'll get club soda right now so it won't set. He stared stupidly at the red stain spreading across the cloth, seeping into the white, and he felt nauseated, he hated the sight of blood, but this was wine, not blood. The stain would come out; she'd said so. Although the lipstick hadn't come out of the handkerchief.

She couldn't have meant *his* handkerchief, someone at the dry cleaners had it; he knew that for a certainty. But he'd heard the word *handkerchief*, and he'd been startled, and his hand had responded with an automatic jerk and knocked over the half-filled glass. That was a product of the axons and neurons in his nervous system; it had nothing to do with fear.

Teresa returned with a damp cloth and soaked the stain, which had taken on the shape of an amputated hand with gnarled, hairy fingers, all pointing at him. There, she said, it's fine. I don't want you to worry about this, all right? Promise you're not upset. I'm not upset, he said, and he wasn't, not about the stain or the hand, because it didn't mean anything.

She picked up her knife and fork and started cutting the hen. He did the same. It was the strangest thing, she said. The detective said they're looking for someone with a handkerchief just like the one she showed me. A witness to something; she didn't explain. Anyway, she said they knew I'd bought some handkerchiefs and had them monogrammed. Isn't that fascinating? She speared a carrot and lifted it delicately to her mouth.

He thought he would faint. Fascinating, he said when he was certain his voice wouldn't betray him. He bent his head and busied himself with cutting the hen into neat, fleshy cubes. He kept his eyes on his plate, cutting, cutting, until he'd removed all the meat and exposed the skeleton.

Anyway, Teresa said, she asked me who I gave the handkerchiefs to. What did you tell her? he asked, amazed at the calmness of his voice, amazed altogether that he was talking, because there was so little air in his chest, so little, and he was finding it increasingly difficult to breathe, he *couldn't* breathe, he was going to die right here because he couldn't, couldn't get any air into his lungs, and his head would fall into his plate of Silk Flowers and lie next to the blood—no, it was wine! He was wheezing now and his eyes were wild with terror and Teresa was saying, what's wrong? and he gestured frantically to the jacket on the sofa. Pocket, he squeaked, and she ran and found the inhalator and he felt the air returning to his lungs and the bands around his chest loosening, and then, and then, he knew he wasn't going to die after all.

I'm all right, he told her when his breathing was normal. It's asthma, isn't it? she said. My cousin has it. Yes, he said, usually it's under control. Maybe it was the wine, she said. Maybe, he agreed, relieved to see that there was sympathy and not distaste in her eyes, because after all, how could he have blamed her?—first one physical shortcoming, now another. But then he'd known from the minute she'd leaned over him in the dentist's chair that she was different. Special.

And now he could lose her! All because of . . . He didn't know how to ask her about the detective, didn't want to know the answer, did you tell . . . ? But then she said, I told the detective I gave those handkerchiefs to my uncle in Canada. I called him Jonathan Merrick, because he's one of the patients I had just that morning. That's amazing, he said (it was all right!). Imagine, a patient with the same initials just that morning. What a coincidence. Yes, she said, and the handkerchief business is just that, coincidence. That's why I didn't see the point in involving you. Right, he said, I have all the handkerchiefs you gave me. You can check. She laughed. You're so silly! She stretched her hand across the table, and he stretched his toward hers, across the plate with the fowl's cadaver and the white cloth with the bloody fingers. What was the detective's name? he asked, their hands suspended in midair, even though he already knew it was Jessie Drake. I'm curious.

Drake, Teresa said. Det. Jessie Drake. I wrote it down, just in case you wanted to talk to her. No, he told her, releasing her hand, I have nothing to say to her.

Later, after he helped her clear the dishes, she kissed him and pressed herself against him, and he knew what she wanted, what she needed. She must have sensed his hesitation. I don't want you to worry about anything, she whispered. Just hold me, that's enough for me right now. And he marveled again at his luck in meeting her, and wondered why a beautiful woman like her was willing to settle for him and what he could offer. Maybe it had to do with her marriage, something that had happened. He wouldn't press her about it; in time she would tell him. And someday he would tell her everything, and he knew she'd understand, because it was clear that she trusted him and believed in him. Needed him.

The lights were on in the bedroom. She turned them off, and they undressed, their backs to each other. Then they were in bed, facing each other, and for a brief moment he thought, *maybe*, but then he knew it would be the same. Hold me, she whispered, kissing his tears, hold me.

Sometime in the night he dreamed about his father. He was in his uniform and snickering at him, "*Not much of a man, are you?*" and as each guffaw grew louder, his father was growing larger and larger, taking up more space. Stop! he yelled, you're using up all the air, *my* air, I can't breathe. But his father kept laughing, laughing, so he had no choice, he had to cover his father's mouth and nose with the handkerchief to stop the laughing, but when he removed the handkerchief, his father's face peeled away with it and revealed Jessie Drake's face. Now it was Jessie smothering him with laughter. Stop it! And the face kept changing from Jessie to his father, back and forth, until he couldn't tell them apart, couldn't stop either of them from making him shrink, and he knew that soon he would disappear altogether.

He woke up in a panic, drenched in sweat, his heart hammering in his throat, and for a moment he didn't know where he was. Then he saw her lying next to him and remembered.

Sweet Teresa.

And he realized with sudden, piercing clarity that he could never be what she needed, that he would never be whole, until he finished *the game* and defeated both of them.

His father and Jessie Drake.

The bitch.

Six days had passed since Thursday.

There had been no message. No bodies.

"Maybe he's sick," Barrows said. "Maybe he stopped."

Pruitt shook his head. "He probably landed on Chance. Or on a property that's already his."

Takamura said, "We have to expand the search for the handkerchief. Check other cities, other states."

"Forget the goddamn handkerchief!" Pruitt snapped.

"John's right, Frank," Barrows said. "It's our only lead."

"It's shit, is what it is. The city should offer a reward for the son of a bitch, get the citizens involved. They got Ramirez." Richard Ramirez, the notorious Los Angeles Night Stalker, who viciously killed and mutilated his victims, had been apprehended by several men while he was trying to steal a car.

"Corcoran is pushing the mayor to get the City Council to do just that," Takamura said. "In the meantime—"

"In the meantime we're talking to the same witnesses over and over. Today's Wednesday. Let's say we're lucky and he didn't kill last week. We won't be lucky twice in a row."

"His sketch is in the papers and on TV all the time," Takamura said. "Every cop knows what he looks like. He has to live somewhere, shop somewhere, bank somewhere, have his hair cut, eat out once in a while. Someone will recognize him."

"So why hasn't anyone recognized him so far?" Pruitt demanded. "A *cop* let him pass by him, for Christ's sake!"

"Come on," Jessie said. "He was thrown by the uniform."

"So what about the guy who *rented* him the uniform, huh? Or a bank teller? We sent copies to every goddamn bank in the city, figuring he's got to withdraw money to play the game. How come no teller's spotted him?" Pruitt paused. "I'll tell you why. It's a shit sketch. The nurse saw him in a disguise. The Podrell woman said the sketch wasn't accurate."

"What about the asthma angle?" Barrows said. "We could show the sketch to clinics and private doctors."

Pruitt said, "Do you have any idea how many doctors there are in this city? How many people with asthma? Jesus, Ray!"

"I don't see you coming up with any better suggestions." Barrows's face was red with anger.

When they left for the day, Pruitt walked with Jessie to the parking lot. They were careful to keep apart, but it was damn hard, she thought, not to touch him.

They had been together almost every night since Thursday.

Helen had said, "Again? So who is it? What's he like?"

"Just someone from work," Jessie said. "Nothing serious."

Brenda had been shocked. "I thought you hated Frank Pruitt! You said he was an asshole. You said he treated you like shit."

"We . . . uh . . . worked things out."

"Oh? It's like that, huh?"

"Yeah." Jessie felt herself blushing.

A pause. "Well, it's about time, girl. But is that smart, sleeping with someone you work with? It must be complicated."

Very complicated; they had talked about it that first night. "We'll handle it," he'd said.

"You were rough on Ray," Jessie told Pruitt now.

"I know. This shit's getting to me." When they neared her car, he said, "Pick you up at eight? We'll take in a movie."

"And dancing?"

"That, too, sweetheart." He grinned and brushed his fingers against her palm.

She watched him walk away, then turned to open the door to the Honda. "Frank!" she called urgently.

He was by her side in an instant. She pointed to the envelope tucked under the windshield wiper. JESSIE DRAKE.

"How did he know this is my car?" she whispered. "How, Frank?" She gripped his arm. "He's watching me, isn't he?"

"He's just trying to rattle you, Jess," Pruitt said softly. But there was something somber besides the anger in his eyes.

There were three cards and a note in the envelope:

A Chance card: "Building loan matures. Collect $150."
A Community Chest card: "Go to Jail."
A "Get out of jail, free" card.

Jessie, I hope you haven't been too worried about my activities. I've had a quiet week, but after last week's double play, I enjoyed the hiatus. And fair is fair. I *did* collect $150 from the bank. And as you can see, I got out of jail! Just a little humor, Jessie. I hope you don't mind.

I don't know if the flag is accurate, but it doesn't matter. It's the symbol that counts. I almost introduced myself to you at the Greek Theater, but I thought better of it. Another time, Jessie. Another place.

I promise.

Stapled to the note was a miniature American flag. It took them a few minutes to figure it out.

39

States Avenue, he'd decided a long time ago, would be associated with the federal government. The federal court was too risky. So was the FBI, although wouldn't that be spectacular, and wouldn't it give Jessie Drake something to think about! The post office was a possibility, but he felt disloyal, even though he could've chosen a station other than the one where he'd worked.

He'd become a postal carrier a year and a half ago. Before that he'd been a bookkeeper for a series of small manufacturers of women's clothing in downtown Los Angeles.

"Be an accountant," his mother had said. *"You're so good with numbers. You're a human calculator, isn't that right, Ed?"* But the CPA exam had loomed over him like a brooding, invincible beast. *"Joe Hooker's kid took it three times and still hasn't passed,"* his father said. *"What in hell gave you the idea you could do it?"*

Years later, it occurred to him that his father had been threatened by the idea of his becoming a professional, of surpassing him in education and position and income. At the time, he'd simply accepted his denigrating appraisal as fact. Again.

And so he had become a bookkeeper.

"A bookkeeper?" his father had sneered. *"Jesus! What the hell kind of man takes a job as a bookkeeper, for Christ's sake? Next thing you know, you'll be in a ballet wearing a tutu."*

He was a competent bookkeeper. He found an elemental satisfaction in balancing debits and credits, in tracking down elusive errors, in righting the wrongs on the silent battlefield of ledger sheets, holding numbers captive under his tireless scrutiny and forcing them to reveal their secrets. Of course, no one ever said, "Great job, Jim." No one ever noticed him.

He'd worked at three companies over a period of eleven years. Two had gone bankrupt. He'd quit the third. That had been over two years ago, after his mother had suffered her stroke and his father had placed her in the facility, even though at the time the doctors had said she could be cared for at home. *"Best thing for her, boy,"* his father had said, wearing a grave expression that looked unnatural on him, like a borrowed, too-tight suit. He'd pretended to feel the pain of separation. *"You think I want this? You think I won't miss her? 'Course I'll miss her. But it's the best thing."*

Maybe it had been the best thing for his father. After three months his visits to the nursing home had all but stopped. *"I can't bear to see her like that, boy. Tell her from me that I love her, all right?"* His mother's removal to the nursing facility had propelled him to take an apartment, something he'd contemplated for years, something his mother had always talked him out of. And one evening, when he'd gone to the house to pick up some books he'd left in his room, he'd surprised his father with another woman. They were sitting in the kitchen, their arms entwined, using chopsticks to feed each other Chinese food straight from the container. They were laughing and didn't hear him come in.

His father was in his boxer shorts and a T-shirt. The woman, an overweight brunette with tousled hair and makeup obviously smudged by lovemaking, was wearing a robe. His mother's robe, a worn pink chenille that should be belted at the waist but wasn't.

They stopped eating when he entered the kitchen.

"I came for my books," he said tonelessly, averting his eyes from the chenille robe and the woman who shouldn't be wearing it.

His father followed him to the bedroom. "Why in hell didn't you call first? What if I was sleeping and thought you were a burglar, huh?"

He didn't answer. He opened the closet door and found the carton of books under a blanket. The ones he wanted were on top. *Lord of the Flies. Crime and Punishment. The Stranger.*

"A man has needs," his father said in his boxer shorts. "Your mother's not well, and I did what's best for her."

He closed the carton and returned it to the closet. With his books in one hand he headed for the front door.

"Now look here. Don't you be judging me, you understand? I wish things were different, but they aren't. And I'm not ready to die yet. Life doesn't always turn out the way you want it."

Disturbing visions started intruding on him at work, popping up between the columns of black numbers, upsetting the balance between the addends and subtrahends, visions of his father and the woman in his mother's pink robe lying on the king-size mattress, visions of his mother wrapped in white sheets in her narrow hospital bed. It dawned on him that now they were all separate. His father in the house; his mother in the nursing home; he in his apartment; his brother in his grave.

He started making mistakes. First it was a few pennies—an annoyance, really, but it was a blow to his pride. Then it was $8.00. Then $32.00. Then $1,226.00. It took him two days to undo his error, and he knew his boss, Al Borbolla, was going to fire him. Borbolla hadn't said anything, but there was a tightness around his lips whenever he passed his desk, which was more often than it had ever been. Before, he'd never even noticed him. Like the others. So he'd told Borbolla he needed time off, his mother was gravely ill. Gee, Jim, I wish I could keep the job for you, but I need a bookkeeper. I understand, he said. *Bastard!* he thought. *Liar!* Tell you what, Borbolla said, file for unemployment. I'll say I let you go.

The unemployment hadn't been enough to pay for rent and utilities and food. Moving back into the house with his father wasn't an option. It would be a declaration of failure; more than that, the idea of living with his father made him physically ill. He didn't want to do bookkeeping; nothing in the classifieds appealed to him. Then one day when he went to the post office, the thought floated into his head. He could be a postal carrier. He was tired of working indoors, of keeping a vigil against phalanxes of numbers that were constantly fighting him. He was in luck: the exam, given once in three years, would be administered that August, one month away. He passed the exam. His name was placed on the register of applicants, and three months later he was hired.

He hadn't intended to tell his father about his new job, but the information had slipped out.

"Well, well. Desperate to get into uniform, huh? My son, the postal carrier. In my day they called it 'mailman.'" He shook his head. "Say, watch out for those dogs. You'd better hope all you come across is poodles and Chihuahuas." He laughed. "You don't mind my joking, do you, boy? It's all in good fun, right?"

I hate you, he said into the receiver after his father had hung up. I wish you were dead.

It shouldn't have made a difference; he should have been

prepared. But his contentment with his job was irrevocably damaged. He was furious with his father, more furious with himself. What had made him think his father would react differently? When would his pathetic need for his approval stop? And he told himself this was the last time he would expose himself to his father's cruelty, the last time he would talk to him altogether.

Ever since he'd found his father with the woman, he'd rarely gone to the house, and then only at his father's insistence, but he'd phoned once a week to report on his mother's condition. His father had asked him to. He'd known that the request had been prompted by guilt, that his father had no interest in her welfare (*"Tell her I'll be there soon, real soon,"* he said every week). But he called, because he was the obedient son; because he needed to talk about his mother to someone, anyone, who knew her; because he wanted to shame his father, who was probably at that minute sitting in his T-shirt and boxer shorts with the woman in his mother's robe, wanted to remind him that his wife (*"Where is Ed? Why hasn't he come?"*) was still alive, God damn him to hell.

And, he admitted to himself later, he called for the same reason he returned to the house, for the same reason it had taken him so many years to leave it, because he couldn't sever the connection, because he was a masochist, drawn to the one person who had the greatest power to maim him, like a downed pugilist clawing his way up the ropes to face his opponent once again, because (and this was the most frightening thought) there was still inside him an atom of unspoken hope that the next phone call or visit would be different, that with his brother dead and his mother gone, his father would need him, see him differently. Love him. And so, even as he replaced the receiver, wishing his father dead, he knew he would call him again and again and again.

After *the game* was over, maybe he'd go back to school. He could use his father's money. He wondered how many years it would take him to become a CPA. Well, he didn't have to decide now. And until he decided, he could get back his job at the post office.

But he couldn't go back! he realized with a jolt. His face was in every post office in the city! He'd worried that his coworkers would recognize him from the sketches in the paper and on TV. But they hadn't—why would they? They'd hardly noticed him at work. He hadn't worried about the people on his route. Mostly, he'd delivered letters to mute mail slots and deposited packages and magazines in front of doors that couldn't bear testimony. Only three people had given him Christmas gifts.

But now that the sketch was in the post office, it was too risky to go back! And that was Jessie Drake's fault, too. The bitch was trying to ruin his life! Well, she wouldn't succeed.

Funny how she'd bumped into him just as he'd left the receiver dangling in Parker Center. Up close, she was even taller than he'd realized, more beautiful. For an instant he'd panicked, had almost run. But she hadn't seen him; she'd seen a mailman in uniform, just as she had when he'd delivered the second note, right to her! Just as she'd seen only a uniformed policeman two rows below her in section C at the Greek Theater.

He wasn't surprised. He'd been invisible most of his life.

At 7:55 A.M. he entered the Federal Building on Wilshire. The FBI was on the seventeenth floor; the Passport Agency on the thirteenth. He'd been surprised to learn there *was* a thirteenth floor. Most buildings didn't have one. But he wasn't superstitious, not about numbers or cracked mirrors. Or opals. The jeweler had said something about opals being unlucky, but opals had been very lucky, for him and for

Teresa. When the elevator doors opened, he entered and pressed "13."

In the main room, already filled with a polyglot crowd of men, women, and children, he waited in line to pick up a passport application. Ten minutes later, with his blank application in his hand, he headed for the rest room.

It was empty. Later in the day, it would be filled with men combing their hair and children having their hair combed before they took passport pictures in one of the curtained booths.

He waited.

For the first time in his fifty-six-year-old life, Samuel Kropp was going abroad. He and Lois would be spending three weeks in Europe—an anniversary gift from the kids. It was the first time, too, that his floor-covering store would be closed. Enjoy, the kids had said, and he would.

The problem was the passport. It was less than three weeks to their departure, and he still didn't have it. Lois, of course, had gotten hers immediately, and she'd been nagging him ever since. I'll take care of it, he told her; I'm not a baby. And here he was, without a passport. It was her fault, really, because if she hadn't nagged, he would've taken care of it right away.

His stomach twisted; he knew he was having the runs. Whenever he was nervous, his system suffered. He looked at the line ahead of him. Sixteen people. He'd never make it. Sighing, he relinquished his spot. I should charge for it, he thought. He slipped his application into the inside pocket of his jacket.

Except for one man, the rest room was empty. When Samuel exited the cubicle five minutes later, the man was combing his hair. Samuel joined him. There was a passport application near the sink.

"First time?" Samuel pointed to the application.

"Yes. What about you?"

"Also." He patted the area where he'd placed the application. He turned on the faucets, rinsed his hands under the flow, and briskly slapped his face. In the mirror, he could see that the man had finished combing his hair. Samuel turned to take a paper towel from the dispenser, and suddenly an arm was locked around his neck, and a handkerchief was pressed against his nose and mouth, and he couldn't breathe, he couldn't. . . .

He dragged the man toward the cubicles at the rear and lowered him onto the tiled floor. When he removed the man's jacket, the passport application fell out. Samuel Kropp, he read. He was grateful that Kropp was wearing a short-sleeved shirt. He took the deposit slip and the $140 and placed it along with the application inside the jacket pocket.

He thought he saw Kropp stir. He pressed the handkerchief once more against Kropp's nose and mouth. He thought again about the other handkerchief. He'd been certain that he'd left it in the jacket he'd given to the cleaners, but that wasn't possible, not if Jessie Drake had it. He'd been thinking about it ever since Teresa had told him about her visit, but he hadn't been able to reconstruct the events. Where could he have lost it? How could he—

With a start, he realized where he was. There was no time to waste. Someone could come in at any minute. He bent down and quickly examined both arms. The veins on the left were more pronounced. He reached inside his pocket for the readied syringe and placed it on the floor next to him. He massaged the area inside the left elbow, then tied rubber tubing around the upper arm. It took him longer than usual to tie it, his fingers were stubbornly inept, and he knew that was because he was nervous about the handkerchief. As a volunteer at Bollard Memorial, he'd watched nurses administer intravenous injections. And he'd watched so many nurses give his mother so many shots that he'd felt like an expert even before his first time with the old Chinese woman. It was easy, especially if you didn't have to worry about the bubble. And there was no one to complain about his technique.

He lifted the syringe. With his thumb against the plunger, he pressed the cold tip of the hypodermic against the now-throbbing gray-blue vein.

A noise.

Footsteps.

Startled, he withdrew the syringe. He untied the rubber tubing and stuffed it and the syringe into his jacket pocket. He felt his chest start to constrict, but with superhuman strength, he willed his bronchial passages to remain open.

A man loomed over him. "What's going on?"

"I'm a doctor," he said crisply. "This man fainted. I was trying to revive him." He stood up quickly and the blood rushed to his head. His eyes clouded. He thought he was going to faint.

"He looks awful! Is he dead?"

"He's not dead. I'm going to call an ambulance. You stay here, in case he needs immediate help. Do you know CPR?"

"Yes. But what if—"

"Good. I'll be right back. Don't leave him for a minute."

Outside the rest room, he had to stop himself from running to the elevators. The hallway was filled with people jabbering in a cacophonous jumble of languages, Spanish, Russian, Iranian, French, and he wanted to scream at them, Shut up! and then the elevator doors opened, and he entered and pressed "Lobby."

The doors closed. He shut his eyes and almost cried with relief. The elevator started moving, but his stomach told him it was wrong, all wrong! He opened his eyes. Instead of going down, the elevator was going up, up to the FBI! He jabbed "14," but the elevator had already passed that floor; he jabbed "15"; too late for that floor, too. The elevator doors opened on sixteen. Two men got in. One was a security guard; the other had on a dark-gray suit. Both wore somber expressions. The doors closed and the elevator ascended to seventeen. No one was there.

The elevator began its descent. He studied his nails as it slipped past sixteen, past fifteen, fourteen. Why was there a thirteen? Buildings weren't supposed to have a thirteenth floor! He knew that the minute the doors opened, they'd be waiting for him, Samuel Kropp and the man who had prevented his death, they'd point at him and say, "He's the one!" All this flashed through his mind in the seconds it took the elevator to go from seventeen to thirteen, but when the doors opened, there was no one pointing at him, only the same people, jabbering away. It was as if time had stopped still, as if the elevator had never left the thirteenth floor. His two silent copassengers exited without looking at him.

When he left the lot, he drove several blocks on Wilshire and turned onto a side street. Then he turned off the ignition and ran out of the car. He remained crouched over the gutter, heaving bitter waves of fear and failure, long after the vomiting stopped.

They had a witness! Jessie could hardly believe it. Two witnesses, actually—Samuel Kropp, the first person to survive an attack by the killer, and Harry Stoddard, the man who saved him.

Jessie and the others had just returned from UCLA Medical Center, where they'd met with Kropp, Stoddard, and Detective Al Recinos. Recinos had immediately contacted the task force after Kropp told him he'd been smothered with a handkerchief.

And now they had the handkerchief. Jessie picked up the

plastic bag holding the handkerchief Recinos had given her. According to Recinos, the paramedics had found the handkerchief on the floor next to Kropp, assumed it was his, and put it in his jacket pocket. "What handkerchief?" Kropp had said. "What deposit slip?"

"It looks much older than the other one," Barrows said.

"But the initials are J.M.," Jessie said. "As in James Miller. I hope Stoddard or Kropp can make improvements on the sketches we have." Stan Gibbins hadn't been able to give a clear description of the man who'd rented the uniform.

Barrows said, "You think the killer will try again, Jessie?"

"When Monica Podrell walked out, he picked a target in the other library. This time he was almost caught, though. Maybe he's scared. Let's hope so."

"More likely desperate and mad as hell at us," Pruitt said.

Mad at *me*, not *us*, Jessie thought with a chill, remembering the note on her windshield and Manny's warning.

"What are you doing?" Pruitt asked Jessie.

Takamura was "in conference" with Corcoran; Barrows and a sketch artist were meeting first with Kropp, then Stoddard.

Jessie was at her desk, studying the items she'd arranged in four vertical rows: the deposit slips and corresponding money; next, the property cards the killer had sent her; the Community Chest and Chance cards; finally, the three notes.

"There's something here we're missing, Frank."

"You want my opinion?" He drank from a can of Diet Coke. "There are thirty-three spaces on the board, if you take away Community Chest, Chance, and Go. He's killed ten people. I say we resign ourselves to twenty-three more."

"Not funny."

"He's always one damn step ahead of us, Jess. Doesn't it ever get to you?" He crumpled the can and tossed it into the trash.

"I keep thinking about the money. Where does he get it? And you were right, Frank. Why *hasn't* a bank teller recognized him?"

"I keep telling you, that sketch is lousy."

"But the killer can't be sure that no one will recognize him. Why would he risk going into the bank every time he has to withdraw money?"

"So he goes to a different branch every time, or he wears a disguise, like he did when he worked at Bollard. And remember, he made most of his moves before we knew about him, before there was a sketch. So he had nothing to worry about." He picked up a file and, leaning against a desk, started reading.

"Right." Jessie was silent. Suddenly, she turned around. "Frank, maybe he doesn't go to a bank at all!"

He looked up. "Then where does he get the money? A fairy godmother? He's using real bills, sweetheart, not Monopoly money."

"Listen to these notes." She picked one up. "This is from the first one. '. . . last Thursday I was collecting a prize for a beauty contest. It's only ten dollars, but it's money in my account.' "

Pruitt put down the folder. "What's your point?"

"This is from yesterday's note: 'I did collect a hundred fifty dollars from the bank.' If he's leaving real money, we can assume he's collecting real money, too. Obviously, he means the Monopoly bank. So what would be the equivalent of a Monopoly bank?"

"What?" Pruitt frowned.

"An automated teller machine!" Jessie stood up. "Think about it. It's impersonal. It avoids risk. It hands out the money like the Monopoly banker. He said he *collected* a prize, *collected* a hundred fifty dollars. *Collected*, not withdrew."

Pruitt shook his head. "That's semantics."

"I don't think so. And it could be a pattern. Because he *collected* money more than just those two times, Frank. He collected two hundred from the bank every time he passed Go. We could figure out the dates by his moves, then try to track him down by a pattern of deposits and withdrawals."

"Let's say you're right, Jessie. Do you have any idea how many ATMs there are in the city?"

There were thousands, Jessie learned, and the number was increasing. Some were specific to one bank. Others, in shopping centers, minimalls, and convenience stores, belonged to one of several systems (like MasterCard, Visa, Plus, Star, Exchange, or Cirrus) that serviced a number of banks. One bank employee had guessed that there were over three thousand ATMS in the metropolitan Los Angeles area.

There might as well be a million, she thought. Banks kept separate records for transactions conducted on each ATM. None of the banks had computer programs that would provide the police with ATM users whose initials were J.M. Unless the police could determine which ATM the killer used—if in fact he *used* an ATM—it would be impossible to trace him through his pattern of withdrawals and deposits.

That night she dreamed she saw him standing in front of an ATM. "Freeze!" she commanded, her gun drawn. "Put your hands on your head and turn around slowly."

"Don't shoot!" But when he was facing her, she saw not the man she knew from either of the sketches, but the cherubic Mr. Moneybanks. He grinned at her and winked.

"Houses and hotels, little lady. That's the ticket. Of course, first you have to get a monopoly."

"Where is he?" she cried. "Tell me where to find him!"

"One step ahead of you. But if you play right, you can catch him. Here. Maybe this'll help." He tossed her a card.

It landed on the floor. She bent to pick it up. "Go to jail. Go directly to jail. Do not pass Go. Do not collect $200."

When she looked up, Mr. Moneybanks had disappeared. Spewing forth from the ATM was an endless flow of Monopoly money.

When the phone rang, she squinted at the luminous green numbers on her clock radio. 4:30 A.M. *They found a body*. She fumbled for the receiver on her nightstand. "Drake," she mumbled.

"Jessie, let me talk to Helen."

Neil? Jessie sat up. "Why are you calling, Neil? Is something wrong?" She tried to keep the loathing from her voice.

"No games, OK? I know Helen's there. Where else would she be? I called our house. I kept getting the answering machine. I just called the camp. They said she took Matthew out two days after camp started! She lied to me!" In a calmer voice, he said, "I want to talk to Helen. Get her, please."

She could hear the controlled anger in his voice. "It's the middle of the night, Neil. I'm not going to wake her up. She'll call you tomorrow." Bastard, she thought. Monster!

"I want to talk to her now, goddammit, not tomorrow!"

"To be honest, I don't think Helen wants to talk to *you*."

"Look, I don't know what lies she's told you. She's—"

"Good night, Neil." Drop dead, Neil. "I'll give Helen your message."

"She ran to her sister the cop for protection, huh? Well, Matthew's my son, and you can tell that bitch I'm driving to Rijad in two days and taking the next available flight to the States. She'll be sorry she did this!" He slammed down the phone.

In the morning before Jessie left for Parker Center, when she was sure Matthew couldn't overhear, she told Helen.

"Oh, God," Helen moaned and clutched Jessie. "He's going to kill me! Help me, Jessie. Please help me! Don't leave!"

"Helen, he has to drive to Rijad first. He can't get here for at least three days. I won't let him hurt you or Matthew."

"But what about Monday? And the day after that? What will I do if Neil shows up when you're at work?"

"You'll call the West L.A. precinct and ask for Phil Okum, my partner. I'll alert him. It'll be OK, Helen." She hugged her.

Midmorning, they learned that the killer had struck again after all. It was Jessie who took the call.

"The apartment manager found the body this morning," Tom Moran of Wilshire Division said. "Seems the dead woman's boss was concerned when she didn't show up for work. Called her all morning, then called her parents. They contacted the manager."

"When did she die?"

"The M.E. guesses sometime last night. There's an injection site on the inside of the elbow. I almost missed it. No signs of violence. No rape. And she's young for a heart attack. Early thirties. That's why I thought to call you."

"Where was the body found?"

"In her bed. She looked like she was sleeping."

Like all the others, Jessie thought. "Suicide, maybe? OD?"

"No syringe. No other marks on her arms."

"Did you find any money on her? A deposit slip?"

"Nope. All she had on was a nightgown. I didn't see any money. I can check with SID, see if they found anything."

The killer had already left $140 with Samuel Kropp.

Maybe he hadn't felt like paying twice. "That's all right. I'll call them." She would also call the M.E. and ask him to rush the lab results. "So where is this apartment building?" If the killer was their man, there had to be a link with States Avenue.

"Wooster Avenue."

Wooster? That didn't fit. Maybe there was a connection with the victim's name. "What's the dead woman's name?"

"Barnett. Her first name is—"

"Teresa!" Jessie whispered. "Jesus Christ! Teresa Barnett!"

40

Teresa Barnett lay with her head propped on a pillow, her hands resting on the comforter. She looked serene, untroubled, as if she'd slipped into death just as she'd slipped between the comforter and the cool sheet, with ease and anticipation of comfort.

Driving to the Wooster Street apartment, Jessie had gone over her meeting with Teresa. Was there something that indicated in retrospect that Teresa had lied? Replaying the scene revealed nothing new. Teresa had presented an innocent face with innocent answers, marked only by reserve and the nervousness normal to someone being questioned by a detective. Now there was no sign of the nervousness, and the quiet had been cemented by death.

It would take a while to do an autopsy and get the lab results; the M.E. had said tomorrow morning. But Jessie knew the tests would show curare. Anything else would be a case of grand coincidence, and Jessie didn't believe in coincidence.

Should she have told Teresa they were searching for a

serial killer, not some fictional, harmless witness? Would that have encouraged her to reveal the name? Maybe, maybe not. Even if she *had* believed Jessie, she might have wanted to protect him. She obviously hadn't feared him even after she'd told him about the handkerchief (she *had* to have told about the handkerchief before Thursday night, Jessie reasoned, or he wouldn't have come prepared to kill her). She had let him into her apartment, into her bedroom, hadn't suspected that he would kill her.

Maybe telling her wouldn't have made a difference.

Or maybe, Jessie knew, she was trying to convince herself that she was in no way to blame for Teresa Barnett's death.

An hour's search revealed nothing in Teresa Barnett's apartment that would lead Jessie to her killer. In an accordion envelope in a drawer of her dresser, Jessie had found the woman's personal papers—a bankbook; her final divorce decree from Donald Mattison; a recent portrait with Teresa and an older man and woman, presumably her parents, all frozen in uncomfortable stiffness against a photographer's swirled gray background; other pictures showing Teresa's transformation from little girl to young woman—Teresa in braces, Teresa in cap and gown, Teresa in a wedding gown gazing wistfully at her bouquet; a diploma from a San Diego city college; a document certifying that Teresa Barnett could practice as a dental hygienist in the State of California.

Her purse contained keys, a makeup pouch with mirror, lip gloss, and blush; a checkbook and wallet; a packet of tissues; a daybook listing bills to be paid—auto and medical insurance, utilities—errands to be run, and appointments, including evening sessions with a "Dr. R." There was a phone index at the end. The page tabbed *M* had been removed. There was no entry under *J*.

A small cardboard box in the bedroom closet contained

Teresa Barnett's financial records: canceled checks; receipts from MasterCard, Sears, the Broadway; utility and phone bills; pay stubs from salary checks issued by Dr. Morris Banneker, D.D.S., a Medical Corporation; an automobile insurance policy.

There was a diary, too, a cloth-covered book in a floral pattern. Jessie found it buried underneath Teresa's nightgowns. It was unlocked. She opened it excitedly to the last entry, flipped backward for the page that would discuss Teresa's first encounter with J.M., that would reveal his full name.

She found the entry, dated August 1, but there was no last name. Just "Jim."

> We went to a movie. . . . Jim seems so sad, so vulnerable, probably because his father died and his mother is so sick. . . . I think he's concerned because I'm taller than he is, but I don't mind. Height isn't important. Jim said he'll call again. I hope so. It's so nice after Don to meet someone decent, caring.

They had gone out four times, Jessie read, each time on a Saturday night. On the second date she'd given him the handkerchiefs. On the third, he'd given her opal earrings.

> . . . so beautiful, too expensive, really, but the look in his eyes didn't let me say no. I'll always treasure them. I can't remember Don giving me anything as nice, not even before we were married. Strange, but I can't remember anything nice about Don at all. There must have been, or why did I marry him?

In the same entry, Teresa had written that she and Jim had made love. Or tried to.

> . . . so sad! He was so embarrassed, so crushed. I told

him it didn't matter, but I'm not sure he believed me. It's true, though. Right now, I just need to be held.

The next entry was dated Tuesday, August 18:

Dr. R. cautioned me about my relationship with Jim, wants me to think about why I'm interested in someone impotent. I hate that word! It's so unfeeling, so clinical. I told her I'm sure his problem is temporary. He has too much on his mind—his mother, for one. And sex isn't that important to me right now.

Why not? she asked. You should think about that.

I told her I would.

There were several later entries, but only one mattered:

Last night I told Jim about the detective and the handkerchief; he thought it was a funny coincidence. I'm so glad now I didn't mention Jim's name. . . .

And later in the same entry:

. . . and he was disappointed again, but he wasn't as embarrassed. We'll work it out together; I know we will. Until then, it's enough to be cherished, needed. I told that to Dr. R., but she seemed skeptical.

Do you want to be his lover or mother? she asked.

I want to feel safe, I told her. With Don, especially at the end, I never felt safe. Jim makes me feel safe. I know I can trust him. Is that so wrong?

What do you think? she asked.

Dr. Morris Banneker, Teresa Barnett's employer, was shocked and saddened by the news of her death.

"A special woman," he told Jessie, shaking his head in

disbelief. "A wonderful hygienist. A very gentle touch. Everyone loved her. Who would do such a thing?"

"We're trying to find out who her friends were. Who she dated. Was she particularly friendly with anyone in the office?"

"In the office?" Banneker looked puzzled. "Oh, patients? I doubt it. Even if she *was* interested in a patient, she wouldn't tell me about it. She knows I disapprove of that sort of thing. It's not professional." He hesitated. "Have you talked to her ex-husband? I think she had a bad marriage, you know."

"Did she talk about it?"

"No. She is— Teresa was a very private woman, Detective. But one time he called here, and I could see she was very angry, very upset. That was when she told me she'd been divorced."

"Did she receive any calls from other men?"

"Not that I know of. She was a quiet woman, Detective, dedicated to her work. Very professional."

Banneker's staff—a receptionist who scheduled appointments, another hygienist, a woman who did the insurance billings, and an X-ray technician—all echoed the doctor's sentiments but had nothing to add. No one recognized the face in the police sketch.

"Could you please check your files for a male patient with the initials J.M.?" Jessie asked Banneker.

The dentist looked uncomfortable. "I think that would be a violation of my patients' privacy."

"I'm investigating a homicide, Doctor. If you insist, I can get a subpoena, but I'd appreciate your swift cooperation."

Banneker hesitated, then nodded. The receptionist checked the files and found three male patients. One was a teenager; two were in their sixties. Jessie recognized one of the latter, Jonathan Merrick, as the "uncle" Teresa had invented.

From Parker Center, Jessie called Teresa's parents in San Diego, Charles and Maureen Barnett. She knew they'd been informed of their daughter's death. Still, she dreaded talking to them, intruding on their grief.

Charles Barnett answered the phone. "Yes?"

Jessie introduced herself. "I hate to bother you at a time like this, Mr. Barnett—"

"I thought maybe you were calling to say it was a mistake."

"I'm sorry," she said gently, not knowing what else to say.

"Yes, well, can't this wait? My wife and I are leaving for the airport. We should be in L.A. by evening to see . . . to see . . ."

Jessie could hear the pain in the silence. "Mr. Barnett, believe me, if I didn't think this was vital, I wouldn't—"

"What do you want?" His voice was husky with anger and pain and bewilderment and resignation, but he answered her questions.

No, Teresa hadn't mentioned she was dating anyone when she'd visited them the previous week. She'd sounded happy, though, happier than she'd been in a long time. Did the initials J.M. suggest anything? No, nothing at all. Girlfriends in Los Angeles? Not that he knew of. She hadn't been living there all that long, just a little over six months. They'd begged her not to leave San Diego. L.A. was too big, they'd told her; there was so much violence. But she'd wanted to get away after her divorce, to make a new start, and how could they have stopped her?

"I still can't believe she's dead!" Charles Barnett cried. "How could this have happened? Why would anyone kill Teresa?"

He lay on his side on his bed, hugging his knees to his chest, the rocking motion of his body keeping time like a metronome to the hoarse, keening moans that issued from his throat. A gnawing pain was crawling, crablike, through his stomach and chest, and his head was throbbing dully from when he'd slammed it, over and over, against the wall, trying to block out the images that wouldn't leave him.

Teresa was dead.

He had waited until her breathing had settled into a steady, unhurried rhythm, until he'd been sure that her eyes were sealed with sleep. Then he reached into his pants pocket for the handkerchief and syringe. A choked sob escaped his lips, and his hands were shaking so badly that for a moment he thought he couldn't go through with it. But how could he not?

Crouching over the gutter just blocks away from the Federal Building, he'd realized that now two more people could identify him, Samuel Kropp and the man who'd saved his life. The police would talk to them, would ask them to amend the sketch that had been appearing daily on the news and in the papers. He tried to convince himself that neither man had gotten a good look at him. Samuel Kropp had seen him for a brief moment; the other man had been concentrating on Kropp's body, lying on the tiled bathroom floor. Maybe it would be all right. He tried not to panic.

But when he was home, he discovered that the handkerchief wasn't there! He ran outside and checked the front seat of the car, but it wasn't there, either. Had it fallen out as he'd been vomiting? And then he remembered. He'd used it a second time to ensure that Samuel Kropp was unconscious. Damn Samuel Kropp!

The papers would mention the handkerchief. And Teresa would read about it, and she would recognize his face from the new sketch. At first she wouldn't believe it, but then she'd start thinking about the other handkerchief, the one she'd given him. Maybe she'd ask him to show her all three. I'm just joking, she'd say, but she wouldn't be joking; it would be a test. And he would fail it, because how could he replace the handkerchief? The police had obviously been all over the city trying to trace the one he'd lost. If he bought a new one, had it monogrammed with his initials, he might as well announce that he was the killer. If he had more time, he could explain everything to Teresa, but it was too soon to tell her, too soon to expect her to understand that what he was doing was right and necessary.

Too soon. And too late. It was just a matter of time before she called the police. He couldn't blame her. The evidence would be there, the handkerchief and the sketch, staring her in the face, and what choice would she have?

So he called her late in the afternoon and asked her out. Instead of Saturday night? she asked, surprised. Saturday night's still on, he said, I just want to be with you. And it was easy to say the words, because they were true. But it was also true that he didn't want to go.

She looked exceptionally beautiful. He found himself staring at her all during the movie (he couldn't even remember what they'd seen), trying to memorize her features, the graceful curve of her neck, the tilt of her nose, her large eyes, her long, silky lashes, her—What? she asked, turning to him, smiling, as she caught his glance. Nothing, he said, you're so pretty. She squeezed his hand tightly and leaned against him.

In her apartment, they listened to an old Barbra Streisand record on Teresa's stereo and sipped lemonade. Dance with me, Teresa said softly, and she stood and pulled him up. She kicked off her shoes and moved closer, and they stood, eye to eye, on the carpeted floor. I can't remember the last time I danced, he said awkwardly. Don't worry, she said. She slipped both hands around his neck. His hands circled her waist. They started moving to the music. Barbra was singing "Oh, My Man," and Teresa's cheek was against his, and then she was rubbing her lips against his with a light, feathery motion, and then they were kissing slowly. In spite of himself, in spite of the handkerchief and syringe that lay waiting in his pants pocket and the dread that surrounded his heart, he was aroused.

In the bedroom they went through their ritual of undressing in the dark. He folded his pants and placed them near his side of the bed, within easy reach. As soon as he slipped under the comforter, she pressed against him, and suddenly, he was overwhelmed with confusing emotions, excitement at his body's instinctive response, love and gratitude for this woman whom he cherished beyond belief, despair born of the knowledge that this was the last time he would ever hold her in his arms, ever. . . . There was a moment when he thought, *this time*, but the moment passed and his hopes were deflated, and he lay sobbing in her arms, not caring now whether she saw his tears, because what did it matter? Don't cry, she whispered, please don't cry. You'll see, everything will be all right. And how could he tell her that it would never be all right? That he was crying not because of his failed manhood, but because he was losing her forever.

Just before he placed the handkerchief on her sleeping face, he thought about taking all his father's money and escaping to South America or Europe, disappearing. Then he wouldn't have to kill Teresa. But he knew that was impossible. He had to finish *the game*. He couldn't abandon it, not even for her.

I'm sorry, he whispered as he leaned over Teresa, ready to position the handkerchief. He had been certain that she was fast asleep, but her eyelids fluttered open. She smiled, slipped her arms around his neck, Jimmy, she whispered, and started drawing his face to hers. Then, quickly, quickly, he had no time, he clamped the handkerchief across her nose and mouth. She stared at him, her eyes blinking away sleep and becoming wide with bewilderment, then terror, then panic. A muffled cry escaped her lips. Her hands flew to her face, pulled at the handkerchief, clawed at his hands. Then they fell to her sides.

Gently, he closed her eyes. He cried as he prepared her arm, cried as he injected the curare into the vein on the inside of her right elbow—Teresa! He held her in his arms, crooning a wordless lullaby, until he was certain it was all over.

From his other pants pocket he took a pair of latex gloves and was about to slip them on when he noticed his hands. Teresa's short nails had left bloody tracks on them; he remembered the amputated hand the wine stain had formed on the white tablecloth and shivered. He slipped on the gloves. He wondered whether he should do something about her nails; the police would probably find his skin particles under them. He decided not to do anything. Skin cells would be forensic evidence only if they caught him. And they would never catch him. The gloves were a sensible precaution. He *had* been fingerprinted when he'd become a postal carrier. He thought about the handkerchief he'd lost in the Federal Building. His hands clenched. There was nothing he could do about it.

There was a cotton nightgown under the pillow. He slipped it over her warm, unresisting body. He placed her in the center of the bed, straightened the comforter, and arranged her arms over it. He went into the living room and took the glasses, filmy with lemonade pulp, into the kitchen. He washed and dried them. Then he went back into the bedroom and rummaged through Teresa's purse. He removed the *M* page from the telephone index of her planner. His name and phone number were on it.

He checked the financial records he found in a cardboard box in her closet. There were pay stubs from salary checks issued by Dr. Morris Banneker. That was the dentist Teresa had mentioned, the one for whom she worked on Mondays, Thursdays, and Fridays. There were no pay stubs from Dr. Stoltz. She'd worked for him only twice, both times on a Tuesday, as a substitute for Stoltz's regular hygienist. He returned the box. The police would learn that Teresa had worked for Banneker, but there was nothing to lead them to Dr. Herman Stoltz.

Before he left, he went to the bed to look at her one final time. She looked peaceful. Beautiful, even in death. The opals were in her ears. Had they brought bad luck after all?

Within a day, someone would report her missing. Dr. Banneker would wonder why she hadn't shown up for work. Then the police would come, but they wouldn't find anything. He thought suddenly about Jessie Drake. He pictured her leaning over Teresa, touching her, his Teresa! He knew there would be an autopsy, that a medical examiner would mutilate her beautiful body, and all because of Jessie! Hate bubbled in his throat.

It wasn't the opals, it was Jessie Drake! It was Jessie who hadn't played fair, Jessie who had come to Teresa with the handkerchief and her insinuations, Jessie who had come between him and Teresa. Jessie who was to blame for her death. He wanted to cry out in his rage and frustration. It wasn't fair!

Instead, he kissed Teresa's cold lips and shut the light.

He had no idea how long he'd been lying in his bed, rocking, moaning. All day, judging from the dark sky outside his window. He felt nauseated, but then he hadn't eaten since Thursday. He didn't think he could eat anything now, but he would force himself. He needed all his strength.

Even without looking at his watch, he knew it was time. He always knew. He struggled to sit up, then wobbled into the kitchen and shielded his eyes as he switched on the light. He took the bowl and filled it with pretzels. He filled a glass with beer and Seven-Up. He brought the bowl and glass to the card table in the living room and sat down in his chair across from his father's seat. His playing piece was still on States Avenue. His first failure. It would be his last, too, he vowed. He took a sip of the adulterated beer, then picked up the dice.

Jessie Drake thought that the game was over, that because Teresa had been taken away from him, ripped out of his life, he wouldn't go on. But he had no intention of quitting. He would make Jessie sorry for what she had done. She would pay!

It wasn't fair.

He would make them all sorry.

He closed his eyes, shook the dice, and let them drop onto the board. He opened his eyes. Two and two. He moved his piece to Community Chest and picked a card. "Advance to Go. Collect $200." That was all right. He threw the dice again. Three and three. Oriental Avenue. He was disappointed, because he'd already purchased the property, and he was anxious to redeem himself after his failure on States Avenue. The last time, in the library, he'd recovered and completed his transaction. This time the thought of the handkerchief and its repercussions, and Teresa, had immobilized him and made another attempt impossible.

At least this week might not be wasted. He'd rolled another doubles. He could throw a third time. He picked up the dice, cradled them in his cupped hands, squeezed his eyes shut, blew on the dice (*"Come to Mama!"*), tossed them, and opened his eyes. One cube said "six." The other one had skittered to the edge of the board and was lying half on the board, half on the table. If he didn't like the number, he could roll the dice again. That was fair.

He looked at the number, then at the board, and gasped with pleasure. He knew without counting where he would land, it was too perfect, he couldn't *believe* what a perfect combination he'd rolled! Just to be sure, he counted the spaces with his index finger (not with the piece—if he used the piece, that would mean he'd accepted the number on the cube that was half off the board), and he was right!

He moved his piece and placed it firmly on the space his finger had just vacated. This would make up for States Avenue.

41

Teresa was a nice woman, Eric Goebel, the fifty-four-year-old apartment building manager told Jessie. Quiet. Kept to herself. Saw her once in a while in the laundry room. She was careful with the detergent and bleach. Never left a mess. Always polite.

Boyfriends? Not many, Goebel said. There *had* been a guy who'd come by a few times. Real short. Had he been there last night? Goebel couldn't say; he'd been out playing poker with some friends. Just for chips, he told Jessie quickly. Had he noticed what kind of car this man drove? Sorry, no.

All the neighbors agreed with Goebel's assessment of Teresa. Several had seen the man Goebels had described. None could say for certain that he'd been there Thursday night, although the elderly, blue-haired woman who lived in the apartment next to Teresa's had heard music through the walls. None had seen the man's car.

Over the next few days, Jessie learned that Teresa had lived a solitary, almost cloistered existence—except for Jim

M. And Jessie had no idea where Teresa had met him. Not at work. Not at church. Charles Barnett had told Jessie that even in San Diego, his daughter had rarely attended services.

Most of the telephone entries in Teresa's daybook were San Diego numbers. Jessie called the few local ones. She spoke to Teresa's Dr. R.—Janice Roseman. The therapist knew nothing about Jim except for his first name. Jessie spoke to Teresa's internist. To her gynecologist. To her hairstylist. Nothing. She spoke to two women. One was a friend of a friend from San Diego; the other had met Teresa at a lecture at the local library. Teresa had occasionally gone shopping with the former, to the movies with the latter. A boyfriend? Teresa hadn't mentioned anyone. Jessie didn't call the temporary employment agency listed in the index—Teresa had had a steady position with Banneker.

No clues. No leads.

Four weeks had passed since Jessie had figured out that the killer was choosing his victims by playing Monopoly, and she was no closer to identifying him. She knew he used curare. (The M.E. had confirmed that as the cause of Teresa's death.) She knew he was white, short, in his thirties. So were thousands of people. Two women had given far-from-perfect descriptions. Samuel Kropp and Harry Stoddard hadn't improved the sketches; both men had only vague, fleeting recollections of the man in the Federal Building.

The City Council had finally offered a thirty-thousand-dollar reward for the killer's capture. That move had generated hundreds of calls, calls that had to be investigated, just in case. . . . In four weeks there had been four more deaths—only three directly related to the game, but Jessie didn't think Charles or Maureen Barnett would be consoled by that distinction.

Dead was dead.

Tomorrow was Tuesday. Teresa would be buried that morning in San Diego, and Jessie would attend the funeral—

standard procedure for any homicide, since the killer might be present. (She worried about being two hours away from L.A.—with Neil's imminent arrival looming over her head, Helen was on the verge of snapping—but Phil had promised to keep an eye on her and Matthew.)

Jessie wondered whether the man who had been Teresa Barnett's lover and her killer would be able to stay away.

He knew Jessie would be at the funeral, searching for him among the mourners, matching their faces against the improved sketch. The knowledge that he couldn't be with Teresa filled him with pain and anger and reminded him again how unfair it all was. It was Jessie Drake's fault. All of it was. He knew she was gloating.

Strange, how life reversed itself. Tomorrow he would be barred from catching a last glimpse of the only woman, aside from his mother, he'd ever loved. Four months ago he'd forced himself to pay his last respects to the person he hated above all others.

Even now, thinking back to that Thursday in March, he wasn't sure why he'd gone to his father's funeral. It had been the perfect opportunity to strike back. But he had put on an outdated charcoal-gray wool suit that had been gathering dust in his closet and gone to the funeral chapel.

It was the same chapel where the service for Ed, Jr., had taken place. After the hospital informed him that his father had suffered another, fatal heart attack, he found a mortuary in the yellow pages that sounded familiar. It would be the same cemetery, too, he learned, but the plots adjoining his brother's grave were taken. We'll do the best we can, the administrator said with hushed somberness and efficiency. Would you like to come down and make the other arrangements? We have a fine selection of—

Just the simplest casket, he said, and felt a wave of satisfaction at denying his father an expensive casket. He was glad, too, that his father wouldn't be next to Ed, Jr. He wondered idly whether they would permit him to erect a tombstone with the inscription "Here lies an old fart." Probably not. He pictured the etched words and smiled.

He didn't call anyone about the funeral, but about two dozen people were at the chapel when he arrived. He recognized two men he'd met at the hospital when he'd visited his father. They'd probably learned of the death and spread the news. The woman who had been wearing his mother's pink robe was there. Today she had on a black wool suit and a small black pillbox hat with a veil. She avoided looking at him. There were no other women, just men, probably policemen come to pay their respects to a colleague. A colleague who'd been fired, not retired. That was why there would be no color guard, no pomp, no official recognition of the twenty-one years his father had been a patrolman. He suppressed a smile. Another victory—not of his doing, but satisfying nonetheless. His father would have been furious and humiliated. Those sons of bitches! They got no right to treat me like this after all those years! But his father was dead, lying in a plain pine box.

Sic transit gloria.

It was an open-casket ceremony. He'd forgotten to stipulate otherwise, and now he'd have to see his father one last time. He braced himself, rose from his seat, and joined the queue heading for the front of the room where the unadorned casket lay.

"Who's that?" he heard someone whisper.

"Must be Ed's son," another man answered.

"What son? I thought Ed, Jr., was killed years ago."

"Someone said there was another son."

"No kidding! Doesn't look anything like Ed."

No kidding.

He felt like leaving. They would think he was overcome with emotion—"Too difficult for him to bear"; "You can see he's keeping it all inside." At worst they would label him cold, insensitive, unnatural in his indifference to his parent's death.

And what of that? It wasn't a criminal offense. He saw himself in a courtroom, facing a jury. Ten were men in uniform, all friends of his father; the eleventh was the woman in the pink chenille robe and the black hat. The twelfth was his mother, thin and drawn in a faded blue hospital gown. The male jurors stood first. "Guilty of great callousness," they intoned one by one. "Guilty." "Guilty." "Guilty." The words swam toward him in widening circles. The woman was next. She stood and lifted her veil, stared at him. "Guilty." Her voice, husky and low, reverberated in the highceilinged room. Then it was his mother's turn. He waited, breathless, to hear her "Not guilty!" because she knew how he'd suffered, knew the endless abuse he'd endured. His mother rose slowly. Her mouth opened, even from a distance he could see her shaping the words, but he couldn't hear anything. "Speak up, please," the judge ordered. "Speak up for the record." She opened her mouth again, and again, then shook her head and sank into her seat.

In an instant he was at the jurors' box. "Say something!" he yelled, knowing it was pointless. She blinked at him, her eyes filled with familiar tears of wistful apology, but it wasn't enough, and he started to shake her, he was determined to rattle the truth out of her. "Tell them!" He shook her frail, bony body, shook her until a restraining arm on his shoulder told him he had to stop.

"Sir? Are you all right?"

With a jolt, he realized that he was in the funeral chapel, not a courtroom, that the hand on his shoulder was real. He turned toward the speaker. It was the nondenominational minister who had delivered the eulogy.

"I'm fine," he told him. "Thank you."

He proceeded toward the casket. He'd never seen a dead body, and the thought made him queasy. His brother's casket had been closed, draped with the American flag that someone had folded after the twenty-one–gun salute and handed to his father.

He stared into the casket. His father looked almost alive, like the statues of celebrities he'd seen in the Hollywood Wax Museum. In death as in life, his complexion was florid. Before, the heightened color had been a product of his drinking and splenetic temper. Now it was the handiwork of a mortician who had applied too much rouge in an attempt to simulate good health. He'd also tried to coax his father's thick lips into a half-smile, to assure the viewers the deceased was at peace. The effect was lopsided, almost a sneer. It was singularly appropriate, he thought, a testimony to his father. Even in death, his personality controlled the muscles of his face.

His father's eyes were closed. He should have expected that; he didn't know why he'd assumed they'd be open, why he was so disturbed that they weren't. It wasn't until after he'd turned away from the casket that he recognized with a shock that what he'd felt was keen disappointment, that he'd been hoping to read in his father's eyes, at the last, some glint of approval.

It was too late. There would be no approval, no mystical reconciliation between father and son that would defy the finality of death. It had been ridiculous to think there would be. And there would be no balancing of the scales, either, no final opportunity to prove his father wrong, to earn, if not his affection, then at least his grudging respect.

The thought gnawed at him as he walked toward the burial grounds; and as he watched his father's casket being lowered into the ground, he was overcome with a strange, unexpected feeling of emptiness, a hollow sensation that made him want to cry. Not for his father, but for himself. Because he realized later that day, sitting in his apartment, that his last chance to defeat his father had been buried along with his body.

He wasn't certain at what point the emptiness became frustration; the frustration, rage. He began seething with the injustice of it all, railing against his father for abusing him, against his mother for not having defended him, against himself for never having confronted him and salvaged his dignity. Against all the people who had wronged him—classmates, teachers, employers who hadn't appreciated his efforts; Al Borbolla, who had fired him after all his hard work, the bastard! his coworkers at the post office. Everyone. And there was no way to get even. No way at all.

He lay in bed for three days staring at the ceiling, not leaving his apartment, eating without tasting, going through the motions of living without any awareness of doing them. The phone rang but he didn't answer it. There was no one he wanted to talk to. There was nothing he had to say. He didn't think it was his supervisor at the postal station. He'd told her he was taking Thursday off to attend the funeral. Why don't you take a few days, she'd suggested, this must be a hard time for you. He knew her sympathy was fake. They were all fakes. He hated them all.

Once or twice, when the phone rang for what seemed to him like ten minutes, the thought crossed his mind that it might be someone at the nursing home calling to tell him that something had happened to his mother. This was the first Saturday since she'd been admitted to the facility that he hadn't visited her. But he didn't pick up the phone. He didn't really care.

By Monday morning he'd compressed the rage into a hard lump that throbbed in his chest with a dull, manageable ache. He called his supervisor and told her he was taking a leave. Then he went to the house.

It was musty but for the most part neat. He wasn't surprised. His father had retained his penchant for military tidiness even after he'd left the army. He supposed he'd have to go through his father's things, give them to the Salvation Army or a thrift shop. And the house itself? It was unlikely that his mother would ever come home. Should he move back? The mortgage payments were low—lower than his apartment rent. Of course, it was his mother's house. She could rent it to strangers or sell it. He'd have to talk to her about it, have to tell her his father was dead. What do you want to do, Ma? But she was in no condition to make a decision. He'd have to see a lawyer about obtaining his mother's power of attorney before she was incapable of granting it.

If he *did* move back, he'd sleep in his parents' room. There was nothing symbolic about that—a psychiatrist might say it was fraught with Oedipal overtones, but the simple fact was that the room was larger and airier and had a view of the backyard.

He walked into the bedroom. The air conditioner had been going for some time, preserving the room and everything in it with its icy breath. Near his father's side of the bed lay a neat pile of clothes and a pair of newly polished shoes. Training dies hard. The bedspread, too, had been carefully folded, but someone had kicked it to the floor. The bed was unmade, the comforter thrown to one side, evidence of the urgent, sudden drama that had invaded the room and snatched its occupant.

There was a half-empty whiskey bottle on his father's nightstand, and two glasses with traces of the amber liquid. There was lipstick on one of the glasses and both pillows. "Lipstick on your collar," Connie Francis had wailed. It was one of his mother's favorite songs, although he'd never understood why. He turned off the air conditioner and left the room.

Except for two six-packs of Coors, the refrigerator was almost empty. There was a pizza box on the kitchen counter next to three empty beer cans. There were whiskey bottles and beer cans all over the house, he'd noticed, votive candles his father had dedicated to the two-headed god of fermentation and inebriation.

The mail slot was in the living room. Walking toward it, he passed the card table in the middle of the room and stopped. The game board was lying on it, open, and he felt his abdomen constrict. There were two game pieces on Go, a purple and a green. The stacks of Chance and Community Chest cards lay in their respective rectangles, waiting to reveal their instructions. Tucked under the borders of two opposing sides of the board were neat piles of pastel-colored Monopoly money arranged in ascending denominations from one to five hundred. The rest of the money was in the "bank," along with the miniature wooden houses and hotels that would eventually dot the board. The dice, each showing one dot, were two eyes staring at him with an unspoken but familiar, malevolent challenge. With one quick motion, he swept everything to the carpeted floor—game board, game pieces, cards, houses, hotels, dice. The paper bills floated hesitantly in the air and were the last to land.

It wasn't what he'd expected. He'd fantasized countless times about upsetting the board, hurling the pieces at his father; now he felt only a disappointingly brief, childlike satisfaction. It was too little, too late. Like all the angry words he'd never voiced. Meaningless. He retrieved the scattered pieces and placed them neatly in the game box.

He looked at the board—a large, colorful, harmless cardboard square. His father had been obsessed with the game, as if winning would make up for *his* father's bankruptcy and suicide, and his own mediocre life. *"If I'd had his money, I wouldn't've blown it, let me tell you, boy. I would've been a winner, goddammit."*

"Winning is everything, boy," but he had never won, not once. Now he would never have a chance to win, and he realized in one illuminating moment that instead of releas-

ing him, his father's dying had been his final victory. "*Come to Mama*."

He sat in the chair that was usually his and placed two pieces on Go. Purple was his father's favorite. He took it for himself and gave his father the yellow. He distributed the money, $1,500 in an assortment of bills. Then he picked up the dice. He jiggled them in his cupped hands and dropped them onto the board. Seven. He moved his piece to Chance. "Advance to Boardwalk." That was an auspicious start; Boardwalk was the most valuable property on the board. He paid the $400 into the "bank" and found the property card. His father's turn. He rolled the dice. Three and one. He moved the yellow piece four spaces to Income Tax and smiled. "Pay ten percent or $200." But even as he withdrew $150 from his father's money, he could hear him. "I didn't roll a four; you did. This is stupid, boy. It doesn't mean shit and you know it." And he wanted to retort that it was his game, his rules, he could do whatever he damn well pleased. But he knew his father was right.

He didn't formulate *the idea* that day. It came to him later, and when it did, he knew it was not only perfect, but necessary and right. *"Power is what counts, boy."* That had been his father's mantra. Now it would be his. With every move, he would prove to his father—to everyone—that he had power, that he was someone to contend with. A winner. And he would get even with the world that had ignored him, that had dismissed him as inconsequential, a nonentity. (*"No kidding? I didn't know there was another son. . . ."*)

He hated them all.

But not as much as he hated Jessie Drake.

42

Officer Maurice Kern of Hollywood Division looked at the two sketches on the bulletin board. He read the intradivision memo tacked next to the sketches. Then he looked at the sketches again.

There was something about the face without the glasses and the extra hair (obviously a toupee) that looked familiar. He'd thought so all along, ever since the task force had circulated the sketch of the man the papers called the Monopoly Murderer, but he hadn't been able to figure out where he'd seen him.

Now he was sure. Well, pretty sure. Sure enough so that he had to make a decision. He read the memo again: ". . . report any incidents involving the use of an automated teller machine and . . ."

The memo had been signed by Det. Jessie Drake. Drake, Kern knew, was the woman whose face was constantly on TV. Kern would have to tell her that, yes, he'd come across an incident involving an ATM. Then she'd want to see the report he'd filed, and that was the problem. Kern hadn't filed a report.

The whole thing had been a waste of time. He'd intercepted a mugging, apprehended the two assailants, and put them in his patrol car, where his partner was waiting. But the victim had disappeared. Kern had checked the area but found no sign of him. That had left Kern with two suspects and the ten-dollar bill the punks had taken from the victim.

Of course, Kern had let the suspects go. Without a victim to bring charges, there was no point in holding them. Technically, Kern was supposed to file an evidence report describing the incident. But for ten bucks? The victim had obviously had similar thoughts. He'd retrieved his wallet (Kern remembered that); that was the main thing. Kern doubted he'd show up demanding his ten dollars. The money would stay in property division awhile and eventually find its way into the city coffers. Not that the city would notice or appreciate it. Ten dollars doesn't go far.

So Kern had pocketed the money and hadn't filed a report. Which meant that now he had to lie to Detective Drake. He could tell her there'd been no physical evidence, that he'd intercepted the mugging before the victim had handed over any money. But what if the victim reappeared and told her otherwise? That's the last thing Kern needed, getting his ass chewed off by a female cop.

But if it involved the serial killer. . . Kern frowned. Maybe he'd tell Drake that in the confusion, he'd forgotten to take the ten dollars back from the suspects. He nodded. That was better.

"Anyway, I thought you ought to know about it," Maurice Kern said to Jessie and Pruitt a half-hour later.

The three were sitting around a table. Takamura and Barrows were out investigating reports from citizens who'd called in response to the reward offer.

Yeah, we definitely want to know about it, Jessie thought. She felt excitement tingling through her. Then she reminded herself not to get her hopes up. The victim Kern had helped wasn't necessarily the killer she was looking for.

But it was amazing that anything had come from the memo she'd sent all the divisions. A waste of time, everyone had told her. (Takamura had raised an eyebrow and smiled.) Pruitt had still been skeptical when Kern arrived at Parker and told them about the mugging at the ATM. But Pruitt wasn't scoffing anymore.

"So no file, huh?" Pruitt was leaning back in his chair, staring at the brown-haired, uniformed officer.

"The guy disappeared. I had to let the suspects go. No case." He shrugged. "There's a resemblance between the guy I helped and the face in the sketch, but they're not identical. He was short. I remember that. It didn't seem fair, those punks picking on him." He shook his head in sympathy.

Jessie said, "Was he nervous? Jumpy?"

"Yeah, he was nervous, but who wouldn't be in a mugging?"

Pruitt said, "You didn't think it odd that he disappeared?"

"I looked for him." Kern's defensiveness was almost palpable. "I thought it was funny, him walking away. But it happens. I thought he figured it wasn't worth his time filing charges, appearing in court, all for a lousy ten bucks. He *did* get his wallet back." He looked steadily at the two detectives.

"So where is this ten dollars?" Pruitt asked.

"I told you. I forgot to take it from the punks."

"Right. I *forgot* you said that." Pruitt smiled.

"It can happen," Kern said to no one in particular.

"When did this incident occur?" Jessie asked.

"I can't say for sure. My partner's on vacation, so I can't

ask him. I'd say four weeks ago." He nodded. "That seems right."

"What day of the week was it?" Jessie asked.

Kern shook his head. "Sorry. I think it was either a Wednesday or a Thursday. Definitely not a weekend."

"Too bad you didn't file a report," Pruitt said. "Then we'd all know."

"I explained what happened." Kern shifted in his seat.

"Let it alone, Frank," Jessie said in an undertone. What was the point of harassing the man? It wouldn't improve his memory. "Which ATM location was involved in this incident?"

Kern hesitated. "I know this is going to sound stupid, but I can't tell you exactly which one because—"

"Jesus!" Pruitt rolled his eyes, then shook his head.

Kern colored. "Can I finish, please?" He addressed Jessie. "I know it was along Sunset near Vine, but there's a lot of ATMs there. And when I came on the scene, the victim wasn't in front of the ATM, so how could I know which one he used?"

"So how do you know there *was* an ATM incident?" Pruitt asked.

" 'Cause the guy told me so, that's how."

"Let's go." Jessie stood up. "Take me to the area."

"Now?"

Jessie accompanied Kern in the patrol officer's car. Pruitt had elected to stay behind, and she was relieved. His presence would have intimidated Kern and made him more on edge than he was.

As Jessie and Kern approached Sunset and Vine, she understood the patrol officer's problem. There were five banks in close proximity to each other: Great American, Home Savings, Bank of America, Wells Fargo, and First Interstate.

"This is where I apprehended the muggers," Kern told

her. They were standing on the south side of Sunset, halfway between Vine and Argyle, a block east of Vine. "See, my partner and I stopped at this pizza place." He pointed to a store in a mall on the northwest corner of Sunset and Vine. "Anyway, my partner was already in the car—he was driving, see?—and I was just getting in when I noticed something suspicious across the street."

"Do you have any idea which direction they came from?"

"No. Sorry."

"So it could've been any of the banks." Except for Great American. The Sunset-Vine branch was the closest to where the two policemen were standing, but Jessie had already noticed that it didn't have any ATMs.

First Interstate was on the northwest corner of Sunset and Argyle; Home Savings, the northeast corner of Sunset and Vine; Bank of America on the southwest corner. Wells Fargo was right next to Bank of America. Each of the banks, she learned within minutes, had two ATMs apiece.

Eight ATMs wasn't as good as only one ATM (that would've been a miracle), but it was still pretty damn wonderful compared to thousands. Eight ATMs was manageable, doable. For the first time since she'd realized they were dealing with a serial killer, Jessie allowed herself to feel a kernel of hope.

"That means we have to get the records for these eight ATMs," Jessie explained to Pruitt and the others. Takamura and Barrows had returned to Parker Center before Kern dropped her off.

"Shit! A guy could get a complex working with you." Barrows grinned at her. "You this good all the time at West L.A.?"

"I got lucky," Jessie said. Damn lucky. She felt great.

"Way to go, Jess," Pruitt said softly and winked.

"What records?" Takamura said. "Kern didn't give you a date."

"He was sure it was four weeks ago," Jessie said. "We check ATM printout tapes for four weeks ago on a Thursday."

Takamura shook his head. "Even if the man Kern saw *is* the killer, we don't know if he was making a deposit or a withdrawal."

"Yes, we do." Jessie walked over to the flow chart on the wall. "Four weeks ago would make it the week of August third. Thursday is the sixth. That's the week he didn't kill anyone, the week we thought he killed the Dehoff woman in Manhattan Beach."

"So that means no withdrawal, either," Barrows said.

"But he *did* make a withdrawal that week. Ten dollars. See?" She pointed to the notation below the date.

"Why ten dollars?" Pruitt asked. "That doesn't make sense."

"Because that's the week he won ten dollars!" She went to her desk and found the letter and Community Chest card she was looking for. "Here's the card he sent: 'You have won second prize in a beauty contest. Collect ten dollars.' We know when he got that card. He discussed it in the first letter he sent. Let me find—here it is: '. . . last Thursday I was collecting a prize for a beauty contest. It's only ten dollars, but it's money in my account.'"

"So we look for withdrawals of ten dollars?" Barrows asked.

"Of twenty dollars. ATMs work in increments of twenty dollars."

"With eight ATMs, there could be hundreds of people who withdrew twenty dollars on that day," Takamura said.

"This happened at night. Kern said between eight-thirty P.M. and ten. That helps. The tapes won't give us the name of the person who made the transaction, but they *will* list the date and time of the transaction, card number, type of transaction—deposit, withdrawal, transfer. Then we'll have to contact the banks and have them supply us with the names of the people who own the card numbers we pull. Then we look for those with the initials J.M."

"Then we have him." Barrows shook his head in admiration. "Your long shot paid off. What about videotapes? We could get them for the days in question and look for someone who resembles the killer. Better yet, we could have Kern take a look at them."

"I checked. Only two of the banks have videos at that location. We could subpoena them, too."

Takamura said, "This could take days."

"We don't have any other leads," Barrows said. "I talked to thirteen people yesterday and three this morning who swear they saw the killer. I didn't learn a thing except that people are eager to win a reward."

Pruitt swiveled in his chair. "Why are you so down on this, John? 'Cause it's not your idea?"

"That has nothing to do with it!" He spoke in angry, staccato syllables. "Maybe this ATM business will help us find the man. I hope so. But today's Wednesday. I don't think we'll find out who he is before he strikes again tomorrow. And how are you going to get these tapes, anyway?"

"We get a *subpoena duces tecum,* John," Pruitt said with exaggerated patience.

Takamura shook his head. "One, a case hasn't been filed. Two, even if you had a subpoena, the banks have ten days to comply with it. And three, the banks will try to get a subpoena quashed. They'll say we're requesting records that violate the privacy of customers other than the ones we're looking for. They'll protect their customers' funds above everything."

Above human life? Jessie hoped not. "We could get a search warrant. Talk to Corcoran, John, ask him to get the

D.A. to write one up himself. We have enough to show the magistrate probable cause and exigent circumstances."

"You're talking about four warrants. One for each bank. You want to access files of not one but four banks and look at transactions of an unlimited number of customers?" Takamura shook his head.

Takamura gave them hourly bulletins:

Corcoran was skeptical, but he was talking with Hanson.

Corcoran and Hanson were now meeting with the D.A. to explain the exigent circumstances and probable cause.

The D.A. had agreed to write the warrants but was worried that because of their broad nature, a magistrate would refuse to sign them.

At 3:30 P.M. Corcoran appeared. He was grinning and waving the warrants. "Judge Hennessey balked about signing, but I told him this was our first solid lead and the killer would probably strike tomorrow." He turned to Takamura. "This ATM wild card sure as hell paid off, John. Hanson's pleased. Damn pleased."

Pruitt said, "The ATM angle and memo were Jessie's idea."

"I told you that, Peter." Takamura's smile was strained, his lips thin.

Corcoran frowned. "Did you? I guess I just don't remember." He smiled at Jessie. "Nice going, Jessie. I knew from the day you walked in that you were going to be an asset to the team."

Sure, Jessie thought. Was it her imagination, or had Corcoran overstressed the first syllable of "asset"?

Corcoran said, "But this isn't about individual credit. You're a team. And the bottom line is, we're finally closing in on the son of a bitch." He made a thumbs-up gesture.

At 3:50, ten minutes before closing time, each of the detectives entered one of the four banks near Sunset and

Vine. Faced with the warrants, the branch managers still insisted on talking to their legal departments before complying. And when they retrieved the printed tapes from the vaults, they insisted on blacking out all data related to card numbers not used to withdraw twenty dollars. While waiting, the detectives examined the ATM videos that were available. The videos showed no one who resembled the killer.

Takamura had been right, Jessie thought glumly when she and the other detectives reviewed their findings. Everyone and his sister had withdrawn twenty dollars on the evening in question. The combined number of bank cards used on all eight ATMs to withdraw twenty dollars between 8:30 and 10:00 on Thursday, August 6, was sixty-three.

For a card number whose owner belonged to the banking institution at which the card was used, Jessie learned, tracing the number took seconds. By 5:00 P.M. the detectives had the names and addresses of the twenty-five card owners who banked with the institution whose ATM they'd used. But identifying the owners of the thirty-eight cards that had accessed the ATM through Star, Plus, Cirrus, or The Exchange would have to wait until tomorrow. The ATM bank branch first had to ascertain the banking institution at which the owner of the card had an account. That involved more phone calls, more questions to legal departments. It also involved obtaining additional search warrants, naming the banks in question.

Of the twenty-five names that the banks had given the task force, two had the initials J.M. One was a woman, Jocelyn Maddens. The male was Jerry Medina. From the bank, Jessie had gone to Medina's De Longpre residence—he was a fifty-one-year-old Latino with black eyes, a full head of hair, and a mustache.

Takamura said, "A whole day spent chasing nothing." He looked pointedly at Jessie.

"We'll get the other names in the morning," Pruitt said. "It won't take long. All the information is on computer."

"By the time the banks open and we get more names, the killer will probably have killed his next victim. We have—what? Thirty-eight numbers to track? With our luck, we'll have at least five J.M.'s."

An officer entered the room. "Detective Drake? This was in today's mail." He handed Jessie an envelope. "I looked for you before, but you were out. I was away from my desk when you came back."

She felt the dread she experienced whenever she received a message from the killer. But receiving it in the mail, she told herself, was less personal than finding it on her windshield.

"What's in it this time?" Barrows asked.

43

The envelope contained a Community Chest card—"Advance to Go. Collect $200"—another note, and two pictures: one of a park, another of a crown. The note was brief:

> You're gloating, aren't you! You think you won. But you're wrong. Dead wrong! Two doubles in a row—it's a sign that luck and justice are on my side.
>
> First a trip to the bank to collect my $200. Then Oriental Avenue—a wasted move, but I don't care, because after that—well, that's for you to figure out.
>
> You didn't play fair. I *always* play fair, *always!*
>
> Do you believe in the Bible, Jessie? I do.

There was no salutation. And Jessie didn't need Manny to tell her that the anger was stronger than ever. Less veiled. *Because of Teresa,* she knew. *He blames me for her death.*

"Why the hell is he bringing in the Bible?" Pruitt said. "And what's with the park and crown?"

Barrows said, "The park could be the Garden of Eden. That ties in with 'Bible.' What could relate to the Garden of Eden?"

"Park Place?" Takamura suggested. "Marvin Gardens?"

Jessie frowned. "How would he get there from Oriental in one move? Park Place is thirty-one spaces away. Marvin Gardens is twenty-three spaces." She moved her finger from Jail and stopped on St. James Place. "St. James Park is in London. St. James Place is ten spaces from Oriental. He rolled a six and a four."

"Something British," Takamura said. "A British church? That would tie in with the Bible. Or the British embassy?"

"Christ!" Barrows whistled. "Should we alert them?"

"Why don't we sing 'Rule, Britannia'?" Pruitt crumpled a paper. "This is stupid. We can't second-guess him. He's proved that." He turned to Jessie. "I don't like the fact that he's so angry at you. This note sounds like a personal threat."

"He's angry about Teresa Barnett. But he plays fair, and I'm not connected to St. James Place." Thank God, she thought. But what about the next move? And the next? What if he *could* fit her into his game moves? Make it "fair"? What if—"I'm so stupid!" she exclaimed.

They stared at her.

"We have to ask the banks to check again through the printouts for August sixth, but look for a deposit of ten dollars made with one of the numbers that made a twenty-dollar withdrawal."

"Why ten dollars?" Barrows frowned. "I don't get it."

"Because the killer plays fair! He tells me that every time. He had to withdraw twenty dollars, because that's the smallest amount the ATM will give him, but he won only ten dollars. So he planned to redeposit ten dollars. That's the ten dollars the punks took from him."

Pruitt said, "If they took the ten dollars, that's the end of it."

"No. He would deposit another ten dollars. He's fair, remember? And he'd *specifically* go to this ATM, to make things right."

"Fine," Takamura said. His face said otherwise. "We'll check with the banks in the morning." He put on his jacket.

The phone rang. Takamura answered it and handed Jessie the receiver. "Your sister." He didn't say "again," but Jessie knew he was thinking it. Helen had called twice before.

Jessie took the receiver. "Go ahead," she told the others. "See you in the morning."

Pruitt signaled her good-bye with his eyes. She'd told him earlier that she couldn't see him tonight; Helen was too anxious about Neil showing up.

"Helen? What's up? Did Neil call?"

"No. Are you coming soon? I'd feel safer if you were here."

"I told you to call Phil if there's a problem."

"I can't take this anymore, Jessie! The waiting is making me crazy! What if he shows up before you get here?"

"I'll be there soon, Helen." She hung up the phone. It rang again immediately, and she picked it up. "Detective Drake."

"Detective, this is Charles Barnett. I have to know—excuse me a minute, please."

Jessie heard another voice in the background, then Charles Barnett whispering "All *right!*" Barnett spoke again. "First of all, I want to thank you for attending Teresa's funeral."

Jessie didn't know what to say. She waited.

"I also wondered whether you've made any progress in finding the person who . . . who killed our daughter."

"Mr. Barnett, we're working on it nonstop and we have some leads. But I can't promise when we'll have something conclusive. Believe me, I know how painful this must be for you."

"How can you possibly—I'm sorry. I realize you're trying to be kind. It's just that I—that we, my wife and I, still find it impossible to believe that this happened."

"I understand."

"It was someone Teresa let into her apartment. But who could that be? Did you check with the dentist she worked for? Maybe Teresa met a patient and went out with him."

"We examined Dr. Banneker's files. He doesn't have a patient who fits the profile of the man we're looking for."

"There was another dentist. We forgot about him."

"What other dentist?" Jessie frowned.

"I don't know his name. My wife just remembered that Teresa mentioned she'd worked for another dentist once or twice on the days she didn't work for Dr. Banneker."

"Did you write the name somewhere, Mr. Barnett? This could be important." It could also be nothing. Probably *was* nothing.

"No. I had no reason to write it down."

Naturally. "I'll see if I can find something out. Thank you for calling. If I learn anything, I'll be in touch."

Jessie looked through her notes. No one at Banneker's office had mentioned that Teresa had worked anyplace else; then again, Jessie hadn't asked. She'd assumed—stupidly, as it turned out—that Teresa had worked only for Banneker. She looked at her watch. 5:50. She dialed the dentist's number. The receptionist answered. Jessie identified herself and asked to speak to the dentist.

"He's with a patient right now, fitting a crown. Perhaps I could help you? Does this have something to do with Teresa?"

"Yes, it does. What days did she work for Dr. Banneker?"

"Let me think." She paused. "Teresa worked here three days a week. Mondays, Thursdays, and Fridays."

"What about the other days?"

"We're closed Wednesdays. I don't know where she worked

Tuesdays. We have another hygienist here that day. She's been with us for years. Sandy—she's the other hygienist? —she gave up her other days, but she held on to Tuesdays."

"Is it possible that Dr. Banneker would know where Teresa worked on Tuesdays? Or maybe someone else in the office?"

"I can check. Please hold." She returned a few moments later. "I'm sorry. Dr. Banneker has no idea. I spoke to the rest of the staff. They don't know, either."

Jessie thanked her and hung up. A minute later, she dialed the doctor's number again. "Sorry to bother you again," she told the receptionist. "Could you tell me whether Dr. Banneker found Teresa through an employment agency? And if so, which one."

"It wasn't through an agency. Teresa responded to an ad I placed in the papers."

In the back of her mind, Jessie recalled something about an employment agency, although she wasn't certain it was connected with Teresa Barnett. Would her landlord know where she'd worked on Tuesdays? Unlikely. Teresa was a private person.

Jessie was about to leave the room when she realized where she'd seen a mention of an employment agency—in the index of Teresa's daybook. Which was now sitting in Property. The good news was that Property was in Parker Center, on the ground floor.

Jessie went to Property, waited while someone found the tagged daybook, and signed it out. Back at her desk, she found the agency under *E* and dialed the number next to it. After five rings, an answering machine picked up the call.

". . . are nine to five-thirty. In case of emergency, please call . . ."

Jessie jotted down the number, hung up, and dialed it. This time she reached an answering service; an operator told her that the manager of the employment agency was out.

"I'll give Ms. Sebrins the message," the operator told her.

Jessie left the number for Parker Center. "Please tell Ms. Sebrins it's urgent." That wasn't necessarily true, but Jessie would have no way of knowing until she spoke to her.

She called Helen and told her she'd be delayed. She waited an hour and a half in the Operations Room. During that time, she called the employment agency several times. Each time the operator told her he still hadn't heard from Ms. Sebrins.

At a little after seven, Jessie called again and left her home number. As she was leaving the room, the phone rang. She hurried to the phone and picked up the receiver. "Detective Drake."

It was Marla Sebrins.

"I'm glad you called," Jessie told her. "I need information about a client of yours. Teresa Barnett?"

"That's the strangest coincidence! I've been trying to contact Teresa. I have some work for her." She paused. "But why are *you* interested in her? Has she done something wrong?"

Slowly, Jessie explained about Teresa.

"I didn't hear a thing about it!" Marla Sebrins exclaimed. "How horrible! She was the loveliest girl, so refined. But I still don't understand why you're calling me."

"I need your help. Could you give me the names of any dentists Teresa worked for? Jobs you arranged for her, I mean."

"As a matter of fact, that's who called about Teresa. Dr. Herman Stoltz, on Wilshire and Crescent Heights. He was pleased with Teresa when she worked for him previously and requested her again." Marla Sebrins gave Jessie the doctor's phone number.

When Jessie called Stoltz, an answering service operator told her Stoltz was on vacation for two weeks. "He's referring all his emergencies to Dr. Hellman."

"Are they associates?" If so, maybe Hellman would know about Teresa. Or J.M.

"No, they don't work in the same office."

"I'd like to speak to him anyway."

Dr. Mark Hellman, Jessie learned, knew nothing about Teresa or any of Stoltz's patients except for those who had contacted him in the doctor's absence. No, he had no idea where Stoltz was. Somewhere in Europe. Had Stoltz left a number where he could be reached? Yes, but the number was in Hellman's office and Stoltz was en route to another city. He was scheduled to call Hellman sometime Thursday to give him a new number.

What about Stoltz's staff? Did Hellman know where to reach any of them? Well, Stoltz's office was closed while he was on vacation, but Hellman happened to know that the receptionist and the woman who did insurance forms were coming in a few mornings anyway. The receptionist had mentioned that to Hellman two days ago. What was the receptionist's name? Andrea something.

"I don't know her last name, Detective," Hellman said. "And the only number I have for her is Dr. Stoltz's office number."

"What time does Andrea get to the office in the morning?"

"I don't know. Probably around eight. That's when my receptionist comes in. But with Dr. Stoltz on vacation, Andrea might not come in until much later."

Terrific, Jessie muttered after she hung up. Stoltz would be calling "sometime" Thursday night. Andrea "something" might meander into Stoltz's office "sometime" during the day.

Thank God they had the ATM lead, she thought as she drove home. One of those numbers *had* to belong to him.

If not, "sometime" tomorrow, the killer would strike again.

"Somewhere."

* * *

Jessie heard the screams as she was opening the side door.

"Don't hit me! Please don't. Please!"

Matthew! The cries were coming from his bedroom.

Jessie ran. Instinctively, her hand went to her gun, then stopped. Why had Helen let Neil into the house? Why hadn't she called Phil? *He's going to kill me, Jessie!* Oh, God! If anything happened to Helen. . . .

"Get over here, I said!"

"Please! I'll be good I'll be good I'll be good!"

"If I have to look for you, Jessica, it'll be worse, I promise! Get over here right now, do you hear me?"

The closet is small and humid and filled with the smell of cedar. The stiff hairs on her mother's mink coat tickle her nose, but she can't sneeze. If she is still, Jessie knows, very still, maybe Mommy will go to her room and lie down and then Daddy will be home, and then—

"There you are!"

Jessie was ten feet away from the bedroom door now.

". . . all your fault Mommy had to leave! All. Your. Fault." A thwack accompanied each word. "Do you know what happens to bad boys like you? Do you?"

Jessie pushed the door open. Oh, God, oh, Jesus! She felt as if she had slammed into her past. Matthew was on his bed, curled in a fetal position, his arms shielding his face. There were welts on his arms and legs. He was whimpering.

"Get away from him." Jessie thought she would vomit.

"You don't—"

"Get the hell away from him this minute!"

Helen moved away from the bed. Her face was white.

"Matthew," Jessie said as calmly as she could. "Matthew, honey, I want you to go into my room right now."

"You have no right to interfere," Helen said.

"Shut up," Jessie whispered. "Just shut the hell up.

Matthew, go to my room," she repeated. "I'll be there soon."

The boy looked at his mother, then at his aunt. Cautiously, he edged off the bed and out of the room.

"He *knew* I had a headache," Helen said. "I told him not to bother me. I had such terrible, terrible pain."

"You're a monster."

"It's because of Neil, Jessie, don't you see that? I just couldn't handle the stress, not knowing when he'll show up, what he'll do. I've never, ever hit Matthew before."

"You're a liar. It's you, not Neil. All along, it's been you." You are some detective, Jessie told herself.

"No! You're wrong, Jessie. Ask Matthew! He'll tell you—"

"He'll lie, because he's afraid of what you'll do if he tells the truth. Just like we lied to Daddy." And to ourselves. "How could you do it, Helen? How could you hit him? He's your child! What kind of mother—"

"Don't you dare look at me like that! Don't you talk to me about being a mother! At least I didn't kill my baby!"

In an instant, Jessie was standing in front of her sister. She slapped Helen hard across the face. Helen raised her arm, the one holding the brush she'd used on Matthew. Jessie twisted the brush out of her hand and threw it to the floor. She hit Helen on her shoulder, again and again.

". . . no better than I am, are you?" she heard Helen whisper.

Jessie dropped her hands. She looked at Helen, then fled from the room.

"It's in both of us, Jessie!" Helen cried, her voice an odd blend of triumph and self-loathing. "You can't run away from that, can you?"

Matthew was on her bed when Jessie entered the bedroom. "Are you OK?" she said softly. She touched his cheek.

He threw his arms around her. "Please don't tell anyone, Aunt Jessie. Mommy said if the police know, a man will take me to a place with strangers. I don't want to live with strangers!"

So that was the "bad man." Not Neil. "That's not going to happen, Matthew. Your dad's coming soon, did you know that?" She stroked his back. His ribs were so thin.

"Mommy said he's going to be angry with me, because I've been bad. She's going to tell him that."

"You're not bad, Matthew." Oh, God, you're not bad.

"I give Mommy headaches."

"The headaches aren't your fault, Matthew. None of this is your fault."

"But will you tell? Please don't tell, Aunt Jessie. Please!" He buried his head in her chest.

Matthew finally fell asleep in her arms. Jessie wanted desperately to talk to somebody—Manny, she needed Manny—but it wasn't fair to bother him at night. She thought about driving over to Frank's, but how could she leave Matthew alone in the house with Helen?

So she spent the night in the king-size bed with her nephew. She called Frank and told him what happened. He offered to come over, but she said no. Instead, he talked to her on the phone for a long time, saying all the right things, but when she finally hung up, Helen's words were still ringing in her ears.

You're no better than I am, are you?

It's in both of us, Jessie!

"You're wrong!" Jessie whispered to the walls. She looked at Matthew. I could never hit him, she told herself. I could never hit *any* child!

But was that true?

Then why had she been anxious about the life that had been blossoming within her? And why had she felt, along with the wrenching loss and pain, a bitter relief when that life had leaked out of her?

She hadn't shared those fears with Gary. It had been easier to let him think she was consumed by ambition than to deal with the truth—that she was masquerading behind ambition, afraid to have a child, afraid she'd be just like her mother.

Like Helen.

You can't run away from it, Jessie!

When Jessie awoke in the morning, Matthew was curled next to her. She showered and dressed quickly, then went into Helen's room. Helen looked at her, then turned to the wall.

"I'm taking Matthew to Paige for the day," Jessie said. "When I get home from work, we have to talk."

Helen said nothing.

Jessie took underwear, a shirt, and a pair of jeans for Matthew. After he was dressed, they ate silently in the breakfast room. Then Jessie took him to Paige.

"Helen has a terrible headache," Jessie told her neighbor.

"Poor thing," Paige said. "A bad day, huh?"

A bad life. Where would it end?

44

He always awoke early on Thursdays, ever since he'd starting playing *the game*, but he never rushed out of bed. He enjoyed lingering under the covers in the still of the morning, playing the day's events in his mind, rehearsing his moves.

At eight the alarm clock rang. He showered and put on a pair of beige twill slacks and a white short-sleeved shirt. He made the bed and went into the kitchen.

Some Thursdays he was so excited he could barely eat, but he always forced himself (*"Breakfast is your most important source of energy"*). Today he found it harder than usual to finish, and though he was tempted to leave the cereal bowl and utensils in the sink, he washed and dried them. The bowl had a new chip. He ran his finger over it and thought about getting new dishes; then he thought about Silk Flowers, and Teresa. His eyes welled with tears.

In the bedroom that had been his parents' and was now his, he opened a dresser drawer and removed the small brown box that had held his checks. Wearing gloves, he withdrew a $100 bill and four twenties. He counted the money remaining in the box: $970. That was correct. He thought again about the $140 he'd left with Samuel Kropp at the Federal Building and was tight with anger, but he couldn't allow his emotions to get in his way. Not today.

He slipped the $180 into his wallet, next to a Wells Fargo slip he'd picked up Wednesday. That same day he'd driven around the area again, done another reconnaissance. He had no way of determining how many people would be there when he made his move, but he couldn't allow that fact to stop him. It was the perfect move, the move the roll of the dice had determined, a sign so clear he couldn't ignore it.

He looked at his watch. It was almost nine. Soon he'd go to the ATM to withdraw the two hundred dollars for passing Go. Then he'd go home, get the syringe, and complete his transaction.

At nine o'clock, Jessie was in the hallway near the fourth-floor offices of Dr. Herman Stoltz. She'd called Stoltz's office every five minutes from eight in the morning. At eight-thirty, when the other detectives had left for the banks on Sunset and Vine, Jessie had driven to the medical building on Wilshire near Crescent Heights Boulevard to wait for Andrea "something" to show up.

Right now, she knew, undercover police were stationed near the eight ATMs, waiting for the killer to show up. Takamura, Barrows, and Pruitt were presenting search warrants and asking the bank managers to scan the printout tapes, this time only for card numbers that had been used to make a twenty-dollar withdrawal followed by a ten-dollar deposit on August 6. With any luck, there would be only one such number. And just in case, the detectives would obtain the names and addresses of the owners of the thirty-eight unidentified card numbers who had accounts at the other banks. If necessary, Takamura would get phone approval from Judge Hennessey to sign his name on a search warrant. Hennessey had agreed because of the clear necessity for immediate action. A phone call from Chief Hanson and the mayor had helped persuade him.

We'll find the son of a bitch, Jessie thought as she waited. And then she'd deal with Helen. Right now she couldn't think about her sister or Matthew or their fractured lives.

She wondered who would learn the killer's identity—Takamura? Barrows? Pruitt? She wanted to be there, to read J.M.'s full name on the printout. But she had to talk to Stoltz's receptionist. It was possible that the ATM mugging had nothing to do with the killer; in that case, their only lead was Teresa, through Stoltz. And if the ATM lead *did* come through, the fact that the J.M. whose name appeared on a bank's computer screen was the same J.M. who had met Teresa in Stoltz's office would be proof of his guilt.

And it would be reassuring to know, Jessie thought, that even if Kern *hadn't* crossed paths with the killer at the ATM (it was an amazing, against-all-odds fluke that he had), we would have eventually uncovered clues that would lead us to him.

At 9:35, Jessie saw a heavyset woman in her thirties approaching. The woman had taken advantage of the absence of employer and patients and was dressed in a baggy cotton knit top that didn't cover enough of her too-tight jeans. She slowed as she saw Jessie standing near the door to the dentist's suite.

Jessie approached her and showed her ID. "Det. Jessie Drake, LAPD. Are you Dr. Stoltz's receptionist?"

The color drained from her face, leaving two clownlike circles of rouge. She nodded rapidly. "What are you—did something happen to Dr. Stoltz? Was there a burglary?"

"No. Nothing like that. Dr. Stoltz is fine. Can we talk inside the office, Ms.—?"

"Panneli. Mrs. Andrea Panneli. Of course. I'm not thinking clearly." She took a key ring from her purse. Her hand was shaking, and it took her a while to undo the two door locks.

They went into the waiting room. Jessie sat on a sofa; the receptionist sat on a chair facing her.

"I'm here about Teresa Barnett. I understand she worked for Dr. Stoltz occasionally."

"Yes. He was very pleased with her. And the patients loved her. As a matter of fact, Doctor wants her to work Tuesdays on a permanent basis. I called the agency that sent her, but I haven't heard from her yet." She looked at Jessie. "She's not involved in something illegal, is she? She made such a good impression on me."

"Mrs. Panneli, I'm afraid I have bad news." Quietly, Jessie explained what had happened, watched as first shock, then disbelief, then horror bleached Andrea Panneli's face of what little color had been left.

"Oh, my God! Murdered! Teresa murdered!" She shuddered.

"I know this is a shock, but I need your cooperation. We're looking for the person who killed Miss Barnett. It's possible that it was a man she met while working here. His initials are J.M."

"Here?" It was a frightened whisper. "I couldn't tell you who that would be. I've only been working here four months. You're *sure* she met him here?" She clutched her throat.

"No. But I'd like to look at your *M* files to see if anyone fits the description of the man we're looking for."

She frowned. "I don't know. Dr. Stoltz is on vacation. There's a law about patients' privacy. Dr. Stoltz could fire me. He could be sued. *I* could be sued."

Jessie tried to control her impatience. "I can get a

subpoena, but I'd be wasting valuable time. This is an emergency."

"I don't understand why—oh!" Her eyes widened with fear and curiosity. "You think he's going to kill someone else?"

"It's entirely possible, Mrs. Panneli."

She rose. "All right, I guess." She sounded uncertain. "But you can't take any of the files out of the office."

"That won't be necessary." Jessie followed her to a room that contained several desks and a wall of files.

"Last name begins with *M*, did you say?"

At nine forty-five, he drove to Sunset and Vine. He parked at a meter and was about to get out of the car when he had the feeling something was wrong. He looked through his windshield. There was no unusual movement, but he felt jittery. It was an irrational feeling, probably an aftermath of the incident at the Federal Building, and he was tempted to ignore it, to walk across the street and withdraw the two hundred dollars. Instead, he pulled out of his parking spot and drove to another ATM a half-mile away.

There was no line in front of the ATM. He inserted his card, punched in his secret code (his mother's birthday—date, month, and year), and indicated that he wanted to withdraw two hundred dollars.

The machine returned his card. The screen flashed a message: "Cannot complete transaction at this time."

He tried to control his irritation. He checked the card to make sure there was nothing wrong with the edges, but detected nothing. He reinserted the card, punched in his code, and looked at the screen. "Cannot complete transaction at this time."

He wanted to kick the machine, but he controlled his anger and returned to his car. He couldn't remember where he'd seen another ATM. He drove around for a few minutes until he found one that had the system to which he belonged.

There was a woman in front of him. She was taking a long time, and he wanted to snarl at her, Hurry up! But then she turned around, and he smiled at her pleasantly.

He inserted his card and punched his secret code, and there was the message again! He reached for his card, he would try one more time, but it wasn't there. The machine had swallowed it.

He felt his chest constrict, felt the breath leaving his body, knew his lungs were going to collapse, like punctured balloons, but he had to wait until he was in his car before he inserted the inhalator into his mouth. Minutes later, after his breathing had calmed, he stared dully at the windshield.

Something was definitely wrong. He contemplated abandoning his plan, but the anger blossoming within him made him more determined than ever to continue. He felt a sense of urgency and was sorry he hadn't prepared fully, that he had to return home before he made his move.

"Here you are." Andrea Panneli handed Jessie three files. "Three male patients with the initials J.M."

Jessie looked at the printed tabs. John McGuire. James Meecham. James Mitchell. She opened the McGuire file and closed it. McGuire was a teenager. James Meecham, she learned, was thirty-five; James Mitchell, thirty-eight. Meecham's last appointment was July 28. Mitchell had been in for a cleaning on June 15. Jessie asked Andrea to check her appointment calendar to see what day of the week those two dates fell on. Both were Tuesdays.

"Can you tell me anything about Meecham and Mitchell?"

"I'm not sure what you want to know."

"Can you describe them?"

"It's a little hard. It's not as if I see them every day." She squinted. "James Meecham is average looking. Not too much hair. Kind of short. Then again, so is James Mitchell." She looked at Jessie. "Maybe if you could tell me what you're looking for. . . ."

I'm looking for a serial killer, Jessie wanted to tell her. *I'm looking for a man who has injected curare into eleven innocent people, one of whom was Teresa Barnett.*

The phone rang. Andrea Panneli answered it, then turned to Jessie. "It's for you, Detective."

Jessie took the receiver. "Drake here."

"Jessie? Frank. I got it!"

Jessie felt her heart thud. "What's his name?"

"James Robert Meecham." Pruitt gave her an address on Waring Avenue. "We already shut down his account. You said he plays fair—this way, he can't make his move."

Jessie opened Meecham's folder. The address was the same.

"John's on his way downtown to get arrest and search warrants," Pruitt said. "We don't want to blow this by acting without proper authorization. He wants you to meet me and Barrows at Meecham's place and wait until he arrives with the warrants. We'll secure the exits, make sure Meecham doesn't leave."

After what had happened, he wasn't sure it was safe to go home, but he had no choice. He checked carefully from his parked car but didn't see anyone. He got out of the car and walked to his front door, wondering if at any moment someone would leap out at him. A cat scurried in front of him, and he almost cried out.

Once inside, he went directly into the bathroom, and as he splashed cold water on his face, he noticed his reflection in the mirror. His right eye was twitching; his expression betrayed his agitation. He stood, staring at the frightened man in the mirror, knew he couldn't leave until he calmed down.

* * *

"What took so long?" Pruitt grumbled when Takamura arrived.

Takamura didn't answer him. "Is he in there?"

"Hard to say," Jessie said. "It's quiet. I haven't seen anyone moving around."

"How many exits?"

"Just the one door. Two windows that face the back. Ray is watching those."

They walked quietly to the front door. Jessie and Pruitt stood on either side of the door, ready. Takamura rang the bell. No answer. He rang it again, several times in rapid succession.

Takamura said, "Let's try a back window." He moved away.

"Forget the window." Pruitt slammed his shoulder against the door several times until he heard a splintering sound.

He pushed the door open. Jessie and the others entered, their weapons drawn, and checked silently, room by room. No one in the small living room. No one in the kitchen.

He was coming out of the bathroom as they were nearing it.

"Police!" Takamura announced. "We have a warrant."

The man backed into the bathroom and shut the door, but Jessie pushed it open before he could lock it. She stood facing him, both hands on the gun aimed at his chest.

"I'm unarmed!" the man cried. His hands were in the air. His eyes were wild with terror. "Don't shoot!" he rasped.

"Keep your hands on your head," Jessie ordered calmly.

"I don't understand why you're arresting me." He was breathing rapidly, his chest heaving. "I haven't done anything!"

"Then why'd you try to run?" Pruitt asked.

"I panicked. I thought you were burglars."

"We said we were the police," Jessie said.

"This is a mistake! I want to call a lawyer!"

"I'm going to read you your rights, and then you can call a lawyer, Mr. Meecham," Takamura said. "You have the right—"

"But I'm not Meecham!" he shrieked. "You have the wrong guy! My names is Kales, Jerry Kales."

Takamura looked uncertain. Jessie kept her gun steady.

"I swear I'm not Meecham! I can prove it." He took a step forward.

"Stop right there!'" Jessie warned.

"I just want to get my driver's license. It's on my dresser, in my wallet."

"Get his wallet, Jessie." Takamura aimed his gun at the man.

Jessie walked into the bedroom and found the wallet. She opened it and stared at the photo on the license. The man standing in front of them in a terry-cloth robe with his hands over his head was Kales. The address listed on the license was correct.

She went back to the hall. "He's telling the truth."

"Shit!" Pruitt exclaimed.

Jerry Kales, they learned, hadn't heard the doorbell because he'd been in the shower. What Kales didn't tell them but they learned for themselves was that he'd panicked when they'd said "Police" because he'd just made a buy of a sizable amount of cocaine and thought he was being busted.

When he was calmer, Kales also told them that Meecham had been the previous occupant of the apartment. No, he'd never met him, but Meecham's mail still showed up at the apartment building. As far as Kales knew, the apartment manager handled it.

The apartment manager, Mrs. Naugle, confirmed what Kales said. "Mr. Meecham moved about four months ago. I was sorry to see him go. Always helpful. Carried my groceries, little things like that. A real gentleman, Mr. Meecham."

"Did he leave a forwarding address?" Takamura asked.

"He wasn't sure where he'd be staying permanently, so it didn't make sense to change his address yet. He asked me would I hold his mail for him, and I said sure. Why wouldn't I?"

"What about a phone number?" Jessie asked.

"No. I've told you all I know." She looked at them squarely. "Who's going to fix the door you broke?" she demanded.

From Mrs. Naugle's apartment Jessie called Stoltz's office and asked Andrea to check Meecham's file for a change of address.

"The address you copied is the only one we have," Andrea reported a few minutes later. "That's where we send his bill." She paused. "When I was looking at the files now, I noticed there's another Meecham. E. Meecham. Should I check that?"

"Please."

"That's an Ella Meecham," Andrea Panneli told Jessie when she got back on the phone. "I've never met her, but I checked James Meecham's file. His mother's name is Ella."

This couldn't be coincidence. "Where does she live?"

Andrea Panneli gave her an address on Cherokee Avenue, less than a ten-minute drive from Meecham's former apartment.

It was taking him much longer than it should to get ready. He couldn't concentrate on what he was doing; his mind was going over and over what had happened at the ATM. He didn't know what it meant, how much they knew, but he knew he had to hurry.

He checked again to make sure that the $180 and the deposit slip were in his wallet. Then he took a handkerchief from a bottom drawer in his dresser, doused it with chloroform, and placed it in a plastic bag to retain the fumes. He took the vial of chloroform and slipped it inside his jacket, just in case. The syringe he'd prepared earlier that morning was in the bathroom. He took it and slipped it into another pocket. Then he closed the door and left.

Instead of returning downtown for a new search warrant for the Cherokee Avenue address, Takamura had gone to Hollywood Division, only blocks away from Cherokee Avenue, and was waiting there for telephonic approval from Judge Hennessey. Barrows and two patrolmen were waiting with Kales in his apartment for detectives from Hollywood. Jessie and Pruitt were on their way to Cherokee Avenue.

The address they were looking for belonged to a small yellow stucco house north of Melrose Avenue. The stucco was cracked in several places. The wrought-iron bars on the front windows were chipped, showing patches of black through the white paint. There was no car in the driveway. Jessie and Pruitt waited for Takamura to arrive with the warrants. To Jessie, it seemed like an eternity; in actuality, it was less than fifteen minutes.

There were no sounds coming from the house—no radio, no running water. Takamura rang the bell several times, but no one was surprised when there was no answer.

"Jessie and I will check out the back. Frank, stay in front."

There was no sign that anyone was in the rear of the house. Jessie forced the lock on a back door. She drew her gun, then opened the door and stepped inside the house. Takamura followed.

They had entered a bedroom. The room looked empty, but they made sure no one was in the room or the closet, then made their way carefully to the front of the house to let Pruitt in. On the way, they passed through the living room and stopped.

"Christ!" Jessie swore softly. She was staring at a card

table on which a Monopoly game was in progress. So this is where he chooses his victims, she thought.

The doorbell rang. Jessie started, then walked to the door and let Pruitt in. "This is the place," she told him. "But he's gone. We'll have to wait until he returns." *From killing whom?*

"Take a look at this!" Takamura read from a green stenographer's pad that he'd picked up from the table. " 'Oriental Avenue—check Chinatown.' Then he writes 'Mae Sung Lee, Bunker Hill.' 'Electric Company—Watts.' And so on." Takamura looked up. "He's written it all down, all his moves and the associations he made."

Pruitt said, "Forget about that. That's history. What did he write for St. James Place?"

"Nothing." Takamura frowned. He looked at the board. "He lied to us. He's not going to St. James after all."

"Why would he lie?" Pruitt said. "He's never done that."

"Where *is* he going?" Jessie asked. "Did he write anything?"

"Yes, and it matches what he's got on the board." Takamura pointed to the purple game piece. "Tennessee Avenue."

"Let me see that!" Jessie grabbed the notepad. Tennessee Avenue, she read. Next to it, he'd written "YES!!"

"Christ!" Pruitt muttered.

Takamura said, "What's wrong?"

Jessie said quietly, "It's the street where I live."

45

"It could be a coincidence," Pruitt said, but it was clear he didn't believe it. "How would he know where you live?"

Jessie was already running, searching for a phone, there had to be a phone somewhere, goddammit! In the kitchen she found a wall phone and dialed her number. After four rings, the answering machine picked up. She waited for the beep, then said, "Helen, this is Jessie. If you're there, pick up. It's urgent."

After a few seconds, she hung up, dialed again, left another message. Helen could be in the bathroom or out of the house, but it was more likely she didn't want to talk to Jessie, not after last night. Jessie didn't want to consider the other possibility, but it was there, screaming at her.

". . . address?" Takamura asked.

Jessie hadn't heard him come in. "What?" His voice seemed to be coming from a distance.

"Give me your address. I'll have West L.A. send two units."

Jessie gave him the address. "Tell them to use caution. If he's in the house with Helen, if she's—" She couldn't finish.

"I'll tell them." Takamura placed the call, spoke quietly into the phone, ". . . sister may be in the house, and—"

"My nephew. My nephew may be there, too!" She closed her eyes, pictured Matthew's face. Please, God, let him be at Paige's.

Takamura hung up. "Someone will be at your house any minute. Frank, drive Jessie to her place. I'll call Hollywood, get some units to come here and wait in case Meecham returns. Jessie, we don't know that your house is the target." He avoided her eyes.

"Yes, it is." The moment she'd realized the killer's game, she'd been struck with the irony—the street she lived on was a property on the board. *But so what?* she'd told herself. *He doesn't know where I live. I'm not part of his game*. Even after his notes had become more hostile, after he'd left one on her windshield, she'd reassured herself—his associations were more creative; he'd never chosen a victim who lived on a street whose name matched a property. Until now. Fair game.

"Let's go." Pruitt touched Jessie's arm.

"I want to try one more time." She dialed the number, waited for the beep on the machine. "Helen, if you're there, goddammit, pick up the phone. This has nothing to do with—"

"Can't you leave me alone! Just leave me alone!"

It was Helen! "Listen—"

"If you called to tell me I'm a monster, I already know."

Jessie forced calm into her voice. "Listen carefully. Don't interrupt. I don't want you to panic, but you may be in danger."

"You talked to Neil, didn't you? What did you tell him?"

"Helen, shut up and listen, goddammit! This isn't about Neil or Matthew. This is about the serial killer."

"Oh, my God!" Helen moaned.

"Two police units are on their way. Until they get there, I don't want you to let anyone in, do you understand?"

"Yes." Her voice was almost inaudible.

"Where's Matthew?"

"He's at Paige's. Oh, God, Jessie! I'm so scared!" she whispered. "I don't want to die. Oh, God! I'll be good, I promise I'll be good. I'll never do anything bad again."

"You're going to be all right. I'm going to be with you soon." *Soon enough?* "Are the doors locked?"

"The front door is. The side door is open. I was sitting in the backyard, thinking. Then I heard the phone."

Was Meecham already in the house, waiting? Should she tell Helen to go to a neighbor? But what if Meecham was outside? "I want you to close the side door right now. I'll wait on the phone."

Less than half a minute later, she was back. "It's locked."

"All right. Everything will be all right." If you said it enough times, did that make it come true?

"When will—" Helen stopped. "Someone's ringing the front doorbell. It's the police!"

"Helen, wait!" Jessie yelled.

Helen dropped the kitchen receiver and ran to the door. Through the peephole, she saw a uniformed police officer.

"Ma'am, we don't want to alarm you, but we received a radio report to come to this address and secure the premises. My partner's in back right now, making sure no one's in the yard."

"I know. My sister just told me. She's waiting on the line. She'll be very relieved to know you're here."

"Are your windows and doors locked?"

"The side door was open, but it's locked now." She noticed his expression. "What's wrong?"

"Maybe it would be a good idea if I checked the house."

"You think someone's in here?" she whispered. "Oh, God!" She opened the door, stepped aside to let him in.

"There's probably no one here, ma'am, but I'll make sure. Keep the front door locked while I'm looking through the house." He waited until Helen locked the door. "If my partner comes, tell him where I am. How many rooms are there?"

"Two bedrooms and a den. Through there." She pointed to a hall. "I forgot! My sister's waiting on the phone."

"I'll talk to her, tell her everything's under control."

Helen nodded and led the way to the kitchen. The policeman waited in the doorway. The receiver was dangling from the wall phone where she'd left it. "Jessie?"

"Helen? What's going on? Why don't you—?"

"Everything's all right. The police officer wants to talk to you." Helen turned toward the doorway with the receiver in her hand. "Officer?" But he wasn't there. Suddenly, steellike fingers locked on her throat. She gagged and dropped the receiver. It clacked against the wall.

"Helen?" Jessie called.

Using both her hands, Helen wrenched the fingers away and lunged for the knife on the sink, it was just inches away, but he grabbed her arm before she could reach it, and pulled her to him and pressed the handkerchief against her struggling mouth.

"Helen!" Jessie screamed into the phone.

He picked up the receiver. "I'm waiting for you, Jessie, but you have to come in unarmed. No jacket. Your pockets turned inside out, your hands over your head. If you don't, if anyone else tries to come in, I'll kill her right away."

When Jessie and Pruitt arrived, there were two black-and-whites with flashing red lights a hundred feet from her house. Paige was standing near the officers, holding Matthew's hand. When he saw Jessie, he ran to her. She hugged him tight.

"Don't let them take Mommy." His eyes were wet with tears. "Please, Aunt Jessie! It's my fault. I'll be good."

Oh, God. "This isn't your fault, Matthew. It's—"

Paige had hurried over; now she whispered in Jessie's ear. "He and Eric saw the police pull up. He's convinced they're here because of Helen. I had to stop him from going to your house. What's going on, Jessie? Nobody will say."

"I can't talk to you now, Paige. Please take Matthew in the house." Jessie turned to him. "It'll be all right, honey," she said, hating herself for offering false hope, unable to do otherwise. She disengaged herself from Matthew and watched him walk away with Paige, looking over his shoulder every few steps.

Jessie turned to the officers. "Where is he?"

One of the officers said, "All the drapes are closed. We were told to approach with caution, not to make any noise."

Jessie nodded. "Give me a bullhorn, please."

The officer took a bullhorn from the trunk of his car and handed it to her. She motioned for Pruitt to follow her. When they were near the walkway to the house, she took off her jacket and handed it to Pruitt. Then she gave him her gun and holster.

Pruitt said, "If it was my sister and she was still alive, I'd go in and blast his brains out before he knew what hit him."

"Frank, he's probably got the hypodermic in place. I would, if I were him. In the time it would take me to lower my arms and draw my gun, it would be all over. He knows we have the place surrounded. Maybe, just maybe, I can talk him out of it."

"You really believe that?"

Jessie lifted the bullhorn to her mouth. "Mr. Meecham, this is Detective Drake. I'm unarmed, and I'm going to come in through the front door." She inverted the pockets of her pants and walked to the front door. She unlocked the door with her keys, then left the keys on the porch. She opened the door and stepped inside.

She passed through the entry hall and looked in the living room. It was empty. She knew they would be in her bedroom. When she was thirty feet away, she called out. "Mr. Meecham, I'm in the hall, near the bedroom."

"I want to see you with your hands over your head. I want you to stay in the doorway."

"My hands are over my head." She walked to the doorway and stopped. Meecham had blocked it with an upholstered armchair.

Meecham was crouching on the far side of the bed, which was against the wall facing Jessie, leaning over Helen. Helen was lying along the edge of the bed, her head at the foot. Jessie could see that he'd tied rubber tubing around Helen's right arm. She was startled to see a gun in his left hand. The syringe was in his right, its tip clearly touching Helen's skin. Meecham's thumb was on the end of the syringe, ready.

She looked at the killer and saw a balding, thin, ordinary man who resembled the face in the sketches. She had the feeling she'd seen him somewhere.

"She's alive, Jessie. I kept my word. Now I want you to turn around slowly, but keep your hands over your head."

She turned with small steps until she was facing him again.

"I thought you might try to sneak in a gun. You lied to me before, Jessie. You lied many times. I had to check."

There was no point in denying his accusations. Nothing she could say would convince him; it would only make him angry.

"In case you're wondering, I copied your address from the trust deed in the Hall of Records. I planned to kill you, but

I watched your house and figured out this was your sister. I like that even better." He paused. "You're lucky the boy isn't here. I'd have to kill him, too, you know."

Don't react, Jessie told herself. He wants you to react.

"Your sister's very pretty, by the way. Teresa was very pretty, too, don't you think?"

Jessie didn't say anything.

"Answer me!"

She started at his vehemence. "She was very pretty."

"But you killed her, didn't you? You knew how much I loved her, how important she was to me, but you killed her anyway."

Softly, Jessie said, "Jim, you know I didn't kill Teresa." Careful, careful. Watch his face.

"Of course you killed her! You didn't hold the syringe, but you might as well have, isn't that right? Well, isn't it?"

Jessie could see the syringe pressed against Helen's vein. "I can see how you would think that."

"If you hadn't gone to her with the handkerchief, everything would have been all right! That's why I waited for you. I wanted you to see what it was like when Teresa died, to feel my pain. Are you going to beg me to spare your sister's life? Are you?"

"Would it matter if I did?"

"You didn't have compassion for Teresa, did you? Fair is fair. I kept telling you that, but you didn't listen. So it had to come down to this. An eye for an eye, just like it says."

Do you believe in the Bible, Jessie? I do. "Jim, I understand how desperate you felt. But you know you can't get away. If you give me the syringe, I promise no one will hurt you."

Meecham's laugh was a bark. "I killed all those people and you'll let me go? You must think I'm stupid. My father always told me I was stupid. 'Gullible means stupid,' he'd say. But I'm not stupid! I brought along my father's gun."

"I know you're not stupid, Jim. I won't lie to you. We

can't let you walk away, but we can get you help. A good lawyer can prove that you were emotionally—"

"*I am not crazy*. I won't be locked up with deranged people!" He had put the gun down. With two fingers of his left hand, he was massaging the vein on Helen's arm.

Jessie licked her lips. "What would be the point in killing another person?" Don't say "my sister." Don't personalize it. You're a cop, not the sister of the woman you hit last night, the woman lying inches from death, the mother of your nephew. "You won. You have a Monopoly. You've showed you can do it."

"It's not the same! And don't patronize me!"

"I'm sorry. I don't mean to upset you, Jim."

"My father *always* patronized me. He was a cop, just like you. Arrogant, just like you, Miss Superdetective Jessie Drake. He called me 'boy,' even when I was way past my twenties. The last time we talked, he called me boy. I AM NOT A BOY!"

Jessie flinched. Helen moaned. It took all of Jessie's willpower to keep from jumping over the chair and lunging at Meecham, from putting her hands around his neck and forcing the air out of his mouth and nose until his tongue protruded, purple and swollen, and his eyes bulged. And if she did that, Helen would be dead.

"We don't have much time," Meecham said in a quieter voice. "How did you get my address? I've been trying to figure that out."

Jessie told him about the ATMs.

"Did you have police waiting for me at the ATM?"

Jessie nodded.

"I knew it. Very clever, Detective." He smiled. "I have to give you credit. But you have to give me credit, too. I really played the game well, didn't I? Did you like the associations?"

"They were very clever, Jim."

"My father didn't think I was very clever. I wanted to show him—" He stopped. "I don't want to talk about my father. I don't want to discuss my father with you."

"That's all right, Jim. You don't have to do that."

"The important thing is that I played fair. I followed all the rules, every roll of the dice. I could have picked any property I wanted, but that wouldn't have been according to the rules. It wouldn't have counted."

"But you lied about St. James, Jim. That wasn't fair."

He smiled. "I *did* land on Tennessee. I lied to you but it was fair—you lied to me. Everything else in the note was true. I landed on Community Chest and advanced to Go. I went again and landed on Oriental. Then on Tennessee." He frowned. "What's that?"

"I didn't hear anything." She was concentrating on what Meecham had just said. Something wasn't quite, something—suddenly, she realized what she'd missed when she'd been in his apartment.

"But you didn't follow the rules, Jim," she said quietly, fighting to keep her voice and face from betraying her emotion.

"Yes, I did!" He paused. "You're trying to confuse me, to get me rattled. I played fair, and you know it."

"Jim, you've been so careful to play by the rules. I admire that. So I'm sure you want to know what you've overlooked."

"All right, Jessie." He smiled. "What did I overlook?"

Out of the corner of her eye, she saw the bathroom door move. Pruitt! Her heart beat faster. "You landed on Community Chest?"

"Yes. I rolled again, because I had doubles. That's the rule. Then I landed on Oriental. I had doubles again so I rolled again."

"But how did you get to Tennessee from Oriental?"

"I told you. I rolled doubles." Something flickered in his eyes. He blinked. "I don't want to talk about this anymore."

"I know you'll want to do what's fair, Jim. You've always been fair. You know what I'm talking about, don't you?"

"I don't know what you mean. I rolled the dice and moved my piece to Tennessee Avenue." His breathing was becoming labored. He felt the bands tightening around his chest. Not now!

"The only way you could get to Tennessee from Oriental was with doubles, Jim. They're twelve spaces apart." St. James was ten spaces from Oriental. She'd checked it out when Meecham had sent the fake clues. And Tennessee was two spaces after that.

"That's right." His voice was hoarse. "I got six and six."

"Doubles." The door was open an inch now, she saw.

"Yes, doubles!" The shout was more like a squeak.

"But you had doubles twice before. Three doubles in a row means you go to jail. It's in the rules. You forfeit your move."

"You're a liar! I didn't get three doubles in a row!"

"You know I'm telling the truth, Jim. It's the only way it could have happened. You lost this move. It won't count." She paused, then spoke in the most quiet, casual tone she could manage. "Give me the syringe, Jim."

"Don't move!" He picked up the gun.

"My hands are still on my head, Jim. I won't move until you say it's OK. But I think you should give me the syringe. You know that's the only fair thing to do."

"I don't know." He was wheezing now. He knew it would get worse, and he couldn't reach for the inhalator in his pocket. "If I give you the syringe, if I . . ." He could barely talk.

"No one will hurt you, Jim. I promise."

Meecham moved the syringe away a fraction of an inch.

"All you have to do is give me the syringe." Her arms felt like lead over her head.

He stared at Jessie. "And no one will hurt me?"

"I promise." She held her breath.

"I don't—" He wanted so much to believe her; he had to get the inhalator. "If I—" *You can't believe the other guy, 'cause he will lie every time.* "You're trying to trick me!"

"Give me the syringe, Jim," Jessie repeated softly.

"Noooo!" he screamed. "For Teresa!" he managed. He pressed the needle against Helen's arm.

The bathroom door flew open. In a flash, Meecham whirled, raised the gun, and pulled the trigger. Jessie heard a shot, then a grunt. Her eyes darted from Helen and the syringe to the doorway. She saw Pruitt clutching his abdomen and falling. His gun clanked onto the hardwood floor.

"Liar!" Meecham cried. "All liars!" He aimed again at Pruitt, but Jessie had reached under the hem of her pants for the gun she'd strapped to her ankle. She fired.

Meecham's right shoulder and arm flew back as the gunshot exploded in the room. The syringe dropped onto the floor. Jessie shoved the chair out of her way and ran to pull Helen away from the edge of the bed. Meecham grabbed the syringe.

"Drop it!" Jessie yelled.

He lunged at her with the syringe. Jessie fired again. The second shot caught him in the chest. He doubled over, then fell against the nightstand. She put her gun in her ankle holster, then snatched the syringe and his gun. She heard a noise. Turning, she saw three uniformed officers entering the room from the hall.

"We heard shots," one of them said. "We—"

"Detective Pruitt's been shot in the abdomen." Jessie pointed to Pruitt. "And the suspect looks bad." She indicated Meecham. "These are his." She handed the syringe and gun to the officer.

"We have a doctor standing by with that antidote."

The neostigmine. Jessie had asked Takamura to call UCLA about it. A chance in a million. . . . She turned to

Helen. She was still unconscious. Jessie checked her pulse. It seemed normal. There was no sign of a skin puncture. "We don't need the antidote. My sister's OK. Please tell my nephew. Tell him I'll be out soon."

The officers hurried from the room.

Jessie covered Helen with the bedspread. Then she ran to Pruitt and knelt by his side. Blood was seeping from his wound. She bit her lip. "Frank." She touched his hand. It was clammy.

He grinned weakly. "I'll be OK," he whispered. "My pride's injured more than anything else. Corcoran will never let me live this down. Your sister OK?"

Jessie nodded. "For a minute there, I really thought he was going to give me the syringe. Then he went crazy."

" 'Cause the son of a bitch heard me. Sorry."

She shook her head. "He was going to kill her anyway, Frank, before you pushed the door open. This way, I was able to get my gun." She had strapped it on in the car. "Thanks for the distraction," she said softly. She gripped his hand.

"Anytime, sweetheart. You left the front door unlocked. I sneaked in, saw that your bathroom connects with the hall. I didn't think he heard me." He tried to shrug, but winced. "You didn't need me. You took care of the bastard."

She looked at Meecham. His skin was pasty. He was staring at the widening circle of red against the blue uniform shirt.

He pressed his hand against the center of his chest. It was warm and sticky. He pulled his hand away and studied it. "It's blood," he whispered. He sounded surprised. "My blood."

He felt queasy, dizzy. He closed his eyes and saw the amputated hand on Teresa's tablecloth. He should have known it was an omen. He shivered. "I'm cold!" he cried.

"So cold!" His teeth were chattering. He started shaking. "Help me!"

Jessie released Pruitt's hand. She stood and walked to Meecham. She crouched at his side and felt his pulse. It was faint.

He was perspiring and shivering at the same time; he couldn't see clearly. "I played a great game, didn't I? I *know* I did. It was very clever. You said so yourself." He coughed up blood.

She had nothing to say. She stared at him.

"I won, didn't I? For the first time. Tell me I won."

She looked at Helen, lying on the bed. At Frank Pruitt, lying on the floor. At Meecham.

"Did I win, Dad?" he gurgled. His hand was icy. "Did I?"

"You won," Jessie said.

There was a final shudder. Then Meecham was still.

Jessie withdrew her hand. She stood and looked at him.

Do not pass Go.

Do not collect $200.

46

"I didn't think you'd come," Helen said when Jessie entered the hospital room. "I know you saved my life, but after last night, the things I said, and Matthew. . . . You must hate me."

"I don't hate you, Helen."

"Well, I hate myself! You were right. I'm a horrible person. A terrible mother." She sighed. "Where's Matthew?"

"With Paige. I checked on him before I came here." That was after Pruitt and Helen had been taken in separate ambulances to Cedars-Sinai Medical Center. After the medical investigator and criminologists had arrived at her house. After she'd briefed Takamura and Corcoran on what had happened in her bedroom.

"What did you tell him?" Helen asked.

"The truth. That you needed rest." Jessie hesitated, then said, "Neil's with him."

"Oh, God!" She sat up. "Did you tell him about . . . ?"

"No, but you'll have to talk to him, Helen. He came just after the paramedics took you away. The coroner's van was still there, and all the reporters and several network television crews. Neil thought—" Jessie stopped.

"He thought something happened to Matthew," Helen whispered. She covered her face with her hands. Then she looked up. "He'll take Matthew away from me, Jess, and I'll never see him again. That's why I took him out of camp after Neil left, why I came here. Neil said . . . Neil said when he got back from Saudi Arabia, we'd have to make major decisions. I knew what he meant—he was going to divorce me and get custody of Matthew. I love Matthew, Jessie! I can't lose him!"

"I believe you." She did. That was part of the anguish Jessie felt.

"It isn't something I plan. I get lonely when Neil's away, and worried, and edgy. The pressure builds and builds, and I lose control, like Mom used to. Don't you ever feel like that?"

Jessie had thought about this before, many times. She thought about it now. "No." She said it again—"No, I don't"—more to herself than to her sister.

"You're lucky. Or maybe it's because you had therapy."

Maybe. "You have to get help, Helen. You and Neil and Matthew. For Matthew's sake, you can't go on like this."

The door opened. Jessie turned around and saw her mother enter. Her father was right behind her.

Frances ran over to Helen's bed. "We drove here as soon as we heard. Thank God you're OK, Helen!"

Arthur Claypool walked to the other side of Helen's bed and gripped her hand. "You're all right?" His voice was husky.

Helen nodded. "Jessie saved my life. She was wonderful." Tears formed in her eyes.

Frances said, "Of course she was wonderful, but you would never have been in danger if you'd listened to me and stayed in La Jolla. It's a miracle you weren't killed. And Matthew." Frances shuddered in her yellow linen suit.

Arthur said, "We're all grateful no one was hurt."

"If your sister insists on putting her life at stake every day, that's her business. But she should know better than to involve you and a young child. Your father agrees with me, don't you, Arthur?"

Jessie looked at her father. He avoided her eyes.

Jessie said, "I'll see you later, Helen. Mom, Dad."

"Where are you going?" Frances said. "We just got here."

Jessie parked her car in her driveway and walked down the block to Paige's house.

"Your brother-in-law took Matthew out to eat," Paige told Jessie. "He said to tell you he'd come to you afterward."

And do what? Jessie wondered. Would Neil take Matthew to a hotel? Would they stay at Jessie's until Helen came home? It's not my decision, she told herself as she walked home.

The red light on her answering machine was blinking impatiently. She pressed the playback button, sat on the floor, and did stretches to relax her tight muscles while she listened to her messages.

"Hey, Jessie, it's Phil. Way to go! Even Kalish is proud, but don't tell him I told you. Can't wait to get you back to West L.A. where the real action is!"

Me, too, she thought.

"Jess, thank God you and Helen are OK. Listen, I've been thinking about us and I . . . uh . . . want to talk. Call me."

Gary. She'd have to talk to him, explain, say the things she'd never been able to say. "You need closure," Manny had said.

"Jess, it's Brenda. Damn, but we're all proud of you! You nailed the son of a bitch, and right in your own house! Call if you want me to come over. I can't wait to see you wow them in the press conference."

Jessie would face the press tomorrow—unless Hanson or Corcoran grabbed the limelight. Which wouldn't surprise her.

She finished her stretches and took a shower. The hot water eased some of her fatigue. She put on a nightshirt and a robe (for Neil), heated a portion of the tuna casserole Helen had made, and went into the den to watch TV.

"Today a grim drama has finally ended," a dark-haired anchorman on a major network intoned. "A veteran LAPD detective is critically wounded, Det. Jessie Drake saves her sister from a fatal injection of curare, and James Meecham, the man who stalked the city of Los Angeles for so many weeks and claimed eleven lives, is dead. But James Meecham remains an enigma. . . ."

Not for lack of effort, Jessie thought.

Even while Meecham's body was bagged and transferred from her bedroom to the coroner's van, Jessie knew, reporters were racing to contact former neighbors, classmates, teachers, employers to reconstruct the killer's history. And they'd probably learn what they always learned:

"A nice boy. . . . Who would believe . . . ?"

"Always quiet, a little withdrawn. . . ."

"I always knew there was something wrong. . . ."

By the time the first "Special Bulletin!" aired two hours later, some facts had already emerged. Until recently, James Meecham had been a postal carrier. (Jessie had a flash of recognition—*that's* where she'd seen him!) His father, now deceased, had been ousted from the LAPD for using excessive force. Before that, he'd almost been discharged from the armed services for the same reason. Meecham's mother was in a nursing home. His brother—"the good-looking one," a neighbor had said—had been killed during maneuvers on a stint in the military.

Meecham's grandfather, it was learned from a distant cousin in New Jersey, had jumped to his death when the stock market crashed during the Depression. The suicide had left Ed Meecham, the killer's father, bitter and resentful.

"My father always thought I was stupid," Meecham had told Jessie. And *"I don't want to talk about my father."*

She turned off the TV and took her empty plate to the kitchen.

It was over.

Meecham was in a drawer in the morgue, awaiting an autopsy that would reveal the fatal damage caused by a bullet from Jessie's gun but would never explain what had made him kill eleven people, what had emptied him of compassion, of morals, of humanity. A bankruptcy of the soul, the Monopoly expert had said. But there is no autopsy for the soul.

Pruitt would be fine. The bullet hadn't done significant damage. Jessie didn't know where their relationship would lead, but she was eager to pursue it, to be with him. It wasn't just the sex—although that was pretty damn wonderful. It wasn't love, yet. Maybe it could be.

And Helen. She would be out of the hospital soon. She would get therapy, or she wouldn't. Neil would stay with her, or he wouldn't. And Matthew? Jessie ached for the boy, wanted to protect him, to make it all right. But he wasn't her child.

Maybe, if things work out, I'll have a child of my own.

And the doubts that had gnawed at her? The fears?

I'm not a statistic, Jessie told herself firmly. I'm not my mother. I'm not Helen.

It wasn't the first time she'd tried to reassure herself with the thought, but it was the first time she allowed herself to believe it.